A.G. Castillo

This is a work of fiction. All of the characters, names, incidents, organizations, and dialogue in this novel are either the products of the author's imagination or are used fictitiously.

Archway Publishing books may be ordered through booksellers or by contacting:

Archway Publishing
1663 Liberty Drive
Bloomington, IN 47403
www.archwaypublishing.com
844-669-3957

ISBN: 978-1-6657-0406-9 (sc)
ISBN: 978-1-6657-0405-2 (hc)
ISBN: 978-1-6657-0407-6 (e)

Library of Congress Control Number: 2021904631

Print information available on the last page.

Archway Publishing rev. date: 04/22/2021

For Mom and Dad, my two favorite angels in heaven.

For Shandi, I still remember.

For Tim, my heart and soul and best friend.

CHAPTER 1

It's all my fault. I did it. I killed him ... I killed my best friend!

Chente sat up in bed and fervently wiped away the memories that rained down his face like a river of tiny razor blades. He violently pushed back the bedspread and gasped for air. His bedroom suddenly felt small—like a tiny coffin buried ten feet below the ground. He was trapped!

He couldn't breathe and frantically got out of bed; he raced to the bedroom window and opened it. He pressed his face up against the window screen and sucked in the cold winter air.

The last couple of nights had been unbearable—tossing and turning in bed, desperately avoiding sleep, and hiding from the haunting dreams that relentlessly pursued him.

Chente shook his head. *What have I done? Oh my gosh, I killed him.* He shivered uncontrollably. He needed to escape.

He closed the bedroom window and tiptoed to the closet. In the darkness, he blindly fumbled around, trying to find his Nike running shoes and his favorite Texas Tech sweatshirt as he made his way to the bedroom door.

"Where are you going, Chen?" asked Victor as he turned on the lamp next to his bed. He looked at his older brother.

Chente jumped. "Damn it, Vic. You scared the crap out of me!"

"Well, you shouldn't be sneaking around in the dark. Where are you going?" he repeated as he leaned on his pillow. It was obvious Victor wanted some answers.

"I'm going out," replied Chente as he took a deep breath, sat on his bed, and began to put on his running shoes.

"As in outside?" asked Victor in disbelief. "Are you crazy? It's freezing outside, Chente. Do you want to freeze to death? What's the matter with you?"

"Quit with the drama already. It's not that cold." Chente sighed. "Look, I can't sleep, and I'm going for a run to clear my mind."

"Oh, because that makes so much sense. I feel so much better." Victor rolled his eyes and sarcastically shook his head.

Chente ignored his little brother and kept getting ready to leave.

"Seriously? You're going to run in the snow?" Victor tilted his head and looked at Chente. "Are you crazy?"

"The roads have been cleared," replied Chente as he looked at Victor and then started tying his shoelaces to avoid his little brother's all-knowing stare.

There was an awkward silence.

"Okay, spill it," insisted Victor with a hint of irritation. "Dude, what's going on?"

Chente exhaled and rubbed his forehead. He paused for moment, cleared his throat, got up, and stared out the window. Everything outside looked so peaceful and quiet. He longed for that. He just wanted to be alone with his thoughts instead of being interrogated by the barking pit bull disguised as his little brother.

Chente knew Victor wouldn't understand. He just wouldn't get it.

"Christmas holidays are over, and we go back to school tomorrow," muttered Chente as he nervously scratched the side of his head. "I don't know if I'm ready to do that."

Chente took a deep breath and slowly wiped the frost off the windowpane. "I have been gone for three weeks now, and I just don't know if I'm ready to—" He stopped midsentence.

Silence invaded the room. Chente just kept shaking his head.

"Chen, it's not your fault," whispered Victor as he quietly tried to comfort his older brother.

Chente ignored Victor's comment and simply kept looking out the window, desperately trying to focus on anything that wasn't this conversation.

"Chen, you didn't do anything wrong."

Those words sent a chill screaming down Chente's back. He turned away from the window and glared at Victor. "That's just it. I didn't do anything!"

Chente walked over to his desk and began looking for the house keys as Victor's eyes frantically searched the room, trying to find a way to convince his overly emotional brother to stay indoors.

"Look. I am just stressed out about college," replied Chente as he quickly changed the subject. "It's January, and I still don't have a clue where I will be going to school next year."

Victor carefully studied his older brother's physical demeanor and shook his head. He knew Chente was deflecting, but he went with the flow to momentarily keep the peace.

"Get serious, Chen. Quit being so edgy," said Victor. "You have amazing grades, and your SAT scores are out of this world. You so got this."

Chente appreciated his little brother's confidence, but he was in the running for a couple of big college scholarships, and he was nervous. He hoped the stars would align in his favor and that these financial opportunities would materialize in the next few months.

"It's not that easy," explained Chente. "I just want to make sure I make the right decision for everyone."

Victor paused and bit his bottom lip. "Wait. What does that even mean?"

"Huh? What are you talking about?" Chente opened the desk drawers and continued to search.

"Well, you just said you wanted to make sure you made the right decision for everyone. What does that mean?"

Chente stopped rummaging through his desk and glanced at Victor. He frowned and shook his head. "I don't know, Vic. I just said that. I don't know why."

"Right. When you say 'everyone,' you must be talking about Violeta."

Chente rolled his eyes and growled under his breath. He didn't have the energy for an argument. "No, I'm not. She has nothing to do with this."

"Liar, liar, pants on fire," said Victor in a singsong voice as he pointed at Chente. "Violeta makes everything her business. Don't let her do this. It's your decision. You do what you want."

Of course, Victor was right. Violeta was their older sister, and she loved barking out orders like a drill sergeant. She always thought she was in charge and made it a habit to be in everyone's business. His younger sister, Vanessa, called her a "*metiche*" when they argued—and that was often.

"Ay, *hermanito*, don't worry so much. I can handle Violeta," said Chente as he found the house keys under his English literature book and waved them at Victor. He walked toward the door.

"Chente, it really is cold outside. You are going to freeze," said Victor as he crawled back into bed.

"Look. I will be only gone twenty minutes. I am just going to run to the park and back. I just want to clear my head."

Victor groaned and shook his head.

"If I am not back in thirty, send a search party and tell them to look for the snowman wearing the Texas Tech sweatshirt," teased Chente.

"What about Mom?"

"She's asleep. She won't even know I am gone."

"Whatever," mumbled Victor as he rolled his eyes and pulled his blanket over his head.

Chente turned off the desk lamp and closed the door to their bedroom. He knew Victor was worried about him, but he wasn't ready to talk about his feelings. Victor wouldn't understand what was happening, because Chente wasn't sure either.

The entire house was quiet, calm, and still. The peaceful serenity was deafening, and it whispered from room to room, making the house feel warm and cozy. There was a faint glimmer of light coming from a corner in the living room—from a single candle on his mother's beautiful altar, which was filled with tiny religious figurines, Catholic rosaries, and family pictures.

In memory of his late father, every morning his mother faithfully knelt before her altar and recited her morning prayers of hope and love to God. She prayed a complete rosary for her children and then a final prayer for her husband. Chente had witnessed this routine many times. She was very devoted.

Chente walked over to the altar, made the sign of the cross, and began to pray. He quietly watched the candlewick dancing back and forth.

• • •

"Just five more minutes. I want to hit a few more crosscourt backhands before we leave," shouted Chente to his friend Carlos, who stood across the net.

"Fine. Five more minutes, and then we are going to Sonic, and you're buying," replied Carlos as he adjusted his baseball cap and wiped the sweat out of his hazel eyes. He quickly gathered the tennis balls that had accumulated against the back fence and consistently pounded serves over the net.

Chente could hear the sirens in the background, but he focused on his ground strokes. His backhand shot had failed him last year at the UIL Regional Tennis Tournament, and he had lost in the semifinals. This year he was determined to win regionals and advance to the state tennis tournament in Austin.

As Chente continued to practice his backhand, he saw Christina's red convertible pull into the parking lot. She frantically got out of the car and motioned to Carlos. Chente could see Christina's long, black ponytail bouncing as she whispered in Carlos's ear.

Carlos turned to Chente with a panicked expression.

Chente darted over to the fence. "What's going on, Christina?"

"Chen, your dad was in a car accident half a mile up the road. It doesn't look good. You should hurry!"

Chente gave Carlos a worried look, dropped his Wilson tennis racket, jumped in his car, and raced away.

"What happened?" asked Chente as he pushed his way through the mass of people, who had stopped to witness the accident.

Valentin looked stunned and wore an expressionless face as they both watched their dad being placed on a stretcher and then into an ambulance.

"I don't know, Chente. Dad wrecked?" said the older brother in a very calm voice. "Mom and the girls are waiting for me in the car. I am taking them to the hospital. We're going to follow the ambulance."

Valentin turned to walk away.

Chente grabbed his older brother's shoulder. "Wait, where's Vic?"

Valentin shrugged.

"He's probably at David's house. I will get him and meet you at Memorial Hospital in Dimmitt, right?" asked Chente.

Valentin didn't turn around. He just nodded and kept walking.

"I am so deeply sorry. We tried everything, but we couldn't save him," announced Dr. Lee to the Jimenez family as Chente and Victor rushed into the hospital waiting room.

Vanessa held on to Mrs. Jimenez, and they both cried on a couch in the middle of the room. The younger sister gently caressed the top of her mother's head and tried desperately to console her mother's heartbreak.

Violeta retreated to a corner window and began to sob, preferring to mourn privately.

Valentin rubbed his forehead and stared at his feet. He slowly nodded at the doctor and sighed. He walked over, put his arm around Victor's shoulders, and walked out of the room. He was running away and hiding.

Chente swallowed hard and leaned his forearm against the door. His legs suddenly felt weak, and he tried to steady himself as the room slowly began to spin. He closed his eyes and quietly inhaled couple of times, trying to regain his composure.

"Are you okay, son?" the doctor asked.

Chente nodded and opened his eyes. "What happened to my dad?"

"It looks like your dad had a massive stroke while he was driving. There wasn't much we could do for him. I am sorry for your loss."

• • •

The sudden noise from the central heating jolted Chente out of his trance. He let out a deep sigh. He couldn't believe it had been ten months since their family tragedy. He picked up his dad's picture and gave it a quick kiss, made the sign of the cross, and stepped away from the altar.

He quietly walked down the hallway, passing all the memories hanging on the wall, to his mother's open bedroom door. There she lay, all curled up with her pillows, fast asleep. Chente was glad she was resting, because the past year had been rough and had taken its toll on her health.

In early November, Chente and Violeta had taken their mother to the doctor because she couldn't shake off a cold and wasn't eating very well. The doctor examined her and found she was suffering from high blood pressure. He also added that she was probably battling some depression.

The doctor gave their mother medication and advised the siblings to keep her environment as stress free as possible. He wanted to see her regain some weight and scheduled a follow-up appointment to see her in ninety days.

After the doctor's visit, Violeta called an emergency brother/sister meeting at her house to ensure all siblings were on the same page.

"Mom is really sick" were the icy words Violeta chose to use to start the meeting.

"What are you talking about, Vi?" asked Valentin as he placed his cell phone down on the table with some concern.

Vanessa and Victor stopped visiting and laughing, and quickly turned their attention to their older sister.

"Chente and I took Mom to the doctor today, and he is concerned—really concerned. Her blood pressure has spiked, and her dramatic weight loss has left her body fragile and weak. He thinks she could suffer a stroke if her health continues to deteriorate."

Victor looked at Chente. "Is Mom going to die too?"

Chente shook his head. "No … it just means that—"

Violeta abruptly interrupted Chente in mid-sentence. "It just means that we have to take care of her, Victor. It means you can't cause problems at school anymore, or she might die."

Victor was horrified by his older sister's response, and his bottom lip began to quiver.

Vanessa furiously lunged at Violeta from across the table. "Why do you have to be such a bitch all of the time?" raged Vanessa. "This isn't his fault. You are such a fucking bitch!"

Valentin held on to Vanessa's swinging arms and restrained her as she continued to scream obscenities at her oldest sister. "Stop it. Nesh, stop it. Fighting is not the answer. This is stupid," insisted Valentin.

Vanessa and Valentin were both right. Violeta was being bitchy, but right now they needed to stick together and make sure they took care of their mom.

Chente turned to his little brother and tried to calmly reassure him. "Vic, Mom is going to be fine. I promise. We know what's wrong with her; we can make her better. We just need to make sure she takes her medicine and that she eats healthy, exercises, and rests."

Victor wiped away the fear from his cheeks and composed himself. He looked at his older brother and nodded.

"Exactly," chimed in Valentin, who was a second-year medical school student at Texas Tech University. "I will call the doctor tomorrow morning and get more information, and we will get on top of this."

"But guys, we have got to pull together for Mom's sake. We need to leave our differences at the door," advised Chente as he gave the two sisters a long and serious stare. "This isn't about us; it's about making Mom better."

"I agree with Chen. This bickering has to stop," added Valentin as he hugged on his little sister. "We have to be united in this."

"I get it, and I agree," replied Vanessa as she shamefully looked away. "Just keep Little Miss Know-It-All away from me, and I'm good."

Violeta rolled her eyes and walked away from the group.

• • •

Chente could hear his mother breathing. Her breaths were steady, full, and healthy. He quietly moved away from her bedroom and swiftly found the front door of the house, opened it, and escaped into the night.

The winter air felt good against his face. He breathed it in—it was clean, crisp, and inviting. Chente looked down the lonely street; it was empty—not a soul in sight. The silence was mesmerizing, and he welcomed it with open arms.

Instinctively, he began to stretch his arm and leg muscles and slowly jog in place. He had sustained a thigh injury in November during a varsity basketball game against Dimmitt, and he didn't want to risk aggravating the muscle again, since it had been slow to recover. He was a fierce competitor and hated watching the game from the bench.

Chente was the starting-point guard for his high school basketball team, and he couldn't think of anything more exhilarating than breaking a full-court press, passing the ball to his teammates for a slam dunk, or hearing the sound of the net when he made a three-pointer from the top of the key. He loved the thrill of winning a close game and the joy and pride it brought to his family as they watched from the bleachers.

He could hear his coach's voice in his head as he continued to stretch. "Chen, the point guard makes or breaks a team. You are the quarterback. You set the pace."

Coach Alvarez was his varsity basketball coach and an Avalon High School alum. He was tough as nails, precise, and very direct. He had high expectations for his basketball players and had an uncanny ability to pull the best out of them.

"Chen, if this team is going to make a long playoff run, you're going to have to step up your game," echoed in Chente's ears.

Chente shook his head, nervously rubbed his hands together, and shivered. He immediately got butterflies in his stomach.

"I wonder what Coach Alvarez is going to say to me now," mumbled Chente as he finished stretching and began jogging down the street to the city park. "Hell, what is he going to do to me?"

Chente hadn't been out of his house in eighteen days, and getting some cardio exercise felt perfect. His body was hungry for exertion and competition, and he missed playing basketball. His personal sabbatical from the world had cost him to miss four basketball games. He was certain the guys on the team would never forgive him.

He accelerated his jogging pace.

Chente had also avoided his school friends for over three weeks, ignoring their phone calls and not responding to their text messages. He missed them and knew they would be angry with him when he returned to school. He had completely shut them out. He had been MIA since—

"Nope, I am not going to think about that," said Chente as he accelerated his jogging pace into a full-blown sprint.

He could see the city park in the distance, and it was lit up with bright holiday lights. He quickly decided to sprint to the park bench by the big oak tree and take a minute to catch his breath. Then he would jog around the walking track twice and head home.

Chente sprinted past the park bench and tagged the oak tree. He was breathing heavily, but it felt good. He put his hands on top of his head and continued to take in the winter air. His breathing slowly calmed, and he wiped his sweaty forehead with his arms. He felt alive.

He quietly stood beside the park bench and admired all the holiday lights. The holiday wreaths on all the streetlamps and the blinking lights on all the trees made the park look very colorful and festive.

He began to stretch in place while breathing in the peaceful silence when he noticed someone else was running on the walking track. He wasn't alone after all.

Chente carefully watched the lonely figure from a distance. He was a strong runner—long, lean, and athletic. His running strides were fluid and graceful but fiercely intense and precise. Chente could see the outline of the man's leg muscles through his black running tights, and they quivered as he ran past him. He was a beautiful athlete running with a sense of purpose, a sense of urgency. Chente was hypnotized.

He noted that the mysterious runner was sprinting the straight part of the track and then jogging only the curves. His regimen was very methodical and deliberate, but he ran with ease and freedom, like he was chasing the wind. He had powerful arms and an impressive posture, and he ran with a passionate flare that made Chente feel flustered inside. The guy was perfect.

The hooded runner finished his workout and began walking toward Chente, who continued to stand near the park bench. Chente grew nervous and began to jog in place and stretch his arms when the runner spoke to him.

"Chen? Is that you?" asked the mysterious figure as he approached.

Chente turned around to look at the hooded runner, but he couldn't see his face because the light of the streetlamp was directly in his line of vision.

"Mr. Jimenez? What are you doing out here?"

The voice sounded vaguely familiar, but Chente was so spooked that he couldn't make out who was speaking to him.

The runner took off his hoodie, exposing a full head of sandy-blond hair. He waved and continued to walk toward Chente with a big smile.

Chente squinted. "Coach? Coach Doss? Is that you?"

"Yes. The one and only," replied Coach Doss as he laughed with his arms extended wide. "Chen, what are you doing out here?"

Chente was mortified. He had just been crushing on a coach from high school; heck, he had practically ravished the man with his eyes. Chente was at a loss for words and curiously nervous. He was speechless. He simply continued to stare at the gorgeous man, who was standing in front of him and breathing heavily.

The first-year high school coach looked bewildered and turned around to see whether someone else was standing behind him.

"Chen, are you okay? Did I scare you?" asked the coach with a hint of humor and concern.

Chente shook the surprise off his face and finally spoke. "No, no you didn't. I mean, no sir, I … I am fine. Thank you."

Coach Doss looked at Chente, nodded, and playfully nudged his shoulder. "Okay, good. What are you doing out here? Do you live nearby?"

Chente was having a hard time processing his thoughts and translating them into the English language. He was cold, confused, and completely captivated by Coach Doss's strong presence; like a magnetic force, he was drawn to him.

"Merry Christmas and Happy New Year," blurted Chente as he stumbled over his words in his attempt to defuse the awkward moment of silence. "How were your holidays, Coach?"

The high school coach paused for a second and chuckled under his breath. He noticed Chente had skillfully avoided his initial question. "They were good." Coach Doss nodded. "I went up to Amarillo and spent some time with the family." The coach rubbed his stomach and dramatically moaned. "And I definitely ate too much!"

"Oh, I know what you mean." Chente grinned as he began to relax. "My mom always makes tamales during Christmas, and she isn't happy unless I eat at least a dozen—in one sitting."

"Yum, I love tamales," replied the coach as he stretched his arms.

"Yeah, me too, but then she wants you to eat her empanadas for dessert," said Chente with a deep sigh. "That's craziness. She literally wants you to roll out of the dining room."

They both slipped into easy laughter.

Coach Doss put his hand up and playfully protested. "Well, my mom is just as bad. She makes a very tasty dressing. She puts brown sugar and …"

Chente tuned out Coach Doss's voice and studied the coach's lips as he spoke. They looked soft and inviting, and his smile was friendly and warm. There was a soothing easiness to Coach Doss that Chente found strangely alluring, and his ocean-blue eyes danced back and forth as he shared his holiday story. It was like receiving a letter from an old friend; he was familiar, comfortable, and inviting. Why hadn't he ever noticed him before?

"What's up with the goofy smile, Chen?" asked the coach as he tried to keep warm by blowing into his folded hands.

"I—I didn't realize I was smiling. I was just enjoying your story," lied Chente.

Coach Doss stared at Chente, made a funny face, and began to stretch his arms again. He took a deep breath and sighed. "Isn't it an amazing night?"

"Yes, sir. It sure is," whispered Chente as he looked up at the sky and exhaled.

"The full moon is stunning. It's like she's marking her territory and letting everyone know that the sky belongs to her tonight."

Coach Doss quietly glanced over at Chente as he spoke and wondered what secrets Chente was running away from tonight. Why was he out jogging on a frosty winter night—alone?

"And the stars," Chente said, "the stars are like her children who excitedly gather around to listen to her whisper magical stories disguised as the cool winter breeze we feel tonight. Yeah, I'd say it's pretty perfect."

Chente took a deep breath of cold air and easily enjoyed the winter scene that surrounded him. He soaked it all in as he exhaled. He casually turned around and found Coach Doss staring at him with a fierce intensity that weakened Chente's legs. The hypnotic-like gaze locked on Chente, and it felt as if Coach Doss were reading his soul.

Chente gave him an awkward smile and began to jog in place.

A gentle arctic breeze made Coach Doss shiver as he carefully watched Chente try to keep warm. "So, Chen … what are you doing out here? It's kind of late, don't you think?"

"I couldn't sleep tonight, so I decided to go for a run," responded the high school senior plainly.

Coach Doss bent down to stretch his hamstrings, and Chente's eyes admired his round, muscular backside. It was flawless.

"So your parents know you are out of the house and running?" asked Coach Doss as he gave Chente a suspicious glance.

"My mom was asleep," said Chente as he continued to stretch his legs. "There was no sense in waking her up to tell her I was going for a run."

"So you basically snuck out of the house?" The coach chuckled with a mischievous grin.

Chente put his hands on his hip and protested, "Seriously? Coach, I am eighteen years old." The high school senior picked up a handful of snow and playfully tossed it at his coach.

"Wow, I'm eighteen? That's your best comeback?" Coach Doss laughed as he wiped the snow off his face.

"Whatever." Chente laughed as he shook his head and inadvertently pushed Coach Doss into the white snow.

Coach Doss continued to laugh as he got up and wiped the snow off. "But seriously, what are you doing out here?"

"Really, I am just out for a run," answered Chente with a hint of irritation in his voice.

Coach Doss smiled at Chente and cleared his throat. "Look, Chen," began Coach Doss, "it's really none of my business. I am just asking because I am surprised to see you here. That's all."

"Well, Coach, I'm kind of surprised to see you here too," replied Chente as he paused and gave him a quizzical stare. The high school senior conceitedly shrugged and grinned.

"Yes, but I haven't been gone for three weeks," Coach Doss stated matter-of-factly. "I haven't missed four basketball games, Chen, with no explanation. I am not the one who won't return a friend's phone call either."

Those words hit Chente in the face like a runaway freight train. The unexpected truth hurt, and Chente quickly looked away, because he couldn't explain his actions. His mind was a frantic mess. Jimmy's death had left him broken, and he was too scared to admit it to himself or to anyone.

"Uh-huh, yep," responded Chente as he nervously kicked snow. "You're right, Coach."

"Listen, Chen, we all care about you. You know that, right? Your friends, your teachers—we have all been worried about you."

Chente nodded and acknowledged his coach's words.

"I don't really know what's going on, but your friends and Coach Alvarez are very concerned and kind of confused," continued the coach.

"Yes, sir," replied Chente. The high student's teeth began to chatter a little bit, and the conversation was getting colder by the second.

The high school coach moved a little closer to Chente, hoping to connect with the basketball star. "We have lost four basketball games in a row. We had the district opener last Friday, and we couldn't break the press against Olton for the entire first quarter. We lost by fifteen."

Chente knew his team was struggling without him. He had kept up with the basketball scores by reading the *Lubbock Avalanche Journal.*

"Poor Beau." Coach Doss sighed and laughed under his breath. "He has had to start in your place, and he can't break a press to save his life. He really wants you to come back to the team in the worst way."

"Yeah, and I bet everyone's mad at me too, right?" asked Chente as his voice began to shake.

"Chen, don't you understand?" replied Coach Doss as he gave Chente a gentle nudge on the shoulder. "Forget basketball for a second." Coach Doss paused and sighed thoughtfully. "Everyone is worried about you. Nobody knows what's going on. Your friends are scared. You need to talk to them."

Chente shook his head and looked up with tears in his eyes. "I'm sorry. I'm really sorry," he whispered.

Coach Doss stared into those big-brown eyes and was instantly captivated. He was looking at a young man who was in obvious pain, and he felt an overwhelming need to hug him and absorb all his misery, but he hesitated.

Coach Doss was a recent college graduate and in the middle of his first year of teaching, and he didn't know Chente too well. The hustle and bustle of his first teaching/coaching assignment had kept him so busy that Coach Doss had been in survival mode since August. It hadn't been until the middle of November, the start of basketball season, that Coach Doss was introduced to Chente Jimenez.

All Coach Doss knew about Chente was that he was a senior, the star basketball player, and easily the most popular boy at Avalon High School. He was your all-American student.

Coach Doss impulsively reached out and pulled the high school senior in for a hug. He gently patted him on the back. He hadn't meant to make Chente cry. He just wanted to make sure Chente understood that he was missed and that people were worried. Chente had a responsibility to communicate.

"Do you want to talk about it?" whispered Coach Doss after a few seconds passed. "It always feels better after you talk about it."

Chente still had his face pressed against Coach Doss's firm chest. He could hear the steady rhythm of his heartbeat. He could smell Coach Doss's musky scent. He could feel his arms around him, gently patting his back.

Chente quickly pushed him away and wiped his eyes. He walked toward the track, looked up at the moon, and wished he could disappear into the night.

"I know I messed up, and I'm sorry," lamented Chente as another tear rolled down his cheek. "But I'm not ready to talk about it."

"Okay," responded Coach Doss and quietly watched Chente wipe away his hurt from his red cheeks.

There was a long pause of silence. The wind picked up and slightly moved the trees back and forth. Chente could hear a couple of dogs barking in the distance as a small red truck passed by the park and turned down the street.

"Hey, Chen, I was sorry to hear about your friend, Jimmy," said the basketball coach. "Is that what's bothering you?"

It was a stab in the dark. Coach Doss had overheard some of the basketball boys guessing that it was the reason for Chente's sudden disappearance.

Chente's body straightened, and he turned around and looked at Coach Doss. "Did you know Jimmy?" he asked with an energetic curiosity.

"No, I didn't. But I heard he was your best friend," replied the high school coach with a calming smile.

Chente gave him a blank stare and slowly nodded as he stared up at the sky. "Yes, he was ... or he is ... I don't even know what to say anymore," whispered Chente and let out a quiet whimper of pain.

"You don't have to say anything, Chen," replied Coach Doss in a very soothing tone. "We don't even have to talk about it right now."

Chente gave Coach Doss a half smile. "Thank you. I better be going home now," said Chente as he glanced up at the sky. "Looks like it might snow."

There were a few dark, ominous clouds rolling in from the north, threatening the moon's dominance of the sky.

Chente began to stretch his legs and then jog in place. He had allowed his body to get cold, and his teeth continued to chatter. He needed to warm up before he jogged home.

Coach Doss carefully watched Chente and also began to stretch. "Well, I better be leaving too. It's really late," announced the high school coach. "Are you going to be okay?"

Chente choked back the emotion that was threatening to reappear, tried to smile, and nodded. He was tired, but he would be fine in the morning.

"I will see you at school tomorrow, right?" asked Coach Doss as he cautiously waited for Chente's confirmation.

Chente glanced at him and nodded again. "Thanks for the talk. I appreciate it," he replied as he took a couple of steps toward the street and stopped. He turned around and looked at Coach Doss for a long time.

"What's the matter?" asked Coach Doss as he shrugged and looked around. "Is something the matter?"

Chente slowly took a couple of steps toward the basketball coach. "Wait a minute, Coach. What are *you* doing out here?" asked Chente with a hint of curiosity. "Are *you* okay?"

"What do you mean?" replied the first-year teacher as he furiously rubbed his hands together and began to jump up and down to avoid the cold temperature.

"Well, you asked me why I was running on a cold winter night. Now, I am asking you," said Chente as he rubbed his hands together.

The smile left Coach Doss's face. He could see Chente's eyes studying his reaction. "I'm just running," replied the coach in a strained voice.

Chente's curious eyes connected with Coach Doss. He slowly nodded. "Running away?"

Coach Doss looked away for a second, then quietly turned back around. "Yeah, Chen, something like that."

Chente kept looking at him with no expression. "Yeah, I get it. Good night, Coach. See you tomorrow." He jogged home as the snow began to fall.

CHAPTER 2

The score is tied 57–57, and there are two seconds on the clock. The fans in the Avalon High School gymnasium erupt into a frenzy as Chente steps up to the free throw line to shoot his free throws.

Chente can hear Coach Alvarez on the bench, cheering him on. He sees his brothers and sisters in the crowd, clapping their hands nervously; his mother has her eyes closed tight.

The referee hands him the basketball.

Chente looks at the basket fifteen feet away. He bounces the ball once. He bounces the ball twice. He picks up the basketball and lines it up with the goal. He bends his knees and … everything stops.

Chente looks around and shakes his head.

No noise. No one is moving. Everyone is frozen.

"What is going on?" he whispers to himself.

Through the corner of his eyes, he sees a subtle movement. It's Jimmy. He walks into the gym, casually waves at Chente, and smiles.

Chente is stunned; he drops the basketball and shakes his head in disbelief. "What are you doing here?" yells the point guard. "Where have you been? I have missed you so much!"

Jimmy continues to smile and nods at Chente. "You are going to be fine, Chen. Whether you make the basket or not, you are going to be just fine."

Jimmy waves again and turns around to leave.

"Don't go. Please don't go. Please don't leave me all alone," screams Chente as Jimmy slowly walks out of the gym.

"Chente ... Chente ... Wake up. Dude, you're dreaming," said Victor as he continued to tug on his brother's shoulder.

Chente opened his eyes and frantically scanned his surroundings. He felt disoriented and lost. He paused for a moment and took a deep breath. He quickly sat up in bed and realized. *It was just a dream. It was only a dream.* He let out a thankful sigh.

"Dude! That was intense," said Victor as he emphatically gave Chente a concerned stare. "You were moving all over in your bed like you were possessed or something. You okay?"

Chente took a deep breath, rubbed his eyes, and yawned. "Yeah, I'm good."

"I didn't hear you come in last night," said Victor with a touch of irritation in his voice.

It was obvious that his little brother was still a little upset about Chente's irresponsible decision to go for a midnight run in the middle of winter.

"Well, as you can see, I didn't freeze to death," replied Chente as he gave Victor a little sarcastic smile.

Victor shook his head, rolled his eyes, and began to tie his shoes.

Chente watched his little brother and slowly realized Victor was already dressed for school and had his backpack waiting by the door.

"Oh shit. What time is it, Vic? Am I late?" asked Chente as he jumped out of bed.

Victor playfully chuckled under his breath. "No, no, no—relax. It's just seven twenty-five. You're not late. I'm just super way early today." He groaned.

Chente sat back down on his bed and exhaled loudly. His right thigh was throbbing, and he gingerly massaged it. He hadn't stretched enough last night after he got home.

Chente gently rolled his neck from side to side and suddenly straightened his back. He quickly turned to his brother with a puzzled expression. "Wait. Why are you ready for school? What's going on?"

"Well, older brother, while you were having your meltdown before the Christmas holidays," replied Victor with a sly grin, "I was getting into trouble at school."

"What do you mean?" asked Chente as he yawned one more time.

"I got into a fight," said Victor as he casually combed his hair in the mirror.

Chente slowly stood up, favoring his right leg. Then he quickly glanced at Victor in disbelief. "Wait. Hold on. Did you say you got into a fight?"

There was a delightful twinkle in Victor's dark-brown eyes when he heard his brother's reaction. He had his older brother's undivided attention. "Well, it was more like a shoving match than a fight," replied Victor casually.

"Are you being serious? Why didn't you tell me?"

"Well, you haven't been around the last few weeks, if you know what I mean," said the little brother as he stared at Chente through the mirror with a trace of bitterness.

Chente ignored Victor's biting comment and sighed.

"Listen, it's no big deal. I shoved Ricky in the lunch line. Can I use some of your cologne?" asked Victor as he picked up Chente's cologne bottle and waved it at him.

"What? Yes, please put on some cologne," said Chente as he shook his head. "Seriously? You got into a fight with Ricky Bennett? Why?"

Victor turned around, looked at his older brother, and pointed his index finger right in front of Chente's face. "Because, Chen, I am tired of him talking shit about you all of the time."

"What? Are you kidding me?" asked Chente, rolling his eyes. "Are you saying you got into a fight because of me?"

"Yep. That's what I am saying. It's all your fault," said Victor with a playful grin; he drenched himself in cologne.

"Victor, it doesn't matter what he says about me. I don't care—nobody cares what Ricky says," said Chente as he stood up. He walked to his cell phone and turned it on.

Victor shook his head and growled softly. "I know, Chente. We should 'kill 'em with kindness,' right? Isn't that what you always say?"

"Exactly," replied Chente as he extended his arms.

"Well, I am not you," snapped Victor. "Sometimes you just have to push back. I am not good at tuning people out like you are, Chente."

Chente held his hands up and protested. "Whoa. Okay, I call a truce." He sighed. "I get it. I have been in my own little world lately. Enough with the snide remarks!"

"Dude, it's not that serious," announced Victor as he went to the closet and grabbed his jacket. "The lunchroom monitor got in between us before I could punch his smug, little raccoon face."

"Okay, okay," said Chente as he lowered his voice. "But Victor, you know Mom doesn't need this kind of stress."

Victor put on his jacket and froze in place. He turned around and looked at Chente in utter disbelief. "Really?" replied Victor as he cleared his throat. "You have been a walking zombie the last few weeks, and you're lecturing *me*? You have no room to talk, brother."

Chente felt the truth smack him in the face, and he looked away, deflated. He wondered where this hostility was coming from. Why was Victor so mad at him?

"Look, Mom doesn't even know it happened. Principal Timms called Violeta," replied Victor with a hint of regret in his voice.

Chente turned around and winced. He swiftly covered his mouth with his hands and shook his head. "Oh wow, are you serious? He really called Vi?"

"Yep, an early Christmas gift from good ole Principal Timms." His little brother smirked.

"What did she do?"

"What she always does," said Victor plainly. "She overreacted. She went on and on about how I need to grow up and be more like you. 'Chente never gets into trouble.' Blah, blah, blah," said Victor as he mimicked his older sister's breezy voice.

"Just ignore that. She was just angry," said the older brother.

Chente felt bad for Victor. He always had to endure "Chente comparisons," and it wasn't fair. Victor was a good kid, and Violeta should have never said those things.

"Principal Timms said he wanted to see us first thing after the Christmas break." Victor sighed. "Why do you think I'm dressed and ready to go? How do I look?"

Victor began to pose like he was a model, while Chente pretended to be a photographer and began snapping pictures with his imaginary camera.

They both laughed, fell on their beds, and sighed.

Victor's cell phone buzzed, and he read the message. "Oh gosh ... She's on her way to pick me up. She just texted me. I think my stomach hurts. I think I am going to be sick too."

Victor painfully looked out the bedroom window. He dreaded seeing his older sister.

"Why is she always so harsh and critical?" Victor groaned. "She's like the Tin Man in *The Wizard of Oz*. No heart!"

"I'm sorry, *hermanito. Tienes* ear plugs?" asked Chente as he winced in imaginary pain.

"She just pulled up on her broomstick. Wish me luck," said Victor as he swiped his backpack off his bed, rolled his eyes, and walked out of the room.

"You don't need luck. You should have bathed in holy water," yelled Chente.

"My day already sucks, and it's only seven thirty," shouted the little brother from the hallway and laughed aloud.

"I feel you ... Mine's gonna suck too," whispered Chente as he rubbed his right thigh muscle and limped into the bathroom to take his morning shower.

Chente quickly bathed and began to towel off. He was a nervous wreck. He was going to have to face everyone today—no more hiding. He knew there would be a lot of questions, and he didn't have any answers.

He wasn't ready to talk about his feelings, and Chente hoped his friends would be a little understanding because Victor was right. He had a keen ability to freeze people out when they pushed too hard. Chente hoped he would be able to hold it together.

He turned off the bathroom light and walked back into his bedroom. He noticed his cell phone light was blinking.

"Let the games begin," he said to himself.

He picked up his cell phone; he had two text messages. One was from Haven, and the other was from Felipe. Haven said, "Good Morning, Chen. Hope ur feeling better. If ur going to school 2day, I want a ride … plz. Just let me know ASAP."

Felipe wrote, "Dude. My dad took my car to work. Can I hitch a ride to school?"

Chente smiled and glanced at his alarm clock; it was 7:42. He responded and told them he would pick them up in twenty minutes. He knew his two friends were concerned and were simply checking in with him.

As he went to his closet and got a T-shirt and jeans, he thought about his conversation with Coach Doss the night before. Coach Doss had given him good and sound advice. He knew he needed to make it right with his teammates and visit with Coach Alvarez as soon as possible. It wasn't going to be easy, but he needed to take the first step.

He walked to his dresser and began to comb his hair in the mirror. He looked at his reflection and whispered to himself, "Chente, you can do this."

"Chente? *Mijo*, come and eat a couple of tacos before you leave for school," shouted a voice from the kitchen.

He paused and cautiously smiled. He slowly put down his cologne bottle and waited for a second and listened. Did he just imagine hearing his mother in the kitchen? Was he hearing things?

He hesitated and quietly listened.

There it was again. The clanking of pots and pans coming from the kitchen, and then the aroma of refried beans and chorizo began to tease his nose, and his stomach started to growl.

"Mom? You're up?" he shouted from his bedroom as he put his schoolbooks in his backpack. He quickly exited the bedroom and entered the kitchen.

Chente pushed back his mother's soft, black hair to one side, gave her a kiss on the cheek, and gently embraced her frail body.

"*Pues*, of course I am," replied his mother as she smiled at her son and flipped tortillas on the stove with her bare hands.

"So you're feeling better?" asked Chente as he closely examined her.

"Yes, *mijo*. I got some sleep last night and feel a little better today. Don't worry so much."

"Yay!" Chente clapped as he reached for a warm tortilla.

Mrs. Jimenez quietly observed her middle son as he made himself a breakfast taco. She knew something else was bothering him, and it frightened her that he always concealed his feelings.

"*Y tú? Cómo te sientes?* How are you feeling?" asked the mother of five as she cautiously watched for his reaction.

"Me? Oh yeah, I'm fine," answered Chente as he shoved the breakfast taco into his mouth and chewed. "Oh my gosh ... Mom, I love your tortillas. They are so good!"

Mrs. Jimenez smiled proudly. It felt good to see her son wearing a smile and eating like a normal teenage boy.

"Mmm, and the refried beans with chorizo too," said Chente as he quickly got up and made himself another breakfast taco. "Mom, this is so awesome. Thank you," he said as he sat down, poured himself a glass of orange juice, and started to drink.

Mrs. Jimenez nodded and continued flipping tortillas. "Take some to Felipe. *Pobrecito*, he's always hungry."

"Yep, and for Carlos *también*. They love your tortillas." Chente smiled.

"Yes, *mijo*, share with your amigos," she said. "They are both such good boys."

That's my Chente, reflected Mrs. Jimenez. He was always thinking of other people and wanting to help. Just like his dad.

"*So, mijo, dime la verdad*," said the mother. "So you're doing better?"

Chente gave his mother a quizzical stare and extended his arms wide. "Yes, Mom, I'm fine. Why do you keep asking me that?"

His mother sighed and squinted. "*Por que?* Chente, *no soy tonta*. I know that something has been wrong with you for weeks. I have eyes in my head," she said. "*No estoy ciega*."

"Mom, really? I know you're not blind," answered Chente as he chuckled under his breath. "Maybe a little deaf, but you can definitely see," teased the middle son.

Chente and his mother had always been close. They had a special connection. In fact, his sister Vanessa always teased Chente and call him a "Momma's Boy," but he didn't care. His mom was the most important person in his life.

But today Chente sensed that his mother was cornering him, so he quickly finished making the breakfast tacos and raced to the living room. "Mom, I am good. Promise. I got to go. I have to pick up Haven and Felipe, and I can't be late for school," he replied as he continued to lie.

He put on his letter jacket, grabbed his backpack, and gave her a quick kiss on the cheek.

"I am so glad you are feeling better!" Mrs. Jimenez smiled at him and waved goodbye as Chente walked out the front door.

Chente got in his car, started the ignition, and drove away. He went up the street a couple of blocks and turned on Avenue C. He pulled up to the driveway of a redbrick house and patiently waited as he casually tried different radio stations.

A few seconds later a tall, blonde-haired girl emerged from the front door. She wore a stylish purple sweater and designer blue jeans. She gingerly walked on the frosty pavement, carefully avoiding the ice patches concealed beneath the morning snow.

Haven Ray was a pretty girl—long, golden hair; big, expressive eyes; and a sincere smile. She came from a privileged and respectable family of five. Her parents were technical engineers and owned a successful software and consulting company in Lubbock, and her two older brothers played college football at West Texas A&M University. They were strong and athletic and annoyingly protective of their little sister.

Haven was the youngest in her family, and her parents doted on their baby girl, regularly buying her expensive designer clothing and fashionable jewelry. But despite the extra familial attention Haven received, she wasn't conceited or arrogant. Instead, the blonde-haired girl was bright, intuitive, and kind; and she was head over heels in love with the Jimenez boy.

Chente and Haven had been dating for about three months, but they had been friends since elementary school. Chente knew Haven wanted the "girlfriend" title, but for some reason, he just wasn't sure that was a good idea.

Haven opened the car door and greeted Chente with a warm smile. Her pretty hazel eyes lit up when she saw Chente behind the wheel. "Hey, Chen, it's so good to see you," she said with an energetic voice.

Chente bashfully nodded and smiled. "Good morning. It's kind of cold outside, right?"

"Yep, but I love the snow," she whispered as she stared out the passenger window. "It's so calming and peaceful."

Chente lowered the radio volume and sighed.

"But anyway, happy New Year!" She giggled as she reached over and gave Chente a kiss on the cheek. Then he reversed the Jetta out of the driveway.

"Oh yes, happy New Year," he said with a nervous lump in his throat. "Uh, we need to swing by and pick up Felipe, too. He needs a ride to school."

Haven nodded and strapped on her seat belt. "So, how is your family? How was your Christmas?" she asked spiritedly.

Haven was in a good mood. She was thrilled to see Chente, and it was obvious she was going to avoid the elephant sitting in the back seat of the car.

Chente made a sad face and incidentally shrugged. "Yeah, it was a little different without Dad this year," he replied with a wrinkled forehead and tense shoulders, "but it was fine."

"Oh, Chen, I am sorry." Haven sighed and covered her mouth. "I forgot about your dad. I am so sorry. I just forgot."

"You? How was your Christmas?" he asked as he casually exhaled and quickly moved on with the conversation. "Was Santa good to you?"

Haven sat up straight in her seat and batted her lovely eyes with excitement. "He was. Santa came through this year." She laughed. "I got a new cell phone and some jewelry from Kendra Scott." She lifted her blonde hair to expose her new earrings.

"Oh wow! Those are pretty." He glanced over at her and made a right turn onto Avenue F. He could see Felipe waiting for them on the curb.

Felipe jumped into the back seat, shook his body, and let out a shivering groan. "Dude, it is so freakin' cold outside." His teeth continued to chatter.

"Yes, it is!" replied Chente as he chuckled under his breath. "But hey, Mom made breakfast this morning. I have some breakfast tacos in my backpack for you. Maybe that will warm you up a little."

"Oh my God, are you being serious right now?" asked the starved boy as he frantically searched Chente's backpack. "Of course, I want them! I am so hungry!"

Chente locked eyes with Felipe in the rearview mirror and smiled. Felipe reached over and playfully swatted Chente on the head.

"Hey, dude, a couple of those breakfast tacos are for Carlos. So don't eat all of them," said Chente as he saw his friend tear into his first taco from his rearview mirror.

Felipe chuckled and nodded. "Oh, excuse me. I am sorry. What's up, Haven? How's it going?" asked Felipe with his mouth full of food.

Haven casually shook her head and smiled. "Hello, Felipe. Happy New Year to you."

Felipe gave her a thumbs-up signal and continued to devour his breakfast with the childish voracity of a starving ten-year-old boy. He let out a gratifying burp after he finished inhaling the first breakfast taco and began to unwrap his second one.

The senior class clown stopped for a second and mischievously looked at his friend in the rearview mirror. He playfully covered his mouth with his left hand as he quietly chuckled to himself and took a bite of his second taco.

Chente lightheartedly shook his head.

Felipe Lopez's family life was a little unstable. His dad was an alcoholic and a regular at the unemployment office, while his mother often left Felipe for long periods when his father became physically abusive. Felipe hated his home life and preferred spending his time with his friends. He regularly ate supper and spent the night with Chente and Victor. The Jimenez house had become his refuge, and Mrs. Jimenez considered him her adopted son.

"*Ay*, Chente! I love your mom's tortillas." Felipe sighed and rolled his eyes in utter delight. "*Y también* these tacos—dude, they are amazing!"

Haven sighed and casually pinned her blonde hair behind her right ear. She quietly turned her attention to the radio and began to thumb through the different stations in search of a good song.

Felipe sat up straight up and curiously looked out the window as Chente made a left turn on Nottingham Street. "*Oyes*, Chente," he said as he nudged the back of Chente's head, "I know you haven't been to school in a while, but dude, you're going the wrong way."

Haven looked away from the radio and surveyed her surroundings with a confused expression. She glanced at Chente and paused. "Hey, Chen, where are we going?"

Chente didn't respond. He remained silent. He kept his eyes on the road without looking at his friends.

Haven softly exhaled as she gazed at Chente. She couldn't read his face. She turned around and looked at Felipe, who shrugged.

"Relax, guys. I am just making a quick, five-minute detour. I promise we won't be late to school," said Chente as he turned into the Avalon Cemetery.

Felipe put the remainder of his taco away and cleared his throat. He rubbed his forehead and sat quietly in the back seat, looking out the window. Haven began to fidget with her cell phone as she casually began to delete old text messages.

Chente pulled up and parked his silver Jetta by the big pine tree in the middle of the cemetery. He left the car engine running and nervously tapped the steering wheel with both thumbs.

The Jimenez boy forced a smile and quietly exhaled. "I need to do something, and I will be back in a couple of minutes," he said as he slowly opened the car door and got out of the vehicle.

"Okay, Chen. Don't be too long. It's really cold out there," said Haven as she tried to smile.

Chente nodded and shut the door; he listened to its lonely echo make its way through the snowcapped trees. He walked down a solitary lane of tall trees and toward a singular headstone, which said, "Beloved Father."

It had been a few months since Chente went to the cemetery to see his dad. He and Victor usually came together. He made the sign of the cross and slowly sat down on a bench as the northern wind softly wailed through the desolate graveyard.

"Hey, Dad," said Chente with a deep sigh. "I just dropped by for a quick visit before school starts. Christmas wasn't the same without you, but we managed. We played some of your favorite mariachi music in your honor."

He felt the cool breeze brush his face like a wintry kiss, which sent chills all over his body. He closed his eyes and smiled. "Just wanted to say hi and let you know I miss you—every single day."

The Jimenez boy was determined not to get too emotional, so he gently outlined his father's name on the headstone with his fingers as he stood up and sighed.

It was a beautiful morning, and the cemetery was so peaceful and quiet. He softly closed his eyes and inhaled the blissful tranquility.

After a few seconds, he opened his eyes and took one last look at his father's grave. He gingerly wiped away the snow from the top of the headstone, made the sign of the cross, and walked away.

He quietly strolled down the same narrow gravel road, which was partially covered in snow, and listened to the northern wind whistle through the icy tree branches of the giant oak trees surrounding the little cemetery.

Chente paused. He rubbed his hands together and anxiously glanced at his parked car in the distance. He had been dreading this moment over the last few weeks, and he could feel the muscles in his legs tense in an attempt to shield him from moving any farther.

He slowly shook his head, softly exhaled, trudged forward another fifty feet, and stopped at an unmarked grave.

"Hey, Jimmy," whispered Chente. He cleared his throat and nervously kicked a pile of snow to the side.

Silence.

Chente closed his eyes and miserably shook his head when he realized the pile of dirt wasn't going to respond.

He couldn't do this. All he wanted was some sort of closure, but it had been a mistake to come here. He turned to walk away, then stopped. He exhaled.

Chente slowly collected his thoughts and tried to calm down. He softly took a deep breath, closed his eyes, turned around, and faced the pile of dirt.

He started again. "Jimmy, I just wanted to come and pay my respects." The Jimenez boy sighed. "I would have come and said goodbye sooner, but your family gave you a private funeral, and well, no one else was invited."

The Davis family was a rich and influential family in Avalon. They were considered "old money" and regarded as one of the town's founding families. The Davis family members were extensive landowners and successfully operated a large feedlot just outside the city limits for their cattle-rearing business. Over the years, the Hispanic citizenry in Avalon, those gainfully employed by the Davis family, began to complain about Mr. Davis's unfair working conditions and minimal wages. There were also whispers on the streets that his cruel employee treatment was because he was a bona fide racist.

In early December, a winter chill had invaded the small West Texas town, and the Davis family had suffered a devastating loss with Jimmy's untimely suicide. Mr. Davis took his only son's unexpected death extremely hard and didn't allow any of Jimmy's friends to attend the private services.

"Get the hell out of here," Mr. Davis had yelled as he charged at Chente, who stood at the entrance of the First Baptist Church. "You are the reason my son is dead!"

"I just want to say goodbye to my friend," whispered Chente as he wiped the tears from his eyes. "I just want to see him one last time."

"Get out!" screamed the mourning father. "Your kind is not welcome here!"

Immediately two big men dressed in black grabbed Chente and pushed him out of the church, warning him not to return.

Now Chente took a deep breath as he remembered. He slowly rubbed his forehead and sighed helplessly. "I miss you, Jimmy. I really hope your heart found some peace," he whispered. "I am sorry, my dear friend. I am sorry that I wasn't there for you when you needed me most. I am sorry that I let you down."

• ● •

Chente turned the corner of Avenue D and onto Broadway Street. He was nervous because Jimmy had sounded really crazy on the phone a few minutes earlier, and Chente had heard harsh screaming and yelling in the background. Something bad was going down at the Davis residence.

When Chente pulled into the curved driveway of Jimmy's house, he could see Jimmy and his dad in an argument. Mr. Davis was shouting at Jimmy, and Jimmy was forcibly shaking his head and shouting back. Mr. Davis grabbed Jimmy and pushed him to the ground.

Getting up, Jimmy sprinted to Chente's car, jumped in, and slammed the door shut. "Go, go, go!"

Chente anxiously sped away as he watched Mr. Davis scream obscenities and wave his arms in the air like a madman. "Dude! What's going on? This is freaking me out," yelled Chente as he drove the getaway car away from all the madness.

Jimmy just sat in the passenger seat, crying hysterically. His demented blue eyes were full of tears as he frantically placed his shaking hands over his blond hair.

"Please, tell me what's happening, Jimmy. Your dad was acting all crazy and shit. He chased the car! What's happening?" asked Chente as he watched his best friend fall to pieces in front of him.

Unexpectedly, Jimmy rolled down his window and began to scream as they drove down the highway. He pounded his right fist on the dashboard three times and kicked like a little boy throwing a tantrum.

"Dude, stop it! Stop it!" begged Chente. "You are scaring me now. Please tell me what's going on!"

Like a light switch, Jimmy immediately turned off his emotions and got quiet. He gradually rolled up the car window and wiped away his tears. He slowly shook his head and gazed out the foggy glass. He took a deep breath and closed his eyes.

"I came out to my parents tonight."

Chente was stunned to silence and didn't know what to say. He quietly absorbed the news and waited for his friend to continue to explain.

"Did you hear me, Chen? I came out to my parents."

"I heard you," started Chente in a calm voice. "What do you mean exactly?"

Jimmy unfastened his seat belt and turned to face his best friend in disbelief. "What do you mean exactly?" repeated Jimmy as he shook his head. "Chen, I told my parents I was gay. I told them that I liked boys and that I was tired of pretending to like girls."

Chente's hand nervously gripped the steering wheel, and he softly exhaled. He could hear the panic in his friend's voice, and it terrified him. He glanced at Jimmy and nodded calmly. "Okay. Then what happened?"

"Well, everything got crazy!" cried Jimmy. "My mom started crying and began to blame herself, and then my dad started screaming and said it was a rebellious phase I was going through. He said his son couldn't be a queer—he wouldn't allow it."

Chente continued to listen and drive. He was nervous. Something in the pit of his stomach wanted to make Jimmy stop talking. He didn't want to know what had happened next. He was frightened.

"You know, my dad is wrong," whimpered Jimmy as he quietly

looked out the foggy window and traced a broken heart with his index finger. "I know this isn't a phase. This is who I am."

Chente reached over and squeezed his friend's shoulder. "Dude, it will be all right. I promise. Your parents didn't see this coming. You caught them off guard," said Chente as he turned down Highway 194 and headed toward Dimmitt. "When things settle down a little bit, you will see that they still love you very much."

"I don't know about that," replied Jimmy with a strained voice. The blond-headed boy sighed quietly. "Maybe … maybe my mom will still love me but not my dad."

"Oh, come on, Jimmy, your dad loves you too," replied Chente as he tried to remain optimistic.

Jimmy frantically shook his head. His expressive eyes were full of agony. "Nope. No way. Not a chance," replied Jimmy as he remembered. "Chen, my dad was so mad. His eyes were full of anger and hate, and the things he said to me were horrible. He will never accept me being gay."

Chente gently exhaled and didn't say a word because he knew his best friend was probably right. Jimmy and his dad had never really gotten along, and this situation would only make their rocky and volatile relationship worse.

Mr. Davis was one of the most successful ranchers in the county, and the Davis family ranching business had been in the family for many generations. Jimmy was the heir apparent and was expected to carry on the family legacy of marrying, having kids, and running the family business—no matter what.

"So Jimmy, are you sure about this?" asked Chente as he glanced over at his friend.

"Yes. I am sure my dad hates me," answered Jimmy as he rolled his eyes and groaned. "I am ruining the Davis name. Wait, I am ruining the family name, and I am going to burn in hell. Those were his exact words."

Chente paused and sadly watched his best friend. "No, I mean are you sure that you're gay? Are you *sure*?"

"What do you mean?" asked Jimmy as he shot a look of horror at Chente. "Of course, I am sure that I am gay."

"Okay. Dude, I was just asking," replied Chente as he nervously nodded.

Jimmy stared at Chente from the passenger seat of the car. He slowly turned and looked out the car window, shaking his head. "So, Chen, I mean, you're gay too, right?"

Chente tightened his grip on the steering wheel and glanced at Jimmy, who was staring at him and waiting for an answer. His heart immediately wanted to jump out of his chest as he tried to regain a normal breathing pattern.

"Are you being serious right now?" Chente said, panicking, "I mean, you are seriously going to ask me that question right now while I am driving?"

"Yes. I am seriously asking you if you are gay too," replied Jimmy as he wiped the tears from his eyes.

Chente shook his head, and his mouth suddenly became dry as he struggled to find words. He needed a drink of cold water. "No … no, I am not … I mean, I don't think so," he finally answered.

"'I don't think so? I don't think so?'" repeated Jimmy as he painfully closed his eyes. "What does *that* mean?"

Chente could hear a hint of anger in Jimmy's voice, and it made him feel anxious and uneasy. He could feel his face getting hot as a million thoughts raced through his head. "I don't know, Jimmy. That means that I am not sure right now. I just don't know."

"What are you talking about, Chen?" shouted Jimmy. "How can you not know? Either you are gay or not! This is not a difficult question."

Chente pulled over to the side of the road and parked his car. He was confused and nervous and ready to explode. He was still unsure about his feelings. He had suppressed those tendencies his entire life and wasn't ready to answer questions. The Jimenez boy simply wasn't prepared to face his truth.

"Why are you yelling at me?" shouted Chente as he rolled down his window and fanned his face. "This is not about me."

"Of course it is," countered Jimmy as he extended his arms wide. "This is about me *and* you."

"What?" Chente gasped in disbelief.

"Aren't you tired of pretending?" shouted Jimmy. "Don't you just want to be yourself?"

Chente pushed his friend away and shook his head as he looked out the car window. He didn't understand how this conversation had spun out of control. How had he become the focal point in this situation?

"Just admit it," hissed Jimmy from the other side of the car. "Just admit it."

"Well, if you are going to force an answer out of me, then I am not gay," shouted Chente as he angrily pounded on the steering wheel. "That's my answer."

"Wow. Unbelievable," whispered Jimmy as he placed his hands over his head, closed his eyes, and exhaled.

Instantly, Chente knew he had hurt his best friend's feelings and tried to recover. He could see the pain on Jimmy's face.

"Look, Jimmy, I … I am not ready to do this. I … I … I don't know if I can do this. I am scared. Maybe I just need some time."

Jimmy didn't say a word as he looked out the car window.

"I … I have all this confusion inside me, and it scares me. I am just not ready for this right now. I … I am not ready to lose my friends and family over this," confessed Chente.

"So I guess I don't count? I thought I was your best friend," replied Jimmy as tears quietly rolled down his cheeks.

• • •

Chente heard a car door slam shut and woke from his memories to find Felipe standing next to him with his hand on his shoulder. Haven had just gotten out of the car and was walking toward them with concern in her eyes.

"Chen? You okay?" asked Felipe as his teeth chattered.

Chente nodded. He wiped the tears from his eyes and regained his composure. "Yeah. I'm good."

"Well, it's eight thirty, and I know you don't want to be late to school," said Felipe as he avoided making eye contact with his friend. "I will wait for you in the car, okay?" Felipe gave Chente a soft pat on the back.

Chente nodded again, and Felipe walked away. Felipe and Haven carefully made their way back to the car and got inside.

Chente listened to the wind howl through the trees; the sun peeked around the clouds and gently kissed him on the forehead.

"Jimmy, of course, you count. You will always be my best friend," he whispered.

Chente took a deep breath and exhaled. He made the sign of the cross and slowly walked away.

CHAPTER 3

The ride from the cemetery to the high school lasted only five minutes but seemed like an eternity for Chente. The awkward tension in the car was undeniable. Both Haven and Felipe were glued to their cell phones, avoided eye contact, and hadn't said a word since they left the graveyard. Chente had never been more grateful for the Maroon 5 song playing on the radio.

The silver Jetta pulled into the high school parking lot. Chente parked the car next to the gym as the school bell rang. "Guys, sorry for being such a downer this morning at the cemetery. It was just something I had to do … so I could move on."

Felipe reached over the car seat and messed up Chente's hair. "Don't worry about it," he said as he opened his backdoor and jumped out. "I'll see you second period." Felipe grinned as he made a peace sign and ran inside the high school building.

Haven quietly studied Chente's face before she opened her door. "Are you okay? Do you feel better?"

Chente exhaled and nodded. "Yes, I do. Thanks for asking." He opened his door, grabbed his backpack, and got out. He met Haven in front of the car, and she reached for his hand.

She smiled and batted her hazel eyes at him. "Of course. I care about you, Chen. You know that, right?"

Chente matched her smile and nodded. Chente knew Haven really liked him, but he wasn't sure how to feel about this or what to do. Haven was such a nice girl, so for now he was going to do his best to be a good friend.

Chente took a deep breath and opened the front door of the building for Haven and walked into the main hallway. He kicked the snow off his shoes and stood there, watching the normal hysteria of a Monday morning.

Life had moved on.

The teachers were standing in their doorways, speaking to each other about their holiday adventures. Girls were exiting the bathroom, laughing, and students were rushing to class to avoid being tardy.

Chente smiled. It was a normal Monday morning.

"Chen, don't be nervous. Everything will be fine," promised Haven as she blew him a kiss and walked away.

"Thanks. See you at lunch," replied Chente as he watched Haven walk down the main hallway and disappear into a sea of high school students.

Chente was an office aide during the first period, and he quickly walked to the administration office. Mrs. Black was busy on the phone, and Principal Timms was in the hallway, corralling students to their respective classrooms. Chente put his backpack on his desk and sat down. He pulled out his cell phone and turned off the ringer. He put it away in his jacket.

The tardy bell rang.

"Good morning, Chen," said Mrs. Black as she got off the phone and smiled. The short and petite high school secretary walked over and gave him a maternal hug. "Hope your holidays were good," she said as she gently pinched his cheeks.

Chente smiled and nodded. "Yes. They were good," he lied.

"Well, honey, I am so glad to hear that," she said as she returned to her desk and grabbed the ringing telephone. In a friendly voice, she quickly placed the caller on hold and turned to Chente. "Honey, would you be a doll and deliver these attendance strips to the following teachers? They must have forgotten to check their teacher mailboxes this morning."

"Absolutely," replied Chente as he snatched the attendance strips and marched out of the office and into the hallways.

Chente walked down A hallway first and delivered attendance strips to Ms. Briones, Mr. Cowder, and Mrs. Vaughan. He waved to a few of his friends through the classroom door windows as he made his way through the hallway. He felt good to be back.

He had only one set of attendance strips left to deliver, and they belonged to Coach Doss. It was a typical first-year teacher mistake to forget to check his box, and he headed to the B hallway and knocked on the coach's classroom door.

Coach Doss answered the door and smiled as morning announcements blared over the school intercom. "Hey, Chen. What's going on?" asked the basketball coach with a puzzled expression.

Chente playfully waved the attendance strips.

"Oh, wow. This is embarrassing. I knew I was forgetting something." The first-year teacher winced as he playfully rubbed his forehead. "Am I fired?"

"Well, not today," whispered Chente lightheartedly as he chuckled under his breath and leaned in close to the coach. "But if it makes you feel better, you weren't the only teacher who forgot." He smiled and casually walked away.

"Hey, Chen?" called out the history teacher as he stood by his classroom door.

Chente turned around.

"Glad you made it to school today." Coach Doss grinned as he made his way back into his classroom.

Chente nodded, and just like that, he felt a lot better. When he returned to the front office, Christina and Carlos were walking out. They had just completed a series of morning announcements and appeared to be bickering at each other about Christina's spontaneous comments over the intercom.

Chente stared at his two friends with a nervous smile as Christina dramatically screamed and threw her arms around his neck. She gave him a friendly peck, leaving her lipstick tattooed on his right cheek.

"Chen! You're back! It's so good to see you," screeched the head cheerleader as she theatrically swung her long, black hair back and forth and hugged her friend. "How was your Christmas? Get anything interesting or expensive?"

"What's up, Christina? Happy New Year!" answered Chente as he quickly wiped his cheek with his hand. "Yeah, Christmas was actually a little different this year."

"Well, I got a Louis Vuitton purse and a diamond bracelet," bragged the feisty Latina as she completely ignored Chente's comment. "See. They are real diamonds too."

Chente let out a little sigh as he pretended to act interested in his friend's bracelet. And even though she was full of herself, it was good to see Christina. She was an old friend of the family. He knew she could be exasperating at times, but under her enormous ego was a good and faithful friend.

"What's up, Chen?" Carlos beamed with a smile.

Chente was even gladder to see Carlos. He and Carlos had been friends for many years. In fact, they had started kindergarten together twelve years earlier. Carlos was a little shy around people he didn't know, but he had proved to be a fiercely loyal friend over the years.

"*Qué pasa*, Carlitos?" said Chente as he hugged his friend.

"Hey, man, thanks for the breakfast tacos. I love your mom's tortillas," said Carlos as he studied Chente from head to toe, making sure he was all right.

"I am shocked that Felipe actually gave them to you!"

All three friends burst into silly laughter.

Principal Timms quickly emerged from the administration office, followed closely by Mrs. Black, who was taking notes on her laptop. He was sporting a crew cut and a black business suit, and he towered over his tiny secretary. He carried a cup of coffee in one hand and a bullhorn in the other. He gave them a stern look.

"I hate to break up the reunion, kids, but you need to get to class." He nodded to Mrs. Black and walked away.

"Yes, sir, Principal Timms," said Christina, and she saluted as he passed by.

"Oh my gosh. You're such a kiss ass, Christina." Carlos laughed as he rolled his eyes.

Christina gave him a horrified look and spectacularly covered her mouth. "Excuse me, but I would not be kissing that ass. Just saying." The head cheerleader giggled as she strutted down the hallway in her fashionable high heels.

Carlos looked at Chente and sighed. "It's so good to see you, Chen. See you next period." He squeezed Chente's shoulder and followed Christina.

The rest of the morning went by smoothly, and Chente blended back into normal high school life with ease. Much to his relief, nobody asked about his whereabouts for the last three weeks. His friends were just thrilled to have him back.

After fourth-period class, Chente, Felipe, and Carlos headed to the cafeteria for lunch. Chente was in the lunch line, inspecting the food, when Ricky Bennett walked over and stood beside him. Chente ignored him and grabbed a slice of pizza and some french fries; he headed to the cashier to pay.

"So it's true. You are back," sneered Ricky as his lanky frame followed Chente to the cashier.

"Are you talking to me, or do you have an imaginary friend, Ricky?" replied Chente as he playfully looked around while he stood in line to purchase his food.

"Very funny." The Bennett boy smirked with suspicious eyes.

Chente quickly paid the cashier and sat down with his friends at their usual cafeteria table. Ricky shadowed him and continued the one-sided conversation. "So, is Coach Alvarez really going to let you back on the basketball team after you missed all those games?"

"I really don't care to discuss anything with you, Ricky," replied Chente.

"Ricky, you make it sound like Chente missed half of the season," replied Carlos as he rolled his eyes and sighed. "Dude, it was only four games."

"And we lost all four games too," added Felipe as he tossed a french fry in his mouth.

"Yeah, but what about all the practices he missed too?" complained Ricky as he shook his head.

"Listen, why don't you let Coach Alvarez worry about that." Carlos smiled as he waved off the red-headed boy. "Now, go eat your lunch like a good little boy."

Felipe stood up and pointed at Ricky with one of his french fries. "What's your problem, Ricky?" asked Felipe as he towered over the Bennett boy. "I don't know about you, but I personally like winning."

Ricky said, "It isn't fair, he can't just—"

"Look, Coach Alvarez better let him play," Felipe said. "Otherwise we will just keep losing. Just saying."

Chente had heard enough and waved off the angry basketball player. "Look, Ricky, I really don't have time for the scene you want to cause right now. Just go eat your lunch and be nice to people." Chente chuckled as he pulled out his cell phone and began sending a text message.

Carlos and Felipe started to laugh as Christina came and sat down at the table. She gave Ricky a disgusted look and brushed her hair back with her polished fingernails. "You heard the man. Get lost. This is a VIP table, and honey, you ain't invited."

Ricky pursed his lips and shook his head. Visibly frustrated by being dismissed by his teammates, he glared at Christina.

The head cheerleader wasn't intimidated as she put her hands on her hips and glared back. She continued to wave off Ricky. "*Ya vete* … Bye … *adios* … No *gringos* allowed."

Ricky left in a huff as the three boys erupted in laughter.

Christina smiled triumphantly and snapped her fingers in a *Z* formation. "And there you have it: Christina to the rescue—again!"

Felipe reached over the table and high-fived Christina, then stole a couple of fries off her lunch tray. "Seriously, Christina, we need to buy you a hot-pink superhero cape with the letters *S* and *B* on it for Super Bitch!"

Christina theatrically fanned her face with her delicately manicured hand and giggled with delight. She playfully gave Felipe the evil eye and sat down.

Chente's cell phone buzzed, and he pulled it out of his pocket and carefully read the text message.

"Is everything okay?" asked Carlos.

Chente nodded. "It's Haven. She's going to sit with Sally today. Apparently, Sally and Dario broke up over Christmas, and Sally is upset or something like that."

"I don't even know what you see in her, Chen. She ain't that pretty." Christina frowned as she rolled her eyes and sighed.

Carlos quickly came to Haven's defense and shook his head. "*Mira*, Christina, really? Why do you got to be like that? Haven is a nice girl, and she's very pretty."

"Whatever. She's boring," complained Christina as she carefully took a bite of her pepperoni pizza so she wouldn't smudge her bright-red lipstick.

Chente ignored Christina and was used to her constant criticism. He responded to Haven's text and continued to eat his lunch.

Felipe let out a big burp and changed the subject. "Hey, guys, did you hear Coach Stoval broke his leg while he was skiing over the holidays?"

"Shut up, dude!" said Carlos. "Are you being serious right now?"

"Really. It was pretty serious too," replied Felipe as he reached over and stole more french fries from Christina's tray. He was still hungry. "I think he broke it in three places. He won't be back until after spring break. I mean that's what I heard." Felipe stood up and got back in the food line.

Christina opened her Louis Vuitton purse and reached for her pink compact and mascara. She mischievously grinned at her friends. "Cool. That means we have a substitute for seventh period," she said with a playful wink. "Yes! Party time!"

The tardy bell rang for seventh period, and Miss Young, the high school counselor, walked into the government classroom with Coach Doss. She handed him a grade book, lesson plans, and some last-minute instructions. Coach Doss looked perplexed and completely overwhelmed.

"Hello, everyone." Miss Young smiled as she stood next to Coach Doss. "You may or may not know, but Coach Stoval had a skiing accident over the holidays and will not be able to return to class until after spring break. With that said, Coach Doss will be taking over seventh period government class until then."

Christina lustfully stared at Coach Doss from head to toe and delicately brushed her long, black hair back and smiled. "Wow. This is definitely an improvement."

Miss Young gave Christina a stern look, and Christina quickly sat up and stopped smiling.

"Now this is a senior class, and I expect you to behave like seniors and be responsible," continued the high school counselor.

The class nodded in agreement.

"Chen? If Coach Doss has any questions, I trust that you will help him?" asked Miss Young.

"Yes, of course," answered Chente as his cheeks turned bright pink. He knew he would be teased relentlessly for being the teacher's pet.

"Okay, then," said Miss Young as she began exiting the classroom, "I will let you get started, Coach Doss. See me after class if you have any questions."

Coach Doss apprehensively looked up and nodded. He got settled at his desk, and he quickly gathered his composure as he placed his brown briefcase next to the filing cabinet.

"For those who don't know me, my name is Coach Doss," he said as he stood up and nearly tripped over the wooden podium at the front of the classroom as he clumsily walked around.

"Hello, Coach Doss," replied Christina as she batted her eyes at him.

The first-year teacher ignored the head cheerleader and continued. "I graduated from Texas Tech last year with a major in history. I am currently teaching world geography and world history. I also coach football, basketball, and track. I have never thought about teaching government, so we are going to be learning together."

Chente gave the new government teacher a reassuring smile and watched him return to his desk and pull out the attendance strips to take roll. He couldn't help but admire how the brown Docker pants hugged Coach Doss's taut backside. It was perfect.

"Okay, guys, I don't know everyone in this class, so let's do introductions," suggested Coach Doss as he peeked at his attendance strips.

Student introductions started from the left of the classroom. One by one each student introduced himself or herself to Coach Doss. After a few minutes, the introductions made their way to the last row of students.

Christina got up from her desk, provocatively stood with her hands on her hips, and smiled at the first-year teacher. "My name is Christina Fernandez, and I have two older sisters, but I am definitely the prettiest. I am eighteen years old, and I am head cheerleader. I plan to attend Texas Tech after I graduate in May."

Christina sat back down at her desk. "Hold your applause, please. Autographs after class, thank you." The head cheerleader grinned.

The students laughed.

Chente hesitated and rubbed his nose. He glanced at Coach Doss as he stood up. Coach Doss's eyes were fixed on Chente. He nodded and smiled.

"My name is Vincente Jimenez Jr., but my friends call me Chen. I am one of five siblings. I play basketball and tennis, and I turned eighteen in October. I am not sure where I will be attending college," said Chente, and he sat back down.

"But you are going to college, right?" asked Coach Doss.

Chente quickly cleared his throat and nodded.

"Coach, Chen is our class valedictorian. He's like a walking brain," teased Felipe. "He's just waiting to see which college is going to give him the most money. Right, Chen?"

Chente could feel his face getting hot as he anxiously adjusted his sitting position. He felt like he was under a microscope, and being in the same class with Coach Doss made him curiously nervous. He felt exposed.

"Oh. Is that right?" The coach nodded. "So which colleges are you considering?"

Chente exhaled and stared at his feet. "I don't really know, sir." He tried to focus on the question and not on the magnetic blue eyes staring at him. "I … I … like Stanford, but the University of Texas is a good school too. Then there's Texas Tech if I choose to stay close to home. So I am not sure yet."

"Wow. That's an impressive list, Mr. Jimenez. Good luck to you," said Coach Doss with an admiring smile.

Chente politely nodded. He didn't like the extra attention and begged the floor to open up and swallow him.

Coach Doss grabbed a manila folder and pulled out worksheets. They were a chapter nine outline. He passed them out and allowed the class to work in pairs.

Carlos moved over and paired up with Chente. He glanced at Chente and then looked around the classroom. "What's the matter with you?"

"It's just embarrassing to be called out like that." Chente groaned as he rubbed the back of his neck.

"Dude, really? You need to chill out." Carlos chuckled under his breath.

"Whatever."

"Dude, Felipe is just proud of you—we all are," said Carlos as he opened his government textbook. "You're getting out of this little town."

Chente retrieved his pen from his backpack, paused, and gave Carlos a puzzled look. "Wait a minute," he whispered. "Carlos, so are you … I mean, you are going to college too, right?"

"Man, I want to, but it costs a lot of money, and I don't know if my family can afford it," replied Carlos as he turned the pages of his textbook to chapter nine. "I don't have scholarships like you."

Carlos came from a very traditional Hispanic family. His father worked at the local feedlot, and his mother stayed home to cook, clean, and raise the kids. Carlos was the oldest in the family. He had two younger sisters and a younger brother, and his dad was counting on him to find a job after high school to help with the household bills.

Suddenly, Chente felt incredibly lucky.

"What about financial aid? Carlos, there's financial aid," said Chente as he closed Carlos's textbook and gave him a pleading look.

Carlos just shrugged and looked at his friend. "Yeah, man, I don't know, Chen."

"We can talk to Miss Young. She's really smart and really good at this college stuff," suggested Chente. "I mean, she really knows her stuff."

The Jimenez boy was on a mission and desperately wanted to find a way for his friend to continue his education.

Carlos's hazel eyes lit up. He had never really considered going to college. He had always thought that completing high school would be the end of his educational career.

"Chen, do you really think I could make it in college?"

"Definitely!" replied Chente with an exaggerated nod. "Of course you can make it in college. You just have to get there."

"Can I go with y'all—you know, to talk to Miss Young?" asked Felipe, who had been eavesdropping on the conversation. "Maybe she can help me too, right?"

Chente began to laugh as he wadded a sheet of paper and tossed it at Felipe.

"Of course. That's a great idea. I have an appointment to see her tomorrow morning during first period. I will schedule you guys an appointment tomorrow too, okay?" asked Chente.

Carlos and Felipe nodded with excitement and gave each other a fist bump.

"Enough with the visiting, guys. I need you to open your textbook and get to work," replied the new government teacher as he walked by and gave them a stern look.

Chente and Carlos breezed through the worksheet in fifteen minutes, and Chente got up and walked to the teacher's desk to submit the assignment. He was excited that his friends wanted to meet with Miss

Young. He was confident that she could help them get on the right path to a college education.

"Hey, Chen, where does Coach Stoval keep the textbook's teacher edition?" asked Coach Doss as he searched the desk drawers.

"I think it's in the filing cabinet—bottom drawer." Chente pointed with a nod.

Coach Doss opened the bottom drawer and pulled out the textbook. "Yep. It's here. Thanks."

"Yes, sir," said Chente as he began to make his way back to his desk.

"Hey, Chen? I don't mean to put you on the spot, but are you really thinking about going to Stanford next year?" whispered Coach Doss.

Chente turned around, took a few steps toward the desk, and nodded. He felt a magnetic pull he didn't understand.

"What a great opportunity that would be for you." Coach Doss beamed.

"Yes, it would be awesome." Chente smiled as he nervously rubbed his forehead. "I mean, I have to be awarded the Presidential Scholarship to go. It's too expensive otherwise."

"Oh, I see." Coach Doss nodded. "Have you applied for it?"

"Yes, sir," whispered Chente as he nervously looked around the room, trying to avoid the captivating blue eyes of the man in front of him.

"And so when will you find out?"

"I should know something by the end of February—good or bad," said Chente with his fingers crossed.

"You know, I have always wanted to go to the Bay Area in California," muttered Coach Doss. "I hear it's a beautiful part of the country."

"I have never been there either," replied Chente as he bashfully shrugged and sighed. "But if I get the scholarship, I think they will fly me and a friend down for college orientation in June."

The bell rang, and students got up and began to file out of the classroom. Chente politely excused himself from the conversation with a nod. He returned to his desk and retrieved his backpack and started to exit the room.

"Well, I hope you get the scholarship, and thanks for your help this afternoon." Coach Doss exhaled as he watched Chente turn to leave.

"No problem, sir. You did good today," replied Chente as he rushed out of the classroom.

Chente hurried down the hallway. He couldn't be late for athletics. Athletes who arrived tardy for practice had to run two miles at the end of the period. He figured he would have enough running to complete just trying to get back on the basketball team.

As Chente made his way through the crowded hallways, he saw Victor standing outside the gym doors, waiting.

"What's up, Vic?" asked Chente as he looked at his watch. "Is something the matter?"

"My stomach hurts, and I am feeling achy all over," complained the little brother. "I don't know what's wrong with me."

"Okay. Have you been to the nurse?"

"Yes, Chente." He moaned and rolled his eyes. "She said I should go home."

Victor never called him "Chente" unless he was serious, so Chente knew he must be really sick.

"Okay, well, if the nurse said to go home, then why are you still here? What's the matter?"

Victor gave Chente a dreadful look as he covered his mouth and coughed. "It's cold outside. It's too cold to walk home. And man, Violeta is our emergency contact. Don't make me call her."

"What do you mean?"

"Dude, I can't handle her twice in one day," complained Victor as he put his hands up in protest. "Seeing her again today will be instant death!"

"Oh, right. I get it now." Chente laughed as he reached into the side pocket of his backpack and pulled out the car keys. "Have the nurse sign you out and go straight home."

Victor nodded and trudged his way down the hallway and back to the nurse's office.

Chente stood outside the gym doors for a couple of seconds. He took a deep breath, opened the door, and walked into the gym.

The boys' locker room was crazy loud as the athletes got ready for basketball practice. There was a little singing, a little laughing, and a little cursing—everything you would expect to hear in a high school boys' locker room.

"So Chen is really back, right?" asked Beau as he put on his workout shorts.

Felipe gave him a thumbs-up. "Yes, he is. The master has returned."

"Thank God." Beau sighed.

Beau was a sophomore and the second-string point guard for the basketball team. He had been elevated to the starting point guard position in Chente's absence, and the transition hadn't gone too well.

"Yeah, well, I don't think it's fair that he just gets to walk back onto the team after missing so many practices and games," grumbled Ricky as he made no attempt to hide his hateful feelings.

"Well, hello, doom and gloom," Carlos sarcastically replied as he put on his basketball shoes. "You're not the coach, so deal with it."

The locker room exploded into silly laughter as Ricky gave Carlos a spiteful look and continued his hateful ranting.

"Guys, seriously, he left us high and dry. He abandoned the team."

Nobody in the locker room cared about what Ricky said.

"Ricky, just give it a rest already—your voice is annoying me. You sound like a barking Chihuahua that never shuts up." Felipe laughed as he shook his head.

"Chen is a senior and has been the starting point guard since he was a freshman. That earns him the right to have a second chance," announced Tre' in a low and powerful voice as he finished tying his basketball shoes and got up to stretch his legs. "The griping and complaining need to stop."

Tre' was a senior and the star of the basketball team. He was a six-six power forward with slick inside moves and a soft shooting range that exceeded just past the free throw line. He was strong and athletic and had several colleges recruiting him for his services. He and Chente had been teammates since ninth grade. Tre' didn't say much, but when he did, everyone listened.

"Now everyone needs to hurry up," said the power forward. "We need to practice. I'm tired of losing."

As Tre' maneuvered his way out of the locker room, Chente was walking in. The six-six basketball star stopped and greeted his point guard with a fist bump. "Sup, Chen? Boy, am I glad to see you."

Now everyone knew where Tre' stood on the topic of discussion, and the locker room grew uncomfortably quiet as Chente walked to his locker and started to get dressed.

Beau was the first to greet Chente with a friendly pat on the shoulder as he maneuvered around the lockers and out to the gym. "I am so glad to see you, Chen. Welcome back."

"Thanks, Beau. See you in a minute," replied Chente as he quietly put on his practice jersey.

The locker room was very still. It was obvious Chente had walked in on a heated conversation between the team, and he had no doubt that it was about him. The point guard was equally sure Ricky was the root of it all too as he slammed his locker shut and left the locker room without saying a word.

Chente turned and watched Ricky storm out of the locker room; he glanced at Felipe and Carlos, who were shaking their heads. "Okay? What did I miss?"

"Trust me, nothing important," remarked Felipe as he stretched his arms.

"Chen, *ya conoces el cabrón,*" muttered Carlos as he slipped his practice jersey over his head. "Man, he's just a pain in the ass. Nothing new. He's just mad that you're back and that you're ten times better than him."

"I don't get him," said Chente as he resumed getting dressed. "Why does he hate me so much?"

"*Celos,*" answered Felipe plainly. "*Tiene celos el cabrón.*"

The three got up to exit the locker room when Coach Doss entered.

"Chen, Coach Alvarez wants to see you in his office before practice starts."

Carlos and Felipe walked out of the locker room, and Chente nodded and stayed behind. He took a deep breath and followed Coach Doss to the coaches' office.

Before entering, Coach Doss calmly put his hand on Chente's shoulders and smiled. "Look, Chen, just relax and don't take anything Coach Alvarez might say too personal," advised the assistant coach. "Just listen and apologize."

Chente nervously nodded in agreement. "Yes, sir."

"Have the guys stretch and start on their ball-handling drills," said Coach Alvarez as he put his whistle around his neck. "We will be out shortly."

Coach Doss nodded as he grabbed a stopwatch off his desk and closed the office door.

Coach Alvarez sat down and reclined in his chair with a clipboard. He calmly and carefully looked at Chente, studying him from head to toe with his eyes.

"So, Chen, tell me, are you okay?"

Coach Alvarez was a hard-ass coach, but he genuinely cared about his athletes. His practices were like boot camp. They were strenuous, organized, and precise; and his military crew cut made him look more like an army sergeant than a basketball coach.

He was an Avalon High School alum, who had played basketball in the same gym he now coached in. His stern brow and his muscular frame demanded respect, and his strategic prowess and attention to detail made him a successful coach. Coach Alvarez lived in Avalon and was committed to his small-town community. He wanted the best for his basketball players on and off the court.

Chente wasn't sure what to say. He respectfully glanced at his basketball coach and worried that he would say something wrong. He wasn't sure that his basketball coach would understand his current distress.

"I don't know what to tell you, Coach," replied Chente as he stared at his basketball shoes.

"How about the truth?" answered Coach Alvarez pragmatically.

The last thing Chente wanted to do was lie to his basketball coach. He admired Coach Alvarez and had too much respect for him to do that.

"See, Coach, I don't know what the truth is right now," confessed Chente without lying.

"I don't understand what that means," replied Coach Alvarez as he sat up in his chair with a confused brow. "Are you in some sort of trouble?"

"No. Of course not. It's nothing like that," replied Chente as he shook his head slowly.

"Okay. Then what is it?"

The basketball player quietly paused and sighed. He shamefully looked at his coach. "See, I have been struggling lately," began Chente.

"Okay," replied the basketball coach. "Is this about your dad and the holidays?"

"Well, yeah, a little of that too, but ..."

"But what?" asked Coach Alvarez as he repositioned himself in his chair.

"See, it's my friend, Jimmy," said Chente, then cleared his throat. "His death ... no, his suicide ... broke me, Coach, and I made some bad decisions.

"There is so much drama surrounding Jimmy's death that still haunts me," confessed Chente as his bottom lip began to quiver.

Coach Alvarez nodded and carefully listened to everything Chente said. He watched Chente's body language and searched his eyes, hoping to find a clue that would help him understand.

"But I did what I think I needed to do to pull me through this," continued Chente with a slight shoulder shrug. "I am very sorry that you and my teammates got caught in the crossfire. I am sorry that I let you down."

Coach Alvarez got up from his chair and let out a deep sigh. He knew this erratic behavior was uncommon for his basketball star. "I am sorry to hear about your friend," said Coach Alvarez in a stern but sympathetic voice. "I am sure that you have not had an easy time with this."

"No, sir."

"But you know that I can't excuse the missed practices and the missed games, right?"

Chente swiftly nodded in agreement. "Yes, sir. I make no excuses. I should have at least called to tell you what was going on," he replied as he continued to stare at the floor.

Coach Alvarez almost began to laugh at Chente's selfless reaction.

"Damn straight you should have called me," answered Coach Alvarez as he slightly raised his voice in an attempt to sound like he was mad. "You will have to run lines if you want to remain on the team. Also, you will have to complete your running before you play another game for me. You got that?" yelled Coach Alvarez as he pounded on the office door.

The head basketball coach wanted to make sure the basketball team outside could hear him.

Chente didn't flinch. He gave his coach a firm nod to acknowledge the terms and conditions to return to the team.

"Of course, sir. I understand."

Coach Alvarez was now putting on a show as he began to pace back and forth in the office. He pointed at Chente and nodded. "Okay. For every missed practice, you owe me two sets of lines, and for every game you missed, you owe me three sets of lines. You got that?"

"Yes, sir. I missed six practices, so that's twelve sets of lines. I also missed four games, so that's an additional twelve sets of lines. That makes the total twenty-four sets of lines," said Chente without pausing to take a breath.

"That's correct," replied Coach Alvarez as he playfully raised his eyebrows and coughed to muffle his laughter.

Chente was all business as he refused to stop looking at the floor. He was too ashamed to face Coach Alvarez. "Yes, sir. I will get started today after practice."

"No, sir, you won't," said Coach Alvarez. "You will start as soon as I excuse you in a few minutes."

Chente looked up at Coach Alvarez with an anxious face. He wasn't sure what was happening.

"I need you to finish your running today, because we have a game tomorrow, and I am going to need you to play." Coach Alvarez grinned as he reached over and playfully smacked Chente on the head.

Chente relaxed and smiled. "Thank you, Coach."

CHAPTER 4

Coach Alvarez blew his whistle and asked the basketball team to huddle up. He had Chente standing next to him when he explained to the varsity players the cardio conditions Chente would have to complete to return to the team. He added that Chente had to complete his running before he could play another basketball game.

"Does everybody understand the conditions?" yelled the head basketball coach.

Carlos immediately raised his hand. "Coach Alvarez, can some of us volunteer to run some lines for Chen?"

"Oh hell, yeah, uh ... I will run two sets of lines for Chen. Can I, Coach?" asked Felipe as he raised his hand and began jumping up and down with excitement.

Coach Alvarez anxiously cleared his throat with a look of surprise.

Carlos, Tre', and Sammy quickly volunteered to run for their senior classmate as well.

Coach Alvarez glanced over at Coach Doss, who simply shrugged.

"Wait. I will gladly run *three* sets of lines for Chen," yelled Beau as he looked at Chente and smiled. "Just *please* let him play tomorrow night," pleaded the back-up point guard as everyone began to laugh.

"We're family, right, Coach?" asked Tre' as he looked around at his teammates. "And in my book, family sticks together."

Most of the basketball boys nodded in agreement, while Chente stood in silence, never expecting this kind of reaction from his friends.

In the corners of his eyes, Chente watched Coach Alvarez mull it over as he paced up and down the gymnasium floor. The basketball coach slowly nodded and finally agreed. He gave the boys a two-minute water break and walked over to speak with Coach Doss.

Ricky stormed into the locker room, disgusted and mumbling obscenities under his breath, while the other boys surrounded Chente. They were glad to have him back on the basketball team.

"Coach Alvarez wants me to take you next door to the practice gym so you can start your running," replied Coach Doss as walked over to Chente with a cocky grin on his face. "Thanks to your fan club, you only have thirteen sets of lines to run."

The assistant basketball coach playfully patted Chente on the back as he kept walking.

Chente thanked his friends and followed Coach Doss out the gym door.

The practice gym was cold and dark, and it had a musty smell. It felt lonely. Coach Doss jogged to the opposite end of the gym, flipped on the lights, and wore a big smile as he walked back to Chente.

"I didn't know you were that big of a celebrity," teased Coach Doss.

"What does that mean?" asked Chente.

Coach Doss laughed aloud and lightheartedly shook his head. "Really? You have fans in the other gym who are willing to run lines for you. That's pretty cool!"

Chente awkwardly smiled and began to stretch his legs.

"Come on, Chen, please tell me you're a little more excited than you're showing."

"Well, of course, I'm pumped up. I am incredibly grateful," replied Chente with a smile. "I am just a little stunned too. I didn't expect that kind of reaction."

"It's a huge compliment that your teammates are willing to step up for you like that," announced Coach Doss as he extended his arms wide. "It says a lot about you. They must really believe in you."

Chente sat down and closed his eyes to concentrate on his leg stretches. "See, I think you got it backward. I think it says a lot about them," said the point guard as he calmly exhaled.

He released and spread his legs and reached to the right. "I'm very lucky that they are my friends and that I am still part of the team."

Coach Doss smiled and slowly nodded. He watched as Chente continued to stretch. "I get it. I see your point," answered the assistant coach.

Chente opened his eyes and glanced up to find Coach Doss staring at him with an intensity that made Chente's heart race in circles. Coach Doss was very handsome, and this fact made Chente very nervous.

Chente quickly stood up and began to jog in place. He was ready to get started. The sooner he started, the sooner he finished—and the sooner he got back on the basketball court.

"How's the right leg doing?" asked Coach Doss.

Chente nodded and smiled. "It's okay, I guess."

"Chen?" replied the coach as he took a couple of steps toward the point guard. "That didn't sound too convincing."

Chente shrugged and confessed, "Okay. Truthfully, it was sore this morning when I got out of bed. I mean, it was throbbing a little bit." Chente grimaced with an anxious grin. "So, I took a couple of Advil before school and then two more at lunch, and it's been fine all day long."

"You have been taking pain medication all day long because your leg was hurting? Seriously?" scolded Coach Doss as he shook his head in disbelief.

"Yeah, well, when you put it that way, it does sound a bit twisted, I guess," replied Chente as he rubbed his forehead.

"Did you stretch last night after you got home?" asked the basketball coach.

"I forgot."

Coach Doss frowned and shook his head in disapproval. "Chen, you have to stretch every time you exercise. You know that," responded Coach Doss as he emphatically gestured with his arms. "And really, you shouldn't have been running in the cold weather last night either."

"Okay. I won't do it again." Chente shivered. "But this gym is pretty cold too."

"Yes, I know," responded Coach Doss. "Why don't you stretch a few more minutes. Just to be on the safe side. We need to be careful if you are going to suit up and play tomorrow."

"Maybe I could get in the whirlpool after practice," suggested Chente. "I really want to get back on the basketball court."

Coach Doss nodded. "That's actually a good idea."

As Chente continued to stretch, he watched Coach Doss grab a basketball off the basketball rack and start to shoot. Coach Doss had a smooth shooting form—elbows in, bent knees, and a good follow-through. He was pretty consistent fifteen feet from the basketball goal.

Chente's thoughts slowly wandered back to the night before. Why had Coach Doss been out late, running in the park on a cold winter night? What was he running from?

Coach Doss saw Chente watching him and smirked. "Yes, I know I'm not the greatest shooter, but I did make second-team all-district my senior year," he said proudly as he playfully flexed his arm muscles.

"Wow. Impressive. Was that like ten years ago or something?" asked Chente as he laughed aloud.

Coach Doss chuckled at the biting comment. "Oh, I see. You like to talk trash," said the basketball coach as he continued to shoot. "By the way, that was four years ago, thank you very much!"

"Whatever, Coach, you're practically walking around with a cane," teased Chente as he continued to laugh under his breath.

Coach Doss's eyes got big, and he shook his head in disbelief as he jumped up and down with enthusiasm. "Oh, oh wait, and this is coming from a kid who is nursing an injured thigh muscle. Really?" roared the assistant coach as Chente smiled and continued to stretch.

"Wait a minute. Wait a minute," said Coach Doss as he abruptly stopped laughing. "How old do you think I am?"

Chente closed his eyes and playfully extended his arms like he was in a deep trance. "I'm feeling twenty-eight or twenty-nine. Definitely borderline thirty."

"What?" yelled Coach Doss in a very exaggerated fashion. "I am twenty-two. Well, I'm going to be twenty-two in June," he quickly added as he shook his head. "You really think I look thirty?"

"So you're twenty-one and a half!" Chente grinned as he covered his mouth with his hand and began to laugh even louder.

"Why is that funny?" asked Coach Doss.

"I'm sorry. I don't know why. It just is," said Chente as he regained his composure.

"Yeah, well, you better get started on your lines, mister," instructed Coach Doss, still pretending to be upset.

"Yep. I'm on it, sir." Chente jumped with a smile and started to run up and down the basketball court.

Chente decided he would run his lines in sets of three. He would take a two-minute break in between to catch his breath, stretch, and drink some water.

The first two sets of lines went well. The adrenaline of possibly playing the following night kicked in, and he completed them with little trouble. However, after he completed his third set of lines, Chente felt a little bit of pain, and his thigh muscle began to tighten up. He didn't mention this situation Coach Doss because he was determined to finish and play in tomorrow's basketball game.

Chente was in the middle of his fourth set of lines when his thigh began to cramp. His running pace slowed down, and he visibly began to struggle.

"Chen, you have to stop. I can't let you go on. You are starting to limp pretty bad," observed Coach Doss.

"Come on, Coach, I just have two more sets, and I am done. I have to play tomorrow," pleaded Chente as he tried to catch his breath.

"No. You are practically dragging your right leg, Chen. No. You are done," replied the basketball coach with a direct tone in his voice. "You have to rest now."

"Please? Please don't do this to me," replied Chente as he looked down at his feet and begged. "Coach, I can't let the guys down—not again."

"Chen, if you keep on running, you will not be playing tomorrow or the rest of the week," answered Coach in a very absolute tone. "You are going to injure yourself further."

Chente knew Coach Doss was right. The pain in his right thigh was excruciating.

"We need to rehab that thigh ASAP," said Coach Doss.

Chente didn't argue any further and dejectedly limped away. He went and sat on the bleachers while on the verge of crying. He desperately wanted to play against Kress and be part of the basketball team again.

He wiped the sweat off his brow, placed his hands over his face, and growled in frustration. He wanted a basketball in his hands tomorrow. He wanted to make things right with Coach Alvarez and his friends. He wanted to prove he belonged on the team.

"Coach, what are you doing?" asked Chente as he wiped the tears of disappointment from the corners of his eyes.

"I am going to run your last sets of lines," replied Coach Doss with a big smile as he removed his hoodie and stretched his muscular legs. "Chen, my man, you are playing tomorrow night!"

"What! Are you being serious? You're going to run for me?" asked Chente as he stood up and hobbled over to his coach with a new surge of energy. "Can you do that?"

"Yep. I guess I am officially part of your fan club." The basketball coach grinned as he extended his arms out, flexed his biceps, and posed. "Yep, I'm on Team Chen!"

Chente threw his arms up in the air and began to laugh heartily at Coach Doss's silly antics, and for the first time in an awfully long time, his heart was filled with pure joy. He felt no pain.

"Now stand back and watch what this twenty-one-and-half-year-old coach can do," said Coach Doss, and he playfully winked at Chente.

Chente watched Coach Doss run. He was a flawless runner—smooth and graceful. His long running strides were effortless. Chente was mesmerized.

Chente and Coach Doss walked into the main gym as Coach Alvarez began to review their offensive sets. Coach Alvarez waved at them as they entered the gym and called a two-minute water break. Chente could tell he wasn't happy simply by the way he walked over to them and placed his hands on his hips.

"So, did you finish your running?" Coach Alvarez bluntly asked Chente.

"Of course, he did," replied Coach Doss as he wiped the sweat off his brow. "But Chen needs to rehab his thigh muscle and get in the whirlpool ASAP."

Coach Alvarez gave Coach Doss a strange glance, then looked at his point guard. "Are you okay? Are you hurting badly?"

"Well, my thigh tightened up while I was running. There's some pain, but I'll be okay for tomorrow," Chente quickly said.

"Okay." Coach Alvarez nodded as he glanced at the assistant coach one more time. "Coach, take Chen into the training room and give him a quick ten-minute thigh massage and then send him back out here. Beau is driving me crazy, and I need Chen to run the offensive sets with the team before I end practice."

Coach Doss nodded in agreement. "Yes, sir, I will take care of it."

"Chen, you will whirlpool after practice," instructed the head coach as he pointed at Chente and walked away.

"Yes, sir," replied Chente.

Coach Alvarez blew his whistle, and practice was back on. Chente followed Coach Doss into the training room. He was so excited that he would be practicing with his team in a few minutes. He missed touching, dribbling, and shooting a basketball; he missed the competition, but mostly he missed the camaraderie of belonging to a team.

Coach Doss motioned the point guard to get on the training table as he went to the supply cabinet and pulled out some muscle ointment. He walked back to Chente.

"Okay, Chen, drop your shorts," said Coach Doss as he tossed Chente a towel.

"Excuse me?" asked Chente.

"Your shorts, Chen, you need to get out of your shorts so I can massage your thigh with this muscle ointment," Coach Doss said plainly. "Cover yourself with the towel."

Chente slid out of his shorts and lay down, facing up on the table. Chente was wearing an athletic jock, so when his exposed butt cheeks rubbed against the cold table, he shivered. He placed the towel over his privates and closed his eyes.

Chente felt the cold ointment splash directly on his leg, and his muscle trembled a little when Coach Doss's hands began to massage the injury with strong circular motions. They were slow and deliberate.

"Communicate with me, Chen, and tell me if I am hurting you, okay?"

Chente nodded. "Yes, sir."

However, Chente felt no pain. As matter of fact, Coach Doss's hands felt wonderful. He was applying just the right amount of pressure on the right spots and rubbing out the tightness of the muscle. His hands were magic.

Chente could feel his thigh muscle slowly begin to loosen and relax. He knew his body was responding to the treatment. Chente could also feel the bulge in his groin getting bigger beneath the towel, and it made him a little uncomfortable.

"So, Chen," said the basketball coach as he loudly cleared his throat. "I know you had a lot on your mind last night. Have things gotten any better today?"

Chente kept his eyes closed and nodded. "Yep, Coach. Things have gotten much better," whispered Chente in a very sleepy voice.

"Good. I'm glad to hear that. I was a little worried," said Coach Doss as he continued to massage Chente's thigh.

"So what about you, sir?" asked Chente.

"What's that?

Chente opened his right eye. "Well, you were out running last night too. Were you able to exorcise your demons?"

Coach Doss paused before he answered. "What makes you think I have demons?"

"Oh, I don't know," said Chente as he closed his right eye again. "I guess it was just the way you were running."

"The way I was running?" asked Coach Doss.

"Yeah. You were super intense and focused," said Chente as he licked his dry lips. "I don't know. It was almost like you were running from something.

"Okay, that hurt." Chente flinched.

"Sorry. I am just trying to loosen it up a little more," replied Coach Doss as he nervously pressed too hard on the muscle.

"Actually, Coach, the outer part of my thigh still feels a little tight," replied Chente as he turned sideways and exposed his naked butt to Coach Doss.

Chente pointed to the direct spot on his thigh with his index finger. "Right here, Coach. Can you hit this spot?" asked the basketball player without opening his eyes.

Chente heard Coach Doss begin to cough and step away from the massage table.

"Hey, Coach? Is everything okay?" asked Chente as he opened his eyes.

There was a knock at the training room door, and Carlos walked in, breathing heavily with sweat dripping down his forehead.

"Coach Alvarez said to come and get Chen. I think he's tired of Beau running the point guard position."

Chente jumped off the table. And in one swift motion, he had his shorts on and was gingerly jogging down the hallway to the gym with Carlos. He paused at the locker room door and nodded and smiled at Coach Doss, who was wiping his forehead. "Thanks for everything, Coach."

Coach Alvarez blew his whistle, and the team congregated in the center of the court. They listened to the breakdown of the good, the bad, and the ugly of the practice session. The head coach's assessment was always very direct and concise.

"Okay, each of you give me ten made free throws and then hit the showers," yelled Coach Alvarez as he walked away with his clipboard.

The team huddled, and Felipe yelled, "Team on three. One, two, three."

"Team!"

Each basketball player grabbed a basketball and began to shoot free throws at the six different basketball goals in the gym.

"So how did it go?" asked Coach Doss with a playful grimace on his face.

"Man, we are rusty and completely out of sync," replied Coach Alvarez. "Beau can't handle my intensity; Ricky's attitude sucks, and the rest are just going through the motions. No passion!"

Coach Doss nodded in agreement. He knew his role was to listen to the head coach vent and blow off steam.

"Tre' is the only one who truly gets it," Coach Alvarez finally said. "Then Chen steps on the floor, and the energy level increases one hundred percent. The team comes alive, and they begin to gel," Coach Alvarez said with a smile. "He's the glue that keeps it all together."

"They trust him," Coach Doss said plainly.

"How's his leg?" asked Coach Alvarez.

"Oh, I almost forgot. He needs to whirlpool it before he leaves for the day. I will go get it ready," remarked the assistant coach as he hurried off.

Coach Alvarez turned his attention to Chente and watched his star point guard shoot his free throws. His eyes were completely focused, and his shooting form was perfect. The ball barely touched the net as it went through the goal. Chente's skills were silky smooth.

"I need to talk to you, Jimenez," yelled Coach Alvarez from across the gym.

Chente quickly jogged over to his head coach. "Yes, sir?"

"So, how are you? How's the leg?"

"I'm good. My leg is at about eighty-five percent."

"Are you sure? Please don't lie to me," replied Coach Alvarez as he searched Chente's eyes for feedback.

"Yes, sir. I'm just glad to be back in the gym with a basketball in my hand." Chente smiled.

The head basketball coach cautiously nodded. "Okay. You need to whirlpool before you leave. Doss is in the back, getting it ready for you."

"Yes, sir." Chente put up his basketball and headed into the locker room.

"How long do I stay in here?" groaned Chente as he got into the whirlpool.

"Twenty minutes, and quit being a wimp," said Coach Doss as he set the timer and walked out of the training room.

Chente rolled his eyes and simply accepted the fact that he was going to have to sit in the whirlpool for twenty minutes. This would make his leg feel better and allow him to play basketball tomorrow night. Chente could live with that.

He leaned back and got comfortable. Slowly, he let go and began to relax. He closed his eyes, and moments later different thoughts flooded his head.

What's the matter with Mom? Why is she losing weight? We can't give her any problems, or she could die. She needs to rest more.

Is Dad in heaven? Can he see us? Can he hear us? Is he proud of me? Why did he have to die?

I miss Jimmy. Why did Jimmy kill himself? Is it my fault?

Haven is such a nice girl? Why can't I like her more than I do? What is wrong with me?

What do I do about college? Do I go far away or stay close to home? Will I like college?

What is up with Coach Doss? Why do I feel a connection with him? He is so handsome. I wish I didn't think he was so handsome.

RRRRRRIIIINNNNNGGGGGG!

Chente reached over and turned off the timer. He had drifted off to sleep for a few minutes, but he quickly regained his composure. He got out of the whirlpool and slipped off his wet shorts. He wrapped a towel around himself and walked across the hallway to the locker room.

Everybody was gone. The locker room was empty, but it had a potent, musky smell of sneakers and sweat. He went to his locker, sat down, and pulled out his watch from his backpack. It was 6:15 p.m., and he needed to get home.

He got up and went to the showers. He dropped his towel and got in. He lathered up under the warm water. It had been a good day, and he was thrilled that he was back on the basketball team and playing tomorrow night.

Coach Doss returned from his classroom. He walked into the gym and quickly turned off the lights. Routinely, he made his final rounds before he locked up the gym and went home for the night.

Coach Doss got to the training room, only to find it empty. He drained the water from the whirlpool and turned off the lights.

"Chen must have gone home," he rationalized to himself.

He checked the equipment room door and the laundry room door, and both were locked.

He walked into the coaches' office to grab his briefcase and noticed that the lights in the locker room were still on. He put down his government book and headed to the locker room. He walked in, immediately heard the showers running, and became annoyed.

"Who left the showers on?" he mumbled to himself as he turned the corner to see Chente completely naked and all lathered up in soap. He stopped in his tracks and simply stared.

Chente had a classic physique. He didn't have an ounce of fat on his body. He was lean and cut with firm pecs and a chiseled abdomen. Chente had a strong backside that connected to long sexy legs. He was perfect, and Coach Doss couldn't breathe.

Coach Doss quietly stepped behind the lockers and exhaled. He felt his face beginning to get flushed, and his groin area stood at attention.

"I shouldn't be doing this," he said to himself and quietly exited the locker room. He returned to the coaches' office, feeling fervently excited and bitterly confused.

About three minutes later, Coach Doss pounded on the locker room door. "Last call. Anyone in here?"

Chente popped his head around the corner as he slid his T-shirt over his head. "I'm almost done. Sorry. I had to take a quick shower before heading home."

"No problem," said Coach Doss without making eye contact. "I'll wait for you out here."

A few minutes later Chente walked out of the locker room, texting on his cell phone. It had escaped his mind that he had given the car keys to Victor earlier in the day and needed a ride home.

"You ready?" asked Coach Doss.

"Yes, sir. Just waiting on a text from Vic," said Chente as he turned off the lights to the locker room and began walking the length of the gym with his coach.

Coach Doss nodded. "Is he your ride home?"

"I hope so. He went home sick today and took the car."

Coach Doss locked the gym doors and unlocked the doors to his truck.

"If he doesn't answer, I'll jog home. I did it last night," said Chente as he playfully glanced at Coach Doss and laughed.

"And the rehab we did today goes down the drain," replied the assistant coach as he shook his head. "Nope, just jump in my truck. I will give you a ride home."

"Oh, okay. That's even better," said Chente as he got into the metallic-blue 4Runner and strapped on his seat belt.

"Where do you live?" asked the first-year teacher as he reversed out from his parking space.

"Eight blocks that way and then make a left." Chente pointed. "We will be the first brick home on the right."

"Oh, that's not too far," said Coach Doss as he turned on the radio.

"It's not. It's one of the perks of living in a small town. Nothing's ever too far."

Chente looked out the window and saw a couple of little kids building a snowman with their father in their yard. He waved as they passed by.

"So today was a good day, right?" asked the coach.

"Yes, sir. It was better than I thought it would be. And look at you, a twenty-one-and-a-half rookie teaching senior government," teased Chente.

Coach Doss looked at Chente in disbelief and started to laugh.

"Oh wow, I am so sorry, Coach. That was so disrespectful," apologized Chente as he quickly put a hand over his mouth. "I can't believe I just called you that."

"Relax. Don't worry about it. That was great, and it made me laugh," replied Coach Doss as he paused at the corner of Avenue A. "Is this you? The house with all of the cars?"

"Oh great. What happened? Why are all my brothers and sisters here?" wondered the Jimenez boy aloud as he anxiously shook his head. "And it had been such a good day."

"Maybe they're here for dinner," replied Coach Doss as he shrugged and glanced at his watch. "It is dinner time, you know."

Chente nervously smiled, unstrapped his seat belt, and opened the door. "Okay, maybe you're right. Thanks for the ride. See you tomorrow," said the high school senior as he shut the door and walked toward the house.

CHAPTER 5

Chente walked in the front door of his house, feeling a little apprehensive. He found Victor wrapped in a blanket and sitting on the sofa, talking with Vanessa. His older brother, Valentin, was in the kitchen, talking on his cell phone, and Violeta was staring out the front window.

"What's going on, guys? Where's Mom?" asked Chente with a hint of panic in his voice.

Violeta ignored him and continued to stare out the window. "Chente, was that your coach who just dropped you off?"

"Is something the matter? Where's Mom?"

"Chente, I'm asking you a question," said Violeta in a stern voice. It was obvious she was annoyed and didn't like being ignored.

Chente stared at her in disbelief and shook his head. "What? Yes, yes, that was one of my coaches," replied Chente as he stared at Violeta and shrugged in disbelief. "He just gave me a ride home. Now, will someone please answer my question?"

Vanessa and Victor began giggling and continued with their secret conversation on the couch, and Valentin stepped into the hallway to finish his phone call.

"You know he shouldn't be giving you a ride home," replied the oldest sister as she shook her head in disapproval. "It's completely inappropriate."

"Oh my gosh! What is the matter with you, Vi?" asked Chente as he dropped his backpack on the floor and growled at his overbearing sister in frustration. "What is your problem? You never stop!"

Chente's voice became louder and more precise. "Do you want me to freeze to death? Coach Doss gave me a ride because Victor drove the car home early from school."

Violeta gasped at Chente's reaction and took a few steps back.

"And stop it. Quit talking to me like I am ten years old," exploded Chente as he pointed at her.

Vanessa and Victor were stunned into silence, and Valentin ran out of the hallway, holding his cell phone in his hand in a bit of a panic. Chente extended his arms out and slowly repeated one more time, "What … is … going … on?"

Vanessa jumped off the couch with a nervous smile. She quickly walked over to her younger brother and gave him a big hug. "Everything's fine, Chente. Calm down, *mijo*," she said in a soft, reassuring voice. "Mom left a note on the table. She's just at a church meeting. She should be back in a little while."

Chente closed his eyes and slowly exhaled. He shook his head and walked over to the refrigerator, grabbing a bottled water. He sat down at the kitchen table, completely drained.

"*Oyes*, Chente, what's going on? Why are you freaking out?" asked Valentin as he placed his hand on his brother's shoulder.

Chente took a deep breath and exhaled. He nervously rubbed his forehead. "I saw all of the cars in the driveway … it looked like … reminded me of …," replied the middle brother as he took another sip of water. "It's cool. I'm fine now."

Vanessa skipped over and hugged Chente from behind. She gave him a bunch of kisses on the head and started to tickle him. Chente began to squirm and eventually fell out of the chair, laughing.

"Now, there's the Chente that everyone knows and loves." Vanessa giggled as she towered over him. "*Bien chiflado*!"

"Well, hello to you too, Nesh," said Chente as he got up from the floor.

Chente and Vanessa had always been close while growing up, and their sibling connection was strong. When Chente was a little boy, he'd had a hard time pronouncing Vanessa's name. Instead of saying "Vanessa," he said "Vanesha." As Chente got older, he had shortened it to "Nesh."

"And Valentin? It's good to see you too, brother," said Chente with a weak smile. "Why are y'all here? Don't y'all have classes? What's going on?"

"What? You mean you didn't know?" asked Vanessa as she sarcastically rolled her eyes. "We have a very important family meeting, Chente. There's lots to discuss."

Chente was puzzled. He glanced at Valentin and then at Violeta, expecting some answers but getting none. He turned to Victor, who had sat next to him at the kitchen table, and asked him how he was feeling.

"I feel a little better. I took some medicine and took a nap until Vi got here," said Victor as he wrinkled his nose.

"Well, you can't afford to miss any more school, so you need to hurry up and get better quick," Violeta replied coldly.

Chente put his hands up and instinctively came to his little brother's defense. "Wait a minute, Vi. Victor went to the school nurse, and she sent him home because he was running a fever."

"Well, I went to the high school and spoke with Principal Timms this morning, because Vic was getting into trouble at school," countered Violeta as she gave Victor an annoying glance. "I was informed that Victor was failing four classes at semester. He runs the risk of repeating tenth grade."

Chente eyed Victor in complete shock. He and Victor went to the same school. How did he not know this? Chente felt horrible.

"Oh wow, is this true, Vic? Are you really failing four classes?" asked Valentin as he calmly sat down at the kitchen table.

Victor nodded and covered his head with his blanket in shame.

"So he's a little behind. We will get him back on track," replied Vanessa as she gave the baby of the family a look of sympathy. "It hasn't been the easiest year for any of us, right?" she added as she uncovered his head and gently patted his back.

"I agree with Nesh," said Chente with a sigh. "I will start tutoring him every night."

"Oh really? Is that so?" asked Violeta as she put her hands on her hips. "Principal Timms also said you missed four days of school prior to the school holidays."

"I did," confessed Chente as he looked at Vanessa. "So what? I own it. I was going through a hard time."

"Oh please, Chente! Please don't tell me it was because your friend committed suicide," said Violeta as she rolled her eyes in disgust and groaned. "Really, Chente, you really think that's a good reason? Because it is not!"

Chente's calm demeanor immediately changed into an icy suit of armor, and he snapped back at his sister with a vengeance. "Well, Violeta, I don't remember asking your opinion," replied the middle brother. "You see, you would have to have friends to fully understand what I was going through. And since you don't ..."

Violeta gave Chente a cold stare and clenched her teeth. "My point is that Mom doesn't need this kind of stress right now," barked the Ice Queen as she pointed at the younger brothers. "You are failing school, and you are skipping school."

"Wait a minute, Little Miss Perfect. Are you saying you never made a mistake?" hissed Vanessa as she stood up and pointed at her sister. "Please don't make me bring up all of the dumb things you did when you were their age."

"Oh my gosh, Vanessa, I can't believe that you're defending them," replied Violeta as she dramatically gestured with her perfectly manicured hands.

"And you don't need to crucify them either," countered Vanessa.

"Oh, my Lord. Dad must be turning over in his grave to hear you speak like this," yelled Violeta as she crossed her arms over her chest.

"Oh, okay, you want to bring up Dad?" retaliated Vanessa as she glared at her older sister. "What happened four years ago, Vi? Who broke dad's heart four years ago? Thank you!"

"Nesh, don't go there," whispered Chente as he calmly reached and squeezed Vanessa's hand. "This is hardly productive."

"Oh my gosh! That's different, Vanessa. I was twenty-two and an adult," screamed Violeta as she theatrically shook her head in horror.

Vanessa rolled her eyes and sarcastically giggled under her breath. "No, Little Miss Know-It-All, that makes it worse because you were twenty-two and an adult!"

Valentin stood up from the kitchen table, quietly walked over to the kitchen window, and sighed. He rubbed his forehead and shook his head. He despised family drama. It made him nervous. Medical school was occupying a lot of his time, and he didn't have the stamina to officiate an argument between his sisters.

"He's only fifteen," said Vanessa as she pointed at Victor.

Violeta waved off her little sister and began rubbing her temples.

"Chente's right. This is not productive," said Valentin as he turned around and got in between the sparring sisters. "We can't be fighting like this. We are brothers and sisters."

The oldest brother looked at all four siblings and sadly shook his head. "If Dad is turning over in his grave, it's because we're constantly bickering and arguing."

There was a long silence.

"Valentin's right. We should be supporting one another instead of fighting," replied Chente as his words broke the tension in the room. He looked directly at Violeta and apologetically smiled. "Vi, I apologize for the comments I made earlier. I was rude, and I am sorry."

Even though his older sister was hard to take sometimes, Chente undoubtedly knew she meant well.

Violeta's shoulders relaxed a little. She slowly nodded and smiled.

"I did skip school a few weeks ago, and I have my reasons," said Chente as he continued his monologue. "You may or may not agree with them, but they are my reasons."

Vanessa grabbed Chente's hand and squeezed it. She knew her little brother was struggling with Jimmy's death.

"Violeta, what Principal Timms failed to tell you is that I work very hard in my classes, and I take my grades very seriously," said Chente.

The oldest sister nodded. "Yes, Chente. I know that."

"Well, what no one yet knows is that I am valedictorian of my senior class," announced Chente as he took a theatrical bow.

"That's awesome, little brother. Congratulations," replied Valentin as he walked over and gave Chente a firm pat on the back.

The room immediately erupted with laughter and praise for Chente and his scholastic accomplishment. Violeta clapped loudly and smiled excessively big, while Vanessa congratulated him with a kiss on the forehead.

"Go on, Chen, and tell them the rest," yelled Victor with an impish grin.

"What? There's more good news?" screeched Vanessa and clapped her hands with excitement. "Come on, tell us, *chiflado*!"

"Well, as you all know, I have been applying to different colleges over the last nine months," started Chente with a nervous grin, "and a few weeks ago, I received notification that I was a finalist for a Presidential Scholarship to Stanford University."

Again, the room was filled with screams of joy and celebration. The Jimenez siblings were united in pride for their brother's academic success. It was like old times.

"That's fantastic, Chente. Stanford is a very prestigious university." Violeta grinned, and her face lit up with pride. "It's one of the best colleges in the whole country. I am so proud for you and our family."

"Congratulations, little brother. Dad would have been proud of you," said Valentin with sentiment in his eyes. "He would have been so proud."

"Thank you. That means a lot to me," replied Chente.

"Chente's also up for a Presidential Scholarship at the University of Texas and at Texas Tech," announced Victor as the youngest brother strategically tried to deflect the attention off himself and onto his middle brother.

"Victor, are you being serious right now?" Chente laughed as he figured out his little brother's ulterior motive.

"What? You need to own your greatness, brother." Victor winked with a sly grin.

Vanessa screamed and danced around Chente. "Texas Tech? Oh my gosh, Chen! Pick Tech! Guns up!"

She made a gun sign with her hands and continued to dance around the room.

"*Oyes, que pasa aquí?*" yelled Mrs. Jimenez as she walked in the front door. "What's all the racket about?"

Vanessa ran to her mother and began to dance with her too. She was so proud of her little brother and so happy to see her mom.

"Chente just told us some good news. *Dile Chen.*" The dancing sister laughed. "Tell Mom your news."

Chente repeated the information to his mother, who of course beamed with maternal pride and gave him a big hug. She always wanted the best for her children. "I am so proud of you, *mijo*. You deserve it. This is wonderful news," whispered the mother of five as she kissed her son's cheek and wiped away her tears of joy.

Valentin hugged his mother from behind and rested his head on her shoulders as she softly caressed his brown hair. "Hello, *mijo*, why are you and Vanessa here? Why aren't you in Lubbock?"

Valentin looked at Violeta, and the oldest sister looked at Chente, who was quick on his feet with a response.

"Well, I asked them to come down from Lubbock so I could share all my good news with everyone at the same time." Chente paused and grinned at everyone in the room. "See, Mom, I am also going to be the valedictorian of my senior class."

Mrs. Jimenez had a blank look on her face. She didn't understand that word. "*Pues, mijo qué es eso?*" She looked at her children's faces, searching for answers. "Is that something good?"

"Of course it is, Mother," said Violeta as she audaciously brushed back her hair. "It means Chente is the top student in his senior class."

Vanessa rolled her eyes and groaned at Violeta's haughty response.

"Mom, it just means he's the smartest in his class," said Vanessa as she tried to break it down even further.

Mrs. Jimenez jumped up and clapped her hands. She smiled proudly as she gave Chente another kiss on the cheek. "I am so proud of you, *mijo*!"

"Thanks, Mom," replied Chente.

Mrs. Jimenez packed Valentin and Vanessa some tamales and fresh tortillas for their trip back to Lubbock. She loved any opportunity she had to feed her kids.

Violeta had already left the house with a dozen tamales, and Victor had gone to his bedroom to rest. Vanessa pulled Chente aside. "Are you doing okay? How was the first day back?" she quietly asked.

"Yes. I am doing better than I thought. It's just going to take some time. But hey, Coach Alvarez let me back on the team." Chente grinned as he gave his sister a thumbs-up.

Vanessa gave him a big hug. "Well, I am so proud of you no matter what, okay? And remember that I am always a phone call away if you need to talk about anything—no judgment."

Chente nodded and forced a smile.

"Thanks, Nesh. I know. See you tomorrow for the game?"

Vanessa nodded and gave him a long, thoughtful look and smiled. She walked over to the front door, said goodbye to her mom, and left.

Chente stood at the door and waved at his brother and sister as the car pulled out of the driveway. He missed Vanessa a lot. She had always been his most loyal confidante and protector as they were growing up. She was always his night light, which kept away the monsters.

Mrs. Jimenez carefully watched Chente and could detect sadness in his eyes. He was concealing something from everybody, but she didn't know what it could be. She was puzzled.

"You miss your *hermanita*, don't you?" asked the mother of five.

Chente looked at his mom and nodded. "Yep. I do."

She knew her children very well and better than they gave her credit. For instance, she knew that tonight's surprise visit had nothing to do with Chente being accepted into Stanford or him being at the top of his senior class. She hadn't been fooled for a second.

"Okay, *mijo,* now that everyone has left, please tell me what's going on," said Mrs. Jimenez plainly.

Chente wasn't about to tell her anything that was going to stress her out. After all, that was what the meeting had been about. They needed to make his mother's life stress free. So Chente looked at his mom and gave her a strange look and lied. "What do you mean?"

Mrs. Jimenez pointed at Chente to sit down on the couch. She gave him a stern look. "*Mira,* I am your mother. Do not lie to me, Vincente."

Chente and his mom had always been able to speak to each other openly and honestly. It was just something they did—something that bonded them to one another.

"*Pues, ya concoces* Violeta, right? You know her. She stresses about everything," said Chente with a nervous chuckle as he sat down and crossed his long legs.

There was a hint of panic in the mother's voice as she nodded in agreement. "Yes? *Qué paso,* Chente?"

"Well, she visited with Principal Timms this morning, and Victor is a little behind in his classes," confessed Chente.

"Okay? No *entiendo,*" replied Mrs. Jimenez with confusion in her eyes. "*Mijo,* what does that mean?"

Chente felt like he was betraying his little brother, but his intuition convinced him that confiding in his mother was the right thing to do.

"It means that Vic needs to do better, or he's not going to pass to the eleventh grade."

"*Ay, Dios mío,*" she said as she covered her mouth with her hands.

Mrs. Jimenez immediately felt responsible for all this. She had been emotionally absent in the lives of her children since the death of her husband. She hadn't been able to cope with the pain of losing the love of her life, and now her children were falling apart. She had neglected them.

"But don't worry about it," Chente quickly replied as if he could read his mother's thoughts. "I am going to start tutoring him, and he will catch up fast. Vic is smart too, you know. He's just a little lazy."

Mrs. Jimenez smiled at her son, because she knew he was trying hard to reassure her and make her feel better. He didn't know it yet, but he was so much like his father.

"*Gracias, mijo.* Thank you for telling me." Mrs. Jimenez sighed as she stood up and dusted off the wrinkles on her skirt. "I am fine."

Chente closely watched his mother as she got up and went to the kitchen. She began to put the dirty dishes in the sink and put away the leftovers in the fridge. She poured herself a glass of wine and looked out the window. "And let me guess. Violeta didn't want me to find out?"

Chente slowly nodded with a half smile. "She's worried about you, Mom. We all are. She called a family meeting to discuss this situation and create a plan."

Mrs. Jimenez quietly exhaled as she turned and faced her son.

"She won't admit it, but I think Vi was pretty scared today that if you found out, you could get sick again."

Mrs. Jimenez calmly sipped on her wine and nodded. "And I bet she and Vanessa got into an argument, and Valentin played referee, right?" asked Mrs. Jimenez as she laughed a little under her breath.

"You got it," said Chente as he chuckled. "I wonder if those two will ever get along."

Her face suddenly got serious, and she locked eyes with Chente. "*Y* Victor? *Cómo está?* Is he okay?"

Chente wrinkled his forehead and sighed. He remembered his morning conversation with his little brother and now realized Victor had been trying to communicate his feelings.

"I think so. Now that I think about it, I think Victor is dealing with losing Dad in his own way," said Chente as he recalled Victor's biting remarks about their oldest sister. "I think Vi stressed him out this morning, and his body reacted by getting sick. I think he's scared that you are going to die too."

Chente got lost in his thoughts and realized he had spoken too freely. He glanced at his mother, and she was wiping the tears from her eyes and shaking her head.

"But, Mom, everything's going to be fine," reassured Chente. "Vic will get it together. I am going to help him. Don't worry."

"I am so ashamed that I let this happen." The mother of five sighed. "But I am getting better, and I will make it up to him."

Mrs. Jimenez gingerly brushed back her black hair and raised her glass. She took another sip of wine and carefully studied her middle son's demeanor. "How are *you* doing, *mijo*?" asked the mother as she glanced at Chente with worry on her face. "*Y no me digas fine.*"

Chente chuckled under his breath as he playfully shrugged. The moment felt authentic and normal. This was the mother he remembered before his dad died—strong, determined, and feisty. "You know, Mom, today was a good day," replied Chente triumphantly.

"That's good, *mijo*. I'm so glad," said Mrs. Jimenez as she relaxed her shoulders and exhaled softly. She tilted her head and admired Chente with a reflective, maternal gaze.

Her middle son had become a strong, handsome, and independent young man right before her eyes. She noticed the strong cheekbones and the expressive brown eyes. In many ways, he was a younger version of his dad—fiercely loyal and always the protector.

"Chente, did I ever tell you the story of when you were born?" asked Mrs. Jimenez as she thoughtfully placed her wine glass on the kitchen table and sat down.

"What? That I was a painful eleven-hour delivery?" Chente grinned as he took a seat beside her. "Yes, you have, and there's no need to repeat it."

Mrs. Jimenez carefully covered her mouth with her hand and laughed. "You were a pain, but not that story."

She got up and went to the kitchen window and looked up at the stars. In a melancholy voice, she traveled back in time. "Do you know that when you were born, your dad wanted me to name you Valiente and not Vincente?"

"What? Are you being serious right now?" asked Chente as he arched his back and laughed nervously. "Dad wanted to name me Valiente? Why?"

Mrs. Jimenez turned and smiled at her inquisitive son. She leaned up against the kitchen sink, calmly reminisced, and recounted the story to him. "It was late in October, and it had been raining all day long. We lived out on the Bennett Ranch, and your dad was really nervous because I had started to have labor contractions. The dirt road to the highway was about half a mile long and very muddy, and your dad wasn't sure that he could reach the interstate in his truck without getting stranded on the side of the road. But you were determined to be born, and we had no choice but to get in the truck and try to get to the hospital."

Mrs. Jimenez took a deep breath, looked at Chente, and caressed his cheek. She loved that he was listening intently and hanging on every word she spoke.

"Your Tia Yolanda was staying with us and became frightened too. She handed me a rosary and said she would stay behind and take care of your brother and sisters. The dear Lord was with us that night, because somehow we made it through the mud and out onto the highway, but it was too late. You were on your way, and there was nothing I could do but tell your dad to pull over on the side of the road. Fifteen minutes later, you were born out in the middle of nowhere."

Mrs. Jimenez paused and cleared the corners of her eyes as she picked up her glass from the table and sipped her wine.

Chente was mesmerized by the story as he envisioned the muddied trail his dad's truck must have left on the dirt road and the sound of the rain pounding on the hood, on the side of a lonely road, muffling his mother's laboring pains.

"Mom, I have never heard this story before," whispered Chente as chill bumps formed over his arms. "How is it that I have never heard this story before? Tell me what happened next."

Mrs. Jimenez cleared her throat, stood next to her son, and smiled. She grabbed his hand and squeezed it. "Well, your dad rushed us to the hospital, where the nurses and doctors quickly took care of me and cleaned you up. Later that night, Dr. Lee came in the hospital room to check on me and was happy that I was doing so well.

"He and your dad stepped outside my room and admired you from the nursery window. Dr. Lee was amazed that you arrived at the hospital unharmed and healthy. He told your dad that you were a brave little boy and that he was certain you were destined to change the world."

Mrs. Jimenez casually finished putting the dishes in the dishwasher and turned it on. She grabbed her glass of wine, walked back to the kitchen table, and sat down next to her son. "After that, your dad told me he wanted to name you Valiente because you were his brave little boy who was going to change the world," said Mrs. Jimenez as she playfully winked at her middle son. "Of course, I told him he was crazy, and I named you Vincente instead. After all, your dad was a brave man too," whispered the mother of five.

Chente loved listening to his mother talk about the past. He had always been the inquisitive kid who asked questions and wanted to know more. "Wow. That was awesome." Chente beamed as he felt a sense of pride fill his soul. "I can't believe I have never heard that story before."

"Oh, *mijo*, your dad was so proud that night," she said as she finished recounting the story. "And now look at you—smartest in your class and getting scholarships to go to college. I guess your dad was right about you."

Chente smiled. He was so glad to see that his mom was feeling better and acting more like herself. He had missed her. He missed the long talks they used to have before the accident. He missed her laughter and the sense of joy and energy she brought to family gatherings. Mostly, Chente missed her infinite warmth and unconditional love, which made him feel safe.

Mrs. Jimenez delicately covered her mouth as she yawned. "It's been a long day. I think it's time I go to bed."

She turned off the light as she walked out of the kitchen. She gave Chente a hug and whispered in his ear. "Remember, *mijo*, that sometimes being Valiente can be as simple as loving yourself."

Chente thought about his mother's parting words as he watched her walk down the hallway and into her bedroom. He sat down on the recliner and began to chronicle everything that had happened earlier that day and realized he was incredibly lucky. He had friends who defended him, a basketball coach who believed in him, and a family who loved him. He was blessed.

Still he just couldn't understand the emptiness he felt in his chest. It was like his soul was searching for something, but it didn't know what it was. And even though it appeared that his life was planned for the next five years with sports, scholarships, and college, Chente felt like he was drifting aimlessly in the wind.

Wait—was it that, or was it that he didn't want to know?

Chente investigated his thoughts a little further.

His mind floated to Jimmy. During their last conversation, Jimmy had practically accused him of being gay. Was Jimmy right? Was he gay? What did that mean? Would he have to give up his friends and family if he were gay? After all, Jimmy had come out to his parents, and all hell had broken loose.

Then he thought about Haven. She was a sweet and pretty girl, and she really liked him a lot. Most guys would have loved to have her as their girlfriend. However, as much as he tried, he didn't feel that way. Was he emotionally defective? Would his feelings change? Did that mean he was gay? So many questions …

Chente stood up and went to lock the front door of the house, and his mind drifted to Coach Doss. He didn't know him that well, yet he felt an immediate connection with him—a physical attraction that was foreign to him. Looking at Coach Doss made him feel nervous inside, and seeing him in his black running tights had stirred feelings he never had before—for anyone. Chente couldn't deny that, and oddly enough, he didn't want to either.

Chente's cell phone began to ring, and it made him jump.

It was Haven.

He let the call go to voice mail. It was late, and he was tired of his thoughts. Chente peered out the living room window and yawned. He turned off the living room lamp and walked to his bedroom, feeling more alone than ever.

CHAPTER 6

"I am glad I caught you before your day got too busy," said Chente as he walked into Miss Young's office as the tardy bell for first period rang. "I just want to touch base with you and get feedback on college options."

"Good morning, Chen," replied the high school counselor as she smiled and furiously typed on her laptop. "Just give me one second while I finish this email."

Miss Young was in her fifth year at Avalon High School. She had been the head volleyball coach/health teacher during her first three years and then transitioned into her current counseling position. She was a petite and feisty student advocate in her late twenties with a contagious smile and warm heart. She was a comforting sounding board for students needing emotional support and a valuable resource for students needing to apply for college. Miss Young loved her job and the students she served.

"Of course," said Chente as he nodded and sat down.

He really liked going to Miss Young's office. It was a place of refuge for all students, and Chente always felt empowered when he left. Miss Young had decorated her office with warm, comfortable couches and chairs. The pastel-colored walls were brightened with positive educational posters and college banners from all over the country. The atmosphere was cozy and inviting.

Chente opened up his backpack. He pulled out and began to review a local scholarship application he was about to submit when the student morning announcements came over the intercom.

He participated in the pledge of allegiance and moment of silence, then he sat back down, closed his eyes, and waited. It was too hard to concentrate on a scholarship application when Christina's voice was blaring through a loudspeaker.

After a couple of minutes, the morning announcements concluded. He opened his eyes to find Miss Young smiling at him from her desk. "Good morning, Mr. Jimenez. Are we sleeping through morning announcements again?"

Chente laughed aloud, made a silly face, put his index finger next to his lips, and said, "Shhh. I was just resting my eyes."

Miss Young smiled. "Of course. How can I help you this morning?"

"I wanted to visit with you about two things," said Chente. "First, I wanted to check and see if you had heard anything about my scholarship applications at Texas Tech, University of Texas, and Stanford. Second, I have two friends who need to see you about possibly getting some advice on going to college."

Miss Young's face lit up with excitement. "Really? That's great. Who are your friends?"

"Carlos Ortiz and Felipe Lopez," said Chente with a smile.

A loud buzzing sound over the intercom interrupted Chente. He quickly covered his ears to avoid the annoying racket. Then the buzzing noise suddenly stopped, and he could hear Principal Timms speaking with Mrs. Black over the intercom.

Principal Timms: "The copying machines in the lounge are out of paper. We need to order some more as soon as possible."

Mrs. Black: "Want me to use local vendors, or do you want me to go to Lubbock?"

Principal Timms: "Local will be quicker. Make sure that the custodians sweep and clean the gym floors for the basketball game tonight. I don't want to hear the parents from Kress saying that our floors are too slippery. We are going to win tonight, and I don't want them to have any excuses."

Mrs. Black: "Yes, sir. I will make sure that one custodian remains on call, just in case."

Principal Timms: "Schedule a department chair meeting for Wednesday after school in the conference room."

Mrs. Black: "What time? Four fifteen?"

Principal Timms: "Also, I need to meet with Mrs. Vaughan. I want to know how her special education students managed to lock her in the classroom supply closet."

Mrs. Black: "Oh my … of course."

Principal Timms: "Oh, and please call Mr. Bennett and let him know that I can't see him today because I am tied up with classroom observations. Huh? What do you mean? … The intercom is on? I hate this piece—"

The buzzing sounded again, and quickly the intercom was turned off.

Chente looked at Miss Young and smiled. "Awkward."

"Well, the school now knows there will be a department chair meeting Wednesday after school," she teased. "They were supposed to have fixed the intercom over the holidays."

"I guess not," said Chente, and he turned his attention back to his friends. "As I was saying, Carlos and Felipe are really good guys, and I was hoping that you could help them with college and financial aid information."

"And they want to go to college?" asked Miss Young as she took notes on her iPad.

Chente nodded.

"Great. Then I will check their grades, and I will call them in after lunch. It's almost too late to be doing this, but we will make it happen," she said confidently.

Chente gave her a big smile. He knew Miss Young would move heaven and earth to help his friends.

"I told my family last night about being accepted to Stanford," announced Chente.

"Oh yeah? How did it go? Were they excited for you?" asked Miss Young.

"Yes, they were," said Chente, "and it made me a little nervous."

Miss Young nodded at her star pupil, intuitively took off her reading glasses, and transitioned into counseling mode. "Why?"

Chente apprehensively looked at his watch—anything to avoid eye contact with the high school counselor. "Well, it is halfway around the country! That's a little scary."

She listened and nodded calmly. "It is, but it's also a little exciting too, right?"

Chente smiled and nodded in agreement. The idea of going to California to attend college was thrilling, but it also made him feel a little uneasy. He had just lost his dad and his best friend, and he wasn't sure that he could handle another major shift in his life.

"You know, Chen, enjoy the process. You have opportunities not many kids your age have," she said casually. "Don't stress about it. Things will fall into place like they are supposed to. I promise."

She put her glasses back on. "Enjoy being eighteen years old."

Chente let out a deep sigh and cleared his throat. "Thank you for saying that. It means a lot to me."

Miss Young instinctively nodded and smiled. "Is there anything else you want to talk about?" Her telephone rang, and she picked it up and listened. She said into it, "Of course I will. I will send him right now."

She hung up the phone and glanced at Chente. "That was Mrs. Black. Principal Timms has a special assignment for you and needs to see you as soon as possible."

Chente straightened in his chair. "Okay. Thank you for your help."

"Keep me posted, and my door is always open," she said as Chente walked out the door.

Chente walked into the administration office to find Mrs. Black and Principal Timms standing behind the counter, discussing his daily schedule.

"Good morning," said Chente. "I was with Miss Young reviewing scholarship applications. You needed to see me, sir?"

"I understand from Coach Alvarez that you will be playing basketball tonight," said Principal Timms as he slapped the counter with excitement.

Chente jumped back and laughed a little. "Yes, sir. I believe that's the plan."

"Well, thank the Lord," replied the high school principal as he clapped his hands together and celebrated. "Little Beau Brockman is going to be a good player one day, but he can't break a press to save his life."

The students at Avalon High School adored Principal Timms. He was bold, brash, and full of perpetual energy— a kid at heart. The high school principal was also an avid sports fan and attended all the athletic functions. He supported his Avalon Longhorns 100 percent.

"Y'all play the Kress Kangaroos tonight, right?"

Chente nodded. "Yes, sir. I believe so."

"Their point guard is pretty good. What's his name?" asked Principal Timms.

"Henry Hamilton, sir," answered Chente, "but I assure you that I am better."

Chente surprised himself by making that remark. He was usually a little more modest about his basketball skills, but there was an intense and personal rivalry with Henry that stemmed back to their freshman year.

Mrs. Black grinned proudly and winked at her student assistant. "Of course you are, Chen, and you will prove it tonight," she said as she walked over and gave him a good-morning hug.

"Now, do you want to tell him about Coach Doss?" asked Mrs. Black as she delicately tapped on the counter. "We have about ten minutes until the bell rings for second period."

Mrs. Black had mastered the job of refocusing Principal Timms, and Chente glanced at his principal and waited for his instructions.

"Coach Doss did me a huge favor yesterday," said Principal Timms. "He gave up his conference period to take on a seventh-period government class."

"Yes, sir. I am in that seventh-period government class," replied Chente.

"Well, Coach Doss is a first-year teacher, and I don't want to overwhelm him so much that he falls behind with his other duties," surmised the high school principal. "I need you to help him by being his student assistant."

Chente tilted his head to the right and rubbed his forehead. "You want me to be Coach Doss's student assistant first period?" asked Chente.

Principal Timms began to holler at a couple of kids, who were exiting the teachers' lounge with candy and soft drinks. He walked away before he answered Chente's question.

Mrs. Black smiled and cut to the chase. "We want you to help him grade papers, make copies, and do any other little tasks he might need help with until after spring break." She smiled. "We don't want his regular classes to suffer because he took on an extra class. Does that make sense?"

"Yes, of course it does. I would be happy to help any way I can," said Chente. "Does he know about this arrangement?"

The telephone behind the counter rang.

"No, not yet. Why don't you go to his classroom and let him know?" she said before she answered the phone.

Chente nodded, grabbed his backpack, and headed to Coach Doss's classroom. He knocked on the door and waited.

Coach Doss opened the door and greeted him with a warm smile. Chente's heart wanted to jump out of his chest. Coach Doss had the most haunting blue eyes he had ever seen. They were intoxicating.

"Hey, Coach," said Chente as he froze in place while staring at his eyes.

"Hey, Chen?" replied the basketball coach with a puzzled look on his face. He paused, looked around, and chuckled under his breath. "Chen, are you all right?"

Chente regained his composure and smiled. He nervously cleared his throat. "Yes, sir. I apologize for interrupting your class, but Principal Timms wants me to be your student assistant first period."

Coach Doss gave Chente an incredulous look and slowly began to laugh. "You're joking, right? Who put you up to this?" The first-year teacher looked down the hallway, waiting for someone to jump out to complete the remainder of the joke.

"No, sir. I'm not joking," replied Chente in a serious tone. "Principal Timms said I should help you make copies and grade papers and stuff like that so you don't get behind. It's because you took on the extra government class."

Coach Doss squinted at Chente and shook his head.

"Sir, I am not joking, I promise." The high school senior sighed. "You can ask him if you don't believe me. I am just doing what he asked me to do."

Coach Doss detected some irritation in Chente's voice. "Really? So this isn't a joke?"

Chente stared at the coach and shook his head. He walked into the classroom, and the students were busy working in groups, trying to complete a map assignment. Beau looked up, smiled, and waved at Chente.

"So you are supposed to be my student assistant and help me grade papers, make copies and, stuff?" asked Coach Doss.

Chente innocently shrugged. "Yes, sir. I have been trying to tell you that for the last few minutes, sir."

"Do the other teachers have student assistants?" whispered Coach Doss as he carefully surveyed the room.

Chente wrinkled his forehead and carefully whispered back to the first-year teacher, "Yeah, I believe it is only until spring break and only because you agreed to teach an extra class?"

Coach Doss nodded.

"I wouldn't get used to it, if I were you," replied Chente with a mischievous grin.

The school bell rang, and the students raced out of the classroom as Coach Doss exploded into laughter. He enjoyed Chente's sense of humor.

"Well, heck, yeah. I would love to have a student assistant—and then the smartest kid in school? I can't go wrong, right?"

"Hey, what can I say? I would have to agree with you, sir. I am pretty awesome." Chente chuckled as he made his way to the door.

"So, Mr. I Am Pretty Awesome, are you excited to be playing tonight?" teased Coach Doss as he put his hand on Chente's back.

"Absolutely! I am so ready. I can't wait to play." Chente beamed since he was unable to contain his excitement. "I'm ready to get this team back on the *W* column!"

Coach Doss kept his hand on Chente's back as they walked into the busy hallway. "I hear Kress is pretty good this year and that you and the Kress point guard have a real heated rivalry thing going."

"Kress is good every year," said Chente. "And Henry, well, he's the second-best point guard in the region—next to me." Chente nodded very decidedly.

The first-year teacher liked Chente's confidence. "Then tonight's game is going to be interesting," he said loudly.

"Well, we're sort of friends," admitted Chente as he felt Coach Doss's hand on his back, making him feel giddy inside. "It's a love/hate relationship. We both hate to lose. It gets intense."

Chente gave Coach Doss a wicked smile, then turned and walked down the hallway to his second-period class.

The Avalon High School gymnasium was a sea of maroon and white. It was loud and full of Longhorn spirit. The student section was going crazy as they danced and cheered to the Avalon High School fight song. The cheerleaders made a victory line extending from the boys' dressing room to the center of the basketball court. There was electricity in the air.

Inside the Longhorn locker room, Coach Alvarez gave his last-minute pep talk, and the boys were trying to psyche themselves up with chest bumps and high fives. The team was in sync—except for Ricky, who was still upset that Chente was getting to play.

Before heading out to the gymnasium, Coach Alvarez announced that Beau was starting the basketball game. And as the door closed behind him, all hell broke loose.

"What do you mean I am starting?" asked Beau in a panic. "Chente's back, and he's so much better than I am."

"He's lucky he's even on the team." Ricky sneered under his breath.

Chente intentionally ignored Ricky's comment and gave Beau a pep talk. "You will be fine. Just keep the ball in the middle of the court and don't pick up your dribble."

Felipe was tired of Ricky's bad attitude and confronted him. "What's your problem, Ricky? Why do you always have to be such a prick?"

"It's obvious." Carlos laughed as he continued to stretch his legs. "He can't stand that Chente is ten times better than him."

Ricky got up and walked toward Carlos with a scowl. "Really? You think I am jealous of Chen?"

"I know you are," hissed Carlos as he stood up and matched Ricky's stare. "You always have been."

"Why do y'all always defend him? He abandoned this team for three weeks," said Ricky as he shook his head in disbelief.

"And we lost every game, you idiot!" yelled Felipe.

Tre' had heard enough and stood up to protest the silly argument. "Guys, we better get our shit together if we expect to win tonight," he said in a low but powerful voice. "Bottom line is that Coach Alvarez made a decision, and it's final."

He slowly looked everyone in the eyes. "Chente is back on the team, and Beau is starting tonight. If you can't live with those decisions, drop your uniform and don't let the door hit you in the ass on your way out."

The basketball team got totally quiet because no one dared to argue with Tre'.

The first quarter didn't start too well. Beau's nervous hands turned the ball over three times in a row, and Kress went up 6–0. Coach Alvarez called a time-out and told Chente to visit with his protégé.

Beau was practically in tears when Chente took him to the side for a quick dose of confidence. "Dude. You got this. No worries," Chente said with a smile. "You can't change what happened during the first two minutes, but you can make some good things happen when you step back on the floor."

The sophomore basketball player tried to focus on Chente's words.

"Listen to me. You can do this," instructed Chente. "On the press, fake right and go left and then hit Carlos as he breaks to the middle. It's open."

Beau regained his composure and nodded. Chente gave him a reassuring wink. "You can do this. I believe in you."

Henry Hamilton gave Chente a quick smirk as he passed by the bench, and Chente took that as a challenge. He would be more than ready whenever Coach Alvarez called for number fourteen.

The next couple of minutes were better for the Avalon Longhorns. Beau did exactly what Chente had instructed, and they broke the press easily for two points. Beau smiled really big as he glanced over at Chente. The teams traded baskets in the next few possessions, and by the end of the quarter, the score was Kress 15–Avalon 8.

Coach Alvarez called Chente to the huddle and began preparing for the second quarter as Ricky rolled his eyes and began to pout. The head coach witnessed Ricky's disgruntled behavior and benched him for the remainder of the half. He wasn't going to tolerate his bad attitude.

Coach Alvarez instructed his point guard to run the motion offenses, and Chente softly disagreed with a little groan.

"What's the matter?" asked Coach Alvarez.

"Coach, we need to run our one-four sets. They are guarding us too tight." Chente grinned with a confident nod. "Start everyone as high as the free throw line, and we can backdoor them all night long."

Coach Alvarez's eyes considered the suggestion for a moment, then nodded. His floor general was back.

The second quarter began with much better results. Chente hit a three-pointer from the top of the key, which sent the crowd into a wild frenzy. On the next possession, he stole an errant pass, rushed down the floor, a no-look pass to Tre', who was trailing on the left.

Slam dunk!

The team was in sync. The halftime score was Kress 24–Avalon 28.

The second half of the game was a hard-fought battle, but Chente played like a madman who had something to prove. He completely took over the game with his consistent shooting and his amazing court vision. His athletic prowess was on full display as he played defense, stole the ball, and hit three-pointers at crucial times of the games. It was obvious that this was his team. Final score was Kress 43–Avalon 51.

After the game ended, Chente waved at his family from the gym floor as he quickly walked over to the cheerleaders and the band to thank them for supporting the team. Chente then jogged to the Kress bench and caught Henry Hamilton before he disappeared into the visitor locker room.

"Hey, Chen, you played a good game," said the tall and lanky, red-headed boy from Kress. "You were on fire tonight."

"Thanks, Henry. You too," said Chente as he smiled and shook his hand. "Hey, man, talk to me. How's your mom doing?"

Henry and Chente were actually on friendly terms. They had attended the same basketball camps and played the same summer tennis tournaments since they were in junior high, and they knew each other very well.

"She's much better. The doctors believe they found it before the cancer could spread. She had her last treatment about a month ago," said Henry as his voice cracked a little. "I will tell her that you asked for her."

Chente squeezed Henry's shoulder. "That's really good news. Please give her a big hug for me, okay?"

"I will. Thanks, Chen." Henry smiled. "Good luck with the rest of the season," said the Kress boy as he playfully hit Chente on the head. He jogged into the visitors' locker room.

Chente walked across the gym floor to visit with his family. They had completely surrounded Coach Alvarez and were taking turns talking to him. Vanessa saw Chente and playfully screamed at him.

"Chente, you were so good tonight. You rocked it!"

Chente just smiled. He was glad that his family was proud of the way he had played. He kissed his mom on the cheek and bumped fists with Valentin.

"Chen, you did great tonight," said the older brother. "You made Henry look like he was a junior high kid trying to play high school basketball."

They both erupted in laughter.

"*Mijo*, I am so proud of you. I was so nervous for you at the beginning," said Mrs. Jimenez in dramatic fashion, "but then you made that three-pointer, and I saw the fire in your eyes, and I relaxed a little."

Mrs. Jimenez softly caressed her son's cheek. "I knew you were going to be fine."

"Whatever, Mom. You were a nervous wreck the entire game," teased Vanessa as she and Valentin continued to poke fun at their mother. "You were clutching your rosary so hard that I thought that your hand would begin bleeding."

Chente tuned them out as he watched Coach Alvarez and Violeta visiting a few feet away. He watched his sister's exaggerated hand gestures and her body posture. He wondered what she was doing and saying that was so important.

"I need to go grab a shower and change," announced Chente as he waved at his family and jogged toward the locker room.

Suddenly, the locker room door flung open, and Ricky stormed out. He gave Chente a dirty look and walked by him in a huff. Chente watched Ricky stomp across the gym floor and meet up with his dad by the exit door of the gym. They both looked over at Coach Alvarez and left.

Chente walked into the locker room, and the guys were excited. They were reliving the game highlights of slam dunks, stolen passes, and three-pointers—making each situation more and more dramatic.

Felipe playfully yelled at Chente from the shower. "*Oyes*, Chen, are you done giving your adoring fans autographs?"

The locker room broke out into crazy laughter.

Chente just laughed it off and shook his head. He leaned over to Carlos. "*Oyes, qué páso con Ricky?* He was very mad when he left."

Carlos groaned. He couldn't stand Ricky Bennett, and he was growing more and more tired of his silly antics.

"*Tú sabes*. He's not the star of the basketball team. He's stupid and immature. Do you want me to continue?"

Beau was listening to the conversation and added his commentary.

"Ricky was pissed that coach benched him. He said he was going to have his dad fire Coach Alvarez."

"Whatever," said Carlos as he put his shirt on and got ready to leave. "Hey, Chen, can I get a ride home?"

Chente nodded.

"I'll wait for you outside," said Carlos.

As Carlos made his way to the door, Coach Doss walked into the locker room with a clipboard in his hand as he shouted out the game stats:

Tre' Washington—19 points, 12 rebounds, 3 block shots
Chente Jimenez—17 points, 6 assists, 4 steals
Felipe Lopez—10 points, 8 rebounds
Carlos Ortiz—3 points, 2 assists, 2 steals
Sammy Diaz—2 points, 1 steal
Beau Brockman—2 assists, 2 steals

"Good job tonight, guys," yelled the assistant basketball coach. "Don't forget that we have a shoot-around practice tomorrow morning at six thirty a.m. It's not mandatory, but some of you could use a little extra time shooting the basketball."

Chente began to take off his shoes and socks when Beau walked over to his locker. "Hey, Chen? Thanks for helping me tonight. I really appreciate it."

Chente fist-bumped his teammate. "Nah, man, you are an important part of the team and a good player," said Chente with added confidence. "And if you work hard, I can totally see you playing a lot more by the time we hit playoffs."

Beau anxiously nodded and smiled. "Thanks, Chen. See you tomorrow."

Chente got up and took a quick shower. He was almost dressed when Coach Doss entered the locker room and looked at him with extended arms.

"What happened?" asked the basketball coach. "I have been waiting on you in the training room to rehab your thigh."

"I am sorry, Coach. I forgot. Can I come in tomorrow and rehab it in the morning before school?" pleaded Chente.

"How does it feel right now? Are you in any pain?" asked Coach Doss.

"It's a little tight, but it's not too bad," replied Chente.

Coach Doss looked at Chente from head to toe and smiled.

"Okay, see you tomorrow. Don't forget," said the assistant coach as he walked out of the locker room.

Chente finished getting dressed, grabbed his backpack, and headed to the locker room door.

"Good game tonight, Tre'. You owned the paint!"

Tre' looked up and smiled. "You too, Chen. It's so good to have you back. See you tomorrow."

Chente walked out of the dressing room to find Haven and Carlos waiting for him by the exit door of the gym. It looked like Coach Doss was on his way out the door as well, since he stood there, talking to Carlos about the basketball game.

Standing beside Coach Doss was a young, pretty girl with long, brown hair and pretty eyes. She wore a chic cashmere maroon sweater, black jeans, and black leather boots to the knee.

Haven saw Chente first, and she smiled. She pulled away from Carlos and walked over to him. She grabbed his hand and congratulated him on a good game. He could tell she was proud of him.

Coach Doss looked at Chente and Haven, who were holding hands. He cleared his throat and glanced away. "Are you the last one in the dressing room?"

Chente looked at the young lady standing close to Coach Doss and slowly shook his head. "No, I believe Tre' and Sammy are still getting dressed."

Chente extended his hand and introduced himself. "Hi. My name is Chente."

The lady smiled. "Hello, my name is Bella."

She looked at Coach Doss, who was strangely quiet.

"I am assuming that you have already met Haven and Carlos?" asked Chente with a curious smile.

She shook her head no, and all three exchanged greetings.

"Well, I have been trying to get to a basketball game for some time now," said Bella. "Aaron has bragged on you for weeks, but school has kept me too busy. Great game, by the way."

Chente politely smiled, then glanced at Coach Doss, who was curiously busy on his cell phone.

Haven and Bella immediately struck up a side conversation, and it turned out that Bella was a senior at Texas Tech studying finance. She wanted to pursue her master's degree right after graduation. It would make her more marketable when searching for a job.

"In the meantime, I figured I better start getting used to this life," she said as she stole Coach Doss's arm and kissed his cheek.

"Why? What do you mean?" asked Haven with a curious smile.

Bella extended her hand toward Haven and showed off her engagement ring. "Aaron proposed to me over the holidays, and of course I said yes."

Bella beamed with joy as Coach Doss forced a smile and avoided eye contact with Chente. "We are planning a June wedding," she said.

Chente's heart sank, but he smiled big and offered them his congratulations. After a few more seconds of conversation, he politely interrupted the small talk. "I hate to break up the girl talk, but I need to get going. We have a six thirty a.m. shooting practice tomorrow morning before school."

The three students quickly exited the gym, got in the car, and left. Haven continued to brag about how lovely Bella's engagement ring was and how romantic a June wedding would be. Chente looked in the rearview mirror and saw Carlos quietly laughing and shaking his head.

Chente pulled into Haven's driveway, and she gave him a quick good night kiss on his cheek and left. Carlos moved up to the passenger seat and exploded into silly laughter.

"Dude! She could not be more obvious!" teased Carlos as he tagged Chente's shoulder "She is so into you!"

"I know she is, but I just don't know," confessed Chente as he glanced over at Carlos.

Carlos got quiet and nodded. "What do you mean?"

Chente's mind was like a Texas twister. He had a myriad of thoughts flying in every direction in his head, and he was having a hard time focusing. It bothered him that he didn't feel a romantic connection with Haven, but finding out Coach Doss was engaged bothered him even more.

"I don't know. It's like something in me that won't allow me to feel more for Haven than I already do." He thoughtfully paused for a few seconds. "I wish I could explain it, but I can't."

Carlos didn't press. He just listened as Chente poured his heart out.

"I mean, I am going to college in six months. What's the point of getting serious, right?" asked Chente, hoping to have his feelings confirmed by his friend.

"You know, Chen, only you know what's right for you. You don't need to justify it to me or anyone," replied Carlos in a quiet and thoughtful voice. "You have been through a shitty year. First your dad and then Jimmy."

Chente pulled up to Carlos's house. Carlos opened the door and hesitated. He turned to his friend, nodded, and carefully spoke. "You know, Chente, for the record, I thought Jimmy was cool. I'm sorry for what happened to him."

Carlos got out of the car and shut the door. He made a peace sign and walked into his house.

On his way home, Chente pushed any thoughts about Jimmy out of his mind. He began to relive moments from tonight's game, and it made him happy. He pulled up to his driveway and parked his car.

Instantly, his mind raced to Coach Doss, and he exhaled. He had a fiancée, and she was very pretty. He remembered looking at the engagement ring on her finger. He felt a sharp ping in his chest.

Wow! Coach Doss is getting married in June.

CHAPTER 7

Chente jumped out of bed as the alarm clock screamed at him to wake up. He frantically searched his desk in the dark until he finally slapped the mechanical rooster into silence.

"What the hell, Chen?" complained Victor as he sat up in bed, visibly startled. "Are you trying to wake up the neighborhood? That damn thing is loud!"

"I'm sorry. I have morning practice at six thirty," whispered Chente.

"Are you kidding me?" groaned Victor, and he put a pillow over his face as Chente turned on his desk lamp to help him navigate through the room.

Chente shook his head and went to the closet to pack his school clothes for the day.

"What time is it?" grumbled Victor as he turned over in his bed.

"It's too early to be talking," yawned Chente. "It's six ten."

Victor looked up from his pillow. "Wait, so how am I supposed to get to school?"

Chente wished he had been able to escape before Victor realized he was going to need a ride to school.

"Maybe you could call Vi for a ride," whispered Chente with a nervous grin.

He could feel the weight of Victor's angry glare on his back as he walked out of the bedroom to brush his teeth and wash his face.

Chente pulled up to the student parking and entered the gym through the rear door. He was the first player to arrive. He went to his locker and put away his school stuff. He quickly put on his workout clothes and basketball shoes. He walked out to the gym, grabbed a basketball, and went straight to the free throw line and began shooting. He had missed two free throws the night before, and that fact didn't sit well with him.

Coach Alvarez soon appeared from the coaches' office in his maroon wind suit and baseball cap; he walked over to Chente and studied his shooting form from head to toe. "You need to keep your elbow in a little bit longer."

Chente adjusted his shooting form and continued to shoot free throws. He was focused and determined to make ten free throws in a row.

"Your shooting was a little rusty last night, but you hustled and played some mean defense," grumbled Coach Alvarez, then walked away while drinking his coffee.

Chente nodded and remained focused on his shooting form. That was as big of a compliment Chente was going to get out of his grumpy basketball coach. Chente recognized it was the head coach's way of saying he had played a good game.

A few minutes later, Beau, Carlos, and Tre' walked out and got a basketball; they began to shoot. Everyone looked tired and sleepy. Ricky walked out of the locker room soon afterward, still wearing the angry scowl on his face from the night before and carrying a huge chip on his shoulders. He looked at Chente and practically growled.

Coach Alvarez took a sip of his coffee and blew his whistle. He instructed everyone to divide up and work on spot shooting.

"You need to make five shots from each spot before rotating. If you finish before the designated end time, shoot free throws," yelled the basketball coach, and he blew his whistle to begin the shooting drill.

The gym echoed with the sound of basketballs bouncing and the vibrating clank of the basketball rim being hit over and over. Chente looked around and noticed that only seven of the ten varsity basketball players had showed up to the voluntary shooting practice session.

After forty-five minutes of practice, Mrs. Black walked into the gym and said something to Coach Alvarez. He nodded in agreement, and she left. Soon the head basketball coach blew his whistle and told the players to hit the showers. He called Coach Doss over and told him something; then he exited the gym doors leading to the main building.

"Hey, Chen," yelled Coach Doss from across the gym.

Chente turned around and jogged over. His legs were feeling a little tired.

"Coach Alvarez wants you to do ten more minutes of spot shooting, and then whirlpool your leg before hitting the showers," announced Coach Doss.

Chente nodded, returned to his basketball goal, and began to shoot.

"I am supposed to rebound for you as you shoot," explained Coach Doss.

Chente dribbled to the top of the key while Coach Doss set ten minutes on the game clock. Chente bent his knees and released—nothing but net. Coach Doss rebounded and tossed it back to Chente as he moved to different spots outside the three-point line.

Chente loved this shooting drill. It was fast, and it allowed him to get in a lot of shooting in a short amount of time.

After three minutes of shooting, Coach Doss called for a quick thirty-second break. "You need to keep your shooting elbow in a little," he instructed.

Chente nodded as he put his arms over his head to open up his lungs for breathing. He was getting a good cardio workout from this drill as well.

"Yes, sir. Coach Alvarez said the same thing earlier. What about my legs? Am I bending my knees enough?"

Coach Doss looked at Chente's legs and smiled. "Your legs look great."

The assistant basketball coach uneasily cleared his throat, and his cheeks immediately turned pink as he tossed the basketball to Chente; they resumed the shooting drill.

Chente caught the basketball and began to shoot again.

Did Coach Doss just check out my legs? Did he just flirt with me? He thinks my legs look great! That is so hot!

The next three minutes of shooting were less impressive. Chente couldn't hit the side of a barn, even if he tried. There were butterflies in his stomach, and his arms felt like Jell-O—not because he was tired but because he was excited that Coach Doss liked his legs.

There was another thirty-second break, and awkward silence filled the entire gym.

"Your fiancée is very pretty," said Chente.

He couldn't believe he just went there.

"Thank you. She's nice too," replied Coach Doss with a half smile. He glanced at Chente and wondered whether his flirting had scared him.

Coach Doss regained his professional composure and began to coach the star basketball player. "Here we go, the last three minutes of shooting. This time concentrate on your shooting form more than the quantity of shots you take."

Chente nodded and focused on the challenge before him.

Coach Doss tossed him the basketball, and Chente caught it, lined it up, bent his knees, and let it fly—swish. He repeated the process until the buzzer sounded three minutes later.

"Good job, Chen." Coach Doss grinned. "I think you hit twenty-two out of thirty-four! That's pretty good!"

Chente closed his eyes, nodded, and walked around with his hands over his head. He was a little winded from the drill, but he felt alive. He loved feeling tired and sweaty after a good workout. He wanted to get back into game-playing shape, and that would take a few more days. He knew that was why Coach Alvarez had him shoot a little extra this morning.

"Why don't you stretch a couple of minutes? I will get the whirlpool ready," suggested Coach Doss as he walked toward the training room.

A few minutes later, Chente walked into the dressing room, and the guys were already out of the showers and dressed. Chente took off his basketball shoes and workout clothes. He swiped a towel, wrapped it around his waist, and headed down the hallway to the training room. Coach Doss was walking out of the training room when Chente arrived, and they bumped into each other.

Chente slipped on the damp floor, and Coach Doss grabbed him by the waist to keep him from falling, slowly steadying him upright. Their faces were only inches apart. Chente could feel Coach Doss's heart racing as their chests pressed up against each other, and he could smell his minty breath on his hungry lips.

Chente could see Coach Doss's curious eyes carefully study his face—his brown eyes, the high cheekbones, and his full lips. He felt the coach's strong hands gently caress the curvature of his back and send an electric current straight to Chente's heart.

"Whoa … whoa …," stuttered Coach Doss as he tenderly stabilized Chente and gingerly let him go. "Dude … dude … we can't have you getting hurt on my watch."

Chente caught his breath and let out a nervous chuckle as his hands softly grazed Coach Doss's toned shoulders. "Well, see I am not as coordinated as everyone thinks I am."

Both guys avoided eye contact and quickly cleared their throats in unison.

"Uh … well … yeah … okay, Chen, the water is ready. I set the clock for fifteen minutes. I have to go to the laundry room and finish washing the uniforms. Holler if you need anything," said Coach Doss as he scurried away.

Chente awkwardly shook his head and watched Coach Doss leave. He exhaled and wiped his forehead. He felt a delightful dizziness in his head that made him feel strangely restless but happy. Why did he feel such a connection with Coach Doss?

He closed his eyes, exhaled again, and regrouped.

Chente got in and let the warm water work its magic. It felt good. He rubbed his right thigh back and forth as he leaned back and closed his eyes. He hoped Victor had found a ride to school … The alarm woke Chente from his nap.

Today he hated alarm clocks.

He crossed the hallway to the locker room. It was empty and quiet. He got to his locker and grabbed his cell phone—8:20. He had to hurry, or he was going to be late to first period. He took off his wet shorts and grabbed the last towel from the shelf. He turned on the shower and quickly lathered and rinsed off. He reached for his towel, dried of, and was headed to his locker to get dressed when his cell phone buzzed.

He read Haven's text: "Where RU, Chen? I will wait 4 you by the gym."

Chente responded that he was getting dressed in the locker room and was on his way. He sprayed on some cologne, swiped his backpack, and headed out the locker room when he heard the showers running.

He stopped. Had he left his shower running in his haste?

He turned around and walked toward the shower area. As he turned the corner, he saw Coach Doss completely naked, taking a shower. Chente froze in place and stared in pleasant disbelief. Coach Doss had an incredible body. It was perfect. His toned legs and muscular butt sent a surge of delightful happiness to Chente's eyes.

Coach Doss lathered up and put shampoo on his head. It was obvious he was trying to shower quickly to get to class on time. He turned around with his eyes closed as he washed off the shampoo from his head.

Chente stood in amazement when he saw soap streaming down Coach Doss's chiseled torso. He quietly turned around and began to walk away when he heard Coach Doss.

"Is someone there?"

Chente paused behind the lockers, trying to gather his thoughts. He didn't know whether he should answer or simply walk away. He remained quiet.

"If someone is in the locker room, I need a towel in the worst way," said Coach Doss as he laughed with embarrassment.

Chente didn't move. He knew his face was hot, and so was the man in the shower.

"Hello?" cried Coach Doss one more time.

Chente walked around the lockers and acted surprised to see Coach Doss in the shower. He was fully drenched and was covering his privates with his hands. He looked mortified to see Chente standing there. Chente didn't know what to say to the naked man, so he just stared and enjoyed the view.

"I didn't have time to go home and shower." Coach Doss winced. "And it seems as though we've run out of towels."

Chente broke out of his lustful trance and chuckled his breath. "Okay? Are there some in the laundry room?"

Coach Doss seemed relieved by the idea. "Yes. I believe I put some in the dryer earlier this morning."

Chente nodded. "No problem. I will go get you one."

He walked toward the door, turned around, and with an impish grin on his face said, "Don't go anywhere, Twenty-One and a Half."

Coach Doss managed a nervous grin.

Chente returned from the laundry room and handed Coach Doss a couple of towels. He smiled. "See you first period," said Chente as he headed for the locker room door and practically ran into Ricky Bennett.

"Watch where you're going," growled Ricky as he walked by him.

Chente just put his hands up, moved out of the way, and kept walking as the school bell rang.

"Sorry to keep you waiting," said Chente as he exited the gym and smiled at Haven. "My rehab lasted a little longer than I thought it would."

Haven batted her hazel eyes, and they began to walk to her first-period classroom.

"I like your light-blue sweater, Haven." Chente nodded. "You look very pretty."

"Aw, thank you, Chen." Haven beamed as she leaned up against him and smiled with excitement.

"So are we still on for Saturday night?" she asked.

Chente hadn't thought past the naked man in the shower and gave her a quizzical look. ". "Remind me again about Saturday."

Haven frowned and playfully hit Chente's shoulder. "Our movie date!"

"Ah, yes. Of course, we're still on. I am looking forward to it." Chente nodded. "I also made reservations at Rosario's so we can grab a bite to eat afterwards."

Haven arched her back proudly. She was pleased with Chente's effort. She waved to him and walked into her first-period class.

Chente hurried back to the front office before the tardy bell rang. He needed to check in with Mrs. Black before he went to Coach Doss's class to be his student assistant.

He turned the hallway corner and saw Principal Timms escorting Mr. Bennett out of his office. The high school principal had a tired expression on his face as Mr. Bennett continued to talk with exaggerated hand gestures and facial expressions. He saw Chente walking down the hallway and stopped.

"Speaking of the little devil." Mr. Bennett smirked with a fake smile. "We were just talking about you, Chente."

"Good morning," replied Chente as he politely nodded.

"I was just telling Principal Timms how much I admired your athleticism," said Mr. Bennett.

Chente could tell Mr. Bennett was upset and that his kind words were soaked in sarcasm and hate. Chente was determined to kill him with kindness and offered him a plastic smile. "Oh, really? Is that so?"

"Oh, yes," said Mr. Bennett with an exaggerated tone in his voice. "Even in my prime years, there is no way I could have ever missed three weeks of practice and still play as well as you did last night."

"Aw, Mr. Bennett how very kind of you to say that," responded Chente with an even bigger smile. "Then our team was fortunate that I played last night and not you, right?"

Mr. Bennett's smile quickly faded as Chente excused himself. "You have a good day, sir," replied Chente with a friendly wink. "Stay warm. It's a bit chilly outside."

Mrs. Black covered her mouth with amusement and winked at Chente as he notified her that he was headed to Coach Doss's classroom.

Coach Doss still had wet hair when Chente entered his classroom. The students were sitting at their desks, writing in their daily journals. Coach Doss was searching for something in his briefcase, so Chente waited patiently.

"Hey, Chen, could you come here please?" asked Coach Doss as he closed his briefcase and opened all his desk drawers.

Chente walked over and stood by the desk.

"I think I left next week's lesson plans at the house as I rushed out this morning," said the inexperienced teacher as he nervously rubbed his forehead with his hands. "Do you think you could walk over to my house and get them for me, please?"

The first-year teacher took a deep breath and shook his head. "They were due this morning, and Ms. Briones is already asking for them."

"Sure," said Chente as he waited for Coach Doss to give him eye contact.

"Thank you," said the basketball coach, and he got up from his desk and began teaching. Coach Doss instructed his students to read and silently annotate the first two pages of chapter thirteen.

"What's the matter?" asked Coach Doss as he quietly walked over to the student assistant.

"Well, sir, I don't know where you live, and I don't have keys to get into your house," replied Chente as he chuckled under his breath. "Would you like me to pick a house and break a window to get in?"

Coach Doss laughed aloud and startled his students out of their slumber. He continued to laugh quietly as he went to his desk and grabbed a set of keys. He walked over and whispered to Chente, "The black Texas Tech key is for the front door," he said. "I live in the third schoolhouse across from the Baptist church, behind the kindergarten building."

Chente nodded. "Where should I look?" He was inches away from Coach Doss's lips.

Coach Doss locked eyes with Chente for the first time since being naked in front of him in the locker room. "On the desk in my bedroom or on the kitchen table," he whispered.

Chente smiled and nodded. "Okay. Be back in a few minutes."

Coach Doss watched Chente as he exited his classroom.

Chente buttoned up his letterman's jacket and exited the high school building through the side door. He put Coach Doss's house keys in his pocket and crossed the street separating the Avalon Elementary campus from the Avalon High School campus.

The high school senior made his way across the elementary playground, where he had played as a child with his friends; then he crossed the street to the school housing section. He reached Coach Doss's front door and pulled out his house keys.

Chente opened the door and entered the house. He shook off the cold and looked around. The house smelled like Coach Doss—cool and fresh with a hint of peppermint. He walked into the living room and stepped into Coach Doss's life.

There was a big, brown leather couch in the center of the room facing a big-screen TV on the wall. He had a matching leather recliner on the left, and next to it was a small table with an antique lamp. The wall behind the couch had a huge, framed black-and-white print of the Golden Gate Bridge. Everything was in its place and orderly.

Wow. Coach Doss is a neat freak!

Chente walked down the hallway to the bedroom and passed a sea of family pictures hanging on the wall. There were a few pictures of an elderly couple, which Chente assumed were Coach Doss's grandparents, and pictures of Coach Doss at various ages with his parents. He was an only child.

Chente entered the master bedroom, and Coach Doss's king-sized bed was perfectly made. His walk-in closet was color coded, with pants and jeans on one side and his T-shirts, polo shirts, and dress shirts on the other. Coach Doss had eleven pairs of Nike shoes, also color coded.

Chente walked over to the desk in the room, and everything was perfect and in its place, but there were no lesson plans.

Coach Doss's kitchen was the best room in his house. He owned a white refrigerator and a black-topped dining room table with matching chairs from the 1950s. His pots and pans and salt-and-pepper shakers were also vintage.

Chente appreciated Coach Doss's sense of style and surmised that the basketball coach was an old soul.

Sitting on his kitchen table was a manila folder titled "lesson plans." Chente picked up the folder and exited the kitchen. He glanced at his cell phone and noticed that he had about ten minutes before second period started.

He walked through the house one more time and made sure all the lights were off. He locked the front door, put the house key in his coat pocket, and started his walk back to the high school.

Chente got to Coach Doss's classroom just as the bell rang. The first-year teacher was scolding a couple of students, so Chente placed the lesson plans on the desk. He waved at Coach Doss and pointed at the lesson plans.

The basketball coach nodded, and Chente left.

Chente made it to second-period English IV class and took his seat next to his friends. He looked at his cell phone and saw he had missed a phone call from Nesh. He texted her that he would call her tonight after practice. She responded that she had news to share.

"*Oyes*, Chente, who are you texting? Haven?" teased Felipe.

Christina overheard; she rolled her eyes and groaned in disgust.

"Someone's jealous," whispered Carlos, and he playfully pointed at Christina and laughed quietly.

"I heard that. I ain't jealous of her," said Christina as she turned and spectacularly swung her long, black hair.

She stood up and posed with her arms on her hip. "Have you seen all of this?" asked Christina as she strutted up and down the front of the classroom like it was a runway for a modeling show.

"She ain't got nothing on me, Carlos!" sassed the head cheerleader as she snapped her fingers in a *Z* formation.

Felipe made a silly face, clearing his throat. "Umm, she's got Chente."

The classroom started to laugh, and Christina flipped him off.

Chente was preoccupied by texting Nesh and didn't hear the silly banter between friends. "Huh? What are y'all talking about?" he asked as the roar of laughter caught his attention.

"Basically, Christina is jealous because Haven is your girlfriend," said Felipe as he ran around the classroom while Christina chased him with her shoe.

"But she's not my girlfriend," said Chente very plainly as he put his cell phone away.

"Boom!" yelled Christina. "*Te dije pendejo.*"

Felipe stopped in his tracks and looked at Chente. "You know she is. Y'all are always together."

Chente shook his head. "No. Dude, we're just friends. I like her, but she's not my girlfriend."

"You tell him, Chen," cackled Christina as she waved her manicured hands in the air. "Chen ain't dumb enough to be picking no *gringa* as his girlfriend."

"No offense," said the head cheerleader as she turned around and quickly apologized to the Anglo population in the classroom.

Christina walked back to her desk and triumphantly sat down. "Besides, I have my eyes set on someone else. Sorry, Chen. You're *bien chulo* and all, but you're my friend."

Chente pretended to be disappointed as he shrugged and smiled.

"Okay, so who are you stalking now?" asked Carlos as he rolled his eyes and sighed.

"Well, I think Coach Doss is really hot!" confessed the head cheerleader as she pulled out her makeup compact and put on bright-red lipstick.

Felipe rolled his eyes and began to laugh loudly as he placed his writing journal on his desk. "I may be *pendejo, pero*. You're *bien pendeja también*!"

"Really, Christina, he's a teacher!" groaned Carlos with a disgusted face.

"He's only been teaching for like four months, and he ain't that much older than us," she said as she put her compact back in her purse. "Plus, I'm eighteen. I am an adult."

The flirty head cheerleader playfully snapped her fingers again and smiled.

"*Ay pero mija*. You are too late. Coach Doss is engaged and getting married in June," replied Carlos as he mimicked her finger-snapping gesture. "Me and Chente met his fiancée last night after the basketball game. Right, Chen?"

Chente glanced at Christina and nodded.

"Well, he ain't married yet," she said with a mischievous grin. "And you know, June is like four months away. Lots can happen in four months."

"Well, you might want to buy a calendar," replied Carlos as he shook his head and sighed. "Because June is *six* months away."

Mrs. Rolando walked into the classroom and scolded the head cheerleader. "Christina, I could hear you all the way down the hallway. Please settle down."

"Sorry, Miss," said Christina as she giggled quietly.

Mrs. Rolando clapped her hands and instructed the class to begin on their journal assignment as she took roll.

Christina turned around and looked at Felipe and Carlos. She whispered, "Coach … Doss … *es* … *muy* … *caliente*!"

She playfully winked at Chente, then turned around and faced the front of the room. She opened her journal and began to write.

Chente quietly exhaled. Even Christina thought Coach Doss was hot.

The rest of the school day was uneventful. Chente went to class and tried hard not to fall asleep. During lunch, Christina and Felipe continued to bicker with each other and put on a show for the rest of the gang. During seventh period, Christina desperately tried to be sexy and get Coach Doss's attention but was unsuccessful. He simply taught the class and paid her no attention.

During basketball practice, Coach Alvarez was a little edgy and complained about everything. They reviewed their press defense and zone offenses, because the Friona game on Friday was going to be a really tough challenge.

"Friona is going to be big and slow," began Coach Alvarez. "They have two post players who are six-six, and their shortest guard is six-two. They are going to want to remain in a slow-paced, half-court game and pound it into the paint all night."

Chente looked around and could see the fear on his teammates' faces. He knew the boys were already intimidated.

"Guys, we can do this," said the star point guard as he tried to generate a jolt of confidence in his teammates. "The bigger they are, the harder they fall, right, Coach?"

"Exactly. We are going to attack them and press all game. We are going to make them play fast, which is to our advantage," said the fiery coach. "Guys, we are quicker and better!"

The boys began to clap loudly and cheer.

After practice, Chente went to the training room to rehab his thigh muscle. Coach Doss was there getting the whirlpool ready for use.

"Hey, Coach," said Chente as he entered the training room.

Coach Doss quickly nodded, said hello, and continued to put some training supplies away in the drawers. There were about seven boxes stacked up against the wall of the training room.

Chente got in the whirlpool and began to massage his thigh in the warm water. He watched Coach Doss frantically open one box after another. He appeared to be very anxious as he walked in and out of the room. He didn't even look at Chente.

"Hey, Coach Doss—is everything okay?"

"Yep. Everything's good," he said dismissively.

"Do you need any help? I could go and get some of the guys to help you put stuff away," said Chente as he awkwardly tried to be helpful again.

"Nope. I am good."

"Really, I am sure they would be glad to help you," replied Chente as he motioned to get out of the whirlpool and help.

"You can help me by draining the whirlpool after you get done," replied the basketball coach in a very chilly tone. "You didn't do that this morning, and I had to wash it out a few minutes ago so you could get in just now."

Coach Doss continued to open boxes.

The comment deflated Chente, and he quietly sat back down in the warm water. Coach Doss had never been rude until just now.

"Yes, sir. I will take care of it," said the injured point guard. "I apologize for this morning."

Coach Doss didn't even acknowledge the apology and walked out of the room.

Chente wanted no part of the toxic atmosphere that overwhelmed Coach Doss at the moment, so he jumped out of the whirlpool as soon as time expired and began to drain it. He felt like he was in the way and wanted to disappear before Coach Doss reappeared.

Chente walked across the hallway and into the locker room. He decided he would skip the showers this afternoon and shower when he got home. He quickly got dressed, grabbed his backpack, and went out the back door just as Coach Doss entered the locker room looking for the point guard.

CHAPTER 8

The car radio was blaring as Chente pulled into the driveway of his house. He was still a little upset with Coach Doss's dismissive behavior in the training room. It was apparent that Coach Doss had been having a bad day, and Chente had received the brunt of it. He shook his head and looked at his cell phone—5:45 p.m. He grabbed his backpack and got out of his car, still wondering what he might have done to warrant the treatment.

I mean, I guess I did forget to empty the whirlpool this morning, thought the teen who tended to take on more blame than was his to take.

The aroma of arroz and frijoles immediately hit Chente's nose as he walked into the house; he instantly forgot about everything else. His mom was cooking again. His stomach did a happy dance.

"Oh my gosh, Mom, are you cooking dinner tonight?" yelled Chente from the living room. "It smells so good."

"Chente? *Mijo*? Is that you?" asked Mrs. Jimenez as she peeked out from the kitchen, holding a spatula and wearing a floral apron.

Chente walked over and gave her a kiss on the cheek.

"Yes, I am cooking. You know I love to cook for my kids," she said as she walked back into the kitchen. "I am making chicken enchiladas *con arroz y frijoles. Tienes hambre*?"

"Mom, I am starving," said Chente, "and the cafeteria food is getting old." He grabbed a freshly made tortilla and began to eat it.

He loved watching his mother cook and maneuver her way through the kitchen. Her movements were easy, effortless, and elegant. She had a special talent for making all her dishes taste so good—with a pinch of this and a pinch of that. She was never one for exact measurements. She was a culinary artist, and the kitchen was her studio.

"Mom, you must be feeling better if you're cooking, right?" asked Chente.

"Yes. I feel fine. Don't worry so much," she said with a stern look. "Now go check on your brother. He is finishing some homework, I think."

Chente looked at her, smiled, and practically skipped out of the kitchen.

"Dinner will be ready in about fifteen minutes," she said as she flipped a tortilla in the air.

Chente walked into the bedroom and saw Victor at his desk, working on his world history assignment—papers everywhere. Chente tried to sound casual. "Hey, Vic, what are you doing?"

Victor looked up at Chente with a deadpan look. "Really? Like I can't hear you and Mom in the kitchen talking about me? You know what I am doing." His attention went back to the open book in front of him.

"Okay," said Chente as he wrinkled his nose and sighed. "So how are you doing? Do you need any help?"

"Well, I have been better—that's for sure," replied Victor. "That red folder has a couple of algebra assignments I finished. You can review them for me if you have some time."

Chente could tell Victor was a little frustrated. He was very smart, but he didn't like school the way Chente did. He didn't want the best grades or to be number one in his class. He didn't want to win awards and scholarships. Victor was different. He was a free spirit, who loved to express himself through art and music. He found studying and pouring over books a waste of time.

Chente quickly glanced at his algebra assignments. "Vic, all of these problems are right. Good job."

Victor sighed and rolled his eyes. "Before you ask, I didn't cheat off anyone either." He put his pen down on his world history textbook and looked Chente in the eyes. He shook his head.

"What's the matter?" asked Chente.

"I don't know how to make y'all understand that I really don't like school. I don't like studying because it's so boring," complained Victor.

"Okay," replied Chente as he calmly nodded and listened.

"Look, Chente, I am so proud of you, but I am not like you. I don't want to go and study at Stanford or Harvard or any place like that," said Victor as he put his hands over his head in frustration. "Does that make sense?" asked the little brother.

"Perfect sense." Chente smiled.

Victor glanced at Chente with a sly look and chuckled under his breath. "I understand algebra, and I get biology. I don't need a tutor. I can get straight As if I want to, but then …" Victor stopped and looked away.

"But then you would be expected to be a younger version of … me," replied Chente with a little smile as he began to understand his little brother's struggle.

Victor looked up, shrugged, and sighed. "No offense, Chen."

"None taken," responded Chente with mixed emotions.

Chente felt terrible and almost responsible that Victor had to endure this pressure all by himself. He should have been more aware. He should have kept an open line of communication with his little brother.

"I just thought that if I failed a few classes, the pressure would go away." Victor chuckled as he got up from his desk and sat down on his bed. "Boy, did that backfire!"

"What do you mean?"

"Violeta!" Victor emphatically said. "She had to call a family meeting and accuse me of trying to kill Mom. Like really?"

They both busted out laughing, breaking the tension in the room.

"Well, you should have known she'd find out," said Chente as he pointed at Victor. "I don't know how she does it. She's relentless. Is being nosy a superhero power or something?"

They both laughed again.

Victor quickly got up, pulled out a binder from under his bed mattress, and showed it to Chente. "This is what I want to do," said Victor as he opened the binder full of his art sketches.

Chente slowly thumbed through the pages in awe. His little brother was an artist—a good one.

"*Ay*, Victor, these are so good," said Chente as he sincerely grinned at Victor with pride. "I had no idea that you could draw like this."

"Well, I really haven't shown them to anyone," confessed Victor as he quietly looked away and retreated within himself. "You know, I started doing this after Dad died," he said softly as he paused and bit his lip. "It helped me escape the madness."

Chente completely understood what Victor meant. The Jimenez household had been a little bit crazy over the last few months. Their dad's untimely death had sent his family into an emotional tailspin.

From the kitchen, Chente heard their mom yell that dinner was ready. Victor quickly put the binder under his mattress again. "Don't tell anyone, Chente," said Victor as he placed a finger over his lips.

Chente nodded and gently promised. "But dude, you need to get those grades up to at least a solid B, and your sister Vi will get off your back."

"Oh, now she's only my sister?" asked Victor with a smirk on his face.

Chente shrugged and laughed. "We'll tell them that you are the next Diego Rivera in a couple of months—when things calm down a little bit."

The brothers exited their bedroom and walked into the kitchen to have dinner with their mom.

"Hey, Chen, what's going on?" asked Vanessa as she adjusted the volume of her cell phone. The college student had just gotten a few groceries at United Supermarket on Fourth and Slide, and was driving back to the Texas Tech campus. Vanessa was in the middle of her third year of college and worked as a resident assistant at the Stangel/Murdough Residence Hall.

"Hey, what's up, Nesh?" responded Chente. "Just finishing some homework."

Vanessa playfully groaned and started to laugh. Her little brother was always studying. "Please tell me you are not that big of a nerd."

"Guilty. Total nerd speaking," Chente said proudly as he turned off the lamp at his desk and sat down on his bed. "And you need to quit already—applying to Texas Tech Law School. Hello?"

Vanessa conceded. "Okay, so we're both nerds."

"Exactly! Now what's going on?" asked Chente as he transitioned to speakerphone on his cell. "What is this news you know?"

"Not so fast, *chiquito*," said Vanessa as she changed the direction of the conversation. "How's Mom doing?"

Chente's voice got excited. "Nesh, Mom actually made dinner tonight. I think she's doing better. Keeping my fingers crossed."

Vanessa let out a big sigh of relief as she turned into her dormitory parking lot. "That's so good. She loves to cook. That's positive," said the sister as she tried to contain her excitement. "And Vic? Is he getting his schoolwork done?"

"It's a long story, but yes. I checked his homework today. Nesh, he's like super smart."

Vanessa could tell Chente was holding back information, but she didn't push. "I believe you. He's just the baby of the family. He's spoiled and a little lazy."

"Yeah, something like that," said Chente.

The middle brother wanted to tell Nesh about his conversation with Victor, but he promised to wait a couple of months.

"And our wonderful sister?" inquired Vanessa. "Is she still being super bitchy?"

"Nesh, you have to stop. Vi is just … she's … yeah, I can handle her. Don't worry," Chente said with a sigh.

He didn't understand why Vanessa had built up so much anger for their older sister, but it was a conversation he didn't want to have right now. He didn't have the energy for any more drama tonight.

"Okay, Switzerland. Maybe you're right," she said, retreating. "Let's just pretend that she's adopted."

They both started to laugh.

"So tell me, sister, what's this gossip you have for me? Is it good?" asked Chente in a playful tone. There was silence on the other end of the phone, and that immediately alerted Chente to prepare himself for something dreadful.

"Now, Chente, you can't get mad," started Vanessa.

There was a long pause.

"Well, that's a great way to put someone on guard," said Chente with a nervous chuckle. "Am I speaking with Violeta or Vanessa?" He stood up and walked to the window. He had an eerie feeling that this wasn't going to be a positive conversation.

"It's about Jimmy," said Vanessa tentatively. "There are rumors about his suicide."

Chente's heart sank, and he closed his eyes, waiting for the worst. He knew word would get out eventually; he just wasn't ready for it to be this soon.

"Go on," said Chente as he braced himself.

"Well, you know Marta, Christina's sister, goes to Tech too, right?" asked Vanessa.

"Yes, she graduated last year," responded Chente.

"Right. Well, the other day I ran into her in the dining hall, and we had lunch together. She told me that she heard that Jimmy had committed suicide because …" Vanessa stopped and took a long breath.

"Because why?" asked Chente impatiently.

The long pause irritated Chente even more, and he wanted his sister to finish her thought. He wanted to hear her say the words. "Because why? Just say it, Nesh," repeated Chente.

Vanessa finished her sentence, "Because he was gay."

There, Vanessa had said it aloud. It was now a reality. People knew or at least suspected that Jimmy was gay.

Chente suddenly felt lonely and didn't respond.

Vanessa's voice became a bit frantic over the phone as she repeatedly reached out to her brother. “Hello? Chen, are you still there?” she asked. “Please answer me. I can hear you breathing through the phone.”

“Yes, I’m still here,” replied Chente even though he was tempted to end the call.

“Well, is it true?” asked Vanessa gingerly.

“Does it really matter?” barked Chente.

“No. Of course it doesn’t matter to me. You know that,” replied the sister as she paused to take a breath. “Still, I would just like to know the truth. He was my friend too.”

Chente knew Jimmy had been tired of pretending and hiding. He had made that very clear during their last conversation in his car.

“Yes. It’s true,” confessed Chente as his brown eyes began to tear up. He leaned his head up against the cold and frosty windowpane.

“So you knew he was gay?” asked Vanessa in disbelief. “Chente, why didn’t you tell me? He was probably going through hell, and he probably needed some support.”

Chente knew his sister was trying to be understanding, but that was the last thing he needed to hear right now. All the guilt he felt about Jimmy’s suicide came flooding back, and he felt a massive tidal wave hit him head-on as he slowly drowned in remorse and regret without a life jacket. He had failed his best friend in his time of need.

“I can’t talk about it right now, Nesh,” whispered Chente.

The emptiness in his heart was overwhelming, and he needed to be alone. He wanted to run away and hide. He wanted a blanket.

“Chente,” said Vanessa with a hint of desperation in her voice. “Don’t shut me out again. Please don’t do that. It’s not fair.”

“Then don’t push,” Chente calmly said. “Nesh, I have to go. I will call you tomorrow.”

“Chente! Promise me that we will talk tomorrow, please.”

The little brother could hear his sister’s distress and finally relented. “I promise,” he said and quickly ended the call.

Chente sat on his bed, not knowing what to think. He stared at the alarm clock on his desk—7:43. He wished he could turn back time.

A few minutes later, Chente felt his cell phone buzzing on the pillow next to him. He didn't want to talk to Vanessa, and she was just going to have to deal with it. He would call or text her tomorrow. He knew she was only trying to help, but today had been a long one, and his body was a little tired. He decided that he would go to bed early.

His cell phone began to buzz again. Chente shook his head and sighed.

"Nesh, I promise I will call you tomorrow," replied Chente as he held his cell phone to his ear. "I just don't want to talk about it anymore today, okay?"

"Hello, Chen? Is that you?" asked the male voice on the other end of the line.

Chente instantly sat up in bed and glanced at the number on his cell phone. He didn't recognize it. "Hello? Yes. This is Chente. Who's calling?" he asked.

"Oh, thank God! Chen, this is Coach Doss."

Chente's heart jumped out of his chest. Why was Coach Doss calling him? How did he have his cell phone number?

"Yes, sir. Is everything all right?" asked Chente.

Coach Doss chuckled on the other end of the phone. He sounded like a kid. "Well, not really. I have been looking for my house keys for about forty-five minutes, and I can't find them. Please tell me that you have them."

Chente shook off the surprise and focused for a few seconds. "Coach, you are locked out of your house?"

Coach Doss laughed again. "It would appear so. I can't find my keys, and I thought that maybe you still had them from this morning."

Chente quickly jumped out of bed and walked over to his closet. "Oh gosh, I don't know. Give me a second to look."

Chente went through his pant pockets and found nothing. In his mind, he tried to retrace his morning movements. His letterman jacket—he had put the keys in his jacket.

"Coach, I am so sorry. I found them in the pocket of my letterman's jacket."

"Heck, yeah. That's great news," said Coach Doss as he hooted and hollered over the phone. "I thought I was going to have to break into my own house, and I wasn't in the mood for a rendezvous with the Avalon Police Department." The basketball coach laughed.

"I am so sorry," repeated Chente.

"Forget about it, Chen, really. I think I remember where you live. I will swing by in a few minutes and get them from you," he said.

"No, sir. It's my mistake. I will run them over to you. I will be there in five minutes," said Chente. "Hang tight, okay?" He ended the call.

Chente got up and went to the bathroom. He brushed his teeth and gargled with mouth wash. He came back to his room and put on his jeans, his Stanford sweatshirt, and Nike tennis shoes. He went to his dresser and sprayed on some cologne. He went to his desk and grabbed the car keys. Chente caught a glance of himself in the mirror as he was walking out of the room, and he stopped.

What was he doing? This wasn't a date.

Chente got in his car and turned it on. He couldn't believe that a few minutes ago he had been in the depths of despair, and now he was anxiously on his way to see Coach Doss. He took a deep breath and reversed out of the driveway. Minutes later he turned the corner and saw the assistant basketball coach waiting by the front door of his house. He looked great.

Chente pulled into the driveway. He turned off the ignition. He exhaled.

"Boy, aren't you a sight for sore eyes." Coach Doss laughed as he stared at Chente with a big smile. "Thank you so much for coming all this way. I appreciate it."

"Well, it was only eight blocks, but it was the least I could do, seeing that I am the reason you are locked out of your house." Chente smiled as he got out of his car.

"I have been meaning to make an extra set of keys, but guess what … I haven't." The assistant coach chuckled. "I simply haven't had any time."

Chente walked up to Coach Doss and handed him his house keys. He felt a hint of static electricity as their hands gently brushed against each other when the exchange was made.

"Do you want to come inside for a few minutes?" asked Coach Doss as he opened the front door of his house and turned on the porch light.

Chente walked in after Coach Doss and closed the door to keep the winter cold outside.

"I like your house. It's cozy," said Chente as he rubbed his hands together.

"Well, thanks, Chen," said Coach Doss as he quickly turned on the lights in the living room and motioned Chente to take a seat on the couch. The assistant coach grabbed the remote control and turned on the TV; he disappeared into the kitchen. A few seconds later he returned with a couple of cans of Dr. Peppers. He handed one to Chente and sat down on the recliner.

"Hey, Chen, I am glad that you came over," said Coach Doss as he leisurely sipped his Dr. Pepper.

"Really? You are?" asked Chente with a hint of surprise in his voice. "Why? You have some papers to grade?"

The high school teacher burst into healthy laughter. "No, you crazy boy," said Coach Doss. "Yeah, man, I was in a terrible mood this afternoon after practice, and I was a complete jerk to you—and you were just trying be nice."

Chente looked down at his shoes, smiled, and shrugged.

"I apologize," said Coach Doss.

"It's okay. We're all a little tired," said Chente as he looked around the room.

He noticed a picture resting on the end table by the recliner. It was an old picture of an elderly man with his arm around a little boy, who held a basketball. "Who's that in the picture?" asked Chente.

Coach Doss picked up the picture and looked at it, smiling. He carefully wiped the dust off the picture frame. "That's me and my PeePaw."

"Oh wow. You were a chubby little boy. How old were you?" asked Chente as he grinned at his coach.

"I think I was eight years old, and we had just won our first Little Dribblers game," replied Coach Doss as he grabbed the picture and traveled back in time. “My PeePaw was my coach, and he was so proud of me.”

“Wow, that’s cool,” replied Chente as he admired the story behind the picture. “To have memories like that with your grandparents must be really special.”

“Yeah, my mom was at the game, and she snapped this picture and captured the last happy moment I had with him.”

“What do you mean?”

“Well, he died in a car accident four days later. He meant the world to me,” replied Coach Doss as he took a drink of his Dr. Pepper. “I cried like a baby for weeks,” he added as he quickly cleared his throat and exhaled.

A long stretch of awkward silence filled the room.

“I’m so sorry. I guess I screwed up again,” said Chente as he threw his hands in the air with a nervous laugh. “I just thought it was such a happy picture.”

“Don’t be sorry. It’s a great picture,” replied the basketball coach as he shook his head. “Actually, it is my all-time favorite picture. I love remembering my PeePaw and the good times we shared.”

Coach Doss got up and excused himself. He walked down the hallway and quickly entered his bedroom.

Chente stood up and walked around the living room, admiring the black-and-white wall prints of the Golden Gate Bridge and the Seattle Space Needle. He rubbed his hands together and shivered as he glanced down the hallway.

The first-year teacher returned moments later, wearing a Texas Tech T-shirt and some Adidas shorts. “Sorry, I had to get into my comfy clothes,” he said with a silly grin.

“Hey, guns up!” replied Chente as he pointed at the Texas Tech T-shirt.

“Guns up.” Coach smiled as he made a gun gesture with both hands.

“So, Coach, did you really play basketball after all?”

“Are you still trash-talking, Jimenez? Still doubting my mad skills?” asked Coach Doss as he pretended to be insulted.

"Maybe." Chente smiled and shrugged.

"Of course I played basketball," replied the assistant coach.

"I mean, past Little Dribblers?" asked Chente as he busted out laughing.

"Hey, I was pretty good too," replied Coach Doss as he playfully tagged Chente on the shoulder and started to laugh too.

"I'm kidding, I'm just kidding," said Chente as he sat back down on the couch and took a sip of his Dr. Pepper.

"Oh, I know." Coach Doss chuckled as he got comfortable on the recliner. "I was a good basketball player in high school but nothing like you. You are really good. It's in your DNA."

"Oh, come now, Coach." Chente grinned. "I have seen you shoot in practice."

"No, Chen, it's not the same. It's like you were born to play basketball," said Coach Doss as he stared at the TV screen. "The way you read the defense and instinctively know which play to call to get us a score, the way you step up and hit a key shot at a crucial point in the game, and the way you break a press—it's so smooth and fluid."

The point guard could feel his face turning bright red.

"You have this commanding presence on the basketball court, but you make it look easy and almost effortless." Coach Doss beamed and glanced over at the high school senior. "The boys on the team crave your leadership."

Chente was completely paralyzed by his words.

"And last night, you were amazing," continued the basketball coach. "You put the team on your shoulders and carried them to a victory. I couldn't take my eyes off you," said Coach Doss as he grabbed the remote and switched the channel to ESPN 2.

Coach Doss turned around and smiled nervously at Chente.

There was something about this kid that made Coach Doss feel at ease. There was a soothing warmth—like coming home and slipping into his comfortable slippers. He just felt right, relaxed, and fearless.

"Thank you," Chente managed to say. "I appreciate your confidence in me."

After a long and awkward pause, Coach Doss finally cleared his throat and scratched his head. "I guess that's why Bella came to the game last night," he said thoughtfully as he sighed. "She had heard me brag about you so much that she had to come and watch for herself."

Chente nodded and quickly changed the topic. "Bella. She's very pretty and seems to be really nice. How long have you known her?"

"I've known her all of my life," responded Coach Doss in a quiet manner. "My parents and her parents are really good friends. My parents absolutely love her."

There was a subtle loneliness in Coach Doss's eyes when he spoke about Bella that left Chente a little bit confused. Shouldn't he be happy?

"So you got engaged over the holidays, huh?" asked Chente.

Coach Doss smiled and nodded.

"So how did it happen? Was it a surprise? Did you get down on one knee?" inquired Chente as he desperately tried to keep the conversation moving.

"Something like that," said Coach Doss as he shrugged. He walked into the kitchen to retrieve a bag of potato chips.

"My dad felt that getting engaged and getting married was the next step after graduating from college. My mom helped me pick out the ring over Thanksgiving, and I popped the question on Christmas Eve."

It sounded like he was checking off items on a grocery store list to Chente, but he pretended to be impressed with the details. "So when is the big day? When will y'all get married?"

"I want to wait a little bit and save some money," said Coach Doss as he tried to sound practical. "But my parents and Bella want a June wedding—as in this June." Coach Doss made an irritated facial expression. It was obvious that he wasn't in favor of the last option.

"Well, can you compromise?" Chente carefully asked. "You know? Like maybe instead of June, you wait until October?"

Coach Doss halfheartedly smiled and shook his head. He looked at Chente and gingerly confessed his inner thoughts. "You know I am just twenty-two years old. There are still so many things I want to do and see before I get married and have kids."

Chente sensed his restlessness, and it confused him. It sounded like Coach Doss resented the idea of getting married. Could this be true?

Coach Doss stood up and aimlessly walked around the living room, mumbling to himself. He quickly walked down the hallway and disappeared into his bedroom.

Chente looked around the room and was a bit puzzled. He stood up and scratched his forehead. He wondered what was going on. Why was Coach Doss playing Houdini?

Coach Doss returned to the living room, full of energy and eager to talk. He was carrying a travel book, and he quickly flipped through the pages. "You know, I've always wanted to go to the Caribbean and go parasailing over the Caribbean water. I want to go sky diving over the Hawaiian Islands. That would be so much fun," he said as his face lit up with excitement.

Chente was stunned by his unbridled enthusiasm. He had never witnessed Coach Doss freely express his feelings this way. He was drawn to his energy.

Coach Doss gave Chente a mischievous smile from ear to ear as Chente took the travel book and started thumbing through some of the locations for himself.

"You know, Chen, I want to go to Egypt. I want to see the Great Pyramids with my own eyes. I want to go to Paris. I want to climb the Eiffel Tower," he said as he extended his arms over his head and began to laugh.

"I don't want a postcard from Mount Rushmore. I want to take a selfie with George, Abe, Tom, and Teddy. I want to go camping in the Grand Canyon and go jogging across the Golden Gate Bridge."

Coach Doss was flying high on his passion and desire for spontaneity. He longed for an unscripted life of chance and adventure, and like a caged bird, he wanted to break free, spread his wings, and fly away.

Chente stood in amazement and watched a highly energized Coach Doss pace back and forth in the living room as he delivered his inspired monologue of hopes and dreams.

"Just do it!" shouted Chente as he put the travel book down on the coffee table and began to laugh at the craziness of the moment.

Coach Doss walked over and grabbed Chente's shoulders; he fervently looked him in the eyes and smiled.

"I want to go. I will go with you," said Chente as he gently smiled back.

"Okay. Let's do it," replied Coach Doss breathlessly.

Chente's electrified body was inches away from Coach Doss—tempting and hungry. And like an energized magnet, he craved his touch. He brushed away a ringlet of perspiration rolling down Coach Doss's forehead and gazed into his ocean-blue eyes.

In that moment, Chente fell in love with Coach Doss.

The close proximity of their bodies was intoxicating and deliriously erotic. Chente knew he wanted to be with him, to feel his skin next to his—but not like this. Something was wrong.

"What's the matter?" Chente tenderly asked. "Are you okay?"

Coach Doss turned away and wiped the mist from the corners of his eyes. He remained silent for a few seconds. He took a deep breath and regained his composure. "It's complicated, and I think you should be going home. It's getting late."

The high school teacher swallowed hard and shook his head. Coach Doss knew he had crossed a line.

Chente nodded in agreement. He was still a bit dazed from all the excitement as he walked to the front door and opened it to go. "Just one last thing, Coach."

"What's that?" asked Coach Doss.

"Dude, quit saying that you're twenty-two years old, because you're not." Chente smiled. "You're still twenty-one and a half!"

The basketball chuckled under his breath.

Chente put his hand on Coach Doss's shoulder and gave him a long, lingering look. Then he walked to his car. He waved and drove away.

Chente gripped his steering wheel as he visualized Coach Doss shutting his front door in his mind. There was no doubt Coach Doss had sent an electrical current through his body that left his soul screaming for his touch. He needed to get home and take a cold shower.

CHAPTER 9

The game was tied 54–54, and Coach Alvarez called a time-out with seventeen seconds left in the fourth quarter. The team huddled on the sidelines by their bench and waited for their basketball coach to call the play.

Coach Alvarez's game plan against Friona had worked perfectly. His full-court press had given the tall and lanky guards from the opposing team a lot of problems, resulting in numerous turnovers. Avalon had capitalized on these mistakes and was now in a position to win the game.

The Avalon gym was charged with hometown spirit. The cheerleaders were in the middle of the gym floor, dancing to a cadence coming from the percussion section of the band. The student section in the bleachers was loud and crazy. A few of the senior boys had painted their faces maroon and white and were jumping up and down, playfully taunting the Friona players.

After a quick deliberation with Coach Doss, Coach Alvarez took a deep, nervous breath and got in the middle of the huddle. He began to draw up the final play.

"Okay, guys, listen up. It's all about spacing and creating one-on-one opportunities for players," he started as he looked at each player.

They each nodded in agreement.

"This is what we are going to do," replied Coach Alvarez as he began to draw up a play on his dry-erase board.

"After inbounding the ball, we are going to go into our one-four set—just like in practice. I want Chen on top of the key and the rest of you, go free throw line extended, to the three-point line."

Coach Alvarez thought for a moment and continued. "We are going to do a 'pick and roll' with Tre' and Chen. Chen, if the lane is open, go hard to the basket. If it is not open, watch for Tre' rolling to the basket on the other side."

Chente looked at Tre', and they both nodded in agreement.

"If the defense collapses on both of you, Carlos will be on the three-point line and ready to catch and shoot."

Carlos winked at Chente and confidently nodded.

"Guys, let's get this done and win this game," yelled the head basketball coach.

The whistle blew, and Chente had the ball on top of the key. He dribbled and waited. Tre' stepped up and set a pick on Chente's defender. Chente drove hard to the lane. The defender guarding Tre' followed him, and out of the corner of his eye, Chente saw Tre' get tangled up with a Friona player and fall down.

Chente glanced at Carlos on the three-point line, but he wasn't open.

Chente took two more dribbles and threw himself up against the six-six post player guarding him. He shot a layup and crashed to floor. The Friona player fell on top of him, and the whistle blew.

Chente opened his eyes and felt a little pain in his right thigh.

"Dude! Are you okay?" asked Carlos as he and Felipe rushed over to help him get up off the floor.

Chente sat up and blinked a couple of times. "Did I make it?"

"Are you kidding me?" joked Felipe as he helped Chente to his feet. "Mr. Too Tall swatted the basketball into the third row of the bleachers."

"But he fouled you," said Carlos. "You're shooting two free throws."

Chente looked up at the clock—two seconds remained.

Coach Alvarez quickly motioned to the referees and used his last time-out.

"Chen, are you okay?" asked Coach Alvarez as he saw Chente slowly limp to the bench and gingerly sit down. Chente grimaced but nodded.

Coach Doss quickly walked over and knelt in front of Chente without making eye contact. He pulled up Chente's shorts and began to apply some heating ointment on his thigh, while Coach Alvarez gave the team last-minute instructions about not fouling.

Coach Doss massaged Chente's thigh with small circular motions, making it extremely hard for Chente to focus on Coach Alvarez.

"You got this, Chen," said the animated head coach as he confidently nodded and looked his point guard straight in the eyes. "After Chen makes his second free throw, Tre', you need to put pressure on the inbounding pass. Don't foul!" he yelled.

"Thanks, Coach." Chente smiled as Coach Doss gave him a quick wink and walked to the end of the bench without saying a word. Chente got up and stretched his legs. His thigh felt a little better.

"No pressure, Chen," said Carlos. "Just pretend you are at practice."

"Yeah, just block out the two hundred people who are here screaming for you." Felipe laughed as Carlos playfully slugged him in the stomach.

As Chente walked to the free throw line, he saw his family quietly sitting in the middle of the bleachers. Vanessa stuck her tongue out of her mouth, and he shook his head at her. He stepped to the free throw line and took a deep breath.

The referee handed him the basketball, and Chente looked at the basketball goal. He got into his shooting stance, bounced the ball three times, lined up the ball, bent his knees, and in one fluid motion shot the ball into the air.

Swish. Nothing but net.

The crowd erupted in a crazy frenzy. The Avalon bench jumped up with excitement.

Chente remained unfazed and calmly shot his second free throw.

Swish. Nothing but net.

Friona inbounded the basketball, and their last-minute desperation shot didn't even graze the basketball goal on the other end of the floor as the buzzer sounded.

The Avalon bench celebrated for a few seconds as the guys gave each other celebratory hugs and fist bumps, then headed into the locker room.

Coach Alvarez was visibly excited as he wiped the perspiration off his forehead and jumped up and down in the locker room with his players. "Friona is ranked number seven in the state, and y'all just handed them their first loss of the year!" he said proudly. "Tonight you showed true grit and great teamwork!"

The locker room roared loudly.

"Don't forget, tomorrow morning the gym will be open for shooting at nine a.m.," said the winning coach as he exited with an extra hop in his step.

The basketball players took a quick shower and got dressed. As they put on their shoes, Chente asked Carlos and Felipe whether they needed a ride home. It was cold outside, and he wanted to make sure his friends didn't have to walk home.

"I have a ride home already," said Felipe with an impish grin. "During seventh period, Christina said she would drive me home after the game."

"I guess all the bickering turned into flirting today?" asked Carlos as he laughed aloud and tagged Felipe on the shoulder.

"*Pues*, look at me," said Felipe as he posed. "She can't help herself."

Chente laughed at Felipe's silly antics. "Good for you, Casanova. Make sure you spray on some cologne," suggested Chente as he pointed at his locker.

"*Y tú*, Carlos? Do you need a ride home?" asked the point guard as he opened the locker room door and walked into the gym.

Haven's eyes got big, and she let out a little scream when she saw Chente exit the locker room. She ran over to him and gave him a big kiss on the lips. She gazed into Chente's eyes and softly caressed his cheek.

"I am so proud of you, baby! You were so good tonight!" whispered Haven as she smiled from ear to ear.

Chente dropped his backpack and coughed a little. He was a little embarrassed when he realized there was still an audience in the gym.

His family had been speaking to Coach Alvarez and had turned around and witnessed the commotion. Violeta was standing next to

Coach Alvarez, and they were both smiling. His mother had a concerned expression, and Vanessa was obviously put out as she rolled her eyes and shook her head.

Bella was at the game again. She smiled, turned, and spoke to Coach Doss, who was staring at Chente. He looked at Bella and nodded, then gave Chente one more painful look and walked out of the gym.

"Well, hello, Haven," replied Carlos. He cleared his throat and chuckled under his breath. He looked at Chente with an exaggerated look of surprise and quickly walked over and gave Mrs. Jimenez a big hug.

"What was that about?" whispered Chente as he tried to regain his composure. "That was a little unexpected."

"What?" replied Haven with sad eyes. "You didn't like it?"

"I didn't say that, Haven. I just wasn't expecting it," said Chente as he tried to avoid another awkward scene. "Thank you for coming to the game and supporting me. Did you like the game?"

"Yes! It was the most exciting game I have ever seen," she said as she grabbed Chente's hand and walked over to his family.

"*Oyes, chiflado,*" said Vanessa as she purposely ignored Haven. "Victor and Valentin went to the Dairy Bee to pick up a few burgers. You need to hurry and come straight home."

Haven turned to Chente and leaned up against him. She batted her hazel eyes at him and smiled. "Will you please give me a ride home?"

Chente glanced at Haven and wondered what was wrong with her. Why was she behaving like this?

"Sure. I was going to give Carlos a ride as well," Chente quickly added.

Haven rolled her eyes and sighed. It was obvious she wasn't pleased. She wanted to be alone with Chente, even if it was for only a few minutes. She was tired of sharing him with Avalon High School.

"Well, maybe I can catch a ride home with Nesh," said Carlos after observing Haven's overreaction.

He looked in Vanessa's direction and shrugged.

"Nope. I can't," replied the overprotective sister. "I have a Toyota Prius, and Mom and Vi are riding with me. Sorry, no room."

Vanessa had her little brother's back. There was no way she was going to let the blonde vampire sink her selfish teeth into Chente's neck. Not on her watch. "Just ride home with Chente and come on over to our house for a burger after Chente drops off Haven, and we can catch up."

The older sister winked at Chente and left.

Chente pulled into Haven's driveway and told her he would call her tomorrow to arrange a pickup time for their date. She smiled and said she was looking forward to it. She waved at Chente as she opened the front door of her house and went inside.

Carlos moved to the front seat, shook his head, and let out a low whistle. "Chen, what the hell is her problem tonight?" asked Carlos as Chente placed the car in reverse. "She was all over you."

Chente thought for a second and shrugged in complete confusion. "I have no idea," he replied as he shook his head. "It was like it was Haven but with a different personality." He looked at Carlos and laughed nervously. "To tell you the truth, she kind of freaked me out by kissing me in front everyone!"

Chente was mystified. Haven had always been shy and unassuming, and she rarely drew attention to herself. But tonight it appeared like she was marking her territory for everyone to see.

"You know, Chen, just forget about it," suggested Carlos as he tried to lighten the mood. "We just beat state-ranked Friona! Let's go get a Cherry Dr. Pepper at Sonic before we head over to the house to eat. I'll buy!"

"Sounds like a plan," said Chente as Carlos playfully tagged his shoulder several times.

Chente drove a few blocks before he hit Main Street. He made a left and pulled into Sonic. Chente placed the drink order, while Carlos looked for a good song on the radio.

"Hey, what do you think about Felipe and Christina hooking up?" asked Carlos as he settled on the local Tejano radio station.

"Do I have to?" replied Chente as they both started to laugh. "You know, I think it's great. Maybe the constant bickering between the two will stop for a little while."

"I doubt it. They both love drama." Carlos sighed as he began to sing along with the radio.

Just then a metallic-blue 4Runner pulled up beside Chente's silver Jetta and parked.

Carlos looked over and whispered, "Hey, isn't that Coach Doss's 4Runner?"

Chente glanced over and saw that Coach Doss had parked next to his car. Coach Doss's fiancée, Bella, was practically hanging out the window and was motioning for Chente to roll down his window. So he did, slowly.

"Well, hello, Mr. Clutch!" yelled Bella. "You played another great game tonight!"

"Thank you," said Chente awkwardly. "I am just glad that we pulled out a win."

There was something a little strange about Bella's behavior, and Chente couldn't put his finger on it. "Are y'all getting something to eat?" he asked.

She rolled her eyes and exhaled. "Yeppers. Your Coach Doss doesn't have anything edible in his fridge," she said as she began to laugh hysterically. "Is that Haven in the car with you?"

Chente wrinkled his forehead and wondered why she was asking about Haven. "No, it's one of my buddies. I already dropped her off at her house. Hey, Coach," yelled Chente.

Coach Doss carefully looked over and waved at Chente. He appeared to be tired, annoyed, and ready to explode.

"Are you going to be at practice tomorrow morning?" asked Chente.

Coach Doss nodded. "Yes, sir. I am."

"Is it okay if I get there around eight o'clock for rehab? My thigh took a beating tonight," said Chente as he rubbed his upper leg muscle. "I'm afraid it will be a couple of Advil tonight if I'm to get any sleep."

"Absolutely," he said, nodding. "I will have the whirlpool ready to go by eight." Coach Doss's tone was a little different—very professional.

Bella's mood drastically changed. She groaned loudly from the passenger seat. "Please ... can somebody please talk about anything but basketball!"

Chente bit his bottom lip and nervously gripped the steering wheel. He wasn't sure how to respond. Was Bella being serious?

The Sonic waitress came and interrupted the conversation. She brought the boys their drinks and left. She was carefully balancing four more large drinks to the jeep three spaces to the right.

"Well, okay, guys, we have to go now. Y'all have a good night." Chente smiled as he rolled up his window and drove away.

"Is it just me, or was that not super weird?" asked Chente as he glanced over at Carlos with a nervous laugh.

Carlos shook his head in disbelief. "Yeah, the fiancée was drunk, right?"

"I am not sure," answered Chente. "And why was she asking for Haven?"

Carlos shrugged. "I don't know, but let's hurry and get to your house. I'm hungry!"

The next morning, Chente pulled into the student parking lot behind the gym a little after eight o'clock. He used the back entrance and went straight to his locker and changed. He grabbed a towel and walked over to the training room. Coach Doss was already there, drinking his coffee and reading the *Lubbock Avalanche Journal* morning newspaper.

"Good morning," said Chente as he got into the whirlpool. "Yes. This feels so good. The water temperature is perfect." The point guard smiled. "Thank you, sir."

Coach Doss just smiled back and continued reading the paper. Everything was so quiet and peaceful. There was a tender easiness developing between the two that made Chente feel strangely safe. He closed his eyes.

Coach Doss turned around and looked at Chente in the whirlpool with his eyes closed. Chente had a calming presence that brought a quiet inner peace to the basketball coach. When Chente walked into the training room, he felt his heart skip, and their souls instinctively link together. It felt automatic. He took another sip of his warm coffee and enjoyed the soothing moment.

About fifteen minutes later, Chente opened his eyes to find Coach Doss standing over him, smiling and holding the front page of the sports section of the newspaper.

The assistant coach dramatically cleared his throat and began to read the headline. "'Avalon Longhorns Upset State-Ranked Friona.'"

"That's so dope." Chente beamed as he sat up. "Coach Alvarez is going to be pumped when he reads that!"

Coach Doss nodded in agreement. "But hold on. I wasn't done," replied Coach Doss. "'Jimenez Hits Late Free Throws to Secure the Win.'"

Coach Doss's eyes got big with excitement, and he started to laugh aloud.

Chente shook his head and got out of the whirlpool in disbelief. "You're kidding, right? It actually says that?"

Coach Doss handed him the paper, and Chente read it for himself as Coach Doss continued to hoot and holler and dance silly around Chente.

"Coach, stop. This is embarrassing! You are embarrassing yourself," exclaimed Chente as he dripped water all over the floor.

Coach Doss swiped the newspaper from Chente's hands and corrected him. "No, this is exciting," he shouted and waved the newspaper in his face.

"I'm talking about your dancing—it's embarrassing." The basketball player chuckled as he playfully covered his eyes. "It is so bad that it's burning my eyes."

Chente secretly loved this moment; he was glad Coach Doss was comfortable enough around him to act a little silly.

"Coach Doss, what is going on in here?" asked Coach Alvarez as he walked into the training room with his coffee cup. "Why are you dancing around like a crazy man?"

The assistant coach stopped dancing and grinned. He handed the sports section to the head basketball coach and waited for his reaction.

Chente quickly got back in the whirlpool to finish his treatment.

Coach Alvarez's face exploded into a huge smile as he read the newspaper headline. He was finally getting some recognition for the years of hard work he had put in at Avalon High School.

"This is awesome, but now we have to back it up and let everyone know we are for real!" said Coach Alvarez as he glanced at Chente in the whirlpool. "How is your leg feeling this morning?"

"It's a little sore, but it always feels much better after a whirlpool treatment," said the star point guard as the timer sounded.

Chente reached for his towel and headed to the locker room to change into his practice clothes. He left the coaches in the training room to talk strategy.

He just wanted to get in the gym and shoot. He loved being in the gym alone. He loved hearing the rhythmic echo of the ball bouncing on the gym floor and the swish of the net as he drained a three-pointer.

After a few minutes of shooting, his solitude was interrupted as the two coaches walked into the gym. Coach Doss was carrying a ladder and headed in his direction.

"Hey, Chen, will you help Coach Doss change the nets? They are starting to look a little worn," said Coach Alvarez as he walked toward his office. "I am going to break down film for our next game."

Chente walked over to Coach Doss, who had already climbed the ladder and was changing one of the nets on the north end of the gym.

"Thanks, Chen. If you will just hold the ladder steady while I'm on it, I will be able to do this much quicker."

"No problem," said Chente as he held the ladder in place and glanced up to admire the view from below. He couldn't help but smile.

"So how's the thigh feeling this morning? Is it sore, or is it throbbing?" asked Coach Doss as he looped the net ringlets around the small hooks of the basketball goal.

"No. It's just a little tight," replied Chente with a small wince. "I must have strained it when that Friona player landed on me at the end of the game."

"Yeah, that was a wicked fall." Coach Doss nodded. "But then you stepped up and hit those free throws, and now people are reading about you in the newspaper. You're a celebrity!"

The ladder wobbled a little, and Chente quickly steadied it. He quietly chuckled under his breath. "Okay, you have to stop. I'm just glad we won—winning is so much fun!"

"Chen, you have ice in your veins," said the assistant coach as he made his way down the ladder and moved to the next goal. He climbed up the ladder again. "You really have no idea how much fun you are to watch, do you?"

The basketball coach glanced down the ladder and saw Chente apprehensively shrug.

"Thank you," Chente said quietly.

"So, you win the game for your team, and you get the girl too! It must be great to be Chente Jimenez," teased Coach Doss.

"Huh? What are you talking about?" replied Chente. "You're crazy."

"Haven," probed the basketball coach. "She's a pretty girl, and the way she kissed you last night after the game ..."

Coach Doss interrupted his own thought as he steadily made his way down the ladder. He looked at Chente and forced a smile. "You can tell she really likes you. How long has she been your girlfriend?"

Coach Doss quickly walked across the gym floor and hurried up the ladder. It was almost like he was running away from Chente's answer.

"It's not like that. We're just friends," answered Chente as he followed the assistant coach to the next basketball goal.

The first-year teacher flinched and looked down the ladder at Chente. "Really? Does she know that?"

Chente nodded in frustration and exhaled. "Why does everyone think I need to be with Haven Ray?"

"That's not what I said," replied the coach pragmatically. "I simply asked if she knew how you felt."

"Yes. As a matter of fact, I have told her many times that I don't want a girlfriend."

Coach Doss was surprised by Chente's unexpected response and lost his balance. Chente dropped the basketball he was holding, quickly reached up with both hands, and grabbed Coach Doss's firm butt cheeks to steady him from falling. Chente kept his hands there until the coach regained his balance.

Chente slowly exhaled. *That was so hot!*

"Why don't you want a girlfriend?" asked Coach Doss as he slowly steadied himself.

Chente paused and took some time to think about the question as he quietly analyzed his heart. "I just don't know if that's what I need right now," he said thoughtfully. "I can't really explain why I feel that way. I guess part of it is because I will be going to college soon, and I, well … I don't know."

Coach Doss appeared to accept his answer, and Chente didn't say anything else on the matter. He carefully steadied the ladder and watched Coach Doss finish installing the last net.

"You know, Haven's behavior last night was so bizarre, though," commented Chente. "It's not like her to just walk up to me and boldly kiss me like that. That was a bit strange."

Coach Doss immediately stopped what he was doing and looked down at the basketball player. "What are you saying, Chen? You didn't like it?"

Before Chente could answer, Coach Alvarez walked out of his office and announced he was going on a taco run and would be back in ten minutes. Coach Doss yelled out his order, and Coach Alvarez disappeared.

"Well, I think I know what happened last night," said Coach Doss with a heavy sigh.

"What do you mean?" asked Chente.

Coach Doss finished securing the net and hurried down. He put the ladder up against the wall next to the bleachers.

"You know that Bella and Haven sat together last night at the game, right?" asked Coach Doss as he walked over to Chente.

"No, I didn't," replied the point guard as he walked over to the free throw line.

"Well, they did. I'm fairly sure that Bella encouraged Haven to kiss you like that," replied the coach. "You know, to just go for it."

Chente laughed at Coach Doss and shot a couple of free throws. "You're kidding, right? Why would she do that?" asked Chente as he shot the basketball a few more times.

The assistant coach's demeanor slowly changed, and he became quiet and pensive.

"What's going on? What are you not telling me?" asked Chente as he stopped shooting and glanced at his basketball coach.

"I'm sorry, Chen. I don't know what to say. It gets complicated," replied Coach Doss. "It's a long story."

Chente wondered why Coach Doss was apologizing. What was he not saying?

"Okay, I am listening," said Chente as he gave Coach Doss his full attention. "Should I be nervous or something?"

"Well, the other night after you returned my house keys and left," started Coach Doss, "Bella called and wanted to discuss June wedding plans. You know, a date, a location, etcetera."

Chente nodded and pretended to be unfazed. He forced himself to smile politely. But truthfully, he felt like someone was throwing invisible darts, and his heart was the target.

"I told her that maybe we should wait a few more months," said Coach Doss. "I told her that maybe a fall wedding would be better."

"Yeah. I bet she didn't take it well, did she?" replied Chente as he slowly shook his head.

"Nope, it was awful. She immediately accused me of cheating on her, and she wanted to know the name of the girl," said Coach Doss as he let out a nervous laugh. "She even accused me of hooking up with a student."

"Wow. Are you serious?" Chente gasped and covered his mouth.

"Well, she had gone to happy hour with some of her friends and had too much to drink. She was really wasted," said Coach Doss. "I told her to sleep it off, and we could discuss it in a couple days."

Chente quietly listened and nodded.

"But instead, she cussed me out and hung up on me," said the coach. He rolled his eyes and sighed.

"Wow! Coach, I don't even know what to say to you," whispered Chente as he shook his head.

"There's nothing to say," said the first-year teacher as he scratched his head.

"Then my parents called me." Coach Doss sighed. "Apparently Bella called them, crying. She told them I had called off the wedding and that I was cheating on her."

"Oh my gosh. No way!" yelled Chente as he tossed the basketball back and forth between his hands. "You're kidding, right? Your parents actually called you? Awkward."

"Good morning!" shouted Beau from across the gym.

Coach Doss turned his attention to Beau, who had just entered the gym for shooting practice. "What's up, Mr. Brockman?" said Coach Doss. "Is there anyone else in the locker room?"

"Yes, sir," said Beau as he grabbed a basketball and dribbled toward Chente. "A couple of guys are on the way out. Hey, Chen, will you shoot free throws with me today?"

"Sure," replied Chente, and he gave Beau a good-morning fist bump.

"Dude, last night was so awesome. The way you walked up to the free throw line and made those free throws. That was so tight." The backup point guard smiled.

His admiration for Chente was obvious.

Coach Doss started to walk toward the locker room and playfully turned around. "Hey, Beau, I keep telling your buddy that he's a local celebrity. Am I right, or I am right?" asked the coach as he threw his arms up in the air and laughed.

"Yep, Coach Doss is right." Beau nodded as he turned around and innocently glanced at Chente.

The Jimenez boy just smiled, walked to the free throw line, and started playing a free throw game with Beau as the other guys exited the locker room.

Chente worked on his shooting for another forty-five minutes and decided to go home. He didn't want to aggravate his thigh muscle, and he needed to rest his legs. He put his basketball on the ball rack and began to walk toward the locker room when Felipe yelled at him from across the gym.

"Hey, Chen, are you and Haven going out tonight?"

Chente turned around and yelled back, "Why do you want to know?"

"*Oyes cabrón, just tell me*," said Felipe as Carlos jogged across the gym to talk to their friend.

"He and Christina want to go on a double date with y'all," teased Carlos as he busted out laughing.

"Oh yeah, like that will ever happen." Chente grimaced. "Christina doesn't even like Haven, remember?"

"*Oyes*, just answer the question," said Felipe as he threw his hands up in the air.

"Okay, yes. We are going to a movie, and then afterward we are eating at Rosario's," announced Chente.

"What movie are y'all going to watch?" asked Carlos.

"You know, I am really not sure. The new one with Jennifer Lawrence, I think," replied Chente with a wrinkled forehead.

"So y'all are for sure going to Plainview?" asked Felipe.

"What's going on?" asked Chente as he nodded. "Why all the questions?"

"Dude, I have never taken a girl out on a real date. I don't know how to do this," whispered Felipe.

Chente chuckled under his breath and gave Felipe a side hug as they walked into the locker room. "Well, I'm no Casanova, but just be yourself," Chente said. "It will all work out."

A few minutes later, the three friends jumped in Chente's car and left the gym. It was a cool Saturday morning, and the boys headed to Isabel's Taco Hut to pick up a couple of breakfast tacos before Chente dropped them off at their home.

Chente began to recount the details of his conversation with Coach Doss as he listened to some mariachi music on the radio and drove home.

It sounded like Bella was a little unhinged and perhaps a little spoiled. How could she call Coach Doss's parents?

He sighed and shook his head. None of it made any sense. Why had Bella sat with Haven at the basketball game? Why did Coach Doss apologize to him? So many unanswered questions.

Chente pulled into his driveway. Those questions would have to take a back seat because Violeta was at the house. There was no telling what she was up to this time around.

CHAPTER 10

Chente carefully opened the front door and quietly walked into the living room. His little niece, Lisa, was sitting in front of the TV, watching *The Little Mermaid*. She was singing and dancing and twirling her long brown and curly ponytail.

He tiptoed over to her and covered her eyes with his hands. The little girl let out a scream of excitement. “I know it’s you, Tio Chin. I know it’s you.”

“No, my name is Lucy, and I want to play house with you,” answered Chente as he playfully disguised his voice into a little girl’s voice.

The little girl giggled uncontrollably and removed Chente’s hands. “See, I knowed it was you, Tio Chin.”

“How did you know it was me?” asked Chente as he picked her up and swung her around the room.

“Because you’re stinky,” she said as she covered her nose and laughed.

Chente chuckled at her innocent but brutal honesty.

Violeta had walked in the room moments before and had witnessed the playful interaction between uncle and niece. She smiled and snapped a picture with her cell phone. “Lisa! That wasn’t very nice of you to say that to your Tio Chin,” said Violeta in her mommy voice.

“I’m sorry, Mommy,” replied Lisa with a sad face.

"Don't apologize to me. Say you're sorry to your Tio Chin instead," said Violeta.

The little girl giggled, walked over, and wrapped her arms around Chente's legs and gave her uncle an overly dramatic apology.

"It's okay, *mija*," said Chente. "I do stink. I have been playing basketball all morning."

He pulled out a dollar bill from his pocket and handed it to her. She screamed, took the money, and ran back to the TV to watch her cartoon.

"She seems like she is always full of energy." Chente smiled as he watched her dance in front of the TV. "Where's Mom?" he asked as he walked into the kitchen to eat his breakfast taco. He went to the refrigerator, grabbed a blue sports drink, and sat down.

"She's taking a quick shower," answered Violeta. "We are going to Plainview to do a little grocery shopping."

"Oh, okay. That's very considerate of you to get her out of the house." Chente smiled.

"Did you see the *Lubbock Avalanche Journal* this morning?" asked the oldest sister as she smiled with prideful eyes.

"Yes," said Chente as he began eating his taco. "Coach Doss and Coach Alvarez were very excited this morning."

He watched Violeta. Something was different about her this morning. She was almost happy.

"Well, last night's game was so exciting," she said as she walked around the table and sat down next to him. "Chente, I knew you were good, but I didn't know you were *that* good."

"Gee, I don't know if that's a compliment or not." Chente laughed.

The older sister playfully hit him on the shoulder and rolled her eyes. "And I saw you kissing Haven after the game too. How long has she been your girlfriend?" Violeta asked with curious eyes.

"She's not my girlfriend," replied Chente in a very straightforward manner.

"But I saw you kiss her last night after the game," uttered Violeta as she raised her voice a little bit.

Chente shook his head in disagreement. "Nope. You saw *her* kiss *me*. There's a difference," he said as he continued to eat his taco.

"Oh, come on. It's the same thing, Chente." Violeta sighed.

"It's *not* the same thing," responded the brother as he stood up and went to the microwave to warm up his second breakfast taco. "What is the big deal, Vi? Are you trying to start an argument?"

"No," Violeta calmly said. "I just don't understand why you won't admit that you have a girlfriend. That's all."

"Because I don't have one," replied the brother. "And I don't know why it matters so much to you."

She carefully looked at her younger brother. "It's very normal for boys your age to have girlfriends, right?"

Chente took a deep breath. He didn't know why Violeta's words irritated him so much, but they did. So he turned around and retaliated with words he was sure would aggravate her. "Then I guess I am not normal."

The room temperature dropped 50 degrees as Violeta's warm demeanor glaciated instantly. She stood up and pointed at Chente. She gave him a cold stare and clenched her teeth. "Why is having a girlfriend a bad thing?" hissed the oldest sister. "I hope this has nothing to do with your friend Jimmy."

Chente pursed his lips and shook his head as he watched the Ice Bitch resurface. "What is that supposed to mean?" he asked with rage in his eyes.

"Chente, you have to know what people are saying about your friend Jimmy, right?"

He just looked at his oldest sister and shook his head. He wondered how they were even related.

"*Pues mija, que dice la gente*? What are people saying about my Jimmy?" asked Mrs. Jimenez as she walked into the kitchen.

Violeta looked away and didn't say anything.

Mrs. Jimenez looked at Chente. It was evident she had walked into the middle of an argument. Chente's cheeks were red, and if looks could kill, Mrs. Jimenez would be calling 911.

"Chente? *Mijo*, what's the matter?"

"It's nothing new, Mom—just Violeta being a bitch again." Chente was breathing fire. "Your oldest daughter wanted to know if I had heard the rumors about Jimmy," he continued as he walked over to Violeta and made her look at him. "Isn't that right, Violeta?"

"*Ay Diosito* ... What rumors?" gasped Mrs. Jimenez as she gently put her left hand over her mouth.

He took a deep breath and tried hard to regain his composure. "Mom, people are saying that Jimmy committed suicide because he was gay."

Mrs. Jimenez tried to digest the rumors for a second or two. She glanced at Violeta and then at her middle sone. "Is that all? Those are the rumors?"

Chente nodded.

"Well, I don't care about that," she said very decidedly and made the sign of the cross across her chest. "All I know is that my Jimmy was a good kid. *Mijito tenia un buen corazón.* May his soul rest in peace."

"So, Mom, like you don't care that people are saying that Jimmy was gay?" asked Violeta with an irritating tone.

"Of course I don't. How could you think that I would care about something like that?" replied Mrs. Jimenez as she dismissed her daughter with her hand. "Now we better get going to Plainview. I want to get back early."

Mrs. Jimenez walked into the living room and grabbed her purse. She put on a light-blue shawl to protect her from the cool morning.

Violeta quickly and efficiently gathered all Lisa's belongings without saying a word. She had a scowl as she stormed out of the house.

"Goodbye, Tio Chin." Lisa waved as she followed her mother out the front door.

"Goodbye, *mija*. Be good," he said as he blew her a kiss.

"*Mira*, Chente, life's too short to worry about things like that, okay?" advised Mrs. Jimenez as she caressed her son's cheek. "And take a nap. You look tired."

"Okay, Mom," replied Chente as he smiled and nodded.

Chente looked at the clock in his room—5:35 p.m. He had overslept. The quick nap had turned into five hours. His body must have needed to rest and recover from last night's basketball game.

He jumped out of bed and took a quick shower. When he returned to his bedroom, he saw his cell phone blinking. He read Haven's text and responded that he would pick her up in fifteen minutes.

He went to his closet and put on some blue jeans and a red sweater. He grabbed his Nike running shoes and slipped them on. He went to his dresser and began to spray on some cologne when his mother walked into his bedroom.

"Are you going out tonight?" inquired Mrs. Jimenez as she admired her handsome son in the mirror.

"Yes. Haven and I are going to watch a movie and grab some dinner at Rosario's," answered Chente. "Why? Is everything okay?"

"Everything is fine," replied Mrs. Jimenez as she sat down on her son's bed and watched him get ready. "Quit worrying so much all of the time."

Chente could see his mother staring at him through the mirror. He turned around. "Really, Mom? What's going on?"

"*Mijo*, you look so much like your dad, especially in that red sweater," she said with a nostalgic smile.

Chente's shoulders instantly relaxed, and he quietly exhaled.

"Red was your dad's favorite color," added Mrs. Jimenez.

"Well, I am going to take that as a compliment," said Chente, and he winked at her through the mirror.

"So, *mijo*, you and Haven are getting along okay?" she asked as she stood and casually made up his bed and fluffed his pillows.

Chente grew suspicious again and gave her a doubtful look. "Yes. Why?"

"*No mas pregunto*," she said. "I ask, well, it's just that I thought I saw a little bit of tension last night when y'all were together. That's all."

"Oh that. Yes. Well, she completely caught me a little off guard," answered Chente as he shook his head.

She nodded. She paused and thought for a second before she

responded. "You know that it's okay if you didn't like her kissing you like that, but I think she really has feelings for you."

Chente sighed and looked out the bedroom window. "Mom, it's just that I am going to college in a few months, and I don't want that kind of a relationship right now."

"Have you been honest with her and told her that?" asked Mrs. Jimenez. Her tone was stern but without judgment.

"Yes. I have been very honest with her," replied Chente.

Mrs. Jimenez nodded calmly. "Okay, so you have been honest with Haven—that's good," she said before she kissed him on the cheek. "Now, have you been honest with yourself?"

Chente wrinkled his forehead and turned around. He didn't know what she meant.

"*Te vez bien chulo, mijo.*" Mrs. Jimenez smiled as she gingerly walked out of the bedroom.

"Stop it, Mom." Chente groaned.

"So which movie are we watching?" asked Chente as he turned his silver Jetta onto Highway 194 and headed to Plainview.

Haven smiled. "I got tickets to the new Jennifer Lawrence movie. Is that okay?"

"Sure. I like her movies," replied Chente with a nod. "What time does the movie start?"

"Six forty-five p.m.," answered Haven as she delicately checked her Kendra Scott earrings in the vanity mirror and primped her blonde hair.

"No problem. We will be there in twenty minutes."

"When is our reservation at Rosario's?" asked Haven as she adjusted her seat belt to avoid creasing her pink blouse.

"I booked our table for nine p.m.," said Chente as he pushed a round button near the steering wheel and sprayed washer fluid on the windshield. The wipers came on and swiftly cleaned the mud off the glass.

"Perfect," she said. "I am so looking forward to spending some alone time with you."

Chente didn't take the bait. Instead, he completely ignored her comment and started talking about the basketball game from the night before.

"It was such a good game," she said as she delicately patted his hand. "The other team was so tall. I can't believe that y'all won."

"Yeah, Coach Alvarez was so happy after the game." Chente grinned. "And then there was an article in the *Lubbock Avalanche Journal* about our basketball team this morning."

"I know. My dad showed it to me." Haven beamed. "They wrote some really cool things about you too."

Chente awkwardly shrugged and said nothing.

"I didn't know that you had scored twenty-one points," she exclaimed. "I guess I need to pay closer attention next time."

The comment reminded Chente of his morning conversation with Coach Doss regarding Bella and Haven sitting together at the game, which Chente still found a little strange.

"Exactly," remarked Chente with a little laughter. "Hey, by the way, where were you sitting? I don't remember seeing you in the student section," commented Chente as he casually kept his eyes on the highway.

Haven started to fidget with the radio. "Oh, I sat with some friends," she said. "The student section was too congested, so we sat close to the entrance of the gym."

Chente gently pressed the issue. "So who did you sit with? Angie?"

Haven found a radio station to her liking and sat back and relaxed. "Uh, no. I sat with Bella. You know—Coach Doss's fiancée," she said very nonchalantly.

"Really? Why?" asked Chente as he suddenly felt the butterflies in his stomach.

Haven casually explained that she and Bella had arrived at the game at the same time and that Bella had mentioned that she didn't know anybody. So they sat together.

Chente kept his eyes on the road and softly exhaled. Why would a Texas Tech student want to sit with Haven? They barely knew each other. It didn't make sense.

"It was all a bit strange," said Haven as she checked her cell phone. "I think she had been drinking a little bit, and I know for a fact that she had been crying."

Chente looked at Haven. "Oh yeah? What makes you say that?"

"Well, for one, I could smell the alcohol on her breath," said Haven as she texted someone on her cell phone. "And two, girls just know when other girls are crying. It's just one of those things," she said as she pushed her hair over her shoulder and smiled.

Chente continued to pump for more information. He couldn't shake the feeling that Bella was playing games and using Haven as a pawn. But why? What was her ulterior motive? "Is she going to be okay?"

"I am not sure," replied Haven. "She said something about wedding dates. I think Coach Doss wants to wait a little longer or something like that. I really was trying to watch you play."

Chente's heart began to race, and he readjusted his sitting position. Was Coach Doss really going to postpone his wedding? Why would he do that? Had he changed his mind about marrying Bella?

Chente could barely breathe and began to cough. He suddenly felt his face getting warm, and he felt flushed. He cracked open the car window and let the winter air in the car.

"Chen, are you okay?" asked the blonde-headed girl. She smiled at Chente and batted her eyes.

"The car just got a little overheated," replied Chente as he wiped his forehead. "I'm good."

Chente watched Haven pull out some lip gloss from her purse. She lowered the sun visor and used the vanity mirror to apply it on her lips. She touched up her mascara as well. Haven used very little makeup. She was naturally pretty.

"So, Chen, have you decided where you're going to college next year?" asked Haven as she put her lip gloss back in her handbag.

Chente regrouped his thoughts and shook his head. He pursed his lips together. "Nope, not yet. I don't have a clue."

Haven studied Chente's face. "I mean you wouldn't go too far, would you?"

"I don't know, maybe. I'm not sure," replied Chente as he casually shrugged. He could see Haven staring at him through the corner of his eye. "What's the matter?" he asked.

Haven looked out the window and shook her head. "I always thought you would go to Tech."

"And I may still," he replied. "But I like Austin too, and going to Stanford would be a dream come true for me!"

Haven didn't share his excitement. The idea of Chente going halfway across the country didn't sit well with her. Chente would go to California and meet someone new and forget about her. She would miss him terribly.

"I won't know anything for another month or so," he said, "Miss Young says I have a really good chance."

"That's great, Chen," said Haven as she forced herself to smile.

Chente pulled into the Movies 16 complex and parked his car. He and Haven battled the icy, blustery West Texas wind as they rushed into the theater foyer. Chente picked up the tickets and walked up to the concession stand to buy some popcorn, while Haven excused herself to the restroom.

"*Órale*, Chente! What a surprise to see you here," yelled Felipe with a playful smile as he, Christina, and Carlos walked into the movie theater a few minutes later.

Chente closed his eyes and shook his head in disbelief. This couldn't be happening.

He turned around let out an incredulous laugh. "Oh wow. What are y'all doing here?"

"What do you mean, Chente?" asked Christina as she batted her fake eyelashes and walked up with Felipe in her arms. "We're here to watch a movie—just like you."

Christina was completely overdressed for a movie date. She wore bright-red leather pants with red stiletto heels and a black, oversized sweater, which exposed her red bra strap on her left shoulder. Her blue eye shadow screamed for attention, and her overprocessed hair looked frizzy under the lights of the movie theater. She was dressed like a cross between Bozo the Clown and a cheap hooker.

"*Dónde ésta La Gringa?*" asked Christina as she played with her ruby-red fingernails. "Is she in the restroom?"

"*Mira*, please, don't start, Christina. We are not in school right now," replied Chente as he waved his finger at her.

"Okay, okay." Christina giggled as she rolled her eyes and walked up to the concession stand with Felipe. She ordered a soft drink.

He looked at Carlos and squinted. "Dude. What are y'all doing here?"

"I'm sorry, Chen. I told them it wasn't a good idea," replied Carlos as he lowered his baseball cap and shamefully covered his hazel eyes. "I didn't even want to come. They tricked me."

"Haven is going to flip out!"

"Yes, I know, and I feel like I am the third wheel on a date from hell," whispered Carlos.

Chente went to the concession stand, picked up his popcorn and soft drink, and waited for Haven to emerge from the back of the theater.

Haven walked out of the restroom and smiled at Chente. She suddenly stopped when she saw Christina and Felipe at the concession stand. She gave Chente a panicked look, bit her lip, and walked toward him.

"What are *they* doing here?" asked the blonde-headed girl as she clenched her teeth and pretended to smile.

Chente just looked at her and didn't know what to say. He couldn't exactly control his friends.

"Well, hello, Haven," said Christina as she smacked her red lips on a cherry lollipop and pranced over with Felipe.

"Hi, Christina," said Haven as she turned around and greeted the pretentious Latina with a warm smile. "Oh my, Christina, I love those pants. They look so good on you."

Chente turned and glanced at Haven. What was she up to?

"Actually, I just love your whole outfit. The way you matched the colors. Did you put it together yourself?" asked Haven.

After a few seconds, Chente could see Christina's icy wall melt.

Haven had her eating out of the palm of her hand, and Chente couldn't help but chuckle under his breath.

"So you want to be a professional stylist?" asked Haven.

"Yes, girl. I am better than Kim Kardashian," replied Christina as she inspected Haven from head to toe. "Listen, maybe I can come over to your house and go through your closet and give you some pointers."

Chente turned and looked at Carlos; he bit his bottom lip to keep from laughing. He quickly took a sip of his soft drink and watched Haven give Christina her undivided attention. Chente was impressed with Haven's kind generosity as she listened to all of Christina's ideas and praised her creative choices.

"Enough of this girl talk," said Felipe as he rolled his eyes. "We have about ten minutes before the movie starts. Let's go find some seats."

"Just let me know when you want me to come over and go through your closet. Girl, we could go shopping in Lubbock one weekend," said Christina as she smiled and followed Felipe and Carlos into theater number four.

Chente playfully glanced at Haven and quietly cleared his throat. "Wow. That was good! Are you a member of the drama club?"

"Kill them with kindness, baby. Isn't that what you always say?" replied Haven with a facetious wink as they watched their friends enter the movie theater. "Besides, she's kind of nice."

Haven grabbed her soft drink from Chente, casually looked over his shoulder, and gasped. "What are *they* doing here?"

"What's the matter?" asked Chente as he turned around and saw Coach Doss and Bella walk into the theater foyer.

"Is tonight Avalon High School Night or something?" whispered Haven as she threw her arms in the air in disbelief. "You have got to be kidding me!"

"Come on. Let's go before they see us," she said, and they quickly turned to walk away.

"Haven? Haven Ray? Is that you?" yelled Bella from across the foyer and waved frantically.

Haven stopped, looked at Chente, turned around, and smiled. She was back on center stage.

"Fancy running into you guys here," said Bella as she gave Coach Doss a sly look. "Are y'all on a romantic date?"

"Yeah, I guess. Something like that." Chente smiled as he sensed Bella's icy tone.

He looked over at Coach Doss, who was staring at him and slowly nodding.

"Hey, Coach. How are you?" asked Chente as he attempted to make polite and insignificant conversation.

"Sure is chilly outside," replied Coach Doss as the girls stepped to the side and huddled into girl talk.

Chente nodded in agreement as he looked out the windows. It was pretty chilly indoors too.

The high school teacher casually walked over to Chente with a mischievous grin. "Are you sure she's not your girlfriend?"

Chente skillfully ignored him and quickly turned the tables. "So the winds of persecution have blown over, I take it?" responded Chente as he ate some popcorn.

"I guess," replied the coach as he shrugged. "It might be a different story tomorrow. Who knows?"

"I see," whispered Chente as he glanced at Haven and Bella, who were visiting. "It's crazy that y'all are here too. I mean, you just missed Felipe and Carlos and Christina. They just walked into the theater."

"I have a confession to make," Coach Doss whispered back. "I heard you guys talking about it in the locker room this morning." He stood back, and his ocean-blue eyes admired Chente from head to toe. "You look good in red." The basketball coach smiled and casually walked over to the concession stand.

Chente just stood there in silence. He was dumbfounded. Did Coach Doss just admit that he wanted to hang out with him? Did he just flirt with him too? Chente felt a subtle giddiness in his chest.

"Okay, great, we will see y'all in the theater," Haven said as she dismissed Bella to the concession stand.

Haven smiled and walked over to Chente, hijacking his arm. As they walked to theater four, she explained that Coach Doss and Bella had reservations at Rosario's too and that Bella suggested that they should eat together.

Chente pretended to be surprised and glanced at Haven. "What? Really?" he replied with a hint of astonishment in his voice. "You have got to be kidding, right?"

"Hush, or she will hear you, Chen," whispered Haven.

"Whatever you want to do. It's up to you, Haven," said Chente as he exhaled. "If you are okay eating dinner with them, so am I."

"What's the matter, Chen?"

"Nothing," said Chente dismissively. "We just need to get into the theater before someone else from Avalon High School shows up."

Chente glanced to the concession stand and saw Bella watching as he and Haven entered the theater. He had an eerie feeling in the pit of his stomach that the evening wasn't going to end well.

After the movie, Carlos and Felipe casually stood around the foyer, talking about their next basketball game, while Christina continued to consume Haven with fashion talk.

Chente exited the men's restroom and spied Coach Doss and Bella exiting theater four together and holding hands. Bella leaned up against her fiancé and smiled. She gave him a peck on the cheek and made a beeline to the ladies restroom.

Chente turned away and gazed out the foyer window, slowly exhaling. He stared out into the darkness, feeling lost and empty. Witnessing the intimate exchange between Bella and Coach Doss had bothered him. It made him feel disoriented and confused inside.

Chente stood back, watched his friends, and smiled. He wished he could cancel his dinner reservations at Rosario's and go with them to the Pizza Hut instead. That would be more fun and a lot less stressful.

"Hey, Coach Doss," said Christina as she sauntered over to the high school teacher. "Did you like the movie?"

Christina batted her long eyelashes and smiled. She casually placed her hand on the coach's shoulder. She was a natural flirt.

"Yeah, it was okay," replied Coach Doss as Bella swooped in; she wrapped her arms around him and simultaneously stared Christina down. The restroom lines were too long, and she wanted to leave.

"Haven," said Bella with a breezy voice. "We will see you at Rosario's."

She glared at the head cheerleader and barely waved at Chente as they left.

"Did you see the way that chick looked at me?" asked Christina. "Hell, if I wanted her man, I could have him, but I don't." She looked at Felipe and purred like a kitten. "I have my own boy toy!"

"I know you just didn't call me that." Felipe smirked as he playfully waved his index finger in Christina's face.

"Time-out," said Carlos as he rolled his eyes. "Can we finish this fight at Pizza Hut? I am hungry."

Chente and Haven walked into Rosario's and waited for the hostess, who was helping another couple to their table. The delicious aroma of Mexican food filled the room, and Chente's stomach started to talk. He had been so stressed at the movie theater that he hadn't eaten any popcorn. Watching Coach Doss and Bella cuddle right in front of him made him feel uneasy and jealous.

"Are you sure you want to eat with Bella and Coach Doss?" asked Chente. "I mean, we could totally meet up with the guys at Pizza Hut."

Chente was uneasy about this idea. He wondered why Bella, a college student, would befriend Haven, a junior in high school. It just didn't make sense. He felt like he was walking into a lions' den.

"Yeah, why?" asked Haven as she innocently brushed her hair back. "We don't have to eat with them if you don't want to, Chen."

"It just sounds like there's some drama there. I want no part of it. That's all," replied Chente. "So that's a no to Pizza Hut?"

"Relax and don't worry much. It will be okay." Haven sighed as she swiped his hand when the restaurant hostess returned and led them to their table.

"Aw, y'all look so cute together holding hands." Bella smiled as Chente and Haven sat down at the table.

Chente watched Coach Doss instantly busy himself with the menu. He didn't even bother to look up.

"Aaron, don't they look adorable together?" asked Bella, and she reached for Coach Doss's hand.

Chente awkwardly glanced at Haven as Coach Doss ignored his fiancée and casually spoke to the waiter about the menu. He ordered chips and salsa for the table.

"So did you like movie?" asked Chente as he cleared his throat and tried to defuse the tension at the table.

Bella turned and glanced at Chente with a plastic smile. "I did. Did you?"

"The ending threw me for a loop, but it made sense after I thought about it a little more." Chente nodded.

Bella barely acknowledged Chente's comments as she abruptly opened her menu and glared at her fiancé sitting next to her.

Chente looked at Haven and smiled. This wasn't going to be fun.

"So, Coach Doss, Chen tells me you are now teaching his seventh-period government class. How's that going?" asked Haven. She sipped on her glass of water.

Coach Doss smiled and gave Haven his full attention. He explained that he had never taught government before and was a bit nervous. He laughed and told her he was still a little lost, but he couldn't say no to Principal Timms when he asked for his help.

"Chen has been a great help in class. Heck, he knows more government than me," said Coach Doss as he let out a hearty laugh.

Bella gave Chente a fake smile and an icy stare. "Well, then it's a good thing you have him in class. Chen, you save the day *again*."

Chente felt the chill in Bella's comments, but he gave her a polite smile.

"Yes. Chen is super smart," Haven said proudly. "He scored over fourteen hundred on his SAT test. Or something like that, right, Chen?"

Chente adjusted his seating position as he nodded and smiled. He cleared his throat and drank some water.

"What? Really? I didn't know that," replied Coach Doss as he shook his head. "Chen, that's an amazing score! I think I scored something like an eleven hundred."

"That's why he has all the colleges recruiting him," replied Haven as she placed her hand on Chente's shoulders and smiled.

Bella raised her wine glass to Haven and grinned as well. "Wow, you must be very proud of your *boyfriend*."

Haven looked down at her menu and nodded. "Chen works very hard; he deserves all the success that comes his way," she delicately said.

"Haven sure is devoted to you. You are incredibly lucky." Bella smiled as she tilted her head to the right; her bright-blue eyes curiously studied Chente's face. She bit her bottom lip and raised her right eyebrow. "How long have you all been dating?"

Chente felt the turn this conversation took. He knew it was making Haven uncomfortable, and he wasn't about to embarrass her in mixed company.

He straightened his posture, cleared his throat, and confidently returned Bella's stare with a fake smile of his own.

"Oh, Bella, you're so right. I am extremely lucky." Chente beamed as he placed his hand over Haven's. "Haven and I have been friends for a long time. She's very special."

Haven looked up at Chente with kind admiration. "We are just friends—very good friends," replied Haven as she delicately brushed her blonde hair over her ear.

"Oh well, how sweet," mumbled Bella. She sipped her wine and slowly brushed her hair back. She scanned the menu as the waiter took everyone's order.

After the waiter left, Chente got up, excused himself from the table, and made his way to the restroom. He went directly to the sink. Chente quickly washed his hands and splashed a little cold water on his face as Coach Doss entered, stood behind him, and watched.

Chente pointed at Coach Doss and tried hard to contain his anger. "What in the hell is going on out there?"

Coach Doss looked away, went to the sink, and nervously washed his hands as well.

"Coach, what is Bella's problem?" asked Chente. "Why is she being so bitchy—and on purpose?"

Coach Doss shook his head. "All I know is that she's been very upset about possibly postponing the wedding date."

"And what does that have to do with me or Haven? That sounds like a problem for y'all to figure out."

Coach Doss looked down at his shoes and didn't respond.

Chente stopped, took a deep breath, and tried to collect his thoughts. "Coach, what are you not saying. This doesn't make any sense."

"Look, Bella has always been very insecure and possessive," started the high school teacher. "She can be really mean when she doesn't get her way."

Chente wrinkled his forehead and tried hard to understand. "Okay, so she's insecure and possessive—lots of girls are that way, Coach. That still doesn't make any sense to me."

Coach Doss paused for a moment. He reached out and grabbed Chente's hands. "Look, let's just have some dinner," Coach Doss said calmly as he gazed into Chente's brown eyes. "Tonight is a little crazy, and I will explain later. I promise."

Chente took a deep breath and nodded. He felt Coach Doss grip his hands tightly, and his touch sent a wonderful sensation to Chente's young heart.

Chente could see the anxiety on Coach Doss's face, and he wondered what was making him so uncomfortable. What was happening?

"Okay. I trust you," Chente whispered as he stared into his ocean-blue eyes.

Coach Doss smiled and softly caressed Chente's cheek with his hand. He turned and walked out of the restroom, leaving Chente breathless.

Chente barely said two words after he returned from the restroom.

He listened to Haven and Bella go on and on about Justin Bieber, the Kardashians, and other TMZ news.

When the food arrived, their conversation shifted to Gigi Hadid, Kendra Scott jewelry, and Louis Vuitton purses. Chente and Coach Doss glanced at each other a few times and smiled.

On the drive back home, Haven thanked Chente several times for a wonderful time. She was excited that she had bonded with Christina and had gotten to know Bella a little better. She was happy she had made two new friends.

Chente was relieved that Haven had enjoyed the night. He was glad she had been oblivious to the underlying drama of the evening.

"Well, I hope you had fun," replied Chente as he pulled up to Haven's house and parked in the driveway.

"I did," she whispered as she reached for Chente's shoulders and pulled him in for a long kiss.

Chente slowly and gently pushed Haven away and stared at her. Haven was beautiful and kind and fun, but he didn't want to kiss her. It felt forced and unnatural. What was the matter with him?

"Is everything okay?" asked Haven as she searched his brown eyes for answers. "Did I do something wrong?"

"No, no, no. It's me," Chente quickly answered.

"What is it?" she whispered.

"Well … we … uh … we are in your driveway," stumbled Chente. "Your parents are home, and it's kind of awkward."

Haven watched Chente for a couple of seconds and then smiled. She nodded and reached for her purse. "Well, I had fun," she said with a nod. "Thank you and good night."

Chente exhaled as he watched Haven enter her house. He slowly reversed his Jetta and headed home with his heart in knots.

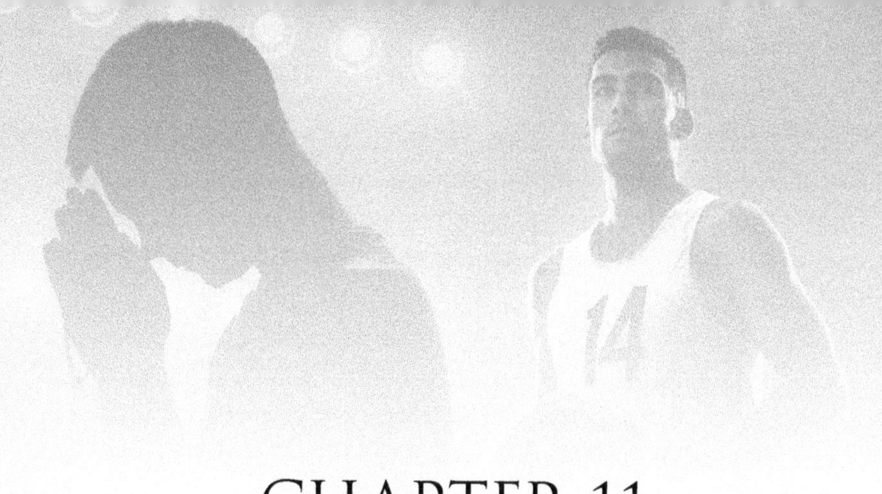

CHAPTER 11

Chente couldn't help but chuckle as he listened to Christina and Carlos make morning announcements to the student body of Avalon High School. Christina's unbridled method of relaying information always left Carlos stumbling to find the correct words to soften her delivery.

Christina: "Listen up, everyone. Valentine's Day is a couple of weeks away, and the student council is sponsoring a Sweetheart's Dance on Saturday, February tenth. So all you lovers, get ready to boogie!"

Carlos: "Uh … she means … boys and girls, get ready to put on your dancing shoes." (Sigh.) "Also, the student council will be selling individual roses for Valentine's Day, and you can purchase one for two dollars. A red rose says, 'I love you,' a pink rose says, 'I like you,' and the white rose says, 'You have a secret admirer.' You can purchase your rose from Mrs. Black in the front office."

Christina: "I know all you freshman boys like me. Cough up a couple of bucks and buy me a rose!"

Carlos: (Clears his throat over the intercom.) "And that concludes our Monday-morning announcements. Always remember—Longhorns, you're number one!"

Coach Doss looked at Chente and shook his head at morning announcements as he monitored the students finishing their quiz.

Chente shrugged and continued to insert grades in the grade book for Coach Doss. He couldn't believe it was almost February and that the regular basketball season was almost over; playoffs were right around the corner.

The Avalon High School basketball team had gone undefeated since Chente's return to the team in January. Felipe had improved his game, and he and Tre' were formidable; they gave the Longhorns a strong presence on the basketball court. And even though Ricky and his father continued to complain about Chente's "preferential treatment," the Longhorn basketball team was sitting in first place and had a really good chance to make a long run in the postseason.

Mrs. Jimenez's health continued to improve. She was sleeping better, and she enriched her eating habits with steady cardio exercise. She began to attend church functions regularly, and she supported the basketball team by supplying them with food on out-of-town games. She was on a clear road for a full recovery.

Haven had also made some positive strides. Since their movie date a few weeks ago, she had acquired a new confidence and independence. She was more relaxed around Chente's friends and not as clingy and insecure. She and Christina had become good friends and often discussed boys and fashion during lunch.

Chente looked at Coach Doss, who was now standing in front of the room, lecturing to his students about the living conditions of the middle class in Russia. He couldn't believe it had almost been a month since he ran into Coach Doss at the city park on that cold January night.

Since that fateful encounter, the first-year coach had taken prodigious care to rehab him back to health by making himself available before school for massage therapy and after school for whirlpool treatments. Chente was so grateful. Gradually his leg had gotten stronger, and gradually Coach Doss had become a staple in his life. There was an unspoken bond that linked their two souls. Chente felt extremely comfortable, relaxed, and serene in his presence. They understood each other without saying a word and shared a trust that often took years to develop.

A loud, shrieking noise sounded over the intercom, and all the students covered their ears and grimaced. Chente could hear Principal Timms speaking to a parent about a concern over the phone.

Principal Timms: "I am sorry that you feel that way, but I don't get involved with that ... yes, I understand that, but I am not the coach ... No, sir, I don't determine playing time ... well, I think that is a conversation for you to have with Coach Alvarez ... Sir, of course, you have the right to call school board members."

There was a long beep, and the intercom went silent. The students in the classroom started laughing. Coach Doss gave Chente a concerned stare.

A few minutes later, there was a knock on the door, and Miss Young poked her head in the classroom. "Good morning, Coach Doss. Would it be possible to see Chen for a few minutes out in the hallway, please?"

"Of course," said Coach Doss as he glanced at Chente.

Chente stood up from behind the teacher's desk and anxiously walked over to the door and out into the hallway. "Good morning. Is everything okay?"

Miss Young faced Chente with a big smile. She clapped her hands and jumped up and down with excitement.

"Yes, Chen. I have great news!"

Chente's shoulders relaxed, and he nervously glanced down the hallway. "Okay, what's going on?"

She handed him a large, tan envelope with the Texas Tech University logo on it. It was from the office of the president.

"Congratulations, Chen." Miss Young beamed as she clapped her hands. "You were just awarded a Presidential Scholarship to Texas Tech!"

Chente looked at the envelope and was completely stunned. He couldn't believe this was happening. He was competing with five hundred other students for this prestigious scholarship and never genuinely believed a Hispanic kid from itty-bitty Avalon, Texas, stood a chance.

"It's a full ride, Chen!" The high school counselor twinkled. "Texas

Tech is paying for everything—your tuition, room and board, books, everything for four years!"

Miss Young was so excited for Chente. "If anyone in this school deserves this opportunity, it is you. You are an excellent student. You work hard, and you're kind to your peers. This is amazing!"

"I don't ... I don't know what to say," Chente finally managed to say as the envelope shook in his hand. "I never thought this would happen."

He instantly thought of how much joy and pride this news would bring to his family. His brothers and sisters were going to be excited, and his mother was going to cry. He gently rubbed the mist out of the corners of his eyes and silently wished his dad were alive to share this moment.

"Hey, Chen, are you okay?" asked Coach Doss as he walked out of the classroom and put his hand on his shoulder. "What's the matter?"

"Nothing's the matter," replied Miss Young as she continued to clap her hands. "He just received some really good news."

"What is it?" asked Coach Doss.

The high school counselor motioned to Chente. "It's just not my news to share."

"Chen? If it's good news, then you should be happy, right?" replied Coach Doss with a concerned brow. "What's the matter?

Chente smiled and held out the Texas Tech envelope. "I was just awarded a Presidential Scholarship—a full ride to Tech."

Coach Doss exhaled loudly, and he threw his arms up in the air. "Whoa! That's tremendous news, Chen! Congratulations!"

"Thank you. Thank you, both," said Chente as he wiped his eyes and slowly exhaled.

"So when are you going to tell everyone?" asked Coach Doss as he playfully tagged the high school senior on the shoulder. "So we can all celebrate!"

Chente paused and considered the question carefully. "I don't think I want to say anything just yet."

"Why?" asked Miss Young and Coach Doss at the same time.

"I am so grateful for this opportunity. Please don't think I'm not," replied Chente as he looked at both of them and grinned. "But I haven't heard from UT or Stanford, and I'd like to before I tell anyone anything. I just don't need the pressure from my family."

"Of course, Chen. That makes sense." Miss Young smiled.

Chente quietly observed Coach Doss's energetic spirit suddenly take a nosedive as he nodded slowly. "Sure. Mum's the word," replied Coach Doss with a forced smile.

The rest of the morning casually floated by. Chente submitted his senior research paper outline during the second period and aced his calculus exam during fourth period. He was on a roll, and nothing was going to break his stride.

At lunchtime, he sat at the usual cafeteria table surrounded by his friends. He quietly observed and laughed at their silly jokes and crazy antics. Midway through the lunch period, Christina and Felipe began to bicker over her brazen comments during morning announcements. The head cheerleader lost her temper and poured her soft drink all over his lap. She and Haven rushed to the girls' restroom and didn't return.

Afternoon classes were uneventful and slow. Chente had to listen to student presentations during sixth period, and Coach Doss was in a melancholy mood during seventh period despite Christina's efforts to flirt with him.

Eighth-period athletics were also very lethargic and slow as Coach Alvarez battled a sore throat. He asked his players to do some spot shooting and a few conditioning drills. He released them early for the day.

As Chente approached his house, he noticed that Vanessa's Toyota Prius was still in the driveway. She had come home over the weekend with a miserable head cold and was hoping their mom's *caldo de pollo* would make her feel better.

When Chente walked into the house, he found his sister on the couch, wrapped in a quilt, and watching reruns of *Will and Grace.* She had her hair up in a ponytail and had a red nose that would rival Rudolph's.

"Hey, Nesh," said Chente as he dropped his backpack by the recliner. "How are you feeling?"

Vanessa gave him a weak smile. "I'm better. I may not look like it, but I feel better."

In a scratchy voice, Vanessa explained that Victor and their mom had gone to the grocery store to pick up a few things and would return soon.

"What's the matter with you?" asked Chente, and he gave her a strange glance as he laughed at the TV sitcom. "Why are you looking at me like that?"

"Is everything okay?" asked Vanessa as she grabbed a tissue and blew her nose.

"Yes. Everything's fine. Why?"

"Because up until a few months ago, you would tell me everything," she said and playfully squinted at him. "But okay, you can have your secrets. I will allow it."

Chente didn't budge. Instead, he went to the kitchen and grabbed a piece of fruit and a bottled water. He returned to the living room to watch TV. He missed having his sister around, and he wanted to spend some time with her without any heavy conversation.

"So how's school going?" asked Chente. Then he bit into his apple.

"It's going well." She grinned. Vanessa knew the direction this conversation was going. "I will be applying for law school in the fall."

"Wow, Nesh. You're going to be a lawyer!" Chente smiled as he shook his head. "I am scared of you!"

"Well, not tomorrow, but eventually, I hope." She laughed aloud and immediately began to cough.

Just then they heard a car pull up to the house.

"I guess that's Mom and Vic," said Chente as he got up and went to the kitchen to toss the remains of his apple. When he returned to the living room, he saw Violeta walk in the front door. She was still dressed in her work clothes with her hair pulled back in a bun. She looked very much like a teacher.

"Hey, Vi. What's up?" asked Chente, who was still in a good mood from his morning news.

Violeta ignored him and walked into the kitchen. She came back to the living room, looking around. "Where's Mom?"

"Hello, rudeness!" said Vanessa as she stared at Violeta. "She's not here."

"What are you doing here?" asked Violeta with a scowl.

Vanessa turned around, ignored her older sister, and continued to watch TV. Chente didn't really understand why they battled all the time, but they were both stubborn, and they were both his sisters.

"She and Vic went to the store to get a few groceries," said Chente. "Is everything all right?" He really didn't want to know what was going on, but he felt compelled to be polite.

"Good," said Violeta very decidedly. "I want to talk to you about something, and I am glad Mom isn't here to listen to this."

Chente cringed at the thought of having a conversation with Violeta. He was having a good day, and his oldest sister was always so extreme and severe and didn't listen particularly well. He dreaded what she was about to say.

"Well, if it's about Vic, he's doing so much better," Chente quickly said. "He has made up some work, and he is now passing all of his classes."

"No. That's not what I want to talk to you about," said the oldest sister as she raised her eyebrows and enunciated every syllable of each word.

"Of course not," replied Vanessa as she grabbed the remote control and changed the channel to the local news. "That would have been way too easy."

"Do you know Amelia Fernandez?" asked Violeta as she looked at her manicured nails.

Chente nodded. "Yeah, that's Christina's oldest sister, right?"

"Well, yes, but she's a first-grade teacher at the elementary, and her classroom is down the hall from mine," said Violeta as she walked across the living room and stood by the recliner.

Chente kept listening. He wasn't following her train of thought and wondered where this conversation was heading. Violeta was always so dramatic.

"Yesterday, we had lunch in the lounge, and she was so excited about her little sister graduating from high school and y'all winning at basketball."

Chente quickly interjected, "Yeah, she comes to our games. I have seen her in the bleachers. She really gets into it too."

"Right," said Violeta. "She said a few weeks ago she had to run up to her classroom late at night because she had forgotten her medication. She said that as she was leaving the elementary campus, she passed by the school housing section and saw your car parked at Coach Doss's house."

Chente slowly nodded and glanced at Vanessa, who rolled her eyes.

"I mean, I went over Coach's house one night a few weeks ago," recalled the middle brother. "But it was because I had to give him his house keys and—"

"So it *was* you! Great," she yelled as she stood up and furiously paced back and forth. "Damn it, Chente, what were you doing there? Why did you have his house keys?"

Vanessa quickly stood up and stared incredulously at Violeta, who was screaming and behaving like a madwoman. She went and stood next to Chente, who was equally flabbergasted.

"Hey! What is your problem?" shouted Vanessa.

Violeta looked directly at Chente. "I thought I was going to have to worry about Victor, but instead it's you. I can't believe this."

"What exactly have I done wrong, Vi?"

Violeta gave Chente a sly look and sarcastically shrugged her shoulders. "I don't know, Chente. What do you think you've done wrong?" asked the older sister as she stood with her hands on her hips, demanding an answer.

"Well, I don't know. I was trying to explain myself, and you went all bipolar on me," he shouted back at her.

Chente didn't understand where his oldest sister was coming from. He took a deep breath. "I am Coach Doss's student assistant during first period. He forgot his lesson plans one morning a few weeks ago, and he gave me his keys to go retrieve them."

"Completely inappropriate," shouted Violeta as she shook her head.

"Will you shut the hell up!" yelled Vanessa. Then she began to cough loudly.

"I put his house keys in my coat pocket and forgot about them," explained Chente. "Later that night, Coach Doss called and asked if I still had his keys. He was locked out of his house. I went over and returned them."

"Since when do teachers have student assistants, Chente?" sneered Violeta.

"They usually don't," replied Chente. "But …"

"Exactly," hissed Violeta as she threw her hands up in the air and pointed.

"No! Not exactly!" Chente shouted back, and he pushed Violeta's index finger away from his face. "You are blowing this way out of proportion. I didn't sign up to be Coach Doss's student assistant. Principal Timms assigned me to Coach Doss."

Violeta stopped shouting and looked at Chente. "What? Why? What are you talking about?"

He exhaled and quietly regrouped his thoughts. "That's what I have been trying to explain, but you keep interrupting me and getting hysterical."

He went on to explain that Coach Doss had taken on an extra class since Coach Stoval's skiing accident. In return, Principal Timms had given Coach Doss a student assistant to help him stay afloat through spring break.

Violeta's demeanor changed drastically. She became much calmer after listening to Chente's explanation.

"I simply drove over to his house that night and returned his keys and came home."

"See, sister, you jumped the gun with your wild accusations and your dirty thoughts," said Vanessa as she pounced on her older sister's erroneous presumption. "*Cochina!* Be sure to go back and tell your gossipy friends the real story."

"Oh, be quiet," growled Violeta. "Aren't you supposed to be sick?"

"I am—so sick of you!" Vanessa laughed as she returned to the couch and began watching TV.

Chente stared at Violeta and stood with his arms crossed. "And?"

"And what?" replied Violeta with a wrinkled forehead.

He put his hands on his hips. "I haven't heard an apology from you, and I want one."

"Okay, little brother. I am sorry. I am sorry, and I should have known better," said the oldest sister. She sighed dramatically.

Mrs. Jimenez walked in with a bag of groceries and paused. "*Ay, Diosito.* Did I hear right? Violeta apologized for something?"

The room erupted in laughter.

Later that night, after everyone had gone to sleep, Chente knocked on Vanessa's bedroom door. He found her in bed finishing some homework for one of her classes.

"Are you feeling any better?" Chente asked as he walked in and closed the door behind him.

"Yes. Thank God! I'm not as congested as I was earlier in the day," she said. "I can actually breathe through my nose a little easier now." She put her book away and turned down the radio.

"So you're leaving tomorrow morning?" asked Chente with a sad face.

"Yep. I have a ten o'clock class."

Chente slowly exhaled as he sat on her bed and leaned up against a pillow. He felt vulnerable, lonely, and frazzled all at once, and he missed his sister. Vanessa had always been his sounding board as they were growing up. He used to tell her everything.

But tonight he was a little guarded. He wanted to talk to Vanessa, but he was scared that she would judge him and not understand his feelings. The thought of losing or disappointing his sister would push him over the edge.

"So, Nesh, I need to tell you something." Chente hesitated. "I should have told you a while ago, but I just wasn't ready."

He began to play with the ends of her blanket as Vanessa searched her little brother's eyes and smiled nervously.

"Okay. What's going on? Is this about Violeta?" she asked with a little laugh. "Because if it is, I can't handle any more of her unnecessary drama today."

"No. It's about Jimmy," replied Chente. He cleared his throat. "You know, the night he killed himself was the same night he told me he was gay."

He glanced at Vanessa and smiled anxiously. He desperately wanted her support.

"What happened?" she carefully asked.

Chente recounted the events that had happened that day in full. He told Vanessa about how he had gone to Jimmy's house because Jimmy called him, crying. Then he described the fight Jimmy had with his parents and how Mr. Davis had run after the car when they left.

"Jimmy was hysterical," he told Vanessa. "He kept saying that his parents didn't really love him but that at least he was being true to himself."

He paused and took a quick breath as his voice began to break. He hated reliving those memories. They burned his heart.

"Then Jimmy looked at me and asked me when I was going to come out," said Chente as he carefully looked at his sister. "When I told him I wasn't sure how I felt, he became angry and shut down," he whispered as he wiped the tears rolling down his face. "He was so disappointed in me."

"It's okay. Just take your time and get it off your chest," whispered Vanessa.

She was very patient and reassuring. Vanessa wanted her little brother to get past this moment in time and heal. She knew he had been hurting for weeks, and now she understood why.

Chente glanced at Vanessa. "Sometimes I feel like it was my fault."

"No," Vanessa said quickly. "This is not on you!"

"*Mijo*, Jimmy's home life was bad, and we all knew it too. He had everything that money could buy, but he didn't have what he craved most—the love of his family."

She paused for a second and sadly shook her head. "Why do you think he practically lived here with us?"

Chente knew she was right and slowly nodded in agreement.

"This wasn't your fault," insisted Vanessa. "You were always a good friend to Jimmy."

"I just can't get the look of hurt in his eyes out of my mind." Chente shivered as he closed his eyes and exhaled. "It haunts me, Nesh, every day."

Vanessa reached for her brother's hand and bit her bottom lip. "I know that you don't want to hear this, but it wasn't fair for Jimmy to do that to you," she carefully explained in her older sister voice. "Whether you are gay or not, it wasn't fair."

"He was scared," replied Chente.

"I am sure he was." Vanessa nodded. "Having the support of your family is always especially important."

Chente remained quiet for a few minutes. He got up and stared out the window, looking at the stars and wondering how different life would be if he had just admitted to Jimmy that he was gay.

Vanessa sighed and finally broke the silence. "So, little brother, are you gay?"

"I think so," said Chente as he continued to look out the window.

"So you're not sure if you are … gay?" asked Vanessa as she playfully giggled under her breath.

Chente heard the humor in Vanessa's voice and started to laugh as well. He turned around and sat on her bed again. "You know, Nesh, up until recently, I didn't know."

Vanessa put her hands on her head. "*Oyes*, Chen, are you trying to confuse me? What does that mean?" She threw a pillow at him and growled.

"It just means that I know who I am, and I feel good about it too." He grinned. "I know that I am gay, and I am totally okay with it."

He repeated those words a few more times. It felt good to finally say them aloud. He felt alive and free. He felt complete.

Vanessa glanced at Chente and smiled. She gave him a big hug. "I am so proud of you! Thank you for telling me."

"Nesh, really? You always say that." Chente laughed as he rolled his eyes and groaned.

"Because I am. You did the right thing, and you did it on your terms," she said as she looked him in the eyes. "And you're sure about this?"

"I am positive," he said confidently and quickly added, "Now, I am not ready to march in a gay rights parade or hang a rainbow flag out on the porch, but I know I am gay."

"Does anybody else know?" Vanessa giggled.

"Not yet. I will tell Mom soon but only when I'm ready," said Chente, and he sighed.

Vanessa nodded proudly.

"For now only you know," said Chente as he smiled at his sister and rolled his eyes.

Vanessa smiled back and threw a pillow at his face. "Yes, Chente, I guess I will keep your little secret."

CHAPTER 12

Early the next morning, Mrs. Jimenez quietly got up and put on her floral robe. She walked down the hallway into the kitchen and turned on the coffee maker. She stepped into the living room, made the sign of the cross, and knelt before her religious altar to begin her morning prayers.

Mrs. Jimenez clutched her Catholic rosary, intertwined it through her fingers, and slowly sprinkled holy water on her religious figurines. Her husband's unexpected death had been very painful, and she had made a "*promesa*" to God to say a rosary for a whole year in his honor.

"*Diosito Lindo, ayudame.* Help me be a good mother to my children. Help me to be strong for them. Grant me courage, wisdom, and patience. Watch over my children and protect them …

"Vincente, *mi amor.* I haven't forgotten you, and I love you. Please help me watch over the kids."

"*Mija*, you need to be very careful when you drive back to Lubbock. Don't be speeding either," said Mrs. Jimenez as she flipped a tortilla with her bare hand. "The weatherman said that a big snowstorm is on its way."

Vanessa and Chente were at the kitchen table, eating their breakfast. She looked at Chente and playfully sighed. "Mom, the snow isn't coming until later this evening. I will be fine," she said. "The storm is coming from the north, and I am going south."

Chente smiled and made a funny face at Vanessa as he reached for another tortilla. "Yeah, if anything happens, it will be our game that is canceled. River Road is next to Amarillo and in the direct path of the storm."

River Road was the last district basketball game on the schedule before the state playoffs began, and if Avalon won, they would be the district champions and the number one seed out of District 4-3A.

"Coach Alvarez has stressed about today's game all week long." Chente sighed.

"*Y tu hermano*? Where is he?" asked Mrs. Jimenez as she turned around from the stove and looked at Chente. "*Dónde está*?"

Chente shrugged and shook his head. "He was in the shower. I don't know."

"Victor!" she yelled. "*Ándale mijo*, or your breakfast will get cold."

"*Oyes*, Mom! The neighbors can hear you!" growled Vanessa as she covered her ears. "So glad you are feeling better."

Mrs. Jimenez gave her daughter a playful look. "Well, *chiflada*, I am glad you're feeling better too."

"I am," said Vanessa. "I have to get going. I have class at ten o'clock."

She got up, headed to living room, and grabbed her backpack from the couch.

Chente snatched her mini suitcase. "I will put this in your trunk."

Mrs. Jimenez handed Vanessa two small bags. "Here, these tacos are for you, and these are for Valentin. Be careful and drive safely."

She kissed her daughter on the forehead and gave her a big hug before she walked out the front door.

Chente opened the car door for his sister. He gave her a hug. "Thanks, Nesh. I appreciate you listening last night." He already missed her.

"Of course, *chiflado*," she said and smiled. "Listen to me. I am proud of you." She blew him a kiss and drove away.

Chente walked back in the house and heard his mom and Victor in the kitchen. He looked at the religious altar in the corner of the living room. He quietly walked over to it and admired his mother's rosaries and religious figurines next to all the family pictures. He looked at his dad's picture and wondered what life would be like if he were still alive.

The bell rang as Chente and Haven walked into the school building. Haven was considering trying out for next year's cheerleading squad and wanted Chente's advice. Unfortunately for her, Chente's attention immediately took a detour to Coach Doss, who was walking out of the teacher's lounge with his morning cup of coffee.

Chente immediately straightened his back and exhaled as he admired Coach Doss's toned pecs under his fitted white polo shirt. His heart was racing.

Coach Doss glanced at Chente and smiled. "Good morning, Miss Haven," he said as he headed to his classroom.

Chente could smell the scent of Coach Doss's cologne as he passed by with his caffeine fix in his hand. He lost all focus and concentration.

"Hey, Coach," said Haven, and she turned her attention back to her question. "So what do you think? Should I try out?" she asked impatiently.

Chente was still admiring Coach Doss's strut down the hallway out of the corner of his eyes. "Do you want to be a cheerleader? You never have before," replied Chente. "Why all the sudden interest?"

Haven smiled and shrugged. "I don't know. I just thought it might be kind of fun," she said as she opened her locker and grabbed some books.

"Then why not? I say do it," advised Chente, and he gave her an encouraging smile.

She nodded very decidedly.

"Yeah, I think I will. See you at lunch," she said, and she hurried to her first-period class. Chente watched her walk away. He was so proud of her. She was becoming more confident and independent.

He walked into Coach Doss's classroom as the tardy bell rang. He walked over to the assistant basketball coach. "Do you think we will play tonight with the storm approaching?"

"I'm not sure," replied the coach. "Coach Alvarez was talking to Principal Timms and Athletic Director Hurley this morning about the different options."

Chente looked at him and wrinkled his forehead.

"You know—like not playing the JV game and starting the varsity game two hours earlier," said Coach Doss.

"Oh, okay. Makes sense."

"But in the meantime, I need you to finish grading these papers, please." He gave Chente a playful wink and began class.

Halfway through first period, there was a knock at the door. It was Coach Alvarez. He stood at the doorway for a few minutes; he spoke to his assistant coach and left.

"Both schools agreed to cancel the JV game and play the varsity game at five p.m.," whispered Coach Doss. "The storm isn't supposed to hit Amarillo until about seven p.m. We should be good."

Chente nodded and immediately started to mentally prepare for the game.

"What was that look for?" asked Coach Doss as he gently nudged Chente on the shoulder.

"Just getting ready for the game, Coach."

"Well, before you psyche yourself out, get on the Internet and make me a list of hotels in Amarillo with vacancies for the night."

"Why?" asked Chente.

"Coach Alvarez wants me to reserve some rooms as a precautionary measure," said Coach Doss as he shrugged. "You know, in case the roads get bad."

"Isn't that a bit extreme?" asked Chente as he started to surf the Internet.

"Yeah, well, he's the head coach and not me." Coach Doss laughed. "Just get me that list before you leave, please."

The boys' basketball team was on the minibus and on the road by 2:30 p.m. River Road was on the north side of Amarillo, about an hour and thirty minute drive up Interstate 20. Chente was the last one on the bus, so he ended up with the seat directly behind the coaches. He put on his earphones and began listening to the playlist on his iPhone, closing his eyes for a power nap.

"Hey, Chen, wake up," said Carlos as he tagged Chente on the shoulder as he was preparing to exit the bus.

Chente opened his eyes. "Are we already here?" He stretched his arms, took off his headphones, and looked out the window. It was already snowing in River Road.

"Yes, we are. We just pulled up a couple of minutes ago," replied Carlos as he quickly exited the bus and hurried into the gym with the others.

Chente got up and put his headphones away. He had gotten some rest and felt rejuvenated and ready to play. He slowly put on his letterman jacket, grabbed his backpack, and walked off the bus. He stood outside for a second and watched the snow fall from the sky.

Coach Doss walked out of the gym and headed to the bus. He saw Chente standing there and looking up at the sky.

"What are you doing?" asked the assistant coach. "Thinking about building a snowman?"

Chente laughed and shook his head. "No, sir, just enjoying the moment—the simplicity of a snowfall."

Coach Doss looked up at the sky and smiled. "Yeah, well, I wouldn't say that to Coach Alvarez right now. He's looking for you."

"Yes, sir."

"By the way, are you going to need to have your thigh wrapped up tonight?" asked Coach Doss.

Chente thought for a second and shook his head. "My legs feel good. I think I'm okay," he said and hurried into the gym.

The Avalon Longhorn basketball team came to River Road ready to play. Chente masterfully dissected their press defense and found his teammates easy baskets. They jumped out to an early first-quarter lead and never looked back.

In the second quarter, the Longhorns played tenacious man-to-man defense, and River Road turned the ball over five times. Tre' and Felipe anchored the paint, accounting for sixteen of the team's eighteen points. Halftime score was Avalon 31–River Road 20.

River Road made strategic adjustments at halftime and came out in the third quarter, playing a suffocating zone defense that neutralized the Longhorns' inside game.

Coach Alvarez called a quick time-out and adjusted the team's offense, allowing for more ball movement around the perimeter and giving the Avalon guards more scoring opportunities. Chente responded by hitting two three-pointers in the first three possessions to keep the opponents at bay.

The final quarter began with the Longhorns' full-court press wreaking havoc on River Road. On the first possession, Chente stole the ball from the River Road point guard and passed it down court to Ricky for any easy score. In the next possession, Chente intercepted an errant pass at midcourt and was driving hard down the lane to score when a River Road player stuck a leg out and tripped him. Chente went flying into the bleachers.

The whistle blew, and the referee called an intentional foul as Chente struggled to get on his feet. There was a throbbing pain coming from his left ankle, and Chente knew he couldn't walk on it. Tre' and Felipe helped Chente to the bench, and Coach Doss quickly put an ice pack on the ankle.

"Where does it hurt?" asked Coach Doss as he gingerly examined the ankle.

The assistant coach was trying to remain calm as Coach Alvarez went ballistic at the referees a few feet away, demanding that the River Road player be ejected for unsportsmanlike behavior.

Chente flinched when Coach Doss's hand touched his ankle. "The outer part of the ankle doesn't feel too good right now." Chente winced as he tried to use humor to defuse the pain.

Coach Doss smiled at him and gave him a sympathetic nod. "Okay. Just keep the ice on it," he said as he rested his right hand on Chente's knee. He looked up at the clock. "We have about six minutes left. I will look at it in the locker room after the game."

The assistant basketball coach hesitated and glanced at Chente, squeezed his knee, and went back to his seat.

Beau took Chente's place on the free throw line. He looked at Chente and smiled after he knocked down the second free throw.

The last six minutes seemed like an eternity as Chente watched from the bench. But when the final buzzer sounded, the score was Avalon 59–River Road 44.

"Okay," Coach Doss said cautiously, "we are going to take off your shoe now, and it's probably going to hurt a little."

Chente nodded and grimaced.

"Hey, Chen, did you see me hit those free throws?" asked Beau as he imitated his shooting form and pretended to shoot an imaginary ball in the air.

Chente smiled. "Yep. You did a good job."

"Well, I have been watching you shoot during practice, and I did the same thing today."

"You also handled the ball very well the last six minutes of the game too. You are getting better and better. It's all mental," said Chente.

Beau smiled really big at Chente and nodded. Then he pointed at Chente's feet. His shoe had been taken off as Beau and Chente were talking.

Coach Doss began to laugh. "That was pretty slick, Mr. Beau Brockman."

Beau waved his hands in front of Chente's eyes. "It's all mental. Right?" The second-string point guard laughed and went to the locker room to shower.

Chente shook his head and grinned, then quickly turned his attention to his ankle as it began to throb again. "So how does it look, Coach?"

"I am pretty sure it's just a bad high-ankle sprain," said Coach Doss as he examined the range of movement in Chente's ankle.

"So are you sure it's just a sprain and nothing more serious?" asked

Chente as he cringed a little bit. "I mean, you are not just saying that, right?"

Coach Doss nodded confidently. "I am almost 100 percent sure. It's swollen and turning blue, but it's just a sprained ankle."

He delicately placed Chente's ankle back on the table. "You need to keep ice on it all night—even when we get home."

Coach Alvarez walked in the training room and sighed. He shook his head and glanced over to Coach Doss. "Well, it looks like we won't be going home tonight. They just closed all traffic on Interstate 20 from Amarillo to Lubbock."

"Oh wow. The roads must be getting pretty bad," replied Coach Doss as he grabbed his cell phone to check on the weather.

"How are you feeling?" asked Coach Alvarez as he walked over to his star player. "You took a hard hit. Are you okay?"

Chente nodded and pretended he wasn't in pain.

Coach Alvarez inspected Chente's ankle. "It looks like a bad sprain. You need to stay off it tonight."

"I will go see if I can get some crutches from River Road's trainer," said Coach Doss, and he walked out of the training room.

Chente watched Coach Alvarez's eyes and body language and began to panic. "So do you think I will be ready for the first playoff game?"

Coach Alvarez thought about it for a minute. "We'll schedule a practice game for Friday that you won't play in, but with some rehab, I think you should be ready a week from now."

Chente was relieved to hear that. There was no way he was going to miss the playoffs, especially since it was his senior year. This was what he had worked for since grade school. A little sprained ankle wasn't going to keep him on the sidelines.

Coach Doss returned with some crutches and some more ice for Chente. "Their trainer said to use these. He said we can return them when we come to their track meet in March," said Coach Doss. "He was very apologetic."

Coach Alvarez walked in the locker room and let the boys know the roads had been closed and that they would be staying the night at the Holiday Inn across town. He started to laugh when the locker room burst into cheer.

He whispered to Coach Doss, "You did reserve those rooms, right?"

When the boys walked out of the gym, everything was white. The sidewalk to the bus was barely visible, and there were mounds of snow on all the vehicles. The snow was coming down hard, and the West Texas wind was howling like a pack of wolves in the distance. It was a cold, wintry night.

Chente allowed Carlos to carry his stuff as he followed him outside. He was determined to make it to the bus using his crutches. He didn't want anyone to help him. He stepped outside and immediately shivered as his teeth began to chatter. It was cold.

Chente gingerly began to make his way down the sidewalk to the bus. He could see Carlos's concerned brow turning around every few seconds to see how he was doing, and this annoyed him.

"Seriously, Carlos, you are making me more nervous by turning around and checking on me," said Chente. "It's not that hard to do this."

Chente took another step, slipped, and fell flat on his back. He was quiet for a second and then he let out a giant laugh.

"Chen, are you okay?" asked Carlos.

The other boys dropped their bags and rushed to help Chente get up. He kept laughing and pushing them away. "Yes! Of course I am fine," he yelled. "We are district champions!"

The star point guard threw his arms up in the air and let out a Tarzan-like yell. The other boys stood there in shock, then joined in on the laughter.

"Let's make snow angels," said Felipe as he began to roll around in the snow. All the boys fell on their back and started to make angels.

"These boys are crazy," said Coach Alvarez as he and Coach Doss got off the bus and watched in amazement. "Sometimes I forget they are kids."

Coach Doss laughed. "Yes. They are crazy. Just like their coach!"

Coach Alvarez gave him a playful smirk, then whistled. "Okay, boys, it's time to go," yelled the head coach as a snowball came hurling through the air at him. He ducked, and it hit Coach Doss right in the face.

The boys gasped, and there was a long silence before they exploded into wild laughter. Even Coach Doss joined in on the fun and started to laugh. "Okay? Who did it?" he asked as he wiped off the snow.

"It was me," said the boy with the crutches, styling an impish grin.

The Amarillo roads were dangerously slippery, and the snow made it hard to see past twenty feet, but the Avalon High School bus cautiously pulled up to the Holiday Inn and parked. Due to the possibility of inclement weather, Coach Doss had reserved six rooms earlier that day.

"Okay, I am going to go in and get our room keys," said Coach Doss. "Y'all need to pair up and decide who will be rooming together."

The boys grabbed their stuff and exited the bus. This time Chente leaned on Carlos as he walked into the lobby, and Felipe carried their bags. Carlos took the room key from Coach Doss, and they made their way to their room.

Chente turned on the light and hobbled to the right side of the room to claim his bed. He and Carlos were roomies, and Felipe and Beau were next door. Chente's ankle started to throb again, so he reached into his backpack and grabbed some aspirin.

"You feeling okay?" asked Carlos as he walked out of the restroom.

"My ankle is hurting a little bit, but I'll live," replied the point guard. "Hey, man, turn on the heater. It's a little cold in here."

Carlos walked over and flipped on the switch for the heater. He continued to explore the room, checking the doors and closets.

"What's this door for?" asked Carlos.

"It's the door that joins the other room with ours," replied Chente as he turned on the TV. "Kind of like a suite—you know, for big families and stuff."

"Oh. So it's Felipe's and Beau's room," said Carlos, and he started to bang on the door.

The door opened, and it was Coach Doss. Chente immediately smiled, and his heart became dizzy with excitement.

"What's up, Carlos?"

"Yeah, I'm sorry, Coach. I thought it was Felipe's room," apologized Carlos.

"It's okay," he said and looked over in Chente's direction. "I know your throwing arm is in good shape," said the assistant coach as he rubbed his forehead, "but how's the ankle holding up?"

"Quit being such a baby," Chente said, chuckling under his breath. "I'm the one with the sprained ankle. It feels fine."

"No, it's not," said Carlos. "Don't get mad at me, Chen, but you were just complaining that it was hurting."

"I took a couple of aspirin," said Chente as he waved off his friend. "It will be fine. I am going to take a quick, hot shower and then lie down and prop it up while I watch TV."

Coach Alvarez entered the room and handed Carlos two toothbrushes and some toothpaste. He told them they were going to walk across the street to eat at McDonald's in a few minutes. He and Coach Doss turned around, entered their room, and closed the door.

"Perfect," said Carlos as he rubbed his stomach. "I am so hungry right now. Want me to bring you back something?"

"Yes, of course, Carlitos," answered Chente. "I am starving too, but I don't want to fall again."

"Quarter pounder with cheese, large fries, and Dr. Pepper?" asked Carlos.

"Yep. In the meantime, I will take a shower and rest this ankle," replied Chente as he grimaced.

Chente quickly called his mom to let her know they had won the basketball game and that they were stranded in Amarillo for the night. He didn't mention the ankle injury. There was no sense in worrying her. He told her he would call her in the morning and hung up.

Chente hobbled to the restroom and started the shower. He took off his clothes and waited a few minutes for the water to get hot before he got in. The hot water running down his body felt good. He grabbed the bar of soap and lathered up. He washed away the sweat from basketball game.

After he was done washing, Chente stood under the shower head for a few minutes, thinking of Coach Doss and the morning he had seen him completely naked in the locker room shower. The point guard smiled as he reminisced.

The injured basketball player sighed, got out of the shower, and began to towel off.

He could feel the effects of the pain medication, because his ankle was throbbing less than before. He looked in the mirror and began to comb his hair. He reached for his black boxer briefs and put them on. He quickly brushed his teeth before he limped out of the restroom.

As Chente staggered to his bed, his foot caught on the strap of Carlos's backpack, and he went tumbling to floor with a loud thud.

"Damn it!" shouted Chente as he reached for his ankle and rubbed it softly, wishing the pain away.

Suddenly, the suite door swung open, and Coach Doss rushed into the room, wearing plaid boxer shorts and a white T-shirt. He looked at Chente on the floor. "What happened? Are you okay?"

Chente shook his head and winced. "I fell coming out of the bathroom and tripped on that damn backpack lying on the floor." He wouldn't let go of his ankle. He was in obvious pain.

"Do you think you can get up?" asked Coach Doss.

Chente shook his head. "Not right now," he said and closed his eyes and took a deep breath. "Give me a few seconds."

Impulsively Coach Doss took Chente's hand, knelt next to him, and slowly began stroking his hair. Chente immediately let out a soft moan and exhaled.

"I know it hurts, Chen," Coach Doss said quietly, "but we need to get you up and off the floor soon. You need to prop your leg up in bed."

Chente slowly nodded but didn't open his eyes.

"Sssshhh, give me a couple of more seconds," whispered Chente as he gently raised Coach Doss's hand and softly kissed it. He placed it on top of his chest near his heart.

Coach Doss's stiffened and froze.

Chente slowly opened his eyes and smiled. "What's the matter,

Coach? Are you okay?" He looked deeply into Coach Doss's ocean-blue eyes and was hypnotized with animalistic desire.

"Please kiss me. I want you to kiss me," whispered Chente.

Chente closed his eyes as he felt Coach Doss's lips gently press against his. Chente slowly opened his eyes and gave Coach Doss a dizzy smile and kissed him again. Hungry, strong, and passionate.

Everything made sense, and nothing made sense.

Chente softly caressed Coach Doss's cheek and quietly traced his lips with his index finger. He was deliriously happy and sure his heart was ready to explode.

Chente wondered if this was what it felt like to love someone. Everything felt perfect, and his heart was full of pure joy.

Chente barely managed to get to his feet. He looked down into Coach Doss's eyes, and without saying a word, Coach Doss read his mind.

The basketball coach stood up and passionately kissed the point guard. Chente could feel his curious hands exploring every inch of his body.

Chente slowly took off Coach Doss's shirt and began to kiss his chest. Chente delicately kissed around Coach Doss's ears until he heard him moan in ecstasy.

"I have wanted to do this for weeks. I have wanted you for weeks," whispered Chente as he pressed up against Coach Doss's toned chest. He could feel Coach Doss's accelerated breathing on his neck.

Coach Doss pulled back and caressed Chente's cheeks. He looked at Chente with unbridled desire and kissed him again. "If you only knew how much I want you too," whispered Coach Doss.

"Show me," pleaded Chente as he gazed into his eyes.

Suddenly, Chente's cell phone began to buzz, and it startled the basketball coach back into reality.

Coach Doss glanced at Chente with a panicked stare. He looked around the room, shook his head, grabbed his shirt, and left the room, shutting the door loudly behind him.

Chente rubbed his forehead and fanned his face. He was dizzy with unquenched desire, and he quietly exhaled. He hungrily stared at the suite door separating him from Coach Doss and slowly fell backward onto his bed.

About twenty minutes later, Carlos returned to the hotel room with Chente's fast food. He took off his coat and shivered as he stood next to the heater and tried to get warm. Carlos excitedly recounted the big argument between Felipe and Ricky at McDonald's to his injured friend. He was completely unaware that Chente's mind was preoccupied with the handsome first-year teacher next door.

Carlos innocently continued to babble as Chente thought about Coach Doss's lips and the hot kissing session he'd had few minutes before. He wanted to explode.

"Dude! Hey, Chente," yelled Carlos as he waved his hands in front of his friend's face.

Chente blinked and shook his head.

"Are you even listening to me?" Carlos laughed.

"I'm sorry, Carlitos. What were you saying?" asked Chente as he sipped his Dr. Pepper.

"Dude, it is freaking cold outside. The snow keeps coming down hard," worried Carlos as he walked into the restroom. "It looks like we are in the middle of a huge storm."

"I agree," replied Chente as he looked at the suite door that separated the two rooms and took a deep breath.

CHAPTER 13

"Mrs. Smith, will you please send Chen and Emma to the principal's office," announced Mrs. Black over the classroom intercom. "Principal Timms would like to have a word with them."

Mrs. Smith jumped out of her desk as the booming voice on the intercom startled her.

"As soon as they complete their chapter quiz, I will send them on their way," she replied.

"Thank you," said Mrs. Black.

The room erupted into teasing laughter, whistling, and snide remarks including, "Somebody's in trouble" and "You just thought nobody was watching."

Mrs. Smith took off her glasses and playfully looked at Chente and Emma, and smiled. She clapped her hands and refocused the students back on their quiz. A few minutes later, both students were done, and the calculus teacher sent them on their way.

"Do you think we're in trouble?" asked Emma as they walked down the long and empty hallway. It was obvious to Chente that his senior classmate was nervous.

Emma was a quiet, studious, and unassuming girl; and it was hard for Chente to imagine her ever being in trouble. He tried to calm her nerves and reassure her. "I don't know why we are being summoned, but Mrs. Black's voice didn't seem to be distressed over the intercom." He smiled.

Emma looked up at Chente as she anxiously twirled her blonde hair with her index finger and nodded. "I hope you're right."

Chente reached over and gave her a friendly side hug. "I am right. Promise."

When Chente and Emma reached the front office, Mrs. Black smiled, wished them a good morning, and escorted them to Principal Timms's office. Principal Timms and Miss Young were reviewing some paperwork when the students walked in and took a seat.

"Good morning," said Principal Timms as he sat at his desk to face the two students.

"Is it?" asked Emma as she nervously rubbed her forehead and tried to smile.

Miss Young gave Emma a sympathetic nod of reassurance. "Yes, of course, it is. We have good news we want to share with you. No one is in trouble."

Principal Timms let out a hearty laugh. "No swats today for you two. Tell them the good news, Lori."

"We are just so proud of both of you," replied Miss Young as she unleashed a huge grin. "Y'all are outstanding students and always lead by example. You both have wonderful futures ahead of you."

The high school counselor paused and looked at Emma. "Congratulations, Emma, you are this year's senior class salutatorian."

Emma quickly placed her hand over her mouth in disbelief. She looked at Chente and shook her head. "Really? I am salutatorian?" yelled the soft-spoken girl as she got up. She hugged Miss Young and started to cry.

She wiped away her tears and started to jump up and down and clap her hands. She laughed and hugged Principal Timms as well.

Chente's heart was full of joy for Emma. She was a genuinely nice girl and worked extremely hard in the classroom. She deserved this honor.

Chente knew Emma's father had lost his job after the Christmas holidays, and her dreams of attending college were placed in jeopardy. Being salutatorian would open financial doors that would make her dream of going to college a reality for her.

"Chen," said Miss Young as she looked at him and smiled. "Congratulations! You are senior class valedictorian."

Chente smiled and gave Miss Young a hug and shook Principal Timms's hand. Emma jumped over and congratulated him as well. His excitement was a little more reserved than Emma's, but he was proud of what he had accomplished. He knew this news would bring pride and joy to his family, and that fact made him even happier.

Principal Timms got on the intercom and announced the news to the entire school. He went on to congratulate the Avalon boys basketball team for their win over Tahoka and wished them luck at the regional basketball tournament this weekend.

After a few more minutes of celebrating, Chente and Emma made their way out of the office. Principal Timms stopped Chente and began talking basketball.

"So how is your ankle holding up?" he asked. "Coach Alvarez said you are doing a little better."

"Yes, sir. I am better. It's been about ten days since the sprain, and my ankle gets stronger every day," replied Chente. "Coach Alvarez makes sure I am in rehab every day after practice."

It had also been ten days since his kiss with Coach Doss in his hotel room awakened his soul. The kiss had been unexpected, spontaneous, and perfect in Chente's mind. He had relived the moment over and over in his daydreams.

However, since then, Coach Doss had avoided him at every turn. He had barely looked at him during first period and always had errands for him to run or papers for him to grade. Coach Doss kept Chente busy, and their interaction in the classroom was minimal.

During basketball practice, Coach Doss coached and interacted with all the players except him. Coach Doss was never rude, but it was apparent that he wanted nothing to do with Chente.

"Well, y'all win two more games, and you punch your ticket to the state basketball tournament," said Principal Timms with a hearty laugh.

"Yes, sir. We are going to do our best," replied Chente as he turned to walk out of the office.

Principal Timms grabbed Chente's shoulder and pulled him in close. "And you need to shoot more, son! The team needs you to shoot more." He cleared his throat and headed into the hallways as the bell for lunch sounded and a stampede of kids headed to the cafeteria.

Chente arrived at the lunchroom a little late, but he was met with a warm reception of congratulations from his circle of friends. It made Chente feel good that he had their genuine support.

"Hey, Chen, that's awesome news," said Carlos as he pulled out a chair next to him for Chente to sit in. "Your mom is going to be super proud!"

Before Chente could sit down, Coach Alvarez and Coach Doss walked into the lunchroom and walked over to the table. Coach Alvarez shook Chente's hand and smiled. "Good job, Chen. I am proud of you!" he said.

"Thanks, Coach," said Chente, and he looked over at Coach Doss, who was smiling and nodding as well.

Without warning, Haven came up from behind and put her arms around Chente. He turned around, and she planted a big kiss on his lips. She looked at him and smiled. "I am so proud of you too!" she screamed.

Chente stepped away from Haven, coughed a little, and tried to regain his composure as his friends went crazy with laughter. Chente wondered why she insisted on embarrassing him like that.

"Whoa, thank you," said Chente as he stared at Haven with a tentative smile.

Chente turned around and saw Carlos and Felipe pointing at him and laughing, while Coach Alvarez shook his head and sighed. Chente's eyes searched the room for Coach Doss, but he had hurried away and was quickly exiting the cafeteria.

"Okay, Miss Haven, I am going to let that pass because of the circumstances, but no more PDA." Coach Alvarez smiled and winked at Chente, then left.

"Yes, sir." Haven grinned.

But all Chente could think of was that he wished it had been Coach Doss giving him a kiss and not Haven, but the basketball coach had walked away without saying a word. Was he ever going to speak to him again?

"Excuse me, my friends," said Felipe as he playfully pushed aside the students in the classroom and escorted Chente to his desk. "I am walking with the senior class valedictorian—please make room."

Chente chuckled under his breath and shook his head at Felipe. He looked at Carlos, who was laughing with the rest of the class. Felipe was being silly, but Chente hated all the attention. He would have preferred just taking his seat and starting class instead of all this silliness.

"Hey, wait a minute, I'm Top Ten. Why does Chen get all of the attention?" asked Christina as he put her compact back in her purse.

"If you're top ten, then I am going to Harvard," said Carlos, and the room of students laughed even harder.

Christina reached over and hit Carlos on the shoulder, pretending to be upset.

The tardy bell rang, and all the students sat down, pulled out their journals, and began to write about the daily topic on the dry-erase board.

Coach Doss had seen Chente and Felipe enter the classroom. Despite his pride for Chente, seeing him kiss Haven in the cafeteria had really bothered him. He didn't like it; he felt restless, anxious, and irritated.

He stood up, surveyed the classroom, and began to return the graded assignments to each student one by one.

"Well, it's obvious some of you didn't study as much as you should have," growled Coach Doss with a sour look on his face. "These are the worst quiz grades of the semester."

Carlos looked at Coach Doss and then at Chente, and frowned. "What's his problem?" whispered Carlos as he leaned toward Chente.

Chente glanced at Coach Doss and shrugged. Coach Doss had

been very edgy the last couple of weeks in class. Maybe he was tired of covering for Coach Stoval, or maybe he just hated being in the same room with him.

"Coach, this quiz was very confusing." Felipe groaned.

"No, sir. It was you who was confused by the look of your grade," replied the government teacher as he handed Felipe his paper. Felipe looked at his grade and sulked as Coach Doss walked past him with a smirk.

Chente heard a few snickers from the students at the back of the classroom. He shook his head to himself. Coach Doss didn't have to be rude, and his biting comments were way out of line. It was okay if he was having a bad day or hated him, but he shouldn't take it out on his friends.

"Mr. Jimenez," said Coach Doss, "I see you shaking your head."

Chente straightened his posture and froze in his seat.

"Your grade isn't very valedictorian either," said Coach Doss as he walked up behind the point guard and placed his quiz on his desk.

Chente glanced at his grade and just smiled. He didn't say anything. However, Felipe was right. The questions on the quiz had been confusing, unclear, and a little misleading; but Chente looked at his paper, put it away, and began writing in his journal.

Chente ignored the comment and decided to take the high road instead.

"Hey, Coach, you're really going to just call Chen out like that just because he's valedictorian?" asked Carlos with an irritated voice.

Christina rolled her eyes and flipped her hair. "Total rudeness!"

Coach Doss took a few steps back and looked at Chente, who appeared to be unfazed and focused on his journal. He immediately felt bad for the comments but was bothered even more that Chente had simply ignored him; he refused to apologize.

Instead, Coach Doss showed his age and threw a few more daggers. "Look, I just mean that he usually makes a better grade. He is better than an eighty-two," replied the first-year teacher as he shrugged. "Maybe if he spent more time studying during lunch instead of—"

"Yeah, maybe," replied Carlos as he shook his head, "but that's not fair to Chen."

Coach Doss turned around and began writing on the dry-erase board.

Chente immediately quit writing, put his pen down, and looked up. He stared at Carlos and shook his head. He could barely contain his growing anger. How could Coach Doss be so impolite and dismissive?

"Really?" boomed Chente as the entire class stopped and looked up from their writing assignment.

"Excuse me?" said the coach as he turned around.

Chente gave him a direct stare and furiously nodded. "You really just said that about me?" replied Chente in a slow and precise manner. "You really think that. Unbelievable."

"Dude, let it go," whispered Carlos as he nervously looked around the classroom. "Don't worry about it. Let it go."

Coach Doss gave Chente a flippant glance and returned to the dry-erase board. "I am not sure that you understand what I—"

"Oh no … no, I agree with you," Chente quickly interrupted him and smiled. "I do usually make better grades."

He paused and continued to stare at Coach Doss. Chente observed some of the students nervously shifting in their seats and looking at each other with a bit of confusion, but he was furious.

Coach Doss nodded plainly. "Okay, good. Now let's get started."

"My grade wasn't very valedictorian like," said Chente as he interrupted again. He glared at the first-year teacher standing in front of the classroom, gave an exaggerated shoulder shrug, and politely smiled.

"It's kind of like your comments about our grades and my activities at lunchtime were very unprofessional and nothing like a *real teacher* would make," replied Chente calmly as he gathered his belongings and walked out of the classroom.

The silence was deafening, and Coach Doss was left speechless while standing in the front of his government class.

Coach Alvarez arrived at the high school gym ten minutes early to prepare for eighth-period athletics. He walked in and saw Chente at the far end of the gym, shooting free throws. Chente's shooting was very disciplined and focused. Coach Alvarez kept away and watched Chente shoot from a distance. His shooting motion was perfect, and time after time the ball barely hit the net as it went through the hoop.

"Mr. Chen, shouldn't you be in class?" asked Coach Alvarez as he walked toward Chente.

Chente nodded and kept shooting.

"Wait, did you just freely admit that you are skipping class?" asked the head basketball coach with a little chuckle.

"Yes, sir. I am skipping class," admitted Chente as he continued to shoot the basketball with intense concentration and acute precision.

Coach Alvarez paused with surprised curiosity and watched Chente shoot for a few more seconds. He wrinkled his forehead and shook his head. "So, do you want to tell me what's going on?"

"Not really, sir," Chente said plainly, "but I will if you make me."

Coach Alvarez was shocked by his response. There was a sound of frustration in his point guard's voice that was so foreign to Chente's personality. What had happened to make his mild-mannered basketball star behave this way?

He continued to watch Chente shoot the basketball for a few seconds. He didn't know how to approach him, so he began to rebound the basketball for point guard under the goal.

"Okay, Chen, I am listening," said Coach Alvarez as he tossed the basketball back to Chente.

Chente shot a few more free throws and sighed helplessly. He was mentally exhausted. The last ten days had been a roller coaster. For the first time ever, he felt so alive. But at the same time, he knew his feelings were one sided.

"I am just tired, Coach." The high school senior sighed.

"What are you tired of?" asked Coach Alvarez.

Well, let's see. It's been almost a year since my dad died, and my best friend committed suicide three months ago. I am gay, and none of my friends know, and I pretty sure I am in love with one of my basketball coaches, who is engaged to be married in June and wants nothing to do with me.

Chente caught the basketball, put it on his hip, and shook his head.

"Of everything. Everything is just happening so fast, and sometimes I can't keep up. Sometimes I don't want to keep up."

And just like that, Chente started shooting free throws again.

Coach Alvarez was stunned. He had never heard Chente talk like this. The calm, soft-spoken boy was gone. Standing in front of him was an angry young man, who was on the verge of snapping.

"Okay. What do you mean? Are you mad at one of your friends?" Coach Alvarez quietly inquired. He looked at Chente, who simply kept shooting free throws.

Chente suddenly stopped and looked at his coach with a flimsy smile. "I'm sorry, Coach. I don't mean to cause any trouble, and I don't mean to be rude. I'm just very sorry."

Coach Alvarez walked toward Chente. "Chen, I don't know what's going on, but I'm getting worried. Are you okay?"

Chente slowly nodded but kept his eyes on the gym floor. He refused to look at Coach Alvarez. He knew that if he did, he would break down, and that was the last thing he wanted to do. "Yes. I am going to be fine, but I have to go home. I can't be here right now."

Coach Alvarez cleared his throat and studied Chente's fragile demeanor, wondering if he should push any further for answers. He decided that the timing wasn't right. "Of course. Go home and get some rest."

Chente turned around and jogged into the locker room.

Coach Alvarez stood in the middle of the gym floor, completely mystified as the bell for eighth period sounded and the basketball boys began to make their way into the gym. Coach Alvarez saw Carlos enter the gym as the tardy bell rang and called him over.

"Hey, Coach, what's up?" asked Carlos.

"Did anything … strange or unusual happen today?" asked Coach Alvarez with concerned eyes.

Carlos winced and looked around the gym in complete confusion. "Uh, well, it's high school, sir. Lots of strange things happen on a daily basis."

Coach Alvarez chuckled under his breath at his player's very honest answer.

"No. I mean to Chente. Did something happen? Is he okay?"

"I don't know, sir. Why do you ask?" lied Carlos as he looked at his shoes.

Carlos didn't want to get involved. Chente was his best friend, and Carlos knew Chente was still struggling with some inner conflict, and he wasn't going to betray his trust.

"Come on, Carlos, I know you know something," said Coach Alvarez with an uneasy voice.

At that very moment, Coach Doss walked into the gym with his briefcase and rushed his way to the coaches' office. He waved as he passed by.

Carlos's face became stone cold as he watched the government teacher cross the gym floor. "Why don't you ask your assistant coach if he knows what's going on with Chen."

Carlos turned and jogged into the locker room.

Coach Alvarez shook his head and wondered why everyone was speaking in riddles today. He walked into his office as Coach Doss was putting on his basketball shoes and getting ready for practice. He sat at his desk, nervously tapping the eraser of his pencil on his coffee mug. He glanced at Coach Doss and wondered what Carlos had meant.

"Is everything okay?" asked Coach Doss as he tied his shoelaces and got up and stretched his legs.

"I'm not sure," said Coach Alvarez. "I walked into the gym about ten minutes ago and found Chen shooting free throws. He was obviously upset about something."

Coach Alvarez paused and gave Coach Doss a long look. "Isn't he supposed to be in your seventh-period class?"

Coach Doss stopped stretching and immediately sat down. "Is he okay?"

Coach Doss's concern for Chente was sincere. He knew he had hurt Chente's pride earlier in class, and he regretted being a jerk to him in front of his classmates. His raw emotions of fear, shame, and anger had escalated over the last ten days, and he had finally erupted today during seventh period.

"I don't know," said Coach Alvarez as he gave a Coach Doss a suspicious look. "He simply said he was tired of everyone. He said that everything was happening too fast and couldn't be here right now. So I sent him home."

The first-year teacher was flabbergasted and dismayed. He had selfishly acted on feelings at the hotel, then pushed Chente away and confused him. And to top it off, he had embarrassed Chente and belittled him out of pure spite. He had retaliated like a jealous boyfriend because he had seen Haven kiss Chente in the cafeteria.

Now Chente was emotionally injured and in need of solitude—all because of him. All because he had kissed the boy of his dreams and then ran away and hid—like a coward. Chente's strong personality couldn't handle his indecisive nature.

"Wow," said Coach Doss as he paused for a few seconds to think. "I hope he's okay."

The assistant basketball coach got up, grabbed his whistle, and walked into the gym for practice.

It didn't escape Coach Alvarez's attention that Coach Doss had never answered his question. "Me too," replied the head coach as he slowly nodded.

Someone knocked on her door.

Vanessa took off her headphones and answered the door to her dorm room. "Hey, Nancy. What's going on?" she asked with a warm smile.

"Just making a very handsome delivery for you." Nancy beamed.

"What do you mean?" Vanessa giggled.

The delivery girl stepped aside, and Chente greeted his unsuspecting sister with a brotherly hug and a big smile.

"I saw him loitering in the foyer, and he said he was looking for you." Nancy smiled.

"Well, this is a surprise for sure," said Vanessa as she gave Chente a questioning look. "Thank you for your help, Nancy. Much appreciated."

"No problem. Anytime." Nancy winked at Chente as she left.

Chente chuckled under his breath; he walked into his sister's dorm room and began to look around as Vanessa shut the door and put her hands on her hip. "What's going on? Is Mom okay?" asked the older sister.

Of course, his sister would think something was wrong with their mother. Chente quickly turned around, apologized, and reassured her that all was well. "Yes, Mom is fine, and so is Vic."

Chente continued to survey the dorm room, secretly visualizing the real possibility that he would have a room similar to this one next year.

Vanessa watched him in silence, wondering what he was thinking and why he was seventy miles away from home.

"Nesh, are all the dorm rooms like this one?" asked Chente as he inspected her tiny kitchen and bathroom.

"No," replied Vanessa. "I am an RA, so mine is a little bigger—more like an efficiency."

"Oh, wow, so the real dorm rooms are actually smaller than this one?" remarked Chente as he made an ugly face and sighed. The reality of college life was slowly creeping in—tiny living quarters, community bathrooms, and dorm cafeteria food.

Vanessa laughed. "Yep. This isn't the Hilton, but it serves its purpose. Quit being such a wimp." She walked to her fridge, swiped a soft drink for Chente, and sat on the couch. She motioned for him to sit next to her.

Chente put his car keys on the coffee table and sat down. He looked at Vanessa and grinned. "I bet you're wondering what's going on, right?"

"Well, Chente, the thought did cross my mind." Vanessa nodded sarcastically.

Chente went on to explain to her that he had been officially named senior class valedictorian during fourth period and that his friends were all so supportive and happy for him. He told her that Haven had created another scene at lunch by kissing him in front of everyone in the cafeteria.

"Chen, you haven't told Haven that you're gay?" Vanessa sighed.

"Really? I just found the courage to tell you the other day. Nesh, please cut me some slack."

"But Haven's your girlfriend. You need to tell her," said Vanessa pragmatically.

Vanessa had never liked Haven for Chente. She always felt Haven was too boring and not enough of a challenge for her little brother. However, Vanessa was a girl, and there was a part of her that felt it was only fair that Chente come clean.

"Oh my gosh. She is *not* my girlfriend, Nesh!" replied Chente as he emphatically threw his arms in the air. "She has never been my girlfriend. I have always been honest with her about that."

"Okay, okay, but she really likes you," conceded Vanessa. "Trust me, Chen, you need to tell her soon before she hears it on her own. Even worse, before she thinks that you used her."

Chente knew Vanessa was right—she usually was. But he wasn't sure he was ready to come out to his friends. He wasn't ready for all the questions. He had lost so much over the past eleven months that the idea of losing his lifelong friends was something he wasn't willing to deal with just yet.

"Look, Chen, I know it's not easy, but you are the bravest person I know. You can do this," Vanessa said as she eased up on the lecturing session and gave him a big hug.

"Why can't you just be my sister right now and not Judge Judy?" whispered the little brother with a heartfelt sigh. "I just need you to be a sister."

"Okay … okay, what's going on?" asked Vanessa as she patiently nodded and giggled under her breath. "Why are you really here?'

"Well, because I have to tell you something, Nesh," said Chente as he gently pulled away from her grip.

Vanessa calmly looked at him and nodded. "I figured as much. Okay. What is it?"

Chente's heart began to race, and he felt like he was going to throw up. His eyes began to tear up, and he softly began to weep. He was exhausted. He was so tired of keeping all his feelings and emotions bottled up, and he was ready to explode and let some of it go.

Vanessa grabbed his hand and simply let him cry. "You know, whatever you tell me isn't going to matter. I will still love you no matter what," she calmly said. "I will always be Team Chente."

That is exactly what little brother needed to hear, and he began to weep even harder. Acceptance and unconditional love felt good. No hiding. No pretending. He felt safe.

Chente wiped away his tears. "I am pretty sure I have fallen in love with someone."

He immediately felt the weight of the secret gone. He could breathe again. He looked at Vanessa and sighed.

"Okay? Is that it?" asked Vanessa with a relieved smile. "Is that what you wanted to tell me?"

Chente just shrugged and nodded.

"Well, little brother, this is good, right?" Vanessa said with a hint of optimism in her voice. "I mean, this is a positive step in accepting who you are, right?"

Chente remained quiet as he slowly wiped away his tears from his face.

Vanessa looked at Chente and shrugged. "Right?"

Chente didn't say a word. He was trying hard to find a way to tell her the whole story. How was she going to react to learn that her little brother was in love with his coach? How was she going to react when he told her he had kissed his coach?

"So tell me. Who is this mystery boy?" asked Vanessa as she playfully tagged her brother on the shoulder. "Do I know him? Is he cute?"

Chente remained quiet. He could hear Vanessa's cell phone buzzing, but she ignored it.

"Chen?" asked Vanessa. "What's the matter?" She cringed and bit her fingernails. "Is it Carlos or Felipe?"

Chente chuckled at the thought of that suggestion. Those two were more like brothers than friends. "Of course not," he said as he shook his head.

Vanessa exhaled loudly. Her cell phone started to buzz again. She looked at it and quickly silenced it. "It is a boy, right?" she asked in a teasing manner.

Chente gave her a silly look. "You should answer your cell phone."

"It's Valentin. I will call him back in a minute," she said. "Quit avoiding the subject and just tell me already." She threw a pillow at him.

He took a deep breath. "It's Coach Doss."

"Chente, stop playing and just tell me. The suspense is killing me slowly," said Vanessa as she laughed and dramatically fell on the couch.

Chente didn't say anything. He watched his sister open her eyes and sit up straight. The smile on her face slowly disappeared.

He shrugged. "I told you," he whispered.

"Shut up!" Vanessa sighed.

Her facial expression said everything else. Vanessa cleared her throat without taking her eyes off her brother and slowly got up. She began to pace the floor. "Chente, are you kidding right now?" she whispered as she bit her bottom lip. "You actually like a teacher? You can't … He can't …"

Chente calmly watched his sister pace. He knew this would be a surprise for her, but he had to tell someone, and in many ways she was his best friend. After she had some time to process the news, he would explain everything.

"Nesh, calm down and let me explain," he said. "I think you are overreacting."

She looked at him, nodded, and sat down.

"Okay, talk to me."

Chente went on to explain to her their chance meeting a few months ago in the park on the night before he returned to school. He recounted how Coach Doss had talked him through his fears and convinced him to return to school.

He also described that it had felt like fate had thrown them together at school when Principal Timms had assigned him to be his student assistant and through basketball practices, injuries, and rehab.

Vanessa quietly listened. She relaxed and smiled. "Aw, Chen, you have a crush on Coach Doss. That's different." She sighed and playfully teased her little brother. "It's kind of cute too."

Chente cringed at Vanessa's idea of his feelings for Coach Doss. It was more than a crush. He wasn't a ten-year-old boy in love with his fourth-grade teacher. It was more than that, but he knew it was her way of dealing with the news, and he let it go. There was no way he was going to tell her he had kissed him in a hotel room.

"So Coach Doss has stolen my little brother's heart." She giggled as she covered her mouth. "He *is* kind of hot, Chen. At least you have good taste!"

"Yes, he is." Chente smiled.

"Wasn't his girlfriend at the last basketball game?" asked Vanessa. "She was very pretty."

Chente wanted to vomit, but instead he nodded and smiled.

Vanessa's cell began to buzz again. This time she picked it up and answered it. Chente could hear her side of the conversation.

"Yeah … he's here. No, I'm not kidding … What? I didn't know that. Okay, I'll tell him," Vanessa said and hung up. She pointed her index finger and gave Chente a scolding look.

"I know what you are going to say." Chente squirmed as he put his hands up to protest.

"Chen? Why didn't you tell Mom you were coming to visit me?"

He could hear the irritation in her voice.

"She's been worried."

"Look, I have my cell phone, but I turned it off," said Chente. "I just needed some time to think some things through, and I wanted to be left alone."

Vanessa shook her head and waved her finger in front of his face. "No, Chente. This is Mom we are talking about and not your friends. You should have at least texted her."

"So you're going to go all Violeta on me now. Really?" Chente sighed as he swiped his keys and made his way to the door. "I will call her on my way home." Chente turned his cell phone on and showed Vanessa.

"Do not ever compare me to Little Miss Perfect. You know I can't stand that, but you know that I am right," said Vanessa as she smacked her little brother on the head.

"That's what Vi always says too," said Chente, and he busted out laughing.

Chente and Vanessa walked out of the building and to the parking lot. He waved goodbye as he drove off.

Vanessa felt a little relieved that Chente was slowly opening up and trusting her again. She couldn't believe her little brother was about to graduate from high school and begin college.

Her little brother had become a young man overnight, and she loved him so much. His fierce independence reminded her so much of their dad. As she walked into the building, she couldn't shake the feeling that she had missed something especially important tonight, but she couldn't put her finger on it.

Chente called his mom on his way home and explained that he had gone to visit Vanessa. He told her he had wanted to see the dorms just in case he decided to go to Texas Tech the following year. He apologized for making her worry and told her he would be home in an hour.

He pulled into the Fast Stop in Shallowater to gas up and get something to drink.

He grabbed his cell phone and saw he had four text messages. The first three were from Haven, Victor, and Carlos—all concerned about his whereabouts.

The last text message was from Coach Doss that said, "I'm sorry."

Chente closed his eyes and exhaled. The anger and resentment in his heart were immediately replaced by endless confusion and restlessness. He rubbed his forehead slowly and shook his head. He got out of his car and walked into the convenience store.

CHAPTER 14

Chente poked his head into Miss Young's office early the next morning and noticed a big bouquet of red roses on her desk. It was Valentine's Day, and he guessed Miss Young's boyfriend was responsible for the beautiful arrangement.

"Good morning, Chen," said Miss Young as she walked up behind him. "Did you need something?"

Miss Young owned a big smile this morning as she pranced into her office. She was always in a good mood, and today was no exception. She was dressed in a pretty floral dress with a pink scarf around her neck to match her shoes. It looked like she was floating on air, and her happiness was so contagious.

"You look pretty today," said Chente with a smile.

"Thank you, sir. How can I help you?" she asked as she sat down at her desk.

Chente took a seat. "I just want some advice about choosing a college."

Miss Young nodded and took a sip of her hot chocolate. "Okay? What's going on? Talk to me."

Chente carefully explained that he was struggling with trying to find the right college to fit his needs. Part of him wanted to stay close to home to be near his family and friends, and the other part wanted something different, new, and unfamiliar. He felt like he was caught in the middle and was feeling a bit claustrophobic.

"I know that I am not making much sense," said Chente as he thumped his fingers on her desk in perfect rhythm. He was nervous, and Miss Young sensed it.

She gave him a sympathetic smile. "Actually, Chen, that makes perfect sense. I am glad that you're conflicted," said the high school counselor as she tried to ease his anxiety.

"You are?" asked Chente.

"Yes. That means you are carefully weighing your options—and that's good. What's even better is that you are blessed with options."

She was right. He *was* blessed. He had a full ride to Texas Tech and had been accepted to all the colleges he had applied to in the fall. He was a lot further along than most seniors in high school.

"Now tell me," she continued with an inquisitive look, "what's really bothering you?"

Chente glanced at her and didn't say anything. Of course, she knew something was bothering him. She was a counselor—smart and intuitive.

She got up, closed the door, and returned to her desk. She smiled and waited.

Chente took a deep breath and began to recount his last encounter with Jimmy. He explained that on the day Jimmy committed suicide he had come out to his parents. He described the explosive interaction he had witnessed between Jimmy and his dad. He paused.

"Looking back at it now," Chente said, cringing, "it was awful. How Jimmy must have felt to hear his dad say all those mean things to him."

He shook his head. He felt anxious and restless inside. It wasn't until then that Chente realized the magnitude of hurt and pain Jimmy must have encountered that day.

Miss Young watched and listened as Chente's story unfolded.

Chente explained to his high school counselor that Jimmy had accused him of being gay and had been completely deflated when he denied the accusation.

"He turned stone cold. It was like I wasn't there anymore," whispered Chente as his voiced cracked. "It was like I didn't exist anymore." He stopped and regained his composure. "He asked me to drop him off at his house, and I never saw him again."

There was a moment of silence.

"And you feel guilty?" asked Miss Young.

Chente looked up, met her soft expression, and slowly nodded. "If I would have just admitted I was gay, he would probably still be here," he quietly whispered.

"Chen, you did nothing wrong," said Miss Young as she tried to reassure him.

Chente looked at her as tears rolled down his cheeks. "My best friend needed me, and I let him down. I can't forgive myself."

"Chen, you weren't ready. There is no fault. It just happened," replied the counselor.

Chente just listened to Miss Young's reassuring words of wisdom, and as much as Chente appreciated her thoughts, he still felt guilty for his friend's death. He should have stepped up and admitted he was gay.

Miss Young's telephone rang, and she answered it. She looked at Chente, nodded, and then ended the phone call. "Looks like Coach Doss is looking for you. Did you tell him you were coming to see me?" she asked.

Chente shook his head and winced. "I didn't think I would take all period."

Miss Young wrote him a pass and reassured him that all would be well. "My door is always open," she said as he left her office.

Chente hurried down the hallway to Coach Doss's class. He didn't understand why Coach Doss was looking for him. His absence should have made him happy.

Chente opened the classroom door and walked in. The entire class turned around and looked at him as he closed the door.

"You're late!" announced Coach Doss as he stood in front of the classroom, leaning up against his wooden podium. There was a weird expression on his face, and Chente couldn't tell whether he was angry or worried.

Chente passively shrugged. "Yes, sir. It's just that I was with Miss Young discussing—"

"Next time you report to me first. Understand?" interrupted the first-year teacher.

Chente nodded. "Of course. I apologize."

The bell sounded, and the students got up and made their way to the door. Beau waved at Chente, and they walked out together.

"Hey, Chen, you okay?" asked Beau as he turned around, looked at his teacher, and shook his head.

"I'm good," replied Chente with a forced smile.

"He has been on a tear all morning. I guess he got up on the wrong side of the bed," said Beau, and he laughed as Haven and Carlos walked up to Chente.

Beau glanced at Haven and dropped his books right in front of her. He quickly recovered them.

"Well, I … I … I will see you tomorrow," stuttered the sophomore student.

"What are you talking about? You mean at practice?" said Chente with a little chuckle under his breath.

"Practice?" asked Beau as he fidgeted with his pen.

"Yeah, as in basketball practice? Beau, we are in the state playoffs." Carlos laughed.

Beau let out a nervous laugh, nodded, and scurried down the hallway.

Just then Coach Doss walked out of the classroom with his coffee cup and stood by his door. He growled at them to get to class.

"Dang. Is he still in a bad mood?" asked Carlos as they walked away.

At lunch time, Christina walked in the cafeteria with a dozen red roses for Valentine's Day. A group of underclassmen had gotten together and purchased the flowers for her. Of course, she flaunted them in front of everyone, and this sent Felipe into a jealous rage.

"Who bought you those?" asked Felipe as he sat down with his cafeteria tray.

Christina brushed back her raven-black hair and basked in the attention Felipe was giving her.

"Well, the note said from the 'Sophomore Studs'—whoever they are." The head cheerleader smiled.

"Are you telling me you actually have a fan club?" Haven giggled as she shook her head in disbelief.

Christina stretched her arm out and looked at her manicured, ruby-red fingernails. "When you're hot, you're hot!"

She glanced over at Felipe, gave him a playful wink, and blew him a kiss.

"Okay, get a grip, Miss Too Hot to Handle. They're not even real roses. They're plastic." Carlos sighed as he rolled his eyes.

Christina shot the bird to Carlos and sat by Haven, who was sulking because she got only a pink rose and a white rose.

"Oh, girl! You got a secret admirer," said Christina as she took the white rose away from Haven. "Chen, you got some competition."

Haven tried to smile, but it was obvious she wasn't happy.

Chente just smiled. He knew Haven was upset, but he wasn't going to lead her on by buying her a red rose. They were only friends.

"They are passing out all of the Valentine flowers in the gym," said Christina.

"Yes, we know. We are going to hurry up and eat so we can run down there to pick ours up," Carlos sarcastically replied.

There was a knock at the classroom door, and it was the Avalon High School student council members delivering Valentine roses to students. Coach Doss gave them permission to enter and make their deliveries.

"Hey, Chen, these belong to you," said Emma as she handed him three roses—two red roses and a white rose. "Happy Valentine's Day!"

Chente was completely surprised. He arched his back and turned around. "Hey, Emma, are you sure all of these are mine?"

Emma efficiently checked her paper list and nodded. "Looks like you have a couple of girls who really like you," she said and gave Chente a friendly smile.

Chente felt his face getting hot, and he nervously shifted in his desk.

"I know this one is from Haven, but who sent me these two?" asked Chente.

Emma shook her head and shrugged. "Chen, I am sorry, but some of the orders are anonymous," remarked the senior classmate.

She and the rest of the student council members completed their deliveries to the other students in the classroom and left.

Chente was completely baffled. One of the red roses had a card from Haven, but the other two didn't. *There must be some kind of mistake.* Chente thought for a second. *Unless, wait, there is no way Coach Doss would send me a Valentine rose. Would he?*

"Wait a minute," said Felipe as he rolled his eyes. "You mean to tell me that you got two roses from someone you don't even know?"

"No," said Carlos. "Chen got two roses from people he doesn't even know, and Cupid forgot about us!"

The classroom erupted in boisterous laughter.

Christina strategically placed her bouquet of fake roses on her desk and sympathetically batted her eyes at her friends. "That's so sad, right?"

Felipe and Carlos entered the locker room, still complaining about Valentine's Day. It seemed like Cupid had shot his Valentine's arrow at everyone except those two. Even Janie the Janitor was sporting a couple of fake roses.

"Man, that's embarrassing. Even Principal Timms got a rose." Carlos laughed as he opened his locker and threw in his backpack.

Felipe was laughing hard as he stumbled to his locker. "What is wrong with us? Do we smell or something?" he asked as he sniffed his armpits and made a weird facial expression.

Carlos shook his head confidently. "Maybe you do, but I don't." He took his shirt off and continued the pity party. "And then Chen gets three roses. Seriously?"

"*Oyes* and get this," replied Felipe as he walked to the urinal, "and he don't even know where two of them came from."

The locker room was buzzing as the guys tried to hurry to get dressed and go out on the gym floor before Coach Alvarez entered and yelled at them.

Carlos shook his head and began to laugh. "*Y no tiene uno, pero dos* secret admirers?"

"*Pues* our friend Chente is a stud!" yelled Felipe as he relieved himself.

Ricky was sitting quietly and getting dressed for practice. He listened to everything Carlos and Felipe were saying about Chente and his three Valentine roses. The more he heard, the angrier he got. He hated Chente and all the lucky breaks life seemed to give him.

"Maybe the mystery Valentine roses came from his best friend Jimmy." Ricky smirked.

The locker room got quiet as Felipe walked back from the urinal. He looked at Ricky and shook his head. "*Oyes*, no one was talking to you. Why do you always have to be an asshole?"

"Really, dude?" asked Carlos. "Have some respect. Jimmy's dead."

Ricky looked around the locker room. Everyone had stopped dressing and looked at him in disbelief. He realized he had everyone's attention and decided to go for the jugular. "Yeah, well, Jimmy was my cousin," he said. "He told me that Chen liked guys—that he was a faggot."

The basketball boys looked at each other and were stunned into silence. Everyone was in complete shock that Ricky was accusing Chente of being gay.

Beau quickly came to Chente's defense. "I call bullshit! Chen is dating Haven."

"He can't even kiss her. She kisses him. Y'all have seen it. He doesn't even like it." Ricky laughed with no remorse.

Ricky started to grossly imitate the coughing scene in the cafeteria a few days ago when Haven had kissed Chente.

"Well, no one is standing in line to kiss you either," retaliated Beau.

Ricky shoved Beau and flipped him off.

“Look, Jimmy was Chen’s best friend, and we all know Jimmy was gay, right?”

“He was?” asked Carlos as he sat down at his locker. “I didn’t know that.”

“That’s enough. Quit fucking around,” growled Felipe as he walked up to Ricky with a stern look.

Ricky put his arms up in the air and laughed. “Look, Jimmy was my cousin, and he was gay. He liked dick!” The Bennett boy scratched his head and shrugged. “Chen was his best friend—it’s not rocket science.”

Felipe looked at Carlos and shook his head. “That’s enough, Ricky. We don’t have time for this shit,” said Tre’ as he stepped to the middle of the locker room and pointed at the Bennett boy.

Ricky ignored Tre’ and continued his bashing. “Look, Jimmy’s dad is my uncle, and he told me.” Ricky made a gun with his right hand and pointed it at his temple. “Why do you think my cousin pulled the trigger?”

Carlos said as he slowly got dressed, “That doesn’t mean Chen is—”

“Gay?” Ricky finished Carlos’s sentence with a wicked smile. He stared at Carlos with pure hate in his eyes. “They were best friends—do the math.”

Anyone could have cut the nervous tension in the locker room with a butter knife.

“Well, by that standard, you’re gay too, right?” asked Beau with an impish grin. “Hell, you probably like to dress up like a girl too, because y’all are cousins.”

The locker room erupted in laughter.

Chente entered the locker room as Ricky shoved Beau to the floor and stormed out. The rest of the basketball team was high-fiving Beau and patting him on the back as Chente began to change.

“What did I miss?” asked Chente.

Tre’ shook his head. “Don’t worry about it, Chen. Hurry, let’s go play some basketball.”

After practice Carlos asked Chente for a ride home. He wanted to check on his friend.

"Sure," said Chente. "Give me a few minutes while I change, and then we'll go."

Chente went to his locker and started to undress. Most of the other guys had cleared out of the locker room. He heard his cell phone buzz and reached for it. It was a text message from Haven, asking him to drop by her house after practice. Chente hoped she didn't have some sort of Valentine's Day gift for him.

"Hey, Chen, do you need to whirlpool your ankle today?" asked Coach Doss as he entered the locker room and picked up the dirty towels off the floor.

Coach Doss had distanced himself from Chente. The hotel incident in Amarillo a few weeks earlier had stirred up some personal feelings that had caused him to pause and reflect about his life—his goals and dreams. It had frightened him in many ways.

From a professional standpoint, Coach Doss knew he could lose his teaching certificate for getting involved with a student. No matter how tempting Chente was and though they were less than four years apart in age, Chente was a senior in high school, and the law insisted that Coach Doss stay away.

From a personal standpoint, Coach Doss missed the ease and comfort he'd felt by being around Chente. He missed his clever wit, his infectious smile, and strong independence. His feelings for Chente were genuine and real, and his soul ached for his warm presence.

As he turned the corner, Coach Doss saw Chente standing by his locker in his tight, black boxer briefs and was stunned into silence.

"Are you speaking to me?" Chente finally asked as he slipped on his jeans. There was a flash of anger in his voice, but his heart jumped out of his chest and began doing jumping jacks when he saw the assistant coach.

Unable to blink, Coach Doss stared at Chente's strong and lean body for a moment and began biting his lower lip. He tried to catch his breath.

"I just want to make sure you are okay," Coach Doss managed to say, "for ... for the game tomorrow."

It was utter torture being this close to Chente, but he couldn't help it. Coach Doss was having a bad day, and his heart was searching for some relief and solace; his broken spirit was thirsty for Chente.

Chente shook his head in disbelief and exhaled. He quickly tied his Nike tennis shoes. "Yeah, Coach. My ankle is fine," he said coldly. "I will be ready to go tomorrow."

Chente was crushed. All Coach Doss cared about was tomorrow's basketball game. He put on his letterman jacket, grabbed his backpack, and checked his cell phone.

"Happy Valentine's Day," Chente said as he walked out the locker room door.

Coach Doss was left standing in his loneliness.

Chente reversed the car and practically peeled out of the student parking lot. He wanted to get far away from school and Coach Doss as possible. He was ready to start college tomorrow and leave all the nonsense behind him. He wanted to disappear—to be invisible.

"*Oyes*, what's the matter with you?" asked Carlos as he held on to the dashboard. "Are you late for a date with Haven or something?"

Chente chuckled under his breath and sighed. Carlos couldn't be further from the truth even if he tried. It was Coach Doss and not Haven who had his heart all tangled up in a knot. It was Coach Doss and not Haven whom Chente had dreamed about at night. It was Coach Doss and not Haven whom Chente yearned to touch, kiss, and love.

"Sorry," said Chente. "My foot slipped." Lying had become second nature for him.

Carlos looked at Chente and knew something was bothering him, but his instincts kept him from pressing the issue. Instead, Carlos changed the subject and asked Chente to swing by Sonic before dropping him off at his house.

After Carlos placed his order at the intercom, he glanced over and saw Chente texting on his cell phone. "Hey? Is everything okay?"

"Carlitos, you have asked me that question at least three times today. Why?" asked Chente.

"You just seem a little rattled lately," said Carlos thoughtfully.

"I'm just texting Haven," replied Chente as he showed Carlos the cell phone. "She wants me to swing by her house after I drop you off. She said her parents aren't home."

Carlos was right. He *was* rattled. Chente didn't want to go over to Haven's house. He didn't want to see her tonight. He knew he needed to be honest with her very soon, and he dreaded her reaction. He was certain she would hate him and that he would lose her friendship forever.

Carlos gave Chente a big smile. "Oh! I bet she has a Valentine's Day gift for you!"

Carlos laughed and tagged Chente's shoulder. Chente cranked up the mariachi music to muffle Carlos's crazy ideas.

When the food order arrived, Carlos paid the waitress, and they left. They were both excited to be playing at the regional basketball tournament in Lubbock the following day. They had worked really hard all season to make this happen.

Chente pulled up to Carlos's house and parked in the driveway.

"Look, I know I am not as smart as you, but we have been friends since kindergarten, and I know you. I know something is bothering you right now," announced Carlos.

Chente was surprised by Carlos's outburst. It had nothing to do with intelligence; Chente was simply behaving cowardly. He wasn't ready to talk about his feelings. So instead he smiled and nodded.

"Carlitos, you are a lot smarter than me. Trust me."

"Dude, whatever. Look, I am here when you're ready to talk, okay?" said Carlos as he playfully hit Chente on the head, closed the car door, and walked into his house.

Chente sat in his car and watched Carlos. He wondered what Carlos would think if he knew that his childhood friend since kindergarten was gay. Maybe one day soon he would find the courage to tell him. He took a deep breath and drove away.

"Hey, Chen, come on in," said Haven as she opened the front door of her house.

Chente quickly walked in and shivered off the cold.

"It's still a little chilly outside, huh?" she said.

"It is very cold," said Chente. "The weatherman says that a northern cold front is blowing in tonight."

Haven walked over to the bar area and offered him a soft drink, but Chente declined. He was coming from Sonic and wasn't thirsty.

"So how did practice go today?" asked Haven as she opened a bottle of Evian water and took a sip.

"It went well. I think we're ready for the regional tournament," replied Chente with a hint of excitement in his voice. "Aside from Ricky, who nobody likes, the team gets along great. With a little luck, maybe we will surprise some people."

Haven smiled. She loved to see Chente excited, and talking about basketball usually did that. He was such a nice guy, and she wanted the basketball team to do well this weekend.

"Where are your parents?" asked Chente as he stretched his legs and sat down on the sofa next to the fireplace.

"My dad took my mom out to eat for Valentine's Day," she quietly said and looked away.

Chente felt so dumb. Of course, her parents were out on Valentine's Day. Why had he brought that subject up? He knew he had disappointed Haven today with a pink rose and not a red one.

There was an awkward silence.

"Look, Chen, that's part of the reason why I wanted you to come over," said Haven while looking at the fireplace.

Chente sensed Haven's uneasiness. He knew she wanted to say something important, and this made him anxious.

"Okay," replied Chente quietly. "Is something the matter?"

Haven looked at Chente, and her eyes began to tear up, but she swiftly regained her composure and smiled tentatively. "I know we are not a couple, but I always hoped that one day you would look at me like

I look at you." She paused and searched for the right words. "But that's never going to happen, right?"

Chente could see Haven's heart was breaking, and he started to panic. He had never meant for this to happen. He remembered what Vanessa had told him a few days before. He should have told her sooner.

"I'm so sorry, Haven. You are one of my best friends, and I love you but not the way you want me to love you," Chente gently said. "You deserve so much more than I can give you right now."

She brushed aside a runaway tear from her cheek. "No, Chen. Don't apologize. You have always been honest about just being friends."

She paused for a moment and gave Chente a weak smile. "But today it became clear to me that we are not meant to be anything more than friends," she softly whispered. She took a deep breath and exhaled. "And I am going to be okay."

Chente reached out and gave her a big hug. "Of course you are. You are a beautiful, intelligent, and kind young lady. Any guy would be lucky to have you as their girlfriend."

"Just not good enough for you, right?" whispered Haven as she held him tightly. She was begging for an explanation, and Chente knew she deserved one.

"It's not that simple," replied Chente as he hugged her even tighter.

He was going to either lose her friendship or gain a confidante with what he was about to tell her, and he was scared everything was about to change.

She softly pulled away and looked at Chente with her hazel eyes. "I don't understand what that means. Are you okay?"

"I'm going to use your answer and say I am going to be okay," replied Chente with a nervous grin.

"What is it?"

Chente could see her searching his eyes for answers. She deserved answers. Chente took a deep breath and exhaled. "Haven, I am gay."

Saying those words were intoxicating to Chente. He wished he could shout them from the middle of the basketball court to his teammates, the fans, and even the opponents. He was growing tired of playing hide-and-seek.

He carefully watched Haven's facial expressions transform from a stunned look to confusion and lastly to realization. He could see her processing the information and trying to make sense of it. She closed her eyes and started to cry.

Chente froze. He had made Haven cry. She was going to hate him.

"Oh, Chen," she said. "It all makes sense now. I thought it was me—that I wasn't pretty enough or good enough for you." She looked at him and shook her head. "And all this time, what you must have been going through."

"Okay? Come again?" said Chente in total confusion. He watched her wipe away her tears and laugh nervously.

"I kept throwing myself at you, and you were always so kind and gentlemanlike." She covered her eyes in embarrassment. "And all along you had to pretend to like me. I am so sorry."

"Wait a minute. I never pretended to like you, Haven," protested Chente. "I do like you. You are an amazing girl."

Chente continued to watch her carefully. Was she really going to be this understanding? He was expecting her to be upset, but instead she was apologizing.

"Oh, I know, silly boy," she said as she laughed aloud. She appeared to be almost relieved that Chente's truth was out. "What I mean is that I have a gay uncle who lives in Austin, who I love very much. He told me how painful it was keeping his sexual identity a secret when he was younger."

Chente nodded and smiled.

"It is a secret, right?" asked Haven as she reached out and gently squeezed his shoulder. "I mean, no one knows, right?"

Chente went on to explain to her that he had come out to Vanessa only the week before. He talked about the fear he had to come out to his friends. He rationalized that graduation was a few months away, and he preferred that everything remain the same until then.

"I don't know, Chen," replied Have with a subtle smile. "I don't think you are giving your friends enough credit. They are crazy about you."

Chente looked at Haven and exhaled. He shook his head. "Maybe so, but I'm just not ready yet. I need to do this my own way and in my own time."

Haven agreed and gave him a big hug. "Well, I think you are brave. Thank you for trusting me enough to tell me. I won't say a word," she promised.

"No, Haven," replied Chente with a firm hug, "thank you for being so understanding and for listening. I really appreciate you so much."

He walked to the door, opened it, and turned around. He felt relieved. His heart was filled with gratitude, and his shoulders were a little less heavy. He felt free.

"See you tomorrow morning—eight fifteen sharp," she said and smiled.

Chente nodded. "Eight fifteen sharp."

CHAPTER 15

The Avalon High School band and Avalon High School cheerleaders loudly marched down the high school hallways, playing the school fight song. Following closely behind, was the varsity boys basketball team, shouting and high-fiving students along the way. It had been a long time since the boys' basketball team had advanced this far into the playoffs, and Avalon High School was celebrating and showing them a lot of love.

When they exited the front doors of the high school, they were greeted by the entire elementary student body from across the street. The students were holding up spirit signs and cheering along with the cheerleaders. The celebration scene was thunderous.

Chente and a couple of the basketball players walked over to the elementary side of the street to shake hands and take selfies with the kids. Chente was clearly the favorite as the elementary students quickly surrounded him, screaming and wanting his attention. He was their superhero.

As Chente made his way to the decorated school bus, he saw Coach Alvarez speaking with Violeta. He shook his head and hoped she wasn't causing problems. Coach Alvarez needed to focus on tonight's game, not the unnecessary drama that always seemed to follow his oldest sister.

"The kids love you, Chen," said Coach Doss as he smiled at the basketball star. "They were hanging all over you like crazy."

"Because he's a superstar," said Felipe as he tagged Chente's shoulder and laughed.

"Yeah, they're a lot of fun," replied Chente as he quickly walked past Coach Doss without making eye contact and sat down in his seat. Chente didn't have time for him right now. His focus was on winning tonight's basketball game.

"Hey, Chen, where are the breakfast tacos your mom packed for us?" asked Carlos as he sat across the aisle from him.

"*Órale*, Chente," yelled Felipe. "I didn't know your mom packed us breakfast tacos. Cough them up, or Carlitos and I are going to give you a wedgie—and it's gonna hurt too."

Chente started to laugh and demanded that they keep their hands off him. He wasn't in the mood for any kind of horseplay. He took a couple of tacos, then gave the rest to Carlos to pass around to all the guys.

Chente's letterman jacket pocket began to buzz, and he took out his cell phone. It was a text message from Henry Hamilton. He was already trash-talking: "Hey, Chen, See you 2nite—may the best man win!"

Chente smiled and quickly responded, "Game on! And the best man will win!"

Chente and Henry were regarded as two of the best point guards in the region and in their respective classification, and they had been rivals since their freshman year when both started for their respective teams. Over the years, they had learned to appreciate one another and had become friends—but neither liked losing.

The guys hung out the windows, waving at the elementary students as the bus drove off. They were on their way to Lubbock and the United Supermarket Arena for the regional basketball tournament. It was an exciting time for the Avalon Longhorn basketball program.

Chente put on his earphones and began to listen to some Maroon 5. He closed his eyes and started to clear his mind from the typical conversation his friends were having around him. He wanted to concentrate on the game.

A few minutes later, Chente felt a nudge on his shoulder. "Really,

Carlos, man, not now," said Chente without opening his eyes. "I'm trying to focus on the game."

A few seconds passed, and he felt the same nudge again. He opened his eyes and saw Coach Doss standing over him. He took out his earphones.

"Hey, Chen," said Coach Doss. "Do you have any more breakfast tacos? I didn't have time for breakfast this morning, and I'm a little hungry." The basketball coach gave him a sad smile.

Chente was surprised to see Coach Doss standing so close to him, and he softly exhaled. Chente could smell Coach Doss's cologne, and it made him feel dizzy with excitement.

Chente casually turned around and asked the guys for the breakfast taco bag. They passed it up, but when it got to Chente, it was empty, and all the players started to laugh.

"No worries. It's cool," said Coach Doss with a little chuckle. "I will get something when we get to Lubbock."

The high school teacher started to walk away when Chente reached in his backpack and pulled out a couple of breakfast tacos he had put away for later. "Hey, Coach," said Chente as he glanced out the bus window. "I set a couple aside for myself. You can have them if you want."

Chente was confused by Coach Doss's erratic hot and cold behavior but handed over the breakfast tacos anyway.

"Are you sure?" The first-year teacher grinned.

"I am. I had breakfast," replied Chente as he glanced at Coach Doss.

"Thank you." Coach Doss nodded.

Chente's eyes locked with Coach Doss's and instantly felt the connection. It was still very real. Chente cleared his throat and quietly put his earphones back, closing his eyes as Coach Doss walked away.

It was halftime, and the score was tied at twenty-one. Both teams had put on a defensive clinic in the first half with intense full-court man-to-man ball pressure. Once the ball crossed midcourt, the Kress Kangaroos reverted to a box and one-zone defense shadowing Chente the entire time and disrupting the flow of the Avalon offense. Kress had limited Chente to six first-half points.

"Carlos and Ricky, you have to hit the open shot," preached Coach Alvarez. "You know they are face-guarding Chen, right?"

Both players nodded.

"Chen has done a good job of penetrating the lane and kicking the ball out to y'all—you guys have to make those shots," he said.

"Felipe," continued the head coach, "are you going to show up tonight? You have got to pick up the slack inside. Tre' has two fouls. Dude, it's now or never. You have zero points," said Coach Alvarez as he glared at his power forward.

The third quarter opened with Henry Hamilton nailing a three-pointer off a pick and roll and right in the face of Ricky. On the next possession, Chente easily broke the press and lobbed a pass over the Kress zone defense to Felipe, who scored and was fouled. Felipe hit his free throw, and the score was tied again. Both teams exchanged scoreless possessions as they continued their impressive defensive stance.

With ten seconds left in the quarter, Chente intercepted an errant pass and raced to the basket, trailed closely by Henry. The Avalon point guard knew Henry was going to try to block his shot from behind, so he quickly faked going right, then reverse-pivoted into a left-handed layup, and scored as the buzzer sounded.

The Avalon crowd busted out into a loud roar as the score was Avalon 29–Kress 27 at the end of the third quarter.

Chente was celebrating with Carlos and Felipe when he noticed Henry on the floor, holding his right ankle and grimacing. He swiftly ran over to see whether his friend was all right.

"Dude, are you okay?" asked Chente as sweat ran down his forehead.

"That was a great move," said Henry. "It was so good that this white boy rolled his ankle." He tried to laugh, but he was in obvious pain.

The Kress coaches rushed out the gym floor and helped Henry up.

Chente watched as the Kress point guard was helped to the bench. Chente reached over and tagged him on the shoulder. "Dude, I'm sorry."

Henry nodded and winked at Chente. "It's all good."

The fourth quarter was completely different. Without Henry Hamilton playing, the Kress Kangaroos were an entirely different team, and Avalon capitalized on it by taking an early six-point lead, which they extended to eight when the final buzzer sounded. The score was Avalon 41–Kress 33.

The Avalon Longhorns were in the regional finals!

After the game, Chente went over to visit with his family, who were all there to support him. He gave his mom a big hug and a kiss on the forehead as she told him how worried she had been that they weren't going to pull out a win.

"*Mijo*, I was so nervous," confessed the mother of five. "Why did number ten from the other team keep following you everywhere you went? Is that fair?"

"Mom, it's because your son is a stud basketball player *y le tienen miedo*. Right, Chen?" Victor laughed as he rolled his eyes.

"I guess. Something like that," replied Chente.

"Your son is being modest, like usual," said Coach Doss as he extended his hand and introduced himself to Mrs. Jimenez. "I am Coach Doss, and it is an absolute pleasure to coach your son."

Mrs. Jimenez gave Coach Doss a warm smile, "*Pues, muchas gracias*. Of course, I am very proud of him, sir."

Chente could see the intense pride in Coach Doss's eyes when he began to explain to Mrs. Jimenez that the Kress defense was designed to prevent her son from touching the ball on offense.

"Kress felt that if they could contain your son, they would win the basketball game," clarified the assistant coach as he turned and looked at Chente and grinned. "But your son is a special player. He simply finds a way to win."

Chente's heart melted when Coach Doss looked at him with his ocean-blue eyes, but his cool outward composure contradicted those feelings so that even his mother, who was looking at him, was fooled.

"It was a great team effort. We all played well enough to win," Chente finally said, and he hugged his mother again. "Everyone stepped up when it counted most."

"Great game, Chen," said Bella as she reached around Coach Doss's waist and gave him a friendly squeeze. "I wasn't sure y'all were going to win."

She exaggeratedly placed her head up against Coach Doss's chest and purred like a skittish cat with sharp claws. "But like Aaron said, you always find a way to win," said Bella with a plastic smile.

There was no doubt in Chente's mind that Bella's compliments were bitter, biting, and insincere.

"Bella? Wow. So good to see you again," lied Chente as he purposely poured over her. "Thank you for coming tonight and supporting the team. Looking more like a coach's wife every time I see you."

Coach Doss's posture stiffened, and Bella was left speechless as Chente quickly said hello to Valentin and Vanessa and excused himself to the dressing room, where the basketball team was celebrating. It felt good to win.

"Yo Tre'," said Chente as he headed to the showers, "thanks for carrying us on your back again tonight!"

Tre' chuckled under his breath. "Yeah, Chen, you too. You played a hell of a game."

The Avalon school bus pulled into the Holiday Inn Express on Fourth and University. Coach Alvarez was still on cloud nine, discussing the game with Coach Doss as the bus doors opened.

"Listen up, guys," said the head coach. "We play Panhandle tomorrow afternoon at six p.m. for a berth in the state tournament."

The bus exploded into craziness and laughter.

"Tonight lights out at eleven p.m. No exceptions," said Coach Alvarez as he got off the bus and made his way into the hotel.

Coach Doss passed out the following day's schedule, and it read as follows:

9:00 a.m.—Breakfast at Holiday Inn Hotel
11:00 a.m.—Shoot-Around Practice at Coronado High School
1:00 p.m.—Lunch at Olive Garden
2:30 p.m.—Back at Hotel

4:00 p.m.—Leave for United Supermarket Arena
6:00 p.m.—Regional Finals Game
8:00 p.m.—Avalon Longhorns Regional Champions

"Chente?" said Coach Alvarez as he stepped back on the bus. "I need you to meet Coach Doss at eight a.m. in the hotel's sauna to rehab your leg."

"The hotel has a whirlpool?" asked Chente in disbelief.

"It's not like what we have in the training room, but it is a whirlpool," replied Coach Alvarez. "Is there a problem with that?"

Chente quickly shook his head. "No, sir. I will be ready at eight a.m."

He grabbed his backpack and glanced at Coach Doss, who was smiling at him. Chente hurried off the bus and walked into the hotel with Felipe and Carlos.

Carlos exited the restroom to find Chente on his bed, playing with the remote control and searching for ESPN. His cell phone buzzed, and Chente glanced at it and grinned.

"Who's texting you? Haven?" asked Carlos as he got under the sheets in his bed.

"No. She texted me earlier," Chente replied as he cracked up in laughter. "This is Henry Hamilton. He's still talking mess."

"I didn't know that y'all were friends," replied Carlos.

Chente was busy typing his response to the Kress boy and didn't answer Carlos until he finished. "Yeah, we have become friends over the years. Through basketball camps and summer tennis meets, we have gotten to know each other a little bit better."

Carlos casually nodded. "How's his ankle?"

"The X-rays say that it's a bad sprain. No broken bones," replied Chente.

Chente's cell phone buzzed a couple of more times. "Now he's saying we won only because he got hurt." Chente laughed. "And I told him that a real man would have played through the pain."

Carlos joined in the laughter and agreed.

"He says that he will get even with me during tennis season."

Chente rolled his eyes and put his phone away and got into bed as well. His legs were tired, and his thigh muscle was a little tight when he had stretched a few minutes before.

"Hey, Chen, did you see Mr. Bennett talking to Coach Alvarez after the game?"

Chente looked over at Carlos. "No. What happened now? Why is he angry this time?"

Carlos shrugged. "I don't know. All I overheard was that you don't pass the ball to Ricky enough."

Chente got up and sat on Carlos's bed. "Are you freakin' serious? Ricky was awful today." His voice got a little louder. "He didn't hit a shot all night—and he was open!"

Chente had passed the ball to Ricky several times during the first half of the basketball game, and Ricky had missed everything. The Bennett boy had even blown a wide-open layup on a fast break in the fourth quarter.

"I know, I know, man," said Carlos as he put his arms up to settle Chente down. "I couldn't believe it either. Just don't kill the messenger."

Chente stood up and began to pace back and forth between the two beds. He didn't understand why father and son weren't simply happy to be in the regional finals. Why did they always have to cause so much drama?

"Chen, why do they hate you so much? Do you think they're jealous?" asked Carlos.

Chente shrugged and exhaled. "I have no idea. Don't have a clue." The point guard sat down on his bed and groaned. "But it's more than just jealousy though. It has to be. They really don't like me, and I don't know why."

Carlos looked at Chente. "Dude, I need to tell you something, but you have to promise that you're not going to get mad at me."

Chente returned his stare and nodded in curiosity.

"The other day in the locker room, Ricky started to talking mess," began Carlos.

He paused and searched for the right words. He glanced at Chente and rolled his eyes and sighed.

"Okay. Go on," said Chente. He had a sick feeling in the pit of his stomach that this wasn't going to be good—that this would be a game changer.

Carlos went on to tell Chente that he and Felipe had entered the locker room, complaining about Valentine's Day. Carlos explained that they had even laughed about the fact that Principal Timms had gotten a rose and they had been forgotten.

Chente laughed a little under his breath. "Yeah, I can see how that might be a little depressing."

Carlos nodded and laughed. "Exactly—but we were just cutting up really. The guys in the locker room were laughing and everything. But then Ricky announced that you had gotten those roses from Jimmy. He said Jimmy was gay."

Chente felt like he had been hit head-on by a bus. This was a level of hatred he hadn't anticipated, and he sat listlessly on his bed, unsure of what to say to his friend.

"Chen, you okay?" asked Carlos. "Dude, nobody believed him. In fact, everyone defended you," added Carlos, hoping to soften the blow a little bit.

Chente sat in silence for a few seconds longer, trying to decide what to do. He knew that if Jimmy were alive, he wouldn't have denied it.

"He's right," Chente finally said. "Jimmy *was* gay."

Carlos calmly nodded and didn't say anything. He waited for Chente to speak again.

"I guess I have always known that," said the point guard, "but truthfully, he came out to me on the day he committed suicide." Chente took a deep breath and slowly cleared his throat. "Yeah, our last conversation ended badly, and I haven't been able to get past it very well. It kind of haunts me still."

Chente stared off into space, wishing he could have their last conversation back again. He would say the right things, and his best friend would still be alive. He longed for Jimmy's crazy fearlessness and loud sense of humor. They had been kindred spirits, and he missed him.

"Obviously, he didn't send me the roses," said Chente with a soft chuckle to break the ice that had surrounded the room. "I still don't know who did. But what a hateful thing to say. Jimmy was his cousin too."

"Yep. The Bennett family are mean people—racists!" growled Carlos.

The room was quiet for a second as Chente processed the information.

"You know, I'm sorry about Jimmy," said Carlos. "I didn't know him that well, but he was cool. He was always nice to me."

"Yeah. He was," reminisced Chente. "I just wish he would have made a different choice, you know?"

"I get it, but it's not your fault, Chen," Carlos whispered.

"Yeah. Everyone says that," replied Chente softly. "But it still feels like it is somehow." Chente sighed and looked at Carlos and smiled. "Thanks though."

There was a big bang at the door that startled Chente and Carlos out of their beds. They waited for a second, and like two little boys, they started to laugh. Chente got up to answer it. It was Coach Doss standing in the doorway.

Coach Doss gave Chente a quizzical look and smiled. He looked in the room and saw Carlos on the floor, still laughing hysterically.

"Okay, you goofballs, five minutes and lights out."

Chente nodded and playfully saluted. "Yes, sir."

"Oh, and Chen, see you tomorrow morning, downstairs, at eight a.m.," reminded Coach Doss as he walked away.

"Yes, sir. I remember." Chente smiled and closed the door.

The next morning Chente didn't wait for the elevators; instead, he raced down the hotel stairs to the gym. Carlos had set the alarm clock to ring at 7:30 p.m., and as a result, Chente had overslept and was running a few minutes late. When he got to the gym, Coach Doss was already there with his coffee cup, waiting on him.

"Coach, I am really sorry for being late," said Chente as he walked up, expecting a reprimand. "It's just that the alarm clock didn't go off like it was supposed to, and now I feel like I am running behind. I hate starting today like this, and I'm sorry for wasting your time."

Chente continued to rattle on—talking unusually fast and hardly breathing. He looked at Coach Doss, who was just standing and grinning.

"Good morning, Chen," Coach Doss calmly said. "Relax. You are three minutes late—no biggie!" He put his arms on his shoulder. "How many cups of coffee have you had this morning?"

"I'm sorry. I guess I just don't like being late," said Chente as he relaxed his shoulders. "And I don't drink coffee."

"Well, I got the whirlpool going. and it's pretty warm if you want to get in," Coach Doss started. "You need to sit there for about fifteen minutes, and then I will give your thigh a quick massage treatment and send you on your way."

Chente nodded and did what he was instructed to do. The warm water felt nice against his cold skin, and after a few minutes Chente was snoozing. He let the water work its magic on his ailing body.

"Hey, Chen," said Coach Doss as he stood over him, "it's time to get out."

Chente grabbed Coach Doss's extended hand and got out. He was inches away from Coach Doss when he stood up, and Chente grabbed a towel and slowly dried off. Chente could feel the electricity in the room.

Coach Doss motioned him to a massage table the hotel had provided and began the massage treatment on his right thigh.

"I didn't see Haven at the game," said Coach Doss as he attempted to break the awkward silence. "Was she there?"

Chente slowly shook his head. "No. She had a family thing she had to go to, but she texted me last night and said she and her parents would be coming tonight."

Chente had thought it was curiously strange that Coach Doss was searching the bleachers for Haven last night. Why would he do that? Surely, he wasn't jealous.

"That's great," said Coach Doss in a quiet, monotone voice. "We need all the fans we can get tonight."

"Well, is Bella going to be at the game tonight?" Chente thought he would return the favor to Coach Doss and see how he responded.

Coach Doss cleared his throat. "You know, I don't know. She has a sorority mixer thing she has to go to …"

Coach Doss didn't finish his thought, and Chente let it go. Bella had definitely been shooting daggers at him last night, and he wondered why. Maybe she was jealous?

"So how are the wedding plans coming along?" asked Chente quietly. "Have y'all agreed on a date yet?"

Chente couldn't help it. He hadn't spoken to Coach Doss in a few weeks, and he was out of the loop.

Coach Doss took his time to respond. "Yes," he finally said. "She picked June twenty-third."

Suddenly, Chente couldn't breathe. It felt like someone was punching his lungs and pounding the life out of him. He sat up and started to cough like he was choking.

"Excuse me," said Chente as he tried to recover from his outburst. "I am still half asleep."

Coach Doss patted Chente's back as he coughed. He rested one hand on Chente's shoulder and continued to gently rub Chente's back with the other until he stopped coughing.

"I'm better now. Thanks, Coach," lied Chente as he continued to clear his throat. "Listen, it's eight thirty-five. I better head up to my room and get ready for breakfast. You know how I hate being late."

Chente tried to smile and awkwardly waved at Coach Doss. He ran up the stairs as fast as he could. When he reached the third floor, he paused and frantically tried to collect his thoughts. His heart felt like it was going to jump out of his chest as he desperately tried to control his labored breathing.

Chente covered his face with his hands as tears came from his eyes like rain from a storm cloud. He sat down and sobbed like a little boy who had lost his way home. He felt silly, foolish, and absurd. How had he allowed himself to think Coach Doss cared for him? How had he allowed himself to think Coach Doss wouldn't get married?

He wiped his tears away and softly spoke to himself. "Chente you can do this—you will overcome this," he whispered to himself. "He's getting married, and there's nothing you can do about it."

Chente paused and took a deep breath. He gently rubbed his forehead, then wiped away his tears. He closed his eyes and concentrated.

"Come on, Chente, focus," he whispered slowly. "Focus on tonight's game. Nothing else matters. Focus on winning!"

He cleared his throat, ran up to the fourth floor, and exited the stairwell.

Coach Doss quietly emerged from the stairwell. He hadn't waited for the elevator either. He had heard Chente crying. He sighed and slowly shook his head as he exited the stairwell.

The rest of the day Chente avoided Coach Doss at every turn. At breakfast and at lunch, Chente made sure they sat at the opposite ends of the table, and he stayed close to Coach Alvarez during basketball practice to make sure he understood the game plan for Panhandle. Chente savored the moment with his friends and made advancing to the state basketball tournament his top priority.

The first half of the game went badly. Early on in the first quarter, Avalon fell behind by four points since it took a little time for the Longhorns to shake off the big-game jitters. And just when they began to get into the flow of the game, Ricky got trigger happy and started shooting the basketball the minute he touched it. As a result, Avalon trailed by five points at the end of the first quarter. Avalon 11–Panhandle 16.

The second quarter was even less productive as the Longhorns continued to struggle to find any offensive rhythm. Midway through the quarter, Coach Alvarez benched Ricky for his erratic shooting, and Tre' picked up his second foul.

"Okay, guys, we are down seven right now. We can't let this game get away from us," warned the head coach. "We have to generate some offense!"

Coach Alvarez glanced at Chente, and the point guard nodded and understood.

When the team returned to the floor, Chente told Beau to run the point while he moved to the shooting guard position. Beau hesitated but did what Chente had instructed him to do.

The personnel change was minor, but it allowed Chente to create offense for himself. In a matter of two minutes, Chente drained two three-pointers and made three free throws to cut the Panhandle's halftime lead to two points. Avalon 23–Panhandle 25.

The locker room was a complete chaos at halftime because Ricky threw a crazy fit for being benched. He and Felipe were yelling at each other when Coach Alvarez intervened.

"Ricky, that's enough," yelled the basketball coach. "I am going to do what I feel is best to get this team to win. If you disagree with my decisions, you can leave your jersey at the door on your way out."

"It's just not fair. It's not fair," complained Ricky as he shook his head in disagreement.

"You're right. It's not fair to us that you keep shooting and missing," yelled Felipe.

"Dude, you need to pass the ball to your teammates," complained Tre'. "You can't just shoot the ball all the time."

"I didn't shoot that much," protested Ricky, and he looked directly at Coach Alvarez. "I didn't."

The head coach looked at Coach Doss, who was holding the first-half stats. "Ricky, you shot eight times and didn't score," the assistant coach quietly said.

Coach Alvarez had heard enough. He announced that Chente was moving to the shooting guard position and that Beau would run the point in the second half. He warned Tre' about his picking up his third foul and pleaded with Felipe to get more involved in the rebounding department.

The team returned to the gym floor with much better energy in the second half. Beau transitioned into the starting lineup with ease, and Chente and Tre' took over the third quarter, combining for eighteen points. Avalon hit their stride and never looked back. When the final buzzer sounded, the Avalon Longhorns had punched their ticket for the state tournament. Avalon 51–Panhandle 41.

The Longhorn bench and the Avalon fans rushed the court to celebrate. It was sweet pandemonium. This was the first time in history that Avalon High School was advancing to the state basketball tournament.

Coach Doss rushed over to Chente, lifted him, and gave him a big hug. "You were amazing!" he yelled as their eyes locked.

"Coach Alvarez is speaking with the KLBK TV station, and they are asking for you," the basketball coach said with a grin. "I guess you are a superstar!"

Chente followed Coach Doss and stood beside Coach Alvarez as the reporter from KLBK finished interviewing him. Coach Alvarez saw Chente and pulled him up front and center and in front of the television camera.

"So tell me, Chente, how does it feel to be going to the state tournament?" asked the reporter.

Chente smiled for the cameras. "It feels great. I can't be prouder of my team. We all worked really hard to get here. Coach Alvarez deserves this. I'm just proud for the community of Avalon."

Coach Alvarez stepped away from the reporter and shook his head at Coach Doss. "You gotta love that kid. He's a natural."

"Yep, I agree." Coach Doss smiled as he pushed past the crowd and led the head coach to his next interview. "He's selfless and poised and says all the right things."

"I understand that you had twenty-two points tonight. Tell me a little bit about that," said the sports reporter.

"Well, I didn't know that," replied the point guard with a little laugh. "Um, you know I think that the real credit goes to Tre' Washington and Beau Brockman. They stepped up and played really well tonight to give us a chance to win."

The reporter smiled, said some nice things about Chente in front of the camera, and went back to reporting the game.

Chente ran to the locker room and encountered Mr. Bennett, who was standing inside the doorway and yelling at Ricky to hurry and get dressed. He had a mean scowl and was obviously upset.

Chente tried to stealthily maneuver around the angry man. He didn't want any problems. He just wanted to celebrate the moment with his friends in the locker room.

"You! I can't believe that Coach Alvarez let you back on the team," hissed Mr. Bennett as he shook his head. He followed Chente into the locker room.

Chente waved him off and kept walking.

"Listen to me, you little faggot. Your kind shouldn't be dressing with normal boys," growled Mr. Bennett. "It's just not right!"

Chente paused and gently shook his head. He slowly exhaled and calmly turned around. He faced Mr. Bennett and grinned. "Wow. You really think that your opinion matters to me," the point guard said with a grin, "but it doesn't. I really don't care what you think. You are a nobody! I don't have time for your hate!"

"How dare you," began Mr. Bennett.

"No, sir!" replied Chente as he raised his voice and pointed directly in the man's face. "No! You need to leave!"

Felipe turned the corner of the locker room and tagged Chente's shoulder. He glared at Mr. Bennett and slowly walked up to the old man.

"Hey, mister, don't hate on Chente because your son sucks!" sneered Felipe as he towered over the middle-aged man. "Ricky shot so many bricks tonight that he practically built a little house on the middle of the gym floor. Your son almost cost us the game!"

The Avalon post player took a few steps and got in Mr. Bennett's face. "Now it's time that you get the hell out of our locker room!"

Mr. Bennett took a few steps back and furiously shook his head, turned around, and walked out of the locker room in a huff.

"What an asshole," said Felipe as he nudged Chente's arm. "Don't listen to him. He's an idiot like his son."

Chente grinned as Felipe threw his arms up in the air. "Dude! We are going to state! Can you believe that? State bound, baby!"

Ricky was already dressed when Chente and Felipe arrived. He was still pouting about being benched and was gathering his stuff to leave. "You know my father is right. They shouldn't let your kind dress with us." Ricky smirked as he turned and faced Chente.

Carlos stood up and walked over to Ricky, putting his hands on his hips. "What is that supposed to mean? Are you being racist now?"

The locker room got quiet and waited for Ricky to respond.

"This has nothing to do with race," replied Ricky as he waved off Carlos and stared at Chente. "It has to do with the fact that Chente is gay!"

Chente didn't acknowledge Ricky or his comments. He continued to take off his shoes and unwrap the tape from his ankle. He wasn't going to let Ricky get the best of him.

"Shut up, Ricky!" shouted Beau. "Why don't you go home with your dad already?"

"It's true. Chente is gay. My cousin Jimmy told me before he killed himself." Ricky snickered as he taunted the point guard. "Yep, that's what my cousin said before he blew his brains out."

Chente bolted to his feet, kicked his locker chair out of the way, and lunged at Ricky. The Jimenez boy got within inches of his face and growled. "Ricky, you better leave, now!"

Chente's fists were clenched, and he was breathing fire. He was ready to punch the teeth out of Ricky's filthy mouth.

Ricky slowly stepped away from Chente and smirked. "Yeah, that's a little too close for me," hissed Ricky as he grabbed his athletic bag. "Sorry, Chen, but I don't kiss boys."

Chente slowly exhaled and regained his composure. He glanced at his teammates, grabbed a towel, and walked toward the showers without saying another word.

A few seconds later, Chente heard a loud crash and quickly turned around. He saw Ricky Bennett on the locker room floor with Beau Brockman towering over him. "Yeah, well, maybe you don't kiss boys, but it's your turn to kiss the floor, you dirty bastard," yelled Beau.

CHAPTER 16

The smell of chorizo and beans woke Chente from his deep sleep. It took him a few seconds to focus and realize he was at home and in his bedroom, still in bed. His mother was cooking breakfast in the kitchen, and the aroma was intoxicating.

Chente stayed in bed under the warm covers for a few minutes longer, enjoying the peace and quiet. His body ached, and his legs were sore, but it was a happy reminder that his basketball team had won the regional title and were now advancing to the state basketball tournament in San Antonio at the end of the week.

Chente glanced at his alarm clock—10:13 a.m.

He needed to get up, but the idea of staying in bed all day was so tempting. He didn't feel like being Chente Jimenez, basketball star and senior class valedictorian, today. He didn't want to be popular today. Instead, he wanted to hide under the covers and simply be Chente—no titles and no labels.

"Chente? *Mijo*? Is everything okay?" asked Mrs. Jimenez as she walked into the bedroom.

Chente slowly poked his head out from under the covers and gave his mother an embarrassed little smile. He quickly nodded. "Yes, I'm good," he answered. "Why?"

Mrs. Jimenez gave him a stern look and shook her head. "*No me heches mentiras*," she quickly said in Spanish in a very no-nonsense voice. "What is going on? *Qué te pasa*?"

Chente sat up in his bed and continued to lie. "Mom, I am not lying to you. Nothing's the matter," replied Chente as he rubbed his eyes and gave her another weak smile.

Mrs. Jimenez wasn't buying it. She pointed at him, sat at the foot of her son's bed, and tilted her head. "Well, I don't believe you, Chente," said the concerned mother as she gave him a long stare and searched his eyes for answers. "I am your mother, and I know these things."

"Well, I am sorry that you don't believe me," replied Chente as he shrugged. "But nothing is the matter."

Mrs. Jimenez shook her head and exhaled. "*Mira*, I am going to tell you a story, and I need you to listen carefully," said Mrs. Jimenez with a joyful twinkle in her eyes. "When you were a little boy, if you were scared or had a problem, you would lie in bed and pull the covers over your head and talk to yourself. *Sabias eso*?"

Chente's eyes began to dance in a childlike manner as he quickly readjusted the pillows on his bed and got comfortable. "I did?" he said as he covered his mouth and chuckled to himself. "Are you sure? I don't remember doing that."

"*Si. Yo y tu papi* thought it was so cute." She smiled. "It was like you would go into your own little world and try to come up with your own solution for whatever was bothering you."

"*Mijo*, why do you think we called you Linus from the Snoopy cartoons when you were little?" teased Mrs. Jimenez as she smiled and giggled to herself.

Chente laughed aloud, quickly covered his mouth, and shook his head. "Seriously? I didn't know that."

He immediately longed for his childhood. Simpler times. When his biggest worry had been learning how to ride his bike around the block. He wanted to negotiate a deal with Father Time and turn back the clock. He wanted to be a little boy again.

"You never wanted anyone to know you were scared or worried," whispered the mother of five as she nodded.

Mrs. Jimenez was happy to hear laughter coming from her son. She knew he had been through an emotional roller coaster lately, and she wanted to reassure him that it was okay to be happy again. She wanted to erase his self-imposed guilt.

"What was even funnier is that you thought that by covering your head under the sheets, nobody could hear you talking to yourself—and we all could."

Chente burst into hearty laughter and gently wiped the corners of his eyes. He was fascinated by this walk down memory lane. He loved listening to his mother tell stories from the past. He had missed her terribly, and he was glad she was feeling better.

"*Vez*?" she asked. "I know something is bothering you. You are under the covers and talking to yourself again."

Chente closed his eyes and exhaled. He stretched his arms out wide and smiled at his mother as she gently grabbed his chin.

"*Ándale*. Now, get up and shower, and we'll talk over breakfast," said Mrs. Jimenez as she walked out of the bedroom and headed back into the kitchen.

Chente playfully saluted his mother as she left, because he understood it was an order and not a request.

The Jimenez boy slowly got out of bed, trudged across the hallway, and took a quick shower. He returned to his bedroom and checked his cell phone. He had a couple of text messages from Carlos and Felipe. They both wanted to make sure he was okay.

Chente also received a congratulatory text message from Henry Hamilton. The red-headed boy from Kress wished Chente luck at the state tournament.

"Chente, *mijo*," shouted Mrs. Jimenez from the kitchen. "*Ándale*. Hurry up before your food gets cold."

Chente put his cell phone down, got dressed, and headed into the kitchen.

"Mmm, it smells so good." Chente smiled as he reached for a fresh tortilla and took a hearty bite. "Oh my gosh, Mom, this is amazing! There is a lot of food. I should have called Carlos and Felipe to come over and eat."

Mrs. Jimenez didn't hold back. She laid a spread of breakfast food for Chente to choose from on the table. She was proud of her son and the way he had played the night before.

"Wait a minute," said Chente as he looked around. "Where's Victor?"

"He went to the movies with Violeta," answered Mrs. Jimenez as she pulled out the cinnamon rolls from the oven and placed them on the kitchen counter.

"What do you mean? He went to the movies with Violeta?" asked Chente as he stopped chewing his food and looked at his mom.

"*Mira*, Violeta, and Lisa were here earlier this morning, and they were going to the movies. Lisa begged Victor to go with them," replied Mrs. Jimenez as she shrugged. "Lisa wanted to see her Tio Chin, but I wouldn't let them wake you up."

Chente was impressed that Victor would go anywhere with Violeta, because they were never on the same page about anything. However, saying no to Lisa was probably too hard for his little brother to do.

"They ate breakfast before they left." Mr. Jimenez grinned. "They were going to watch some Walt Disney cartoon."

Chente made himself a couple of potato, chorizo, and cheese tacos. He added refried beans and cheese to his plate, and poured a glass of orange juice. He sat down and began to eat. He loved his mom's cooking. It always made him feel safe.

"Dang, Mom, this so good." Chente beamed as he continued to eat.

Mrs. Jimenez grabbed a plate and served herself some food. She sat down next to Chente and began to eat. She missed her quiet times with all her children, but her connection to Chente was different; she was drawn to her middle son. Chente's disposition was remarkably similar to his dad's—strong, reliable, and fiercely independent.

"So Chente, what's going on in your world?" asked Mrs. Jimenez.

Chente glanced her way and continued to eat. A lot was going on in his world that he wanted to keep private. However, he knew how unyielding his mom could be, so he took another bite of his taco before it started to spill.

"Well, I received the Presidential Scholarship to Texas Tech a few weeks ago," he said casually. "It's a full ride."

Mrs. Jimenez paused with her fork in her mouth. She looked at Chente and didn't know what to say. She didn't understand the process of applying for college and scholarships. All she knew was that she wanted her children to get as much education as possible.

"*Mijo*, that's wonderful, right?" she asked with curiosity in her eyes.

"I think so. Texas Tech is a good university." Chente smiled.

He explained that this scholarship would pay for all college expenses for four years if he decided to attend Texas Tech. He added that he was still waiting to hear back from the University of Texas and Stanford before he made his decision.

"Ay, *mijo*, I am so proud of you," said the mother of five with a sigh. "My prayers have been answered. *Diosito es muy grande*."

Mrs. Jimenez tenderly cupped her son's chin with her hands and smiled as she made the sign of the cross. It was so obvious that she was relieved that his college future was secure.

"But please, I just want to keep this news between us for now," said Chente.

"Why? Is something the matter?" she asked.

"No, not exactly. I just don't want pressure to make up my mind," he said with a deep sigh. "I want this decision to be mine without any outside interference."

"And you think your brothers and sisters will try to tell you what to do?" asked Mrs. Jimenez with a little laugh before she sipped her coffee.

Chente raised his eyebrows and nodded with exaggeration.

"Of course, they will want to give you their opinion, especially Violeta," said the mother of five. "*Pobrecita*, she thinks *que sabe todo*."

"Oh yes, Mom, poor Violeta." Chente laughed. "I feel so sorry for her."

"Well, you know what I mean," she said. "But *mijo*, I promise I will say nothing."

She got up and kissed him on his head. She took her plate to the sink and asked, "Okay? So *qué más*?"

Chente chuckled to himself. His mother was relentless.

"What do you mean?" he asked as he got up to get more orange juice. "I mean, I am crazy excited that we are going to the state tournament this week. I am kind of nervous but mostly excited."

"*Ay*, Chente. I was nervous last night during the game," said Mrs. Jimenez as she poured herself another cup of coffee. "But I am so glad that y'all won. Coach Alvarez looked very happy."

"He was, but as usual, there was drama in the locker room with Ricky," confessed Chente. "I am getting so tired of him, and so is the team."

Chente told his mom about how Ricky was arguing with Coach Alvarez during halftime, and he described what Ricky had said about Jimmy. Mrs. Jimenez carefully listened to her son as he recounted yesterday's events. She didn't interrupt or offer any advice.

"Ricky just makes me mad when he talks about Jimmy being gay," said Chente as he growled. "He makes it sound like it's evil or bad. It's just not fair."

Mrs. Jimenez remained silent.

"Jimmy isn't here to defend himself," replied Chente in a broken voice.

Mrs. Jimenez nodded at her son and smiled calmly. "Chente, was Jimmy gay?"

"Yes." Chente exhaled slowly. "Yes, Mom, Jimmy was gay."

"Then what's there to defend?" asked Mrs. Jimenez as she wrinkled her forehead and titled her head to the left. "If I know my Jimmy, he wasn't ashamed of it; nor was he trying to hide," she said as she casually sipped coffee and smiled.

"You already knew, didn't you?" asked Chente as he gave his mother a long stare.

"When you are as old as I am, you can see the signs," she said plainly. "*Pero la verdad es*, that I had heard *el chisme* a few months ago, but it doesn't matter to me. Nothing changed. I still love Jimmy."

"So it shouldn't matter what Ricky says?" asked Chente.

"Toss it to the wind and let it go. It won't change anything, right?" asked Mr. Jimenez as she reached for Chente's cheek. "*Mijo*, don't give negative energy any power."

Chente slowly nodded. His mother was right again.

"But Mom, there's so much you don't know."

"Okay, then tell me. What don't I know?" asked Mrs. Jimenez as she straightened her posture and smiled at Chente with a wrinkled forehead.

Chente looked at her and grinned again. "I am gay too," said Chente plainly.

"*Gracias, mijo,*" replied Mrs. Jimenez as she gazed at her son and smiled. "Thank you for trusting me enough to tell me something so personal. I love you just the same—maybe even more." She got up from her chair and hugged her son.

Chente gripped his mom like she was slipping out of his hands. He found an indescribable comfort in his mother's unconditional love, and he felt lucky to have it.

"How long have you known?" whispered Chente.

"I didn't know for sure until now," she said. She kissed his forehead and placed her hands on his head, gently playing with his hair. She softly began to hum a sweet lullaby. "You know, your dad and I always knew you were very private and guarded about your feelings—very different from your brothers and sisters."

"Dad knew?" Chente sighed as he looked down at his feet. "He is probably rolling over in his grave."

"Don't say that," she said in a scolding tone. "Give your dad some credit. As a matter of fact, he's the one who brought it to my attention—your friendship with Jimmy."

"Mom, Jimmy and I were only friends." Chente laughed as he shook his head.

"Okay, *mijo*, that's fine," said Mrs. Jimenez as she nodded. "My point is that your dad was very observant and aware. He knew his children well."

She delicately wiped the corners of her eyes and sighed. "You know,

I wanted to have a talk with you a couple of years ago, and your dad said *que no*," she recalled as she traveled back in time. "He said to leave you alone. He said you would figure it out because you always did."

Chente was astonished. His father knew he was gay and was open-minded and accepting. Could this be real?

"Really, Mom?" Chente asked pleadingly. "Dad was okay with me being gay?"

"He was more than okay. He loved you very much, *mijo*," replied Mrs. Jimenez.

"Oh, Mom, you don't know what this means to me. I feel as though the weight of the world has been lifted off my shoulders."

Chente's heart was as light as a feather. He closed his eyes and imagined himself soaring through the clouds. "It's like I have been given front-row tickets to a Maroon 5 concert," he said as he laughed aloud like a little boy.

His mother joined him in his excitement as she playfully got up and pretended to dance a waltz with her son.

"Your dad loved all of his children, but Chente, he always said that he felt a close connection with you," said the mother of five.

Chente carefully listened with a surprised face. "Why with me?"

"I know you don't see it. Maybe you just can't yet," said Mrs. Jimenez, "but y'all are so much alike." She stopped dancing, playfully took a bow, and delicately gave her middle son a hug. "Oh, and he loved to watch you play basketball."

"I remember. He always waited for me to get home after the game to talk strategy." Chente smiled as he reminisced about the past.

Chente slowly realized he missed his father more than he had thought. His death had left a void in his soul that would remain there for the rest of his life.

"Remember that time when you were little and were shooting baskets one Sunday morning on the side of the house?" Mrs. Jimenez laughed.

Of course, Chente remembered. It had been an early, cold Sunday morning, and his dad was on the side of the house, changing the oil on his truck. Chente was about ten years old and had just gotten a brand-new basketball for his birthday. He went outside to practice his free throws while his dad worked on his truck. Suddenly the girl's bedroom window flew open, and Violeta shouted at him to stop shooting because she was trying to sleep.

Chente was laughing so hard that he could barely finish the story. "Dad told her to be quiet because I needed to practice my free throws. Man, Violeta was mad at me for a whole week."

"Speaking of the devil," said Mrs. Jimenez as she got up from the kitchen table and peered through the window, "her car just pulled up the driveway."

"I wonder what happened," said Chente as he wiped his laughing tears from his eyes.

Victor walked in, rolled his eyes, and growled in utter frustration. "She thinks she knows everything," he said as he threw his jacket on the couch and stormed down the hallway.

Lisa walked in a few seconds afterward, crying at the top of her lungs. She had a big wet spot on her pants, and it was obvious she'd had an accident. She went straight for Chente and put her arms up in the air to be picked up.

"What's the matter, *chiquita*?" he asked quietly as he picked her up, held her in his arms, and stroked her long, curly hair.

"I had a accident, and Mommy is mad at me," said the little girl as Violeta walked in with annoyance etched on her face.

"Chente, don't spoil her," complained Violeta. "I can't believe she used the restroom in her pants."

"Vi, she's four years old," replied Chente with a look of horror.

"No. Wait a second," replied Victor as he ran into the living room and pointed at his older sister. "She told you she needed to go to the restroom as we were leaving, but you were on your cell phone, and you were in a rush to leave. Not exactly mother-of-the-year points for you, Vi."

"If you heard her ask to go to the restroom, why didn't you take her?" asked Violeta as she put her hands on her hips.

Victor started to clap his hands wildly. "You are unbelievably good at shifting the blame onto someone else. It's like you have mastered the art of blaming other people for your mistakes," sneered the youngest brother as he glanced at his mother and brother and shook his head in disgust. He stormed down the hallway and slammed his bedroom door.

Mr. Jimenez looked at Chente and was completely unfazed. "Remember that I love you. We can finish our conversation later," she said to Chente as she took Lisa from his arms.

"I think your favorite *abuelita* has some clothes you can change into. Just come with me, and we'll clean you up," whispered the grandmother as she wiped the tears off the little girl's cheeks.

"What was Mom talking about? Y'all keeping secrets again?" Violeta smirked as she squinted and looked at Chente.

"I don't know, Vi. I guess it's a secret." Chente grinned as he shrugged and walked down the hallway.

"You know I'll figure it out," said Violeta as she rolled her eyes.

Chente walked into his bedroom and found Victor lying on his bed with his headphones on. He was visibly upset and sketching on a tablet of paper. Chente waved at him to get his attention.

"What's going on?" asked Victor as he removed the headphones.

"No, little brother, that's what I want to know," said Chente as he sat across from him and at his desk. "Why did you just go off on Vi?"

He rolled his eyes as he threw his hands up in the air. "Because I get tired of her and the way she acts. I sometimes wonder how we are even related," he confessed as he sat up and shook his head. "You know she is so wrapped in herself that she neglects everything else."

Chente knew exactly what Victor was talking about. Violeta always made her needs the top priority. That was why she and Vanessa didn't get along. Vanessa couldn't stand her self-centered nature.

"That's just the way she is, unfortunately," said Chente, trying to play the middle.

"No, Chen. I am not putting up with her any longer. I am going to start calling her out," said Victor. "She needs to understand that her selfish actions have consequences. Like today and Lisa's accident. That's totally on her."

Chente sighed and nodded in agreement with Victor. He pulled out his cell phone and started rummaging through his text messages.

"You know, I don't know who she was talking to, but you were the topic of conversation for a little while when she was on her cell phone," announced the little brother. "She kept saying that it couldn't be true but that she would find out."

Chente pried his eyes away from his cell phone and stared at Victor. "Hold on," he said with a perplexed expression. "Are you sure she was talking about me? I mean, are you sure? Why would she be talking about me?"

Victor stared at Chente and nodded in an exaggerated frustration. "Yes, I am sure. She got off the phone and started to interrogate me about you when she should have been paying attention to Lisa."

Victor was still bothered over the situation, and Chente had a strong suspicion that it was more than just Lisa's accident. He watched his brother continue to sketch.

"So Vic, what kind of questions was Vi asking you?" probed Chente.

Victor continued to focus on his sketching, and after a second or two, he replied. "She asked me whether you and Haven were still seeing each other. She asked whether I knew Jimmy was gay."

"What?" asked Chente as he sat straight up at his desk.

"Yep. That's our beloved sister for you. But that's just the way she is, right?" asked the little brother while effectively throwing Chente's earlier analysis of Violeta's behavior back in his face.

Victor continued to work on his sketch. "Of course, I told her that your relationship with Haven was none of her business and that everyone knew Jimmy was gay."

"You knew Jimmy was gay?"

"Chente, please, everybody knew Jimmy was gay. It was the worst-kept secret at Avalon High School," replied Victor as he chuckled under his breath. "Relax. Being gay is totally in right now."

Chente couldn't help but chuckle at Victor's last comment. Why didn't he give his little brother more credit? It was obvious he was wise beyond his years.

"Oh wait. She did ask one more thing," remembered Victor. "She asked if I knew Coach Doss and wondered what I thought about him."

"Really?" asked Chente, and his eyes widened as he fought to maintain his composure. "What did you say?"

"I didn't," said Victor. "That's when Lisa announced she had wet her pants, and all hell broke loose. Who knows? Maybe she wants to date him," suggested Victor as he shook his head and went back to sketching. "Good luck to Coach Doss!"

"Yeah, maybe," said Chente as looked out the window and watched Violeta drive off.

Chente quietly jogged around the walking track at the city park. Tonight he needed a little distraction, so he told his mom he was going to the park for a little exercise. The last couple of weeks had been a little hectic, and he needed a little solitude to clear his mind.

Chente loved being outside. Feeling the cool wind brush against his face made him feel alive. Exercise was one of Chente's best friends, and it usually brought focus and clarity to his life. Chente rounded the last lap and walked to the park bench by the big oak tree to stretch.

"I guess we were both thinking the same thing tonight."

Chente quickly turned around and saw Coach Doss in his black running tights and black hoodie. The coach was smiling at him.

"Wow. It's been a long time since we've been on the same page on anything," replied the high school senior as he glanced at his coach from top to bottom, then resumed his stretching exercises.

Coach Doss didn't say anything. He stood next to Chente and started his stretching routine on his legs.

"Wait. Don't tell me. You had to clear your mind?" Chente said.

"Exactly." Coach Doss chuckled under his breath as he nudged Chente's arm. "Dang, Chen, you can even read minds tonight."

"It's a talent." Chente grinned as he stood up.

"I know you must have heard this a zillion times, but you played so good last night. It was hard to take my eyes off you," said Coach Doss as he glanced at Chente and winked.

"Thanks, Coach. It was a good game," replied Chente while completely ignoring the flirty gesture. "I am just so glad that we won."

Chente was determined to hold his ground and not let Coach Doss fluster him. He needed to stay mentally strong.

"Why are you shaking your head?" asked Coach Doss as he began to stretch his arms. "Is something the matter?"

Chente's heart was ready to explode, but he was tired of pretending. He was tired of the hot and cold reactions from Coach Doss. He wasn't going to play games any longer.

"I have a better question for you." Chente smiled with a hint of anger in his voice. "How's Bella tonight?"

It was time to put the cards on the table for everyone to see.

"I don't want to talk about her right now," Coach Doss quickly replied as he locked eyes with Chente and smiled.

Chente's posture straightened up, and he chuckled under his breath. "Why not? She's your fiancée, right?"

Coach Doss remained silent and slowly began jogging in place.

"Aren't y'all getting married in June?" asked Chente as he extended his arms out wide. "It's June twenty-third, right?"

Coach Doss exhaled and gradually stopped jogging in place. His eyes narrowed and slowly roamed in every direction like he was searching for something he had lost. He rubbed the sweat off his forehead and looked up at the starry sky.

Everything was wrong, and yet everything was clear. This wasn't how he wanted his story to continue. He couldn't get married to Bella, because he loved Chente. His heart was screaming for Chente. The core of his soul was begging for Chente.

For the first time in his short life, Coach Doss caught his breath and let go. He wasn't going to fight himself any longer, and he was done pretending. The sense of freedom was overwhelming, and Coach Doss started to laugh. He extended his arms in the air and started to spin around in circles.

"What's the matter with you?" asked Chente as he looked around to see whether anyone else was watching. "Have you gone mad?"

Coach Doss grabbed Chente by the arms and continued to laugh. "Yes! Yes! Yes!" he shouted as he continued to spin in circles. "Yes! I have gone mad. Madness is my middle name."

"Coach Doss, what are you doing?"

"I am madly in love with you, Chen," whispered the high school teacher as he reached for his student. "Simply and madly in love with you."

Chente quickly pulled away and shook his head in disbelief. "What are you doing to me? Stop doing this to me," whimpered the basketball star as he put his hands on his head and began to walk away.

Coach Doss prevented Chente from leaving by quickly reaching over and embracing him from behind.

"Don't leave. Stay. Please stay here—with me," whispered the coach. "Just listen to me for a second."

Chente was breathing hard, and his voice was labored and strained. "I can't do this."

Coach Doss gently placed his hands on Chente's chest. "What do you mean, Chen?" asked Coach Doss. "What can't you do? What do you see happening between us?"

"I thought I knew, but I am not sure anymore," replied Chente as his heart was all at once filled with confusion and excitement.

"Please trust me, Chen," Coach Doss said with a smile. "Just listen to me for a second."

Chente slowly shook his head as he gazed into those ocean-blue eyes and sighed. "No. You can't say things like that to me. I don't play like that. Please stop playing with my feelings. I am not a yo-yo."

The high school senior's frantic eyes glistened in the moonlight.

"I'm not strong enough to lose someone again—my heart can't handle it. Do you hear me?" whispered Chente as he slowly walked away.

"Don't go," shrieked Coach Doss in desperation. "Please, please don't go." He reached for Chente's hand and squeezed it. He pulled him in closer and used the big oak tree to shelter them from sight.

"Why are you doing this?" asked Chente as his accelerated breathing sounded like he had just run a marathon.

"Because I am pretty sure I have fallen in love with you," whispered Coach Doss as he gingerly pulled Chente in for a gentle kiss.

Chente timidly pushed away, but an unseen magnetic force pulled him right back into Coach Doss's loving arms. "What are you doing? We are in the middle of the park?" said Chente.

"Relax, Chen, it's almost ten," replied the assistant coach. "No one is out here, and no one can see us behind this huge tree."

Coach Doss gently gazed into Chente's brown eyes and whispered in his ear. "Did you hear me? I think I have fallen in love with you, Chen."

Chente was completely out of sync and didn't know what to think. Everything was happening too fast, and he needed time to process. "What are you talking about, Coach? You are engaged to be married in a few months. You have a fiancée."

Coach Doss didn't hesitate for a second. "I will call Bella tonight and call it all off." He paused, took a deep breath, and grinned impulsively. He was delirious with happiness. "I just need to know that you love me too."

"You can't really be serious," muttered Chente while shaking his head. "Coach! You could lose your job. You could get fired!"

"Trust me, Chen."

Chente's heart began to hop, skip, and jump at the same time. "Of course I love you. I am crazy about you," confessed the point guard.

Chente threw caution to the wind, wrapped his arms around Coach Doss, and kissed him. As soon as their lips touched, it was exactly as Chente remembered. His heart was dizzy with joy and happiness.

Chente gently pulled away and softly exhaled. "Are you sure about this?"

Coach Doss was mesmerized with the man in his arms. "Absolutely sure," he said as he tenderly outlined Chente's lips with his index finger and then kissed him one more time. "But we are going to have to wait a few months."

"Why? What's the matter?" panicked Chente.

"You are still my student—for another three months anyway." Coach Doss smiled and then made sad eyes.

Chente relaxed and chuckled under his breath. "Yes. That is right. You could get into serious trouble. We both could."

"That's why we will need to keep a distance," surmised Coach Doss. "You need to focus on basketball, the rest of your senior year, and going to college."

Chente nodded in agreement.

"If you still have feelings for me after graduation," whispered Coach Doss, "I will go speak with your mother and go from there."

"I'll be worth the wait. I promise," said Chente as he rested his head on Coach Doss's chest and closed his eyes. For the first time in his life, he felt absolute and unbroken. Chente was in heaven.

CHAPTER 17

Chente's alarm clock was screaming at everyone to wake up. He quickly reached over and turned it off without opening his eyes. He rolled over on his bed, yawned, and stretched; he wasn't ready to get out of bed.

"Hey, Vic, you get in the shower first today," he said.

"Wake up, Chen," said Victor as he yawned. "I am already out of the shower, and Vi is on her way to pick me up for school."

The youngest Jimenez brother was putting on some of Chente's cologne and combing his hair in the mirror.

Chente opened his eyes and looked over at his little brother. "What? Why? What's the matter?" he asked. "Are you in trouble again?"

Victor glared at Chente from the mirror and flipped him off. "Really? Again?" Victor shook his head and checked his cell phone. "That's Vi; she will be here in two minutes."

Chente sat up in his bed and scratched his head. "So what's going on?"

Victor started to put his books in his backpack. "It's just a progress meeting Principal Timms set up back in January. You know, to check up on me—the family delinquent."

"But your grades have gotten better, right?" asked Chente with a little concern.

Victor looked out the window, rolled his eyes, and sighed. "Ugh!

Cruella Deville is here—right on time," groaned the little brother as he turned to Chente and nodded. "Yes, big brother—five As and three Bs."

"Hey, that's great, Vic!"

"Well, I certainly can't let on that I am actually smarter than you, can I?" Victor winked as he ran out the bedroom door, laughing.

Chente jumped in the shower and got dressed. There was extra pep in his step this morning, and Mrs. Jimenez noticed as soon as Chente gave her a good morning kiss. He practically skipped to the stove, where he grabbed a tortilla and made himself a breakfast taco.

"So your jog last night did you some good, I see," said Mrs. Jimenez as she flipped another tortilla in the air. She wasn't sure what had happened, but it was good to see her son in a good mood.

"Yes, Mom, last night was exactly what I needed." Chente grinned. "I have a good feeling. Like today is going to be a great day."

He poured himself a glass of orange juice as he recollected the agreement he had made with Coach Doss. They would play it cool until after graduation, and then they would finally be able to be together. Just the thought of it made him smile stupidly.

"Well, good, *mijo*," she said. "When are y'all leaving for San Antonio? I think that Violeta, Victor, and I are planning to go. She was looking for a hotel room last night when she called looking for you."

Chente was reading his text messages as he listened to his mom. "Really? Is Nesh going?"

"*No se*," answered Mrs. Jimenez. "She said she was going to try but had to see what her work schedule looked like first." She started to pack a couple of tacos for Carlos and Felipe. "*Tu otro hermano* is too busy with medical school, but he said he would listen to it on satellite radio."

Chente nodded. "I am pretty sure we are leaving on Wednesday," he said. "Our first game is Friday morning, and then the championship game is on Saturday."

He looked at his cell phone. It was time to go. He grabbed the breakfast tacos and his backpack, and headed out the door to his car. He waved at his mom as he drove away to school.

In the silence of the car, Chente's mind raced back to last night.

Jogging in the park. Coach Doss kissing him. Coach Doss loving him. The day was brand new, but it was already a great day—because Coach Doss loved him.

Chente drove to Haven's house and picked her up for school; he listened to her praise him for Saturday night's performance.

"Thank you," he said. "I'm just excited that we get to play for a state championship in a few days." Chente could see the pride in Haven's eyes as he pulled up to Felipe's house.

"Well, I thought that y'all played really well. Especially after Ricky didn't play anymore." She giggled to herself as Felipe opened the rear door. "Why was he shooting so much?"

Chente knew Haven didn't really understand basketball. She just watched because he played.

"Because he's a ball hog," answered Felipe as he got in the car and laughed. "Oh, and by the way, good morning. Coach Alvarez should kick off him the team for the way he talked back to him at halftime."

"Easy, tiger," said Chente as he handed Felipe the breakfast tacos his mother had made. "Hey, man, and a couple of those are for Carlitos."

Felipe gave him a big, hungry smile and took them quickly. "Yeah, Chente, you're too nice," said Felipe as he bit into his taco. "Ricky is a jerk. You should have punched him Saturday night, especially after what he said."

Haven looked up from her cell phone and glanced at Chente. "What happened?

"Nothing that's worth worrying about," replied Chente as he shook his head calmly. He pulled into the high school parking lot and parked.

"Dude! How can you be so calm about it?" asked Felipe with his mouth full of breakfast. "He accused you of being gay!"

Felipe was obviously still worked up about the locker room incident. He had never liked Ricky, and this last episode had him truly angry. Chente worried that things could soon get physical between the two of them.

Haven gave Chente a worried glance and calmly reached for his hand. "Why give negative energy a platform, right, Chen?" Haven smiled. "Ricky isn't worth it." She trusted Chente and was going to support him and his decisions.

Chente nodded and winked at Haven. He was grateful for her friendship now more than ever. He looked out the car window in agony. He hated keeping his sexuality a secret from his friends, but he just didn't feel the time was right to come out. He would tell them soon.

Christina pulled up beside Chente and waved as she got out of her car. Felipe jumped out of the back seat and walked her into the building.

"Are you okay, Chen?" asked Haven with concerned eyes. "I mean, I know this can't be easy for you."

"It sucks. I should tell Carlos and Felipe for sure—maybe even Christina," replied Chente as he made up his mind. "I will tell them over spring break."

Haven nodded and squeezed his hand. "They are going to be fine. They love you now, and they are going to love you after spring break too." The blonde-headed girl smiled and got out of the car as the school bell sounded.

Chente and Haven entered the high school as Violeta was leaving Principal Timms's office. She was wearing a stern face and looked upset as she rushed by them and out the front door.

"Hey, wasn't that your sister?" asked Haven as she watched her pass by.

Chente slowly nodded as he watched Violeta leave the building.

"She looked mad. I hope everything's all right with Victor," said Haven.

"Yeah, me too." Chente sighed. "Okay, thanks for everything. See you at lunch," he said to Haven as she walked down the hallway to her first-period class.

The front office was a madhouse—a typical Monday morning. A couple of teachers had called in sick at the last minute, and Mrs. Black was trying to find substitutes for their classrooms. In the meantime, she was using a couple of the instructional aides to help cover, and Mrs. Black informed Principal Timms that she would be in Mr. Wood's classroom until he arrived. He had car trouble but was on his way.

Chente nervously walked down the hallway to Coach Doss's classroom. He felt the butterflies in his stomach as he got closer to the door. What if Coach Doss had changed his mind this morning? What if he still wanted to marry Bella?

Chente exhaled and walked into the classroom as the tardy bell sounded. Coach Doss looked up from his desk and gave Chente a warm smile. Chente's heart melted. He felt better.

"Good morning, Chen," said Coach Doss. "I need you to finish inserting these grades into the grade book, please. When you finish that, please start to grade the quizzes in the maroon folder."

"Okay, no problem," replied the high school senior.

Coach Doss gave Chente a quick nod, got up in front of the classroom, and started to lecture.

A few minutes later, a loud beep sounded, and the morning announcements interrupted the classroom flow. The students put their pens down and listened to the voices of Carlos and Christina over the intercom. The lunch menu and student organization meetings were quickly announced, and Christina ended with a shout-out to the Longhorn basketball team.

"Listen up, everybody. The Avalon Longhorn basketball team traveled to Lubbock this weekend and competed in the regional basketball tournament. They kicked butt, took names, and brought the regional championship trophy back to Avalon High School. Woo-hoo!

"They are competing at the UIL State Basketball Tournament this weekend in San Antonio. Go get 'em guys! We know you are number one!"

Chente looked over at Beau, who grinned from ear to ear, as Coach Doss answered the classroom door. Miss Young was there to cover the classroom because Principal Timms wanted to speak with him. Coach Doss gave the students a reading assignment and walked out the door, promising to be back shortly.

Miss Young walked over to Chente and quietly asked him about the basketball game. She was excited they had won and was planning to attend the state tournament over the weekend. She loved San Antonio and was ready to eat some good Mexican food on the River Walk.

Their conversation eventually transitioned over to college choice. Miss Young said she anticipated hearing from the University of Texas and Stanford in a few days. She was a nervous wreck but hid it well. "My sources tell me that the scholarship recipients will be notified by the end of the week. Gosh, I am so nervous for you."

She started to laugh and watched the students complete their assignment.

Chente smiled. "I have a good feeling about it all. I think everything will work itself out like it is supposed to."

There was a painfully loud screech on the intercom followed by the voices of Principal Timms and Coach Doss on the intercom.

Principal Timms: "Coach Doss, there have been some concerns brought to my attention about your relationship with Chente Jimenez."

Coach Doss: "Oh really? I don't understand."

Principal Timms: "Well, there are allegations that your relationship has become inappropriate."

Coach Doss: "Excuse … excuse me? What do you mean?"

Principal Timms: "Well, for example, has Chente ever been to your house."

Coach Doss: "Yes, sir. I sent him to my house to retrieve some lesson plans I had forgotten on the kitchen table."

Principal Timms: "Is that the only time he's been to your house?"

Coach Doss: "Yes, sir … wait, no, sir. He came later that day to give me my house keys. He had forgotten to return them to me. I was locked out of my house. What's this about?"

Principal Timms (coughing): "Well, there are rumors about you two … you know, that you two are very friendly."

Coach Doss: "I … I don't understand."

Principal Timms: "The rumor is that perhaps y'all prefer an alternative lifestyle. You know, that y'all are gay."

Coach Doss (long pause): "Oh really … wow … well, I can't speak for Chente, but I am not gay. Sir, I am getting married in June."

Principal Timms: "Of course, Coach." (There was a loud door knock in the background.) "What? Damn it! Not again!"

There was a loud screech, and then the intercom was silent again.

The students in the classroom sat in silence. A few glanced over in Chente's direction and awkwardly looked away. They were embarrassed for him.

Miss Young gripped Chente's hand and whispered that he should go and wait in her counseling office. Chente was in complete shock. Numb. He looked at Miss Young and nodded, and like a robot, he got up and walked out of the classroom.

The Jimenez boy looked down the hallway toward Miss Young's office, and in his mind, it stretched for miles. He slowly started his walk of shame. How was he going to recover from this? He had practically been outed to the entire school over a broken intercom.

He finally got to Miss Young's office door. He opened the door. He entered the office. He closed the door and sat down in the darkness. He needed to gather his thoughts. He closed his eyes and tried to wish this day away. The day had started so promisingly, and now all he wanted was for the walls of this office to swallow him alive.

As he sat in the dark office with his eyes closed, Chente suddenly felt warmth and peace in his heart and a calming presence fill the room. He heard someone softly whisper in his right ear.

"Mijo, you're going to be fine."

"Dad?" Chente quietly asked as teardrops raced down his face like raindrops on a windowpane. "I'm scared." There was no hiding under the blanket this time. Chente was fully exposed.

"No, mijo, you're strong. Be brave. You are brave."

Chente kept his eyes closed. He didn't want his dad's voice to go away.

"What do I do?" whispered Chente. "What do I do?"

"Be yourself. Just be yourself. Acuerdate, tu eres … valiente!"

Miss Young opened the door of her office and turned on the light.

"Chen? Are you okay?" she asked with a panicked expression on her face. She placed his backpack by his chair and sat down beside him.

Chente was still trying to digest the whole situation. He still felt numb. He wiped away his fear from his cheeks.

"I am so mad I could spit fire," growled Miss Young. "I told Principal Timms that he needed to have that damn intercom fixed months ago! Now look at what's happened!"

Chente took a deep breath and exhaled. He thought about what his dad had said. He felt a calming presence fill his soul.

Tu eres valiente.

"Chen, I am so sorry that this has happened," said Miss Young. "Do you want me to call your mother and explain all of this? I mean, she probably needs to know."

The basketball star completely tuned out Miss Young's voice. *Maybe there is a reason why this happened. Is this destiny telling me to step up—a second chance to be honest?*

Tu eres valiente.

"No, not right now. That's the last thing I want anyone to do," replied Chente. "I want to be the one who talks to her. I want to explain. I will make her understand that everything is going to be okay."

Tu eres valiente.

"Right. Okay, then, what do you want me to do?" Miss Young frantically paced her office floor. "How can I help? What do I do?"

"Nothing." Chente said plainly, and with every moment, he was getting stronger, and his vision became clearer. "Just let me think for a second."

Tu eres valiente.

Miss Young nodded but was visibly confused and rubbed her forehead. "So, Chen? You don't want me to do anything?" she asked again as she continued to wear out the carpet on her office floor.

"Exactly." Chente nodded reassuringly. "I just need some time to think this through."

Tu eres valiente.

"Okay. I am confused," answered the high school counselor as her eyes blinked a couple of hundred times. "What? Talk to me. Tell me what you are feeling right now."

"Miss Young, it's just that—I am gay," replied the high school valedictorian in a calm voice. "It's really okay."

Miss Young paused, regained her composure, and sat down at her desk. She professionally nodded as she soaked in the news. "I see. Okay, very well, Chen."

The high school counselor nervously scratched her head.

"I mean, this isn't the way I wanted to come out," explained Chente as he chuckled nervously, "but it's here, and I am tired of hiding and pretending. It's exhausting!"

The Jimenez boy sighed and let go of all the negative energy. He sat in silence for a few seconds, thinking. He could feel his dad's presence embrace him. He could feel his dad's love surround him.

"You know, Miss Young, I like myself. I am not ashamed of who I am, and I need my actions to start reflecting that," he said as he exhaled. "I am brave. I am strong. I can do this."

Miss Young's face was beaming with pride. "Of course, you can," replied Miss Young with a confident nod. "Chen! Of course, you can!"

"Can I call my mom now, please?" asked Chente as he exhaled. "I want her to hear this from me. I want to explain so she knows I am okay."

Chente hung up the phone and quietly sat in his chair. He took a deep breath and exhaled. He was glad he was able to visit with his mother before word got out of the intercom incident. He reassured her that he was fine and that they would talk more after school.

"How did it go?" asked Miss Young as she sipped her hot chocolate. "Was your mother upset? Is she okay?"

"She took the news in stride," replied Chente. "Obviously, she was concerned for me and wanted me to come home. But she understood my reasons for staying at school."

Miss Young nodded.

"I came out to my mom a few days ago," said Chente. "She knows I am gay and is very supportive."

"I am so proud of you, Chen." Miss Young sighed.

"We will talk some more when I get home this afternoon," said

Chente as he nodded confidently. "She had some questions about the broken intercom."

There was a desperate knock at Miss Young's door, and Principal Timms frantically barged into her office. He looked at Chente and shook his head furiously.

"Look, I am so sorry, Chen," blurted the high school principal. "I didn't know the intercom had malfunctioned, again."

"Principal Timms, how long have I been telling you to fix that intercom?" scolded Miss Young.

"I know. I know," agreed Principal Timms as he nervously glanced at Chente and then the high school counselor. "I am so terribly sorry."

Chente exhaled and nodded. He knew his high school principal was a good man and would have never intentionally done anything to hurt or embarrass any student.

"So, have you called your mother? Is she on her way to visit with me?" asked Principal Timms. "Are you wanting to go home now?

"I did call my mom and explained," replied Chente. "She was a little confused, but we will discuss it further later today when I get home."

The school bell sounded, and it was time for second period. Chente swiped his backpack off the floor and darted for the door. He was going to class.

"What are you doing? Where are you going, son?" asked the high school principal as he placed his hand on Chente's shoulder. "You can't go to class."

"Why not? That was the bell for second period," Chente said pragmatically and glanced over to Miss Young for some help.

"So you're not upset?" asked Principal Timms as he sat down in complete disbelief. "You're not mad at me?"

Chente gave Principal Timms a long look. Chente knew he wasn't to blame. "Well, I am not exactly thrilled, sir," replied Chente as he made his way out the door, "and you need to fix that intercom."

"I don't understand," replied Principal Timms.

"Sir, what I am trying to say is that I am a little rattled but okay," explained the high school senior as he paused at the office door and exhaled. "I fine because … because I *am* gay."

"What did you just say?" asked Principal Timms. "Wait, what …"

Chente looked at Miss Young and shrugged. He didn't know what else to say.

"Go to class." The high school counselor sighed as she shook her head and walked Chente out the door. "I got this."

Chente casually walked through the hallway to his locker, where Haven greeted him.

"Hey, Chen, how are you doing?" she asked as she instantly searched his eyes. "Are you going home?"

Chente had never been more grateful to see her in his entire life. He felt so naked, exposed, and unprotected; and Haven was the security blanket he needed. He took a deep breath and gave her a brave smile.

"No. I'm not going home. I am done hiding," replied Chente as he shook his head. "I am good. I think."

"What the hell happened? There are rumors, Chen," whispered the blonde-headed girl.

"I have no idea where all of this came from," explained Chente as he displayed his best fake smile and tried to remain calm and collected.

"And then Coach Doss? Really?" asked Haven as she raised her voice a little bit and frowned. "'I can't speak for Chente, but I am not gay? I am getting married this summer'?"

Chente calmly shrugged and smiled because he knew they were being watched. He didn't have time to think of Coach Doss's betrayal. He had to freeze him out momentarily and think of himself. He was in survival mode and determined to walk with his head high. He was determined to beat this.

"That son of a bitch," hissed Haven as she rubbed her forehead. "I hope Bipolar Bella gives him hell and makes his life miserable!"

Chente covered his mouth with his textbooks and began to laugh. Haven rolled her eyes and giggled as well.

"Haven, I can't do this right now. I have to get to class," he said as he grabbed her hand. "Thank you for being here for me."

"Absolutely. I will see you at lunch," she said as she smiled to keep from crying and walked away.

Chente walked into second-period class and watched his friends immediately stop talking. He grabbed his usual seat behind Emma, took out his homework, and placed it on Ms. Rolando's desk.

"Hey, Chen, have you decided where you will be going to college in the fall?" asked Emma as Chente sat back down. "How many options do you have lined up?"

Chente smiled at Emma as she gently squeezed his hand. He was so grateful that Emma was being kind. He knew it was her way of trying to break the ice and showing her support.

"Nope, not yet. I hope to make that decision after spring break," he answered with a friendly nod. He took a deep breath. "What about you? Have you decided?"

"Yes, I have," she said and clapped her hands excitedly. "Mary Ann and I are going to be roommates at West Texas A&M University."

He looked at both girls and congratulated them. He was so pleased that everything had lined up for Emma so nicely. She deserved her shot at success.

"We are going to visit the campus over spring break." Mary Ann smiled as she finished brushing her hair at her desk. "I am so excited!"

"Good for you both. That sounds like fun." Chente nodded.

The tardy bell sounded, and the students got their journals out and started to write. Chente's heart deflated because none of his friends attempted to initiate conversation. They didn't even acknowledge him. His fears had been confirmed. He had known that coming out would change everything.

"Chen? How are you holding up?" whispered Carlos as he reached over and nudged Chente's shoulder with his pen.

Chente shrugged and nodded.

"Dude. It will be okay." Carlos smiled.

Felipe looked over at Carlos and Chente, shook his head, and turned around. Chente guessed he was upset with him.

"Miss Rolando, Carlos and his friend are whispering, and I can't concentrate on my writing," groaned Christina as she raised her hand.

"Are you kidding me?" asked Emma in utter disbelief as she slammed her pen on her desk. "All year long we have had to endure you chewing and smacking your bubble gum like a camel, and now you're complaining about a little whispering?"

Emma shook her head in complete disgust. Her gentle and quiet nature had been replaced by fiery spunk.

"I wasn't talking to you, *gringa*!" yelled Christina as turned around and glared at Emma.

"Whatever, Christina. Let me get my shades out of my purse so I can see past your bright-red lipstick," replied Emma as she rolled her eyes.

Emma was feisty and determined to hold her ground as the classroom burst into chaotic laughter, making Christina incredibly angry.

Miss Rolando clapped her hands and yelled at the class to settle down. "Obviously, everyone heard the intercom malfunction earlier this morning, and I think we need to address the elephant in the room," suggested the English IV teacher.

"What? No! That's crazy," replied Emma as she shook her head in disagreement. "With all due respect, it's really none of our business."

"It's up to Chen to talk about it if he wants to. Not us," said the senior class salutatorian.

Miss Rolando sighed and nodded in agreement. "Of course."

"I don't mind ... talking about it," replied Chente as he cleared his throat, took a deep breath, and exhaled. "It's true. I *am* gay."

He paused and tried to smile. His hands were shaking. "Does anyone have any questions, comments, or concerns I can clarify?"

Chente felt like he might as well get all the questions out in the open sooner rather than later.

The classroom remained quiet for a second or two, and then Carlos got up from his desk and gave Chente a hug. "You are still my best friend. I don't care about all that other stuff. You and I can talk about it later."

Chente's shoulders relaxed, and he exhaled. He was relieved Carlos was trying to understand.

"Chente, you are like the brother I never had. That will never change," said Felipe quietly as he cleared his throat and nervously looked around the room. "But why couldn't you tell me yourself?"

Chente said, "Felipe, it's just that—"

"I know I'm not smart like you," he said as he sniffed loudly. "Did you think I wouldn't understand?"

"No! Gosh, no, Felipe," said Chente. "I am sorry I made you feel that way, but it's nothing like that. You are like my brother from another mother."

Felipe's posture straightened, and he quickly wiped his eyes again.

"I wanted to tell you guys, but things got crazy busy with basketball and stuff," confessed the point guard. "So I decided to tell my close friends over spring break."

Chente went on to explain that he hadn't accepted he was gay until the last few months. He explained that Jimmy's death had forced him to realize a lot of different things about himself. He explained that he was still learning about himself and trying to come to terms with Jimmy's unexpected suicide and the death of his father.

"I never meant to disrespect any of you or our friendships," said Chente as he paused and looked at his friends. "I wanted to tell you, but I was a little scared that I would lose your friendship. Y'all have been my friends for a long time," said Chente as he shrugged. "Every single day it felt like I was swimming upstream and drowning above water—I couldn't breathe."

"I get it, Chen," said Tre', who had been sitting quietly in the back of the room, soaking in the information. "But I think we should be apologizing to you."

"I don't know what you mean," replied Chente as his face registered confusion.

"We are supposed to be your friends," remarked the six-six basketball star as he extended his arms wide and spoke very deliberately. "You shouldn't have to be making a speech about who you are. None of this should matter because you are our friend—gay or straight. You are still the same Chen."

Chente bit his bottom lip to keep from crying. He simply nodded at Tre' and smiled.

The room was awkwardly quiet as they all considered Tre's point of view. Felipe looked at Chente, put his fist up against his chest, and smiled. Chente knew that was his way of saying things were cool between them.

Christina's hand shot straight up in the air as she brushed her long, black hair to the back. She had been listening intently over the last few minutes. "Okay, so wait," replied the head cheerleader as she wrinkled her forehead and processed the information she had just heard. "So, like, Chen, like, you really don't like girls?"

The entire classroom moaned in unison.

Emma rolled her eyes and sighed. "Unbelievable!"

CHAPTER 18

Carlos and Felipe took on the role of Chente's bodyguards during lunch as the star point guard was sandwiched between the two in the lunch line. They were being overprotective and practically growled at anyone they thought might have given them a dirty look. Chente was sure a couple of freshmen had gone to the second serving line simply out of fear.

"Guys, y'all are acting like a couple of bullies," said Chente. "Y'all can't be rude to everybody in the serving line."

Felipe flexed his biceps and playfully glared at the other students. "Sure, we can. It's so easy."

"Chen, we aren't being bullies." Carlos laughed. "We just want everyone to know we got your back."

"And I appreciate that," said Chente, "but look at the second serving line."

All three boys turned around and saw that the second serving line was backed up to the cafeteria restrooms. They looked at each other and busted out laughing.

The three boys paid for their lunch and took a seat at their usual cafeteria table. Christina was already sitting down, eating her low-fat yogurt, and polishing her nails. She looked at Chente and studied him a little while. "So like, Chen, you never answered my question about liking girls."

Felipe and Carlos let out a groan.

"What?" she asked in a high-pitched voice. "Look, y'all, I just want to know. I want to get all educated on this LGBTQ stuff."

"I'm surprised that you even know your alphabet," said Carlos. He and Felipe started to laugh while Christina rolled her eyes and focused on Chente again.

"Seriously, though, I just want to know," she said.

Chente smiled. He was glad Christina was trying to find a connection with him and wanting to understand how her lifelong friend suddenly liked boys.

"Okay," said Chente, "I will try to explain it the best way I know how." He paused, looked at Christina, and smiled. "See, it's like you, Christina. You are an exceptionally beautiful girl. You could probably have any boy in this cafeteria."

"You know that's right," roared the head cheerleader as she snapped her fingers.

Carlos shook his head, rolled his eyes, and pretended to choke his neck and die. He knew Chente was stroking Christina's ego a little to let her down gently.

"Except for me," Chente said plainly. "There is something in my DNA that won't allow it. It's not who I am."

He looked at his friends, and he had their attention. He realized all three really wanted to understand what he was going through.

"When did you notice this?" asked Felipe.

"Yeah, like, did you just wake up one morning and decide that you liked guys?" asked the fashionista as she ate her yogurt.

Chente cleared his throat. He thought for a second and tried to explain himself. "You know, I guess subconsciously I always have kind of known I was different, but I always pushed those feelings away. I would get super focused on school or on basketball or on tennis. I didn't want to think about it."

Chente's friends were spellbound. They hung on to every word he said.

"When Jimmy died, I was forced to search my heart and evaluate my feelings," he said as he took a small bite of his pizza.

"Why? Was he your boyfriend?" asked Christina.

Carlos threw a french fry and hit her on the forehead.

"No." Chente chuckled under his breath. "Despite the rumors, Jimmy and I were only friends. I didn't care for him like that." Chente looked down at his food and started to play with it.

"So, like Chente, do you have a boyfriend or two or at least someone you like?" Christina smiled really big.

"*Oyes*, do you think you're Ellen or something?" protested Carlos.

Chente smiled at his friends. He was lucky to have them want to understand who he was slowly becoming. He was lucky that they were supportive and kind.

"No, Christina. I don't have a boyfriend or anything like that. For a minute I thought ..."

"Hey, guys," said Haven as she interrupted Chente's last comment. "I know this is sacred territory, but can Beau and I sit with y'all today, please?"

Chente smiled really big at Haven and gave her a quick wink. "Of course, you can. Please sit down," he said with a bit of surprise in his voice. "There is plenty of room here."

"Hey, Chen, how are you doing?" inquired Beau. The sophomore point guard was obviously nervous, but he was trying to be cool by sitting at the senior cafeteria table.

Chente nodded slowly and fist-bumped Beau. "Dude, I am great. Thanks for asking."

He looked at Haven and gave her a little hug. He really approved of his replacement. Chente sat back down and watched his friends laugh and banter back and forth. He felt loved.

Chente casually got up from the table to buy another sports drink. He grabbed the blue one and stood in line to pay when he saw Coach

Alvarez and Coach Doss enter the cafeteria. He quickly paid the cashier and turned to walk away when he ran into Ricky.

"Watch where you're going, gay boy," shouted Ricky. "I don't want all of your gayness to rub off on me."

Chente put his hands up in the air and avoided the Bennett boy.

The mindless chatter in the cafeteria quieted, and the students looked in their direction. He knew Ricky was trying to cause a scene in front of everybody.

"I apologize. I didn't see you there," replied Chente as he calmly took a deep breath and tried to discreetly walk away.

Ricky blocked him in and cornered Chente. There was anger and hate in the Bennett boy's eyes, and he taunted Chente. "Are you apologizing for being gay or for lying to everyone? You are such a fake!"

Chente noticed that students were turning around at their tables to see what was going on. He saw Carlos and Felipe walking up, and he waved them down. This was his fight.

Chente calmly shook his head and chuckled under his breath. "Oh, no way. I don't apologize for being gay. I know who I am."

He stepped onto the nearest cafeteria table, looked at the student body, and clapped his hands to get their attention. "Excuse me for interrupting your lunch, but I have an announcement to make. My name is Chente Jimenez, and I am gay. No shame here."

There was a little pause of confusion; some students were bewildered and shocked by the announcement. Then the cafeteria burst into loud applause and encouraging cheer.

Chente looked over to his friends, and they were jumping up and down and screaming for him, their arms up in the air with smiles of pride. And out of the corner of his eye, he spotted Coach Doss by the exit doors, clapping his hands and smiling. The coach lowered his head and discreetly left the cafeteria.

Chente jumped off the table and smiled at Ricky. "See, little boy, no shame and no hiding. You must have me confused with one of your imaginary girlfriends," said Chente as he smugly turned around and walked away to the cheer and laughter of his peers.

"You fucking faggot," shouted the Bennett boy and lunged for Chente while his back was turned, but he was met by Victor's right hook and crashed to the floor. The cafeteria got quiet and then erupted into cheers again.

Chente turned around and saw Victor standing over Ricky, who lay on the floor with a bloody nose while groaning in pain. Chente shook his head at Victor, who simply shrugged with no remorse.

"Victor? What did you do? You don't have to defend me," said Chente.

"Chente, really?" Victor laughed. "I wasn't defending your honor; I just don't like this piece of shit."

Victor had a big, impish grin as the cafeteria monitor escorted him to the office.

After all the excitement at lunch, the rest of the day seemed dull in comparison. Fifth and sixth periods were excruciatingly boring, and almost every student in the high school said hello to Chente in the hallway during passing periods. Victor was right; being gay was the new "in" thing.

Chente walked to seventh period, expecting to see Coach Doss, but instead Miss Young was using this period to speak to seniors about college stuff—applications, scholarships, and deadlines.

In the middle of class, Chente received a text message from Vanessa.

Vanessa: "Did you really come out to the entire high school?"
Chente: "Yes."
Vanessa: "What? Why? You okay?"
Chente: "Long story. Will talk later. I'm great."
Vanessa: "Valentin and I are headed home in a couple of hours. Family meeting at six p.m.?"
Chente: "What? Didn't know about meeting. See you then."

Before practice started, Coach Alvarez asked to speak to Chente in his office. Chente quickly got dressed and headed to Coach Alvarez's office.

"Coach, you wanted to see me?" asked Chente as he knocked on the office door. He was a little nervous about meeting with Coach Alvarez and hearing his thoughts about this crazy day.

"Hey, Chen. Come on in and shut the door," said Coach Alvarez as he paused the basketball video he was scouting. He inspected Chente top to bottom. "So how are you holding up? You okay?"

Chente nervously nodded and sighed. "It's been a long day, but I'm good."

"Tell me about it," said Coach Alvarez. "I sent Coach Doss home today. He was still pretty shaken up over the intercom fiasco."

Chente maintained his composure and nodded. *Coach Doss was shaken up?*

"Well, Coach, you don't have to worry about me." Chente nodded. "I am really good. I have really good friends, and we've talked through the whole thing."

"I am so glad to hear that. Good for you," said the basketball coach.

"Are you going to be okay?" asked Chente with a hint of doubt on his face.

"I'm not sure what you mean."

"Your starting point guard is gay. Are you going to be okay with that?" asked Chente as he extended his arms wide and smiled.

"Oh, I am completely fine with this. You are still the same Chente to me." The head coach paused and looked at Chente. "You know my door is always open, right?"

Chente nodded. "Yes. Thanks, Coach."

There was an awkward silence.

"Coach, I really want to win state, so if that's all, can I please go and practice my free throws?" asked Chente with an impish grin.

"Yes. Get out of here." Coach Alvarez smirked.

After practice, Chente drove Felipe and Carlos to Sonic for a quick snack and a drink. They pulled up and quickly ordered. Through the rearview mirror Chente watched Felipe text someone on his cell phone, while Carlos sat in the passenger's seat, looking through his backpack and searching for his wallet. Chente smiled. He loved how easy their friendship was.

In that moment Chente felt blessed to have them in his life. He knew he had dropped a personal bomb on them today, and they could have easily turned their backs on him and bolted. Instead, they embraced him and the unexpected news, and continued to be fiercely loyal friends.

Chente quietly thanked God for his blessings.

"Hey, guys, can I tell you something?" asked Felipe as he continued to play on his cell phone.

Carlos looked at Chente. "So are you going to come out too? Because if you are, then I will come out *también*, and we can all be gay together."

The three boys looked at each other and exploded into laughter.

"Carlos, you are such a *pendejo*," said Felipe as he reached over and hit him on the head. "No, I am serious. I need to tell you something, and I need advice."

Chente got serious. "Okay. We're listening. Is something the matter?"

Felipe squirmed a little bit in the back seat. "Guys, I really like Christina, but I don't know if she likes me. It's like she doesn't take me serious."

Carlos stopped laughing. He glanced at Chente and made a scary face. Christina was a big flirt and had always had a thing for Chente. He didn't want to see his friend get hurt.

"So does she know you like her? I mean, have you told her?" asked Carlos.

Felipe shook his head and said no.

"What's holding you back?" asked Chente. "I mean, she's pretty and you're handsome—it could work."

He was trying hard to be optimistic for his friend. Felipe was a good person with a kind heart. Christina would be lucky to have him as her boyfriend.

"Well, honestly, I always thought she liked you," whispered Felipe as he stared at Chente.

Why is there always an awkward silence after truth is spoken?

Chente froze and gave his friends a blank stare, but Carlos didn't hesitate for a second.

"Well, that just isn't going to happen, now is it? And you won't know how she feels if you just sit around crying about it all of the time. Just tell her how you feel."

Chente was grateful Carlos took the lead and gave Felipe a little bit of tough love.

"We can help you if you want," offered Chente in a desperate attempt to lift his spirits.

Felipe smiled really big. "You will?"

Chente and Carlos nodded in agreement. "Of course, we will help," said Chente. "You could send her some real red roses before we leave for San Antonio."

"And sign it 'Love, Your Secret Admirer' and keep her in suspense," added Carlos. "I'm telling you she will eat that up." Carlos started to laugh with devilish excitement.

Felipe nodded and smiled. He liked the idea.

"Okay. Sounds great, but I don't know how to do all that," he said nervously as the Sonic waitress dropped off their food and drinks.

"Let me take care of it tonight," said Chente. "I will place the order online. You can pay me back later this week. Okay?"

Felipe gave Chente an impish grin and nodded.

Chente reversed his car and drove away.

Chente pulled into the driveway of his house and parked next to Valentin's car. He took a deep breath and grabbed his backpack from the back seat. As he entered the front door of the house, he noticed the headlights of Violeta's car coming down the street. He already dreaded this family meeting.

"Hey, Valentin, when did y'all get here?" asked Chente as he walked into the living room.

The older brother was sitting on the recliner. He was on his phone, texting someone. Chente could tell he was miles away, in his own reality. He didn't want to be here, and he was quick to state the obvious.

"Hey, Chente, what's all of this about? Why are we meeting again?"

Chente shrugged. "I don't know. I didn't call this meeting."

"Well, I'm in medical school, and I can't just drop everything and come down whenever one of these family meetings are called." Valentin sounded tired and irritated. He went right back to his cell phone.

Vanessa and Victor appeared from the kitchen. Vanessa quickly walked over to Chente and gave him a big hug. "How are you doing? Are you okay?"

Chente didn't have a chance to answer because Violeta walked into the house. She was still in her professional clothes and obviously annoyed about this called meeting. "Okay? What's going on? Why are we meeting?" she asked.

Chente threw his arms up in the air. "Again, I don't know. I didn't call this meeting. I thought you did."

Violeta rolled her eyes. "Nope, not me."

Vanessa looked confused. "Then who did?"

"Where's Mom?" asked the oldest sister as she directed her questions at Chente. "Is she doing okay?"

Chente fired back, "Vi, I just pulled up from practice two minutes ago. How should I know?"

"Well, you *do* live here, Chente," replied Violeta as she placed her hands on her hip. It was apparent she was in a mood to argue, again.

"And you claim to be all-knowing Violeta, so why don't you know?" replied Chente as he gave his oldest sister a long stare and walked away. "And drop the prima donna attitude. It's getting old."

"You are my hero, Chente," whispered Vanessa as she covered her mouth and giggled.

"So, who called this meeting? Don't tell me I drove all this way for nothing," whined Valentin as he stood up from the recliner with an anxious face.

Victor stood in the middle of all of them and shouted, "SHUT UP!"

Everyone stood in shock—speechless.

"I called this meeting, and I need everyone to just be quiet," said the youngest brother as everyone gingerly took a seat.

Chente had never seen Victor like this. His little brother was focused, determined, and a bit upset. His forehead was wrinkled, his eyes were stressed, and his bottom lip began to quiver as he spoke.

"I have something to say, and I want to be heard," began the youngest Jimenez brother.

"Well, get on with it then," replied Violeta with a frigid stare. "Some of us have places to be."

Vanessa wanted to choke Violeta with her eyes, but the little brother tuned her out and continued. He was determined to speak his mind. "Something happened today that made me ashamed to be part of this family," said Victor and looked directly at Chente. "It was mean, calculated, and unforgivable."

He paused and took a deep breath. His eyes began to tear up.

"What happened, Vic?" asked Vanessa as she quickly scanned the room.

"Today Chen was outed to the entire school," announced Victor.

"What are you talking about?" asked Valentin as he glanced at Chente and then at Violeta.

Violeta gasped. "Exactly what does that mean?"

Chente calmly raised his hands, looked at all his siblings, and interjected, "That means I am gay, and it was announced to the entire school over the intercom." He took a deep breath and exhaled. He looked at Victor. "Is that what you are trying to say?"

Victor nodded and looked at his brothers and sisters.

Valentin and Violeta glanced at each other and said nothing, while Vanessa reached for Chente's hand and gave it a squeeze. "How are you doing?"

Chente smiled. "I am better than I thought I would be. My friends have been amazing and understanding and supportive."

"Wait. Hold on," shrieked Violeta. "Are you telling me you are gay? You-like-boys gay?"

"That's the only kind of gay there is Violeta," said Vanessa, smirking. The younger sister was finding pleasure tormenting the older one.

"No," said Violeta as she shook her head. "No. You can't be gay, Chente. What about Haven? She's your girlfriend."

The oldest sister stood up and rubbed her neck. She walked to the living room window and closed her eyes. She inhaled and then exhaled.

"I have never had a girlfriend," said Chente calmly.

Violeta turned around, faced her brother, and continued to shake her head in disbelief. "But Chente, you don't look gay. You don't talk gay." She nervously put her hands up to protest. "No. I won't believe it. It's just a phase you are going through, right?"

"Well, are you going through a heterosexual phase?" Chente promptly asked.

"Of course not." Violeta grimaced.

"And neither am I," said Chente plainly.

Vanessa reclined on the sofa and was having fun watching her older sister anguish over this announcement.

Valentin's reaction was quite different and more reflective. He watched and listened to his sibling's conversation and said nothing. He was still processing the news that his younger brother had been outed to the entire school.

"Okay, stop for minute," Valentin calmly said. "What do you mean that it was announced to the entire school? What exactly happened?"

Chente explained the intercom malfunction. Apparently there had been rumors that Chente and this teacher might be having inappropriate relations.

"Who was the teacher?" asked Valentin in utter disbelief.

"Coach Doss," answered Chente, and out of the corner of his eye he saw Vanessa glance over at him.

"Well, Chen, I hate to ask," said Valentin, "but there was no truth to that rumor, right?

Chente cleared his throat and shook his head. *I can't tell them right now.*

"Of course not," replied Victor. "Coach Doss is engaged to a woman and is going to be married in June."

"This is absolutely crazy. Complete madness," responded Vanessa.

"How did this rumor get started? I mean, who would do something like this?"

"I don't know. My guess is Mr. Bennett had a talk with Principal Timms. He hates me and wants Ricky to be the star of the basketball team," surmised Chente.

Vanessa nodded in agreement. He was probably right. It sounded like something Mr. Bennett would do.

"No. It wasn't Mr. Bennett," said Victor as he shook his head. He stood up and started to pace back and forth the living room floor.

Vanessa anxiously watched her youngest brother. "Vic? What do you know?"

"Victor? Do you know who started this rumor?" asked Valentin.

"I heard you talking to Principal Timms this morning after our meeting," said the little brother as he slowly turned and looked at Violeta. "You said Coach Doss was a bad influence for Chente, and you questioned his motives."

Victor was breathing hard, and he pointed at Violeta. "You said you feared that their relationship had crossed the line and had become inappropriate ... That's what you said ... I heard you."

Victor's words were a gut punch for Chente. He was dumbfounded for a couple of seconds before he looked at Violeta with hurt in his eyes. He slowly put his hands on his head and walked to the kitchen without saying a word. He had to be alone for a minute.

Valentin looked at Vanessa with his mouth wide open, completely speechless.

Violeta stood up and glared at Victor. "You little brat. I can't believe you were eavesdropping on a private conversation. How dare you!"

"That's all you have to say?" shouted Vanessa. "You dumb, self-centered bitch! Do you know what you just did to Chente? You fucking bitch!" screamed Vanessa as she lunged at Violeta and slapped her hard across the face. "I hate you!"

Valentin grabbed Vanessa and restrained her as she continued to scream. "He's your little brother! He's your flesh and blood! You are supposed to protect him! I hate you!"

Victor started to cry, and Chente reappeared from the kitchen and stood by his little brother as Violeta burst into tears and began to cry as well.

"That's what I was trying to do," she said pathetically. "I didn't know this would happen. I didn't know."

Vanessa kept screaming at the older sister. "This is all your fault, you stupid bitch!" yelled Vanessa as she broke free of Valentin's grip and rushed over to console Victor. "You are dead to me!"

"I didn't mean for this to happen. I promise," Violeta said through her tears. "I am sorry, Chente. I never meant this to happen."

Chente didn't say a word. He had lost his ability to speak. It was his sister and not Mr. Bennett who had caused all this drama. She was the reason he had been outed to the entire school. Violeta was the reason he would never be able to love Coach Doss.

Mrs. Jimenez walked in the front door with a horrified look on her face. "*Qué pasa aquí,*" she said as she closed the door behind her. "I could hear you as I walked up the driveway. What is happening?"

She looked around the room, but no one was talking. She quickly walked over and hugged Victor. "*Por que lloras, mijo*?"

Mrs. Jimenez panic was real, and she looked at Chente for answers. "*Mijo*, are you okay?" she asked. "Why is everyone crying? Will someone please answer me?"

"Hey, Mom," said Chente as exhaled. He got up, hugged her, and seated her on the couch. "I just came out to all my brothers and sisters."

"And you made them all cry?" asked the mother of five as she shook her head in complete confusion.

"Yeah, I guess it looks that way, right?" replied Chente as he looked around the room at his brothers and sisters and chuckled to himself. He carefully recounted to her the events of the day—the intercom mishap, his conversation with his friends, the lunchroom fight with Ricky, and Violeta's involvement.

Mrs. Jimenez gently put her hand on Chente's cheek and calmly smiled. "*Mijo*, it sounds like you had a long day. Are you doing okay?"

"Yeah, Mom, I am fine." Chente sighed. "What's done is done, right?"

"Oh no. No, no, no. It's not that simple," she said as her whole demeanor changed. She glared at Violeta and slowly shook her head. "*Y tú que tienes?* What is wrong with you?"

"Mom, let me explain," replied Violeta as she stood up to protest.

Mrs. Jimenez pointed at Violeta and gave her a stern look. Violeta got quiet; she knew her place.

"Violeta, what were you thinking?" said Mrs. Jimenez. "I am the mother, not you. If you were worried, then you should have talked to me."

"I was thinking of the family and our reputation," responded Violeta. "I was trying to preserve our good name," she said as she wiped the tears from her eyes.

Valentin was alarmed by his sister's response. He placed his hand on his forehead and began to gently shake his head back and forth. "Really, Vi? That's what concerned you? That's what you were trying to do—preserve our good name?"

"What are you trying to say?" asked Vanessa, who was ready to use her older sister as a punching bag again.

"Of course," Violeta responded to Valentin. "One's reputation is especially important in a small town. Daddy would always say that. Remember?"

"I kind of remember that," interjected Vanessa as she tilted her head to the right and pretended to think aloud. "Was that before or after you got pregnant and had an illegitimate child?"

"Nesh, don't go there," said Chente.

"You know she's implying that being gay tarnishes one's reputation, right?" asked Vanessa as she looked at her little brother. Vanessa was ready to go to war—civil war.

"I know what she means, but she's wrong," replied Chente as he quietly looked away.

"Guys, you know Daddy is rolling over in his grave right now, right?"

stated Violeta, showing no remorse for her callous comments. She stood firmly on her position.

"You shut your mouth right now, Violeta," screamed Mrs. Jimenez. "Don't you dare speak on behalf of your father! Do you hear me?"

Everyone was startled by their mother's emotional outburst.

"Mom," said Violeta in a weak voice.

"No! No! No!" screamed Mrs. Jimenez. "Don't you ever disrespect your father's memory like that!"

Violeta began to cry, and she ran out the door and drove off.

The four remaining siblings remained quiet for a few minutes as they huddled around their mother and tried to console her shattered spirit.

"Mom, are you going to be okay?" asked Valentin as he hugged her and softly told her to quit crying. "Everything is going to be fine."

"Chente is strong, and he's going to be fine," said the oldest brother as he carefully watched Chente, who stood by the living room window. "And Vi, well … she will … I don't know." Valentin sighed.

"Please, don't say she will learn." Mrs. Jimenez giggled as she wiped her eyes. "*Por que tú ya la conoces*. You know your sister."

Valentin chuckled under his breath and quietly agreed with his mother's assessment. "Victor, please get Mom a glass of water," he said.

Vanessa gingerly walked over and stood by Chente. "A penny for your thoughts, little brother," she said as she hugged him from behind.

"You know I feel sorry for Vi," said Chente thoughtfully. "She really can't see the harm she did here today. She really can't."

"Because she is more comfortable with blame than with accepting responsibility," said Vanessa in an irritated voice. "She's always been like that."

Chente thought for a second and smiled. "Perhaps. But you know she kind of did me a favor though. Her actions this morning forced me to face my truth, and I am so relieved that there is no more hiding and pretending."

"Oh my gosh, I am going into sugar shock," said Vanessa as she grabbed her throat. She smiled at her little brother. "Leave it to you to find the silver lining."

Valentin walked up to Chente and gave him an unexpected hug. "I love you just the same. Just be happy, brother," he said. "Maybe we can talk really soon."

Chente nodded.

"Thank you."

"But Mom, I have to leave. Medical school is kicking my butt this semester," announced Valentin with a mild groan. He and Vanessa said their goodbyes and headed back to Lubbock.

Mrs. Jimenez went to the kitchen and couldn't decide what to cook for dinner.

"Let's just go get some Sonic," suggested Victor.

Mrs. Jimenez considered the suggestion and put up the pans. "Sound good to me," she said decidedly. "I'm going with y'all."

"I'm driving. Come on, Chen, let me drive," shouted Victor.

"Only if you tell Mom about lunch," bargained Chente as he dangled the keys in front of his little brother.

"Okay," he said as he took a deep breath spoke really fast. "Mom, I punched Ricky Bennett in the face during lunch because he was making fun of Chente. I may have broken his nose." Victor squinted as he anticipated his mother's wrath.

"That's good, *mijo*," she said as she made her way to the front door. "He's a little jerk and probably deserved it."

Chente and Victor grabbed their jackets and looked at each other in amazement.

"Oh, and Chente is still going to drive us to Sonic, because I want to get there and back safely." Mrs. Jimenez giggled under her breath. She was still in charge.

CHAPTER 19

"I can't believe we made it to the state tournament," Chente said as he made himself a bean and chorizo taco. "I am so pumped!"

"Yes, Chente, we are all proud of you. *Necisitas comer,*" instructed Mrs. Jimenez. "You are not going anywhere until you sit down and eat."

Chente playfully stood at attention and saluted his mother. "I packed a couple of dozen of breakfast tacos for the boys. These two bags are for your coaches—*pobrecitos*. They work so hard too."

Chente casually cleared his throat as he thought about Coach Doss. He had tried very hard to minimize face time with Coach Doss over the last couple of days. He told Principal Timms that he thought it would be best for everyone that he no longer assist Coach Doss during first period. Principal Timms agreed and understood.

During government class, Chente focused on his studies and never asked any questions. At basketball practice, Chente stayed close to Coach Alvarez and avoided Coach Doss as much as he could. He stopped going to rehab for his leg injuries and showered at home after practice.

However, despite his efforts to erase Coach Doss from his everyday life, Chente's soul was broken without him.

"So, are you ready for me to drop you off at school?" asked Victor, who walked in the kitchen in his pajamas and house slippers. His hair was sticking up in every direction, and it looked like a West Texas tumbleweed.

"Yes. Let's go. I don't want to be late," said Chente. "Coach Alvarez said the bus for San Antonio would leave at six forty-five sharp.

Victor grabbed Chente's suitcase and walked outside to the car. Chente snatched the breakfast tacos and kissed his mom goodbye. He and Victor left. They picked up Felipe and Carlos along the way.

When Chente arrived at the high school, the three boys loaded their suitcases on the bus and reserved their bus seats for the ride to San Antonio. Chente waved at Victor as he drove away and entered the gym. Chente walked to the coaches' office to drop off the breakfast tacos and ran into Coach Doss.

"Hey, Chen," said Coach Doss.

"Good morning, sir. Coach Alvarez?" asked the basketball player without making eye contact.

Coach Doss coughed nervously and pointed to Principal Timms's office. "He's in a meeting with Principal Timms and Mr. Bennett."

"He is. Why?" asked Chente, breaking his own rule and looking at the coach in front of him. Instinctively Chente became nervous.

"Daddy Bennett is upset that Ricky is suspended from the team for fighting, even though it's in the athletic code of conduct that Mr. Bennett signed at the start of the season."

Coach Doss shook his head and let out a deep sigh.

Chente had a feeling this scenario wouldn't end well. Mr. Bennett had a lot of money and friends on the school board. He was stubborn, opinionated, and used to getting things his way. He knew Coach Alvarez was in a serious battle in Principal Timms's office.

"Well, my mom made breakfast for y'all. She thought y'all might be hungry," said Chente and handed him both bags of breakfast tacos.

"One bag is for Coach Alvarez, and the other one is for you."

"Thank you, Chen. As usual, your mom was right. I am so hungry," replied the assistant basketball coach.

"Yes, sir, my mom is great," said the point guard as he awkwardly nodded and turned to walk away.

"Hey, Chen, don't leave just yet," said Coach Doss. "I need to talk with you." His voice sounded strained, fragile, and desperate. Almost as though he were in pain.

Chente stopped but didn't turn to face his basketball coach. He slowly shook his head and pleaded softly. "Please don't do this to me again." The pain and hesitation in Chente's voice were apparent.

"I'm sorry, Chen. I am so sorry," whispered the coach as he walked away.

Chente rushed into the locker room, found a stall, and locked himself in to be alone. He needed to regroup. After a few minutes, he exited the stall, went to the sink, and splashed cold water on his face. He wanted to erase any trace of hurt and tears.

"Chen, are you feeling okay?" asked Carlos.

"Yeah, I'm just splashing some water on my face to wake up," lied Chente.

Carlos gave him a suspicious look and nodded. "Okay … well, we're leaving in three minutes. Come on. You know Coach Alvarez won't put up with tardiness."

The two boys walked out of the gym and ran into Ricky and Mr. Bennett. Ricky's nose still looked like an oversized red balloon, and Mr. Bennett wore a scowl. It was obvious he was upset.

Carlos and Chente avoided any eye contact with the father and son, and hurried to board the school bus. Mr. Bennett deliberately shouted at Chente as he boarded. "Mr. Jimenez, I promise. I will get the last laugh."

"We sure will, you faggot," yelled Ricky.

Chente just looked at them and shook his head.

Felipe rolled down his window as the bus was leaving and shouted, "Hey, Ricky! You look like Bozo the Clown!"

The basketball team erupted in laughter as the bus drove away.

The boys slept on the bus until they stopped in Big Springs for their first restroom break. Felipe ran over to Carlos and Chente, who were stretching their legs behind the bus.

"Look what Christina just sent me," Felipe said as he held up a picture of Christina holding a bouquet of roses. "She wants to know if I am her secret admirer. What should I do?"

"Why do you sound like a scared little girl, Felipe?" asked Carlos.

Chente chuckled under his breath. "What Grumpy means is, what do you want to do?"

Felipe looked completely lost and scared, and he didn't know what to say. "Come on, Chen, just tell me what you would do if you were me. Please?"

Carlos began to laugh at seeing Felipe act so pathetically. "You know, I would be straight up with her and tell her the truth. I would tell her how you feel," he said with added confidence. "Take a chance. I have a feeling that the results will be positive."

Felipe nodded in agreement, smiled really big, and walked away. "Thanks, buddy."

"*Oyes*, now you're playing Cupid?" asked Carlos as Coach Alvarez and Coach Doss walked up behind them, discussing something quietly.

"Hey, Chen, what did Mr. Bennett yell at you when you were getting on the bus?" asked Coach Alvarez.

Chente could tell Coach Álvarez was a little stressed and had probably gotten little sleep over the last few days. Chente looked at both coaches and shrugged. "I don't know. Something like he would have the last laugh," replied Chente as he rolled his eyes. "I think he was just mad that Ricky wasn't going to go to the state tournament."

"It sounds like a threat to me," said Coach Doss, and he looked at Coach Alvarez and waited for his thoughts. Coach Alvarez thought for a second, shook his head, and grew more concerned.

"What is it?" asked Chente as he watched both coaches' body language.

"I think you should go ahead and report it," suggested the assistant coach, and he put his hand on Chente's shoulder. "We have to protect Chen."

"What are you talking about? Protect Chen from what?" questioned Carlos.

"From whom?" snapped Coach Doss.

"Whoa … whoa … whoa," exclaimed Chente as he held his hands up. "Can someone please tell me what's going on here? Y'all are freaking me out."

Coach Alvarez gave Chente a concerned look and pulled him aside and away from the bus, with Coach Doss and Carlos following closely behind.

"I am sorry, Chen. I don't mean to scare you, but Mr. Bennett was extremely angry when we suspended Ricky from the basketball team."

"Okay, but what does that have to do with me?" asked Chente with an agitated look on his face.

"He blames you for the suspension," said Coach Doss.

Chente was flabbergasted. He couldn't wrap his mind around the idea that he was being blamed for Ricky's actions. "Ricky is a jerk by his own merit. I have nothing to do with that."

Coach Alvarez agreed. "Yes, we know that, but Mr. Bennett doesn't see it that way and is going to find someone to blame." The basketball coach shrugged and sighed. "For whatever reason, Chen, he is blaming you."

Chente let out a heavy sigh and shook his head. He knew exactly why he was being targeted, and it had nothing to do with playing basketball, not really. It was because Chente was gay and Mr. Bennett was a twisted homophobic racist, who used his wealth and status to bully and terrorize people around him.

Chente was tired of taking the high road. This time he wasn't going to back down. If Mr. Bennett wanted to start a fight, Chente was ready and willing and determined to beat him at his own game.

"Chen, are you okay?" asked Carlos, who was watching him closely.

"Let him blame me because I really don't care anymore. I refuse to be scared of Mr. Bennett. If he thinks I'm going to flinch, he's wrong,"

Chente's words were razor sharp. No more Mr. Nice Guy. Chente was on the verge of snapping.

Coach Doss looked at the basketball star and nodded.

"It's not that simple, Chen," said Coach Alvarez. "Mr. Bennett is very wealthy and very influential throughout the state. He has friends everywhere."

"What are you saying, Coach?" asked Carlos with a trace of fear in his voice.

"I'm just saying he's a powerful man, and he made some very cruel comments and accusations this morning in Principal Timms's office."

Chente had grown tired of the conversation and wasn't listening.

"I don't care. I am not going to be afraid for the rest of my life. I refuse to give Mr. Bennett any power over me. He's a bully, and so is his son."

"Chente it's just that—"

"No, Coach Alvarez, with all due respect, I am done with this conversation. We have all worked too hard to get here, and I will be damned if I let Mr. Bennett and Ricky ruin it for me," said Chente, and he stormed off.

The three of them stood there quietly. They knew Chente was right, but they also knew Mr. Bennett was a real threat.

"Carlos, are you rooming with Chente in San Antonio?" asked Coach Alvarez.

Carlos nodded. He knew why Coach Alvarez was asking.

"I won't let him out of my sight," Carlos said. "I promise. Felipe and I will have his back."

"I will make sure that our room is next to theirs at the hotel," added the assistant coach.

Carlos nervously bit his bottom lip. "Coach, do you really think Mr. Bennett will try to do something to hurt Chen?"

"Yes. I am afraid so. He was really angry," said Coach Alvarez as he slowly nodded.

The next day the basketball team got up early, ate breakfast, and boarded their school bus. Coach Alvarez had planned for an early-morning practice at Alamo Heights High School. He wanted to be sure to review the game plan for their semifinal opponent, Shelbyville.

"They are going to be very disciplined and well coached," said

Coach Alvarez. "They are more of a half-court team and won't make many mistakes. We are going to have to beat them because they won't beat themselves."

"So like Vega?" asked Felipe.

"Exactly like Vega," replied Coach Alvarez. "We are going to press and try to get them out of their comfort level. We want to run the ball."

"Do they play man or zone on defense?" asked Carlos.

"Mostly a match-up zone, but they will run a man defense every now and again to shake it up," said Coach Doss. The assistant coach had been breaking down film and helping Coach Alvarez scout all week.

"Bottom line, guys," said Coach Alvarez. "We should win tomorrow. We are better than them. We are quicker and a lot more athletic." He looked at his team and smiled. "We are the best team in the state—I have no doubt."

After practice, the basketball team went to the Alamodome and watched the afternoon session of the state tournament. They would be playing in the same gym the next day. It was a good opportunity for everyone to get a feel for the venue, the size of crowd, and the magnitude of the moment.

"Where are you going?" asked Carlos as he watched Chente get up from his seat.

"I'm going to get something to drink. Wanna go with me?" asked Chente. "I don't need a bodyguard, but I don't want you to get into trouble with Coach Alvarez," he sarcastically added and rolled his eyes.

"*Oyes*, don't be a hater." Carlos laughed as he tagged Chente on the shoulder. "We just want to be sure our Manu Ginobili is safe."

Carlos tagged Felipe's arm. "Do you want to go?"

Felipe was glued to his cell phone and busy texting like a madman. "No. *Por favor*, just bring me back a Dr. Pepper and some popcorn."

"Who are you texting?" asked Chente as he looked over his shoulder.

Felipe smiled really big and gave them a wink. "My girl, Christina."

"Oh, she's your girl now?" asked Chente with a surprised voice. He chuckled under his breath. "Man, those roses must have been laced with magic."

"Does she know she's your girl?" asked Carlos.

"She will when we get back," replied Felipe with a confident wink, and he lowered his baseball cap and went back to his cell phone.

"Okay, Casanova," said Chente. "We'll be back in a couple of minutes."

Chente and Carlos made their way down the aisle, out to the foyer, and to the concession stand. The lines were long, so Carlos decided to go to the restroom while Chente stood in line and waited.

Chente was excited to be at the state tournament. He looked around and soaked it all in. This was something he had dreamed of doing since he played Little Dribblers in elementary.

"Hey, country boy, what are you looking at?" a familiar voice said.

Chente turned around to find Henry Hamilton grinning at him.

"Hey, buddy." Chente laughed as he gave him a quick fist bump. "What are you doing here?"

"I decided to skip school and come watch you play." The boy from Kress chuckled.

"Well, I am sure that was a tough decision to make—Chemistry, English IV … or go to the state basketball tournament in San Antonio," teased Chente as he playfully weighed the options in both hands.

"Actually, it was an easy decision," insisted Henry. "I'm one of your biggest fans when we are not playing against each other."

"You mean when I am not beating you," joked the boy from Avalon.

They both laughed and continued to talk. Chente noticed Henry was wearing a walking cast on his right leg and casually asked about it.

"The X-rays showed a small hairline fracture, and I am wearing this as a precautionary measure." Henry groaned. "Trust me, I will be ready to go for spring tennis."

"So when I beat you on the tennis court, you'll lean on this as your excuse—right?" Chente laughed.

"Whatever," said Henry, and he playfully nudged Chente's shoulder.

Both boys just stood there for moment and looked at each other. There was an easiness between them Chente had failed to notice before.

He liked Henry, but up until now he'd never noticed Henry's very handsome features—the green eyes, high cheekbones, and pouty lips.

"Mr. Hamilton, what in the heck are you doing here?" asked Coach Doss as he walked up behind him. "Are you hurt?"

Chente detected a hint of irritation in Coach Doss's voice.

Henry gave him a friendly smile and explained that the boot on his foot was to allow his ankle to properly heal and that it was kind of a nuisance. "But I will have it off in about ten days, and that is plenty of time to challenge Chente in spring tennis."

"Oh, wow. So y'all play tennis, too?" asked Coach Doss as he looked at both of them.

"Yes, sir. We're frenemies on the tennis court too," chuckled Henry as he glanced at Chente, who had become oddly quiet. "We have had some epic three set matches. We go way back."

"Wow, that's great," muttered Coach Doss under his breath.

Henry's cell phone buzzed.

"Hey, my folks are looking for me. I got go, Chen," said Henry as he reached around and gave Chente a big hug. "It was really good seeing you."

"Wait, before you leave, tell me how your mom is doing," said Chente as he grabbed Henry's arm.

Henry nodded slowly and looked relieved. "She's good. She's in full remission. We are incredibly grateful. Thanks for asking."

Chente squeezed his shoulder and smiled. "Be sure to tell her I said hi."

"I will and good luck tomorrow. Y'all got this." Henry smiled and playfully nudged Chente as he turned to walk away. "Hey, wait. I almost forgot." Henry beamed. "My family is going to Ruidoso for spring break. Harry and my parents want to do some skiing."

"Oh, wow, that sounds like fun." Chente nodded as he moved forward with the concession stand line. It was barely crawling.

"Really? Then come with us. I can't ski," groaned Henry as he pointed at his foot, "but we can ride snowmobiles or go dog sledding. What do you say?"

"Seriously? Yeah, okay," replied Chente as he gave it some thought. "Let me get through this weekend, and I will call you next week."

Henry's face lit up, and he smiled. He gave Chente a long, thoughtful stare. "Promise?"

Chente nodded. "Of course. It really does sound like fun."

Henry waved at Coach Doss, who was standing nearby, and limped away.

Chente turned around, saw Coach Doss's dejected facial expression, and wondered what that was about. He continued to look over the crowd, hoping to see Carlos returning from the restroom.

"It was good to see Henry, huh?" asked Coach Doss as he carefully watched Chente's reaction.

Chente shrugged and casually nodded. "Hope he gets that cast off his foot really soon." He wasn't in the mood for small talk. He wanted Carlos to hurry up and return from the restroom.

"Henry likes you," whispered Coach Doss.

Chente looked at Coach Doss, rolled his eyes, and sighed. "We've been friends for a long time. He has a nice family."

The silence was excruciating.

"No, I mean he *likes* you more than just as a friend." Coach Doss's voice was faint, distant, and agonizing. It was almost as though his heart was being tortured by speaking those words.

Chente carefully studied Coach Doss's face. "I don't understand you," he finally said. "Now you're jealous?"

"Yes, I am," whispered the assistant basketball coach. "I want to be able to hug you in public. I want to be the one to take you away to the mountains for spring break." His voiced cracked. "It's just not fair."

That comment ripped out Chente's soul. He shook his head and started to walk away. He didn't have the energy to have a conversation to nowhere.

Chente's pain and hurt resurfaced, and he went straight for the jugular. "Yeah, well, you're getting married in June, right? I mean, that's what you announced to the whole high school."

Coach Doss smiled sadly and shook his head. "Chen, you have no idea how sorry I am for that. No idea. How I wish I could have that moment in time back, to do it all over again—but I can't. It will haunt me the rest of my life."

The concession line moved forward, and Coach Doss was shoved into Chente. Their faces were inches apart. Their chemistry was electric.

"Here comes Carlos," observed the basketball coach and with a heavy heart. He slowly turned and walked away.

"The lines at the restrooms are super long too," groaned Carlos as he continued to dry his wet hands on his jeans. "Let's get something to eat. I am starving."

"Yeah, me too." Chente nodded as he turned around and watched Coach Doss slowly walk away.

Swish. Nothing but net.

Chente hit his second three-pointer from the top of the key to bump their lead to six. The Avalon Longhorns got off to a quick start against Shelbyville and were following their game plan perfectly. As a result, they were leading at the end of the first quarter. Avalon 16–Shelbyville 10.

Beau was playing with a newfound confidence and was making great decisions with the basketball. Tre' was a dominant force in the paint on both ends of the floor, and Avalon's pressing man-to-man defense was disrupting Shelbyville's offensive flow. The Longhorns were able to capitalize on a couple of early turnovers to take the lead.

"Okay, guys, good job for the most part," yelled Coach Alvarez. "We need to contest every shot they put up and then block out. I want every rebound. No second-chance points."

The boys nodded in agreement and jogged out to begin the second quarter.

"Just play," said Chente. "You are doing a good job. No fear!"

Chente was giving Beau a last-minute pep talk as they walked to the other end of the basketball court to prepare for their man-to-man press. The Shelbyville players jogged onto the court as well and prepared to inbound the basketball and resume play.

Chente found his player to guard and got into his defensive position.

The player looked at him and pushed him to the floor. "You are too close to me, you faggot."

The official blew his whistle and called a technical foul on the Shelbyville player.

Carlos and Beau ran over to Chente and helped him up. Felipe walked over to the Shelbyville player and gave him a long stare. Coach Alvarez called a time-out and summoned his players over to a huddle by the bench.

"Chen, are you okay?" asked Beau. "What happened?"

Chente just shook his head in disbelief and stared at the Shelbyville player as he walked to the bench. "He called me a faggot and shoved me to the floor."

Coach Doss handed him a water bottle, and Chente took a swig.

Coach Alvarez paused and looked at him closely. "Are you going to be okay?"

Chente nodded and looked at his teammates. His eyes were on fire. "Yeah, I'm good," he said. "I am going to show them that this faggot can play some basketball."

Chente gave them a confident grin, walked back on the court, and calmly sank his two free throws.

The Avalon Longhorns completely dominated the second quarter. The homophobic comment made by the Shelbyville player fueled a fire in the hearts of the entire team, and Shelbyville was made to pay for it. Avalon put on a clinic and took a giant lead into halftime. Avalon 35—Shelbyville 18.

Coach Doss and Coach Alvarez were quietly discussing something as they entered the locker room at halftime. Coach Alvarez looked upset and irritated. He quickly glanced at Chente, mumbled something to Coach Doss, and sent him on his way.

"That's what I'm talking about!" he yelled at the team and clapped. "Great job! That's what I call teamwork. In fact, that's teamwork at its best!"

"That's right," said Tre', and he walked around the locker room and gave everyone a high five. "See what we can do when we work together as a team?"

"Now we just have to match the same intensity in the second half," added Coach Alvarez, "and we will be in the championship game."

The entire team erupted into a cheer. Ricky Bennett's absence in the locker room had lifted the ominous cloud of negativity. Everything felt fresh and exciting.

"There is one thing I want to caution you about before the second half begins," warned Coach Alvarez, and he quickly glanced at Chente. "Apparently, there have been several postings on social media about Chente."

Everyone stared at Chente in confusion.

"What does that mean?" asked Carlos.

"Well, someone has leaked information about Chente's sexuality to every media outlet," said Coach Alvarez. "Facebook, Twitter, Instagram. All have received anonymous information about Chente being gay."

Chente shook his head in disbelief. This was the work of Ricky Bennett and his dad. They were angry with Coach Alvarez's decision to follow the rules and suspend Ricky from the basketball team for fighting. They were trying hard to distract the basketball team and embarrass Chente in the process. They were playing dirty.

Chente looked at his teammates and apologized.

"What? Why are you apologizing?" asked Felipe. "There is no way we would be at the state tournament without you on our team."

"Exactly! No apologies needed," said Tre'.

Carlos stood up and began to preach about team unity and pride. "We are more than a team. We are brothers, and we stick together no matter what!"

"If being gay will make me play like Chen, then heck, maybe I want to be gay too," said Beau with an impish grin.

The locker room explode with laughter, and the tension was gone.

"That's good," said Coach Alvarez. "No room for distractions. Don't let them get into your head. Just play ball."

The Avalon Longhorns returned to the basketball court in the second half more determined and more focused. The team was in sync, and they put up a united front. Nothing was going to derail them from winning this basketball game.

The inside/outside combination of Tre' and Chente was simply too much for Shelbyville to handle. When they focused on shutting down the paint, Chente drained a couple of three- pointers, forcing them to rethink their defensive strategy. When the final buzzer sounded, Avalon had easily won. Avalon 59—Shelbyville 41.

After the game, a couple of local TV stations wanted to interview Coach Alvarez, Tre', and Chente. After some casual congratulation remarks, the TV reporter asked Coach Alvarez about their next opponent, Thorndale.

"Well, we are going to play hard and see what happens," replied Coach Alvarez. "They have a good basketball program, and we have a lot of respect for them."

The TV reporter turned his attention to Chente, and he read out some stats, "Twenty-one points and five assists. I'd say that's a fairly good night, right?"

Chente smiled for the camera. "You know, I am just glad that we came out with a win. I think we played very well. It was one of our best games this season." He was smooth and humble. He was always sure to put the team first.

"Well, we've been getting reports from several media outlets that you came out to your entire high school a few days ago. Would you like to comment on that?" asked the TV reporter as he cleared his throat.

Chente was stunned to silence. Did the reporter really ask him if he was gay on TV?

Tre' got in front of Chente and shielded him. "Dude, really? Man, you are crazy! Do you report for *The Jerry Springer Show*?"

Chente could hear the irritation in Tre's voice.

"The real news story here," Tre' said, "is that we are in the state championship game."

CHAPTER 20

Tre' and Chente hurried into the locker room, followed closely by Coach Alvarez and Coach Doss. What should have been one of the most exciting day of their lives had been clouded by homophobic gossip and trash news reporting.

"I can't believe the reporter asked that question," screamed Coach Doss. "I want to know the local TV station so I can report him to his supervisor."

"It's all about getting good ratings," said Coach Alvarez. "Let's not overreact. Chen, you okay?"

Chente nodded and smiled. He was a little stunned but oddly enough, not too bothered.

Coach Alvarez looked at Tre' and patted him on the back. "That was quick thinking on your part. Your answer was perfect."

Tre' looked at Chente and smiled. "Thanks, Coach. I am going to hit the showers."

As Tre' walked away, Carlos and Felipe ran over to Coach Doss and showed him something on their cell phone. Coach Doss put his hands on his head and looked irritated. He motioned Coach Alvarez over and whispered something. He glanced at Chente and gave him a forced smile.

"It has to be Ricky," said Felipe as he shook his head in anger. "He is such a little bastard. I am going to beat his ass when I get home."

Carlos quickly interjected, "Simmer down, dude. It's an anonymous posting. It could be anyone."

"Do you really believe that?" replied Felipe. "Please do not tell me you're that dumb."

Carlos waved off Felipe and looked at Coach Doss and Coach Alvarez. He was waiting to hear their thoughts on the matter. Both coaches were reading the posted comments off Carlos's cell phone and wearing anxiety on their faces.

Chente stood in the background and watched quietly.

Coach Doss walked away after he was done reading. "I am with Felipe. These anonymous postings reek of Ricky and Mr. Bennett."

"I agree," Coach Alvarez said calmly, "but there is no way of proving it."

Coach Alvarez thought for a second as Coach Doss and Felipe continued to encourage each other's anger for the Bennetts. "I just don't want this to be a distraction for the basketball team."

"What about, Chen?" asked Coach Doss. "He's a sitting duck for more homophobic bullying."

"No, he's not." said Carlos, "We can make sure he's safe on the basketball court."

"That's right. No one will touch him on our watch." Felipe nodded as he clenched his fists like he wanted to box.

"Oh my gosh. Listen to yourselves," exclaimed Coach Doss. "We aren't in Pakistan. We aren't at war. We are simply trying to win a state championship."

"Then what should we do?" asked the head coach.

Coach Doss shook his head. "I don't know. Maybe we should report this to the UIL authorities?"

"And tell them what?" replied Coach Alvarez. "Do we tell them about the anonymous postings outing one of our basketball players? Will that make the situation better or worse?"

Coach Doss looked deflated. "I just wanted to protect Chen."

"We all do," said Carlos.

"Guys, stop it already. I am fine. I don't need anyone to protect me," replied Chente as he exhaled. He had heard enough.

"I think everyone is just trying to help," countered Coach Alvarez with a serious facial expression.

"I know. I appreciate it too," replied Chente with a nod. "Why are we worried about any of this? The posting simply says I am gay, right?"

Carlos nodded.

The point guard nonchalantly shrugged. "Guys, I *am* gay. No harm done, right?"

Coach Doss gazed at Chente with amazement and pride.

Chente looked at Coach Alvarez with a mischievous grin. "With your permission, I have an idea that will end all of this—and beat Ricky and Mr. Bennett at their own game."

Coach Alvarez cautiously nodded and hesitated. "Okay. What is it?"

Chente shook his head and exhaled. "Nope. You and Coach Doss have a lot of work ahead of you to prepare for Thorndale. I've got this. Trust me. I just need to make a few phone calls."

Coach Alvarez said, "But Chen—"

"Please, Coach Alvarez, trust me. Everything will be okay," replied Chente with a confident nod. "You just need to focus. We are here to win a state championship. You and Coach Doss, get to work. Leave the rest up to me."

The Avalon basketball team strolled down the sidewalks of the San Antonio River Walk, enjoying the colorful lights and the sound of mariachi music surrounding them. Coach Alvarez had made early dinner reservations for the entire team, and the players were soaking up the Mexican-influenced culture of the Alamo City.

"I could totally live here," said Felipe. "I like the weather, I like the culture, but mostly, I really like all the pretty girls." He looked at Carlos and Chente and burst into laughter.

"*Oyes*, so what about Christina?" asked Carlos. "I thought she was the one your heart desired. *Qué pasó?*"

"It's all good," replied Felipe. "I can looky but no touchy."

They walked into the restaurant, and after a short wait, the hostess escorted them to their table. Chente quietly excused himself to the restroom, and a few seconds later, Coach Doss followed.

They ran into each other in the next room while Chente was listening to a mariachi band performing for the restaurant and singing to the guests as they ate. "Chen, what are you doing?" asked Coach Doss.

Chente motioned for him to keep quiet. They both listened. Chente was completely mesmerized by the mariachi vocalist. "This was my dad's favorite mariachi song. He and I used to sing it all of the time. I must have sung that song over a hundred times," he softly reminisced. "It is such a sad song though."

"Dude, you can sing? Like really?" asked Coach Doss with hint of surprise in his voice.

"A little bit, but I'm not that good." Chente cringed as he continued to watch and listen to the female vocalist. "It was something my dad and I had in common—something we did together. We both love the passion in mariachi music."

"It's beautiful. What is she singing about?" asked Coach Doss.

"The song is called 'Volver, Volver,'" replied Chente as he glanced at his coach. "She's consumed by madness. She longs to return to the man she loves, but she can't."

Coach Doss looked at Chente. "Why can't she return?"

Chente shrugged. "I don't know. She just can't." He listened for a little longer, then silently walked away, leaving Coach Doss listening to the impassioned vocalist with a newfound appreciation for mariachi music.

When Coach Doss returned, he had a surprise waiting for him at the table.

"Hi, babe," said Bella with a huge smile. "Surprise!"

Coach Doss's fiancée got up and threw her arms around Coach Doss, giving him a big kiss. A couple of players quietly laughed at Coach Doss, because the assistant coach appeared to be more upset than happy to see her.

Chente casually turned and watched the couple from the end of the table as he dipped his tortilla chip into the cheese dip and tossed into his mouth. He sensed Coach Doss's displeasure and awkwardness.

"Bella? What are you doing here?" asked Coach Doss.

"What do you mean, you big silly? I am here to offer support and to watch Avalon win their first state championship tomorrow." She turned around and gave Coach Alvarez a smile.

"Well, we appreciate all the support we can get," Coach Alvarez said with a smile.

Coach Doss looked displeased. "Where are you staying? You know I am working, right?" whispered the assistant basketball coach.

"Will you join us?" Coach Alvarez got up and added a chair to the table, making room for Bella to sit down.

"I would love to," replied Bella. "I am staying at the same hotel as you. Your parents and I flew down here to watch the game."

"My parents are here? Are you kidding me?"

Bella looked at Coach Doss with a hint of irritation on her plastic smile. "Sweetie? Of course, I am not kidding," she said as she took his hand and kissed it. "Well, your mother and I are here. Your dad and my dad had a work conference thing to attend in Tennessee or Kentucky or something like that."

The waiter brought Bella a fresh glass of ice water, and she took a sip and smiled. "We have all heard so much about Coach Alvarez and the basketball team—and of course, Chen. You go on and on about Chen and how good he is." Bella peeked down the table and waved at Chente with an icy smile.

Chente pretended not to be listening as he continued to visit with Carlos and Felipe. "*Oyes, la* girlfriend *de* Coach Doss is a little crazy," whispered Carlos as he leaned into Chente. "Does she have something against you?"

Chente pretended to be confused and shook his head. "*Por que*? I don't think so. I don't even know her that well. Why do you think that?"

Felipe chuckled under his breath and covered his mouth.

"Because she kind of freaked out when she got to the table, and you and Coach Doss were not here." Felipe couldn't stop laughing. "Maybe she thinks the rumors about you and Coach are true."

Carlos gave Chente a worried look and shrugged.

"Whatever," said Chente, and he continued to munch on the tortilla chips on the table.

"Yeah, something's not right," said Carlos as he wrinkled his nose. "Coach Doss is not happy that she's here. He barely kissed her. His whole body language is off."

Carlos kept looking at the couple. "And what's up with her coming down with his parents? Super weird, right, Chen?"

"Yeah, well, that's not our problem," said Chente as he tried to change the subject. "Dude, I have a media circus I am trying to control. Don't have time to worry about Coach Doss and his Barbie."

The food came, and the basketball team had a great meal. They managed to forget about the state tournament and had a good time being friends and acting like silly teenagers.

During the appetizer portion of the meal, Felipe got Beau to try some authentic Mexican hot sauce, and the table erupted in laughter when Beau's forehead began to sweat and his eyes began to tear up.

"Wow. That was so hot. That cleared my sinuses." Beau laughed as he finished drinking a glass full of cold water.

The restaurant's mariachi band made its way to the table just as the team was getting ready to leave. Coach Doss got up and handed the band a twenty-dollar bill; he spoke to the vocalist about singing a song. She nodded and walked over to Chente.

"*Perdón muchacho, mí nombre es* Cecilia and I understand that you and your dad had a favorite song?" asked the beautiful singer as she tipped her mariachi hat and grabbed Chente's hand. "Please help me sing it?"

Chente gave her a desperate look and shook his head.

"No. What do you mean? I … I … I really can't sing." He glanced at Coach Doss and continued to shake his head.

The entire basketball team began to cheer wildly for Chente to get up and sing with the band. One of the band members took off his mariachi hat and put it on Chente, and the basketball team cheered even louder.

"*Órale*, Chen, you can do it. It's time to represent," yelled Felipe as he laughed and pointed at his friend.

"I will take the first verse, and you harmonize—to warm up your voice. Then the second verse will be your solo," whispered the vocalist.

Chente was horrified. "What? What do you mean—my solo? I haven't done this in a super long time. This is going to be bad."

Cecilia could hear the apprehension in Chente's voice, and she tried to reassure him with a gentle smile. "It's okay, we do this all of the time. Just relax and do the best you can. Most of the people in here have been drinking anyway. They won't know the difference. Besides, I will be harmonizing."

She gave him a pretty smile and winked at him as the mariachi band began to play.

Chente looked around. There was nowhere to hide. He looked over at Coach Alvarez and Coach Doss, and they were both smiling and clapping. Felipe and Carlos were screaming and yelling, while some of the other members of the basketball team were recording the event on their cell phones.

He took a deep breath, decided to live in the moment, and chose to sing his heart out in memory of his dad. He would do it for his dad.

Cecilia opened her mouth, and her voice was absolutely stunning—strong, confident, and passionate. It wouldn't be difficult to harmonize. They began to sing together. It was obvious that Cecilia was a seasoned professional. She knew how to work the crowd and entertain.

The restaurant crowd clapped and cheered as Cecilia finished the first part of the song. Chente heard Mexican *gritos* from the audience, confirming the appreciation of her amazing voice.

Cecilia looked at Chente and nodded and smiled. "Give it up for my friend, Chente."

The mariachi band kept playing and crowd politely clapped.

Chente took a deep breath and closed his eyes. He wanted to feel the torment and agony of the words, to live their shameless suffering. Memories of his dad and Jimmy flooded Chente's heart. He opened his eyes and was no longer in the restaurant.

He had traveled back in time …

He was eight years old, and his father was strumming his guitar, smiling at him as his brothers and sisters sat on the couch, listening to them sing. He could smell the arroz and frijoles from the kitchen as his mom walked in and blew him a kiss.

Nos dejamos hace tiempo
Pero me llego el momento de perder
Tu tenias mucha razon,
Le hago caso al corazon y me muero por volver

Y volver, volver a tus brazos otra vez,
Llegare hasta donde estes
Yo se perder, yo se perder,
Quiero volver, volver, volver

The mariachi music slowly came to an end, and Chente slowly slipped back into reality. He looked around the restaurant and saw Coach Alvarez with an agonized expression. He looked at Coach Doss and his friends. They were all astonished into silence until Felipe let out a Mexican *grito*, and then the room exploded into applause.

Chente was a little embarrassed that he got caught up in the moment. He looked over at Cecilia and awkwardly smiled.

"*Mijito*, I thought you said you couldn't sing." The mariachi vocalist smiled as she walked over to him and gave him a hug. "That was pretty good—very emotional!"

Chente bashfully shook his head. "I'm sure you are being kind, but thank you," he said as he returned the mariachi hat to the band member. "I appreciate you and your band for singing that song. It brought back many good memories."

"No, sir. Thank your coach over there," replied Cecilia, and she pointed at Coach Doss. "He was incredibly determined that we sing that song for you. He said you had a rough week."

He looked over at Coach Doss, who was arguing with Bella. The emotional fiancée pointed at him and furiously walked away.

"I guess I will thank him a little later," Chente said and bid her farewell.

"*Oyes*, I didn't know you were a younger version of Alejandro Fernandez," said Carlos as he and Felipe ran up to Chente and fist-bumped him.

"*Órale*, Chente! My brother, you can sing!" exclaimed Felipe. "That was awesome!"

Chente started to laugh. "Dude, you obviously don't listen to mariachi music. That was average at best. I was pitchy in the middle for sure," said Chente as he shivered. "But I appreciate the love."

The three made their way out the front door of the restaurant when Chente glanced over and saw the Hamilton family sitting a couple of tables away. He waved at them and walked over to say hello.

"Dang, Chen! You got some pipes," said Harry Hamilton as he got up and greeted Chente with a big hug. "Dude, it is so good to see you."

Chente was mortified. "Oh gosh, don't tell me you saw that."

"Sure did," said Harry as he laughed. "Four years of high school Spanish, and I still don't know what you sang about, but I felt it, and you sounded really good."

The entire family smiled and nodded in agreement.

Chente's cheeks turned bright pink, and he quickly changed the subject. "So Harry, how's college going? You like it?" he asked. "Did you pass your first year?"

"Barely! I am a studly sophomore now." Harry grinned as he playfully flexed his biceps and looked at his little brother, Henry, and winked. "I love Tech. I can't wait for Henry to join me next year."

Chente looked at Henry and playfully nudged his shoulder. "So you have decided to go to Texas Tech next year?"

Henry watched Chente and smiled really big. He made the guns-up signal with his hands. "Yep. I'm going to be a Red Raider. What about you? Do you know where you're going to college?" asked Henry as he glanced at his parents.

"No. I haven't decided yet, but I am really considering Texas Tech," replied Chente as he duplicated the guns-up signal.

Chente noticed Henry relax a little and look over at Harry with a grin. He wondered what was going on. What was he missing?

Chente turned his attention to Mrs. Hamilton. He walked over and gave her a big hug. "Mrs. Hamilton, you look so good and healthy. I am so happy that you are doing well."

Henry's eyes followed Chente.

"Well, I just decided I wasn't going to let cancer get the better of me," responded the mother of two with a perfectly friendly smile. She looked at Chente. "It is so good to see you. You played wonderful today!"

"Thank you. One more game." Chente exhaled. "It's now or never, right? Let's hope that things fall into place tomorrow."

The boy from Avalon quickly shook Mr. Hamilton's hand and exchanged polite pleasantries, while Coach Doss walked up to the table. "Hey, Chen, I apologize, but we have to leave," announced the basketball coach. He politely nodded at Henry and waited for Chente.

"Well, it was good to see y'all. Try the enchiladas—they were really good," said Chente as he started to walk away with Coach Doss.

"Hey, Chen, we really want you to go with us to New Mexico over spring break," said Henry with an anxious smile. He looked at his family and they all nodded in agreement. "Please think about it," requested the boy from Kress.

"That sounds like fun." Chente smiled. "Thank you."

"And Chen, we'll see you tomorrow. Good luck," said Henry.

"Keep your fingers crossed," said Chente as he walked away with Coach Doss to the Avalon bus.

"See I told you he liked you." Coach Doss smirked with a hint of regret in his voice.

Chente just absorbed the comment and didn't respond. He wasn't in the mood to argue or fight. He was exhausted and ready for bed. If Coach Doss was jealous, then that was something he was going to have to deal with on his own. He was going to embrace the inner peace he had found tonight.

"Thank you for tonight," said Chente.

"Why are you thanking me?" asked Coach Doss with a mischievous grin.

"You are such a bad liar." Chente smiled and playfully rolled his eyes. "You were the one who asked the mariachi to come and sing for me. I know it was you. Thank you," he said as he reached out and nudged his shoulder. "This was the best night I have had in a very long time."

Coach Doss could barely contain his happiness as he quietly watched Chente get on the school bus.

The Avalon Longhorns had battled the Thorndale Bulldogs for the state championship for three quarters and were trailing by two points. Avalon 45–Thorndale 47.

Coach Alvarez huddled the team and was scrambling for a strategy to get his team over the edge. "We have the ball to start the quarter," he said. "Chen, run our motion offense off the one-four set and look for the back door cuts. They are overplaying on defense."

The team nodded in agreement.

"After we tie up the game, hustle back and get into your matchup zone defense," he instructed. "Let's plug up the paint and force them to shoot from the outside."

The team again nodded, except for Chente, who was quietly shaking his head in disagreement.

"What's the matter, Chen?" asked Coach Alvarez.

"I think we need to press," said Chente confidently. The other starters looked up when he made that suggestion.

Coach Alvarez disagreed. "They are too disciplined, too fundamentally sound to press."

"But Coach, we haven't even tried," countered the point guard. "Look, it's the last eight minutes. They aren't going to be expecting it, and maybe we can get them rattled and get a couple of easy baskets."

Tre' looked at Chente and then at Coach Alvarez. "I agree with Chen on this one," said the six-six power forward.

Coach Alvarez looked at Coach Doss. Then he looked at his two star players and nodded. "Okay. After we score, jump into our two-two-one press. We need to push them to the sidelines and trap."

The buzzer sounded.

"Guys, we can do this," shouted Chente, and he stepped on the floor to compete for the Class 3A state championship.

Avalon inbounded the basketball, and Chente set up the offense and quickly found Beau cutting back door for an easy layup. Avalon swiftly jumped into their 2–2–1 press and quickly got two steals and two easy baskets before Thorndale called a quick time-out. Avalon 51–Thorndale 47.

The Avalon bench went crazy when the starters ran to the sidelines and huddled up. Coach Alvarez looked at Chente, smiled, and gave him a thumbs-up. "Good call, Chen."

The head basketball coach wiped the sweat off his forehead and continued coaching. "Listen, guys, Thorndale is going to adjust to the press, so slide back into your matchup zone and get every rebound."

The next six minutes felt like an eternity for the Avalon basketball team, but when the final buzzer sounded, they were crowned state champions. Avalon 55–Thorndale 52.

The Avalon fans went crazy, and the band began to play the school fight song. Chente looked up in the stands and searched for his family. He spotted Victor and Vanessa. They both had painted their faces maroon and white, and were jumping up and down in delirious excitement. He spotted his mother sitting calmly beside them with a rosary in her hand. Chente waved at her, and she blew him a kiss.

After the state championship trophy presentation concluded, the coaches and the seniors on the team were escorted to a large media room to answer questions. It was part of the ritual after the state championship game. It gave the media an opportunity to report on the basketball games.

As they walked into the room, Chente waved at a short and pudgy

TV reporter with round glasses and a maroon tie, who was sitting on the front row.

"Chen? What's going on?" asked Coach Alvarez.

"Sir, I told you I had everything under control. Trust me." Chente nodded with a confident grin.

Coach Alvarez looked at Coach Doss and at the other seniors, and they all shrugged. They didn't know what was going on either.

After fifteen minutes of continual basketball game-related discussion, the short, pudgy TV reporter with the round glasses and maroon tie raised his hand. "I have one last question," he said as he ruffled through some notes. "This question is for Mr. Jimenez."

Chente looked up at the reporter. "Yes, sir. What's your question?"

The reporter looked at Chente and smiled. "We received reports from various media outlets that you came out to your high school friends last week. Is that true? Are you, in fact, gay?"

"Chen, you don't have to answer that," said Coach Doss as he stood up and lunged at the reporter.

"That is completely irrelevant. How dare you ask that sort of question. We are leaving," yelled Coach Alvarez as he motioned to get up.

"Coach Alvarez, it's okay. I don't mind answering that question," said Chente. "Do you have a minute?"

"Yes. Take your time," replied the reporter.

All the cameras in the room pointed at Chente.

"Dude, you don't have to do this," whispered Carlos as he tugged on Chente's jersey.

"Yes, I do. I am not going to run from this," said Chente, and he smiled at all of them. "Guys, I am going to do this my way. Trust me," he finally said with a casual wink.

He turned his attention to the reporter and his camera man. "Let me start by saying that today belongs to my coaches and my teammates. We just won our first state championship for our school and our community, and I couldn't be prouder." He nodded as he looked at Coach Alvarez and his teammates. "We all deserve this moment."

Chente looked at all the reporters, the camera men, and the lights in the room. He paused for a moment to reflect. He gathered his thoughts and almost lost his nerve. "You asked me if I was gay," he said as he looked at his friends and cleared his throat. "Here is my answer to that question.

"My name is Vincente Jimenez Jr. I have a loving mother, two beautiful sisters, and two amazing brothers. My dad was my hero, and he died eleven months ago. I love to play basketball and tennis. I am an avid reader and love to watch scary movies. I have an incredible circle of supportive friends, who are fiercely protective."

He calmly turned and smiled at his senior buddies. "I am senior class valedictorian, and I plan to attend college in the fall. English is my favorite subject in school, Maroon 5 is my favorite band, and I love my mom's homemade tortillas. They are the best," he said, and he turned and chuckled a little bit when he heard Felipe agree about his mom's tortillas.

Chente took a deep breath and exhaled. He smiled at the reporter and nodded. "And after all of that, sir—yes, I am gay." The entire room was quiet. He looked at the reporter and patiently waited. "Did I answer your question?"

The reporter finished taking notes on his notepad and grinned. "I think so, but let me recap for you just in case," replied the reporter. "What you are saying is that being gay is a piece of your identity but doesn't define who you are. Is that right?"

Chente proudly sat up straight in his chair and nodded. "That is exactly what I meant. Thank you."

Chente showered and was dressed when Coach Alvarez walked into the locker room. He looked at Chente, shook his head, and grinned. "You staged all of that, right?" asked the head coach as he nervously tapped his heel on the floor. "That reporter, the question, all of it."

Carlos and Felipe started to laugh hysterically as they high-fived each other.

"It took you more than thirty minutes to figure it all out, Coach!"

teased Felipe. "Our boy Chente is valedictorian of our senior class. He's pretty smart!"

Chente finished tying his shoes and exhaled proudly. "Yes. That was Vanessa's friend from Tech. He just graduated last year and works for a local TV station here in San Antonio," explained the point guard. "My sister called him and helped me pull some strings."

Coach Doss quietly listened and admired from afar as he gathered stat books and other athletic gear into a bag.

"Still, that was really brave, Chen," said Coach Alvarez.

Chente thought for a minute. "I don't know about that," reflected the Jimenez boy. "I just know I am tired of running away from the truth. That's not who I am."

"No, I get it," agreed the head coach.

"Plus, I wasn't about to let Ricky and his dad think they got the better of me," said Chente as he quietly gathered his things. "I wanted to take control and tell my story my way."

"Damn right!" said Felipe. "I am still going to kick his sorry ass."

Carlos rolled his eyes. "No, you're not, because Christina probably already did!"

They all let out a huge roar of laughter.

"Guys, stop for a minute," said Chente. "No more doom and gloom. We just won state! Let's celebrate!"

They all yelled in excitement.

"Let's wear our gold medals around our necks and head to the River Walk," suggested Felipe. "I bet we get a lot of girls that way."

Carlos hit Felipe on the head as they walked out of the locker room. "Please tell me you're not that stupid." Carlos pointed at Chente.

"*Oyes*, dude, I am sorry," replied Felipe as he let out a wicked laugh. "Who knows? Maybe Chente will get lucky too and find himself a good-looking dude!"

CHAPTER 21

The Avalon Longhorn basketball team returned from San Antonio to a warm welcome from the Avalon community. There were numerous banners, streamers, and balloons throughout the community as the bus made its way to the high school. When the bus turned the corner of Longhorn Drive, a crowd of fans and the Longhorn band greeted them.

Coach Alvarez got off the bus, hoisting the state championship trophy over his head, and the crowd roared with pride. One by one the players exited the bus, and they were met with a congratulatory handshake from Avalon ISD superintendent Barbara Reyes and Avalon mayor David Herrera.

Superintendent Reyes took the microphone and gathered everyone's attention. "It is with great Longhorn pride that I welcome back our state champions!"

The fans began to clap, yell, and whistle.

"On many levels, it took a lot of courage and '*ganas*' for these young men to travel to San Antonio and battle for this title," stated the superintendent. "They represented Avalon ISD and our hometown very well. Thank you for making us so proud!"

Mayor Herrera took the microphone next, and when the applause died down, he extended his warm congratulations to the basketball team as well. "Superintendent Reyes and I have been visiting all day long, and we have decided that we want to continue to celebrate this amazing achievement. We are organizing a community pep rally and parade for our champions on Wednesday night at the football field."

His announcement was received favorably by the crowd. They cheered, and the band began to play the school fight song.

The basketball players waved at everyone as they made their way to the locker room.

"Mr. Jimenez, may I have a moment, please?" asked Superintendent Reyes as she gently put her hand on his shoulder. "I just want to personally congratulate you on a fine tournament. I am going to miss watching you suit up for Avalon High School."

"Thank you," replied Chente. "I appreciate that. I am going to miss playing basketball with my friends too."

He took a deep breath and grinned. "But tennis is next, and I am looking forward to that."

Superintendent Reyes smiled and shook his hand once again. "I am so pleased to know a young man that is so fearless and genuine. Keep on being a role model for everyone." She extended her arms and gave him a hug. "I will see you on Wednesday." She smiled and walked away to greet other parents in the crowd.

"What was that about?" asked Carlos.

He and Felipe were still playing bodyguard and had waited for Chente by the front door. Felipe was scanning the crowd, looking for Christina.

"She was just being kind," said Chente, and out of the corner his eyes he spotted his family. He motioned Carlos and Felipe to follow as he walked over to them.

Vanessa had her arms extended and was screaming for a hug. "Oh my gosh, Chente, I am so proud of you. You don't even know." She wrapped her arms tightly around him.

"I'm getting the picture. Nesh, I can't breathe," he said and coughed. He laughed as she loosened her grip.

"I am so thankful for you." Chente smiled. "Your reporter friend really came through for me."

Valentin had been waiting patiently for his turn to congratulate Chente. His older brother had sacrificed valuable study time to make the trip from Lubbock. He felt it was important to be there for his little brother in person and show his support. His dad would have wanted that.

"Hey, Vanessa, quit hogging him up. He's our brother too," teased Valentin, who had a smile extended from ear to ear. "Little brother, I am so proud of you. You played your ass off! Damn, you were amazing!"

Chente was surprised to see Valentin. His older brother was usually too busy to be involved with the family, and to see him excited and to hear those words coming out of his mouth made Chente's eyes a little misty.

"Thanks, Valentin. I'm glad you're here," replied Chente as he choked back his emotions. He reached and hugged his oldest brother and bridged the distance that was so often there.

Chente walked over to Victor, who was standing beside his mom. He reached out, fist- bumped his little brother, and laughed. Chente was so connected to Victor that he knew that was his little brother's way of congratulating him without getting too sentimental.

"Damn, Chen, do you always have to be so dramatic?" asked Victor as he laughed. "I mean, coming out on the school intercom is one thing, but coming out on national TV? Really?"

"Dude, be quiet. What are you talking about?" asked the basketball player as he looked at the youngest Jimenez brother.

Victor stopped laughing and awkwardly glanced at his mom. "Chente, your coming-out story is all over CNN and ESPN."

"What?" Chente said, laughing. "You're kidding, right?"

Vanessa covered her mouth with her hands and shook her head. "Nope. Victor is telling the truth."

"Oh my gosh. You aren't kidding." Chente gasped.

"My reporter friend from San Antonio texted me a couple of hours ago to warn me," said Vanessa.

"Yeah, ESPN ran the report about forty-five minutes ago, and CNN did shortly after." Valentin nodded as he looked at his watch.

Chente hadn't known. He and his teammates had been on a bus all day, with spotty Wi-Fi access.

"What's going on?" asked Carlos as he stepped closer to Chente.

"I was trying to tell you, but Valentin interrupted," replied Vanessa. "My reporter friend said the national media outlets picked up your interview early this morning."

A loud silence overcame the group, and they all looked at each other, not knowing how to react. Chente looked at his friends with a hint of fear in his eyes.

"*Órale*, who cares?" Felipe laughed as he shielded Chente with a hug. "You spoke the truth, right?"

Chente slowly nodded. Felipe was right. He had nothing to fear. He wasn't going to let this news deter his excitement to be home with a state championship trophy. "Exactly. Don't fear the truth, right?"

"Chen, you're a superstar. Dude, we're talking about ESPN! That's crazy!" teased Felipe as he started to playfully dance around his friend in an attempt to melt the icy tension.

Chente moved closer to his mother and let her love on him a little. Her motherly touch made him feel special and safe.

"My brave little boy. I am so proud of you." She gingerly kissed his forehead and smiled. "*Tu papá esta muy orgulloso de ti.*"

He looked at his mom and simply nodded, resting his forehead on her shoulder as she caressed his hair.

"*Mijo, dile* a Carlos and Felipe to come over to the house," said Mrs. Jimenez. "I am fixing a big dinner tonight to celebrate."

"I'm so there, *señora*," said Felipe with a big grin. It was obvious he had been eavesdropping.

"You have no shame, Felipe," said Carlos as he laughed and shook his head. "Thank you. I will be there too after I run home and check on my mom."

Chente paused and gave Carlos a quizzical look. "Is everything okay?"

Carlos awkwardly looked at Chente and smiled. He quickly nodded and avoided answering the question as he began speaking to Vanessa about Texas Tech. Chente studied Carlos's body language for a few seconds, then excused himself from his family.

As the three boys entered the high school building, Chente stopped and noticed Coach Alvarez and Violeta were standing beside the bus, speaking very quietly. They were standing close to each other, and he was holding her hand.

On Monday morning, Miss Young was waiting for Chente as he entered the building and quickly escorted him into her office. She congratulated him on his success on the basketball court and winning the state title, but she was even more impressed by the manner in which he had addressed his sexuality with the media.

"Chen, I was blown away that you had the sense and the nerve to do what you did," the high school counselor said with a smile. "I mean, you took the bull by the horns and made it positive—on your own terms. Very clever and very brave."

Chente laughed and nervously shook his head. "Trust me, I was scared to death, but I was glad that it worked out in the end." The high school senior paused and reflected. "You know, I have learned that coming to terms with your sexuality is a personal thing, whether you are gay or straight."

Miss Young nodded in agreement and went into counselor mode and listened.

"I think whoever made those anonymous postings about me had cruel intentions," speculated Chente. "But they motivated me to get ahead of the story and steal their thunder."

"Well, I'm proud of you," she said. Miss Young locked eyes with Chente and smiled. "It took a lot of courage to do what you did. Please remember that my door is always open if you need to talk."

"Thank you," replied Chente.

Miss Young walked over to her desk, reached into her desk drawer, and pulled out two envelopes. "Well, we have heard back from the University of Texas and Stanford last week, but you were in San

Antonio," she said nervously. "I didn't want to distract you, so I kept these envelopes in my desk."

Chente inhaled sharply as his eyes got really big. He immediately felt a tightness in his stomach and around his neck.

"So here you go," she said. "You can open them when you're ready." She handed Chente the envelopes and waited.

Chente took the envelopes and looked at Miss Young as she closed the door to her office. "I just want to thank you for all your help. No matter what happens in a few minutes, I couldn't have done this without you."

Chente opened the envelope from the University of Texas first. He read the letter and smiled proudly. "I got it! I got the Presidential Scholarship."

He put his hands on top of his head and let out a big sigh. He looked at Miss Young and started to laugh with incredulous joy.

"That is amazing! I am so happy for you," Miss Young said with a giggle. "A full ride to UT is an incredible opportunity!"

The high school counselor was genuinely happy for Chente. Attending the University of Texas in Austin would be a wonderful experience for her prized pupil. It would be an opportunity for Chente to learn and grow—educationally and personally.

After a few minutes of celebrating the Presidential Scholarship offer from the University of Texas, Chente opened the envelope from Stanford. This was the scholarship he truly wanted. "I am too nervous to read it myself," he said as he put down the envelope. "Would you read it for me, please?"

Miss Young smiled confidently and nodded. Chente handed the letter to her.

She unraveled the letter and carefully studied its contents. She looked up at Chente with no expression on her face. She handed him the letter and began to jump up and down. "You got it too! Oh my gosh, Chen, you got the scholarship!"

"Are you serious? I got the scholarship? Are you sure?" asked Chente as he slowly stood up from his chair. "Are you positive?"

Miss Young laughed, grabbed Chente by the arms, and began to shake him. "Yes, I am sure. You got a full ride to Stanford. Oh my gosh! This is incredible!"

"I can't believe it!" he whispered. He sat down on her desk and shook his head. "This has always been my dream. I have always wanted to go to Stanford."

He thought of all the times he had stayed up late to study for tests, the times he had come early to school for tutorials, and all the times when he hadn't gone out with his friends due to finishing his homework. Those sacrifices had paid off.

"I am so happy right now" was all Chente could manage to get out. "I am just so happy."

"So, Chen, you have a lot of good options," said Miss Young as she took a seat beside her star pupil. "You have three quality universities pursuing you. This is an amazing opportunity."

He smiled and nodded. "I am truly grateful too."

"What are you thinking?" she asked.

"What I am thinking? Seriously?" The high school senior laughed as he placed his hands on his head. "I'm thinking this is all a dream. I'm pinching myself to make sure this is real."

"No, I understand. It's surreal." Miss Young smiled. "But your SAT scores were out of this world, and now you have been blessed with great circumstances."

Chente composed himself for a second and slowly reviewed the letters one more time. "Is there a deadline to decide?"

"I believe the national date to respond for college admission is May first, but I will double-check and make sure," replied Miss Young.

Chente thought for a minute and grinned. "I am just going to enjoy the moment and let it sink it for a couple of weeks. I want to share the news with my family and get feedback from my mom." He still couldn't believe this was happening.

"I think that is a good plan. There is no rush to decide," said Miss Young as she wrote down a couple of notes. "I would think you may want to visit the campuses before you decide," she said.

Chente nodded with excitement. "Yes. Absolutely, yes. I would love that."

"I am not positive, but I believe the Stanford scholarship pays for an orientation trip for two in June. Let me get confirmation on that for you," said Miss Young as she regained her composure and was all businesslike.

"That would be perfect," said Chente. "Thank you for all of your help!"

"It is absolutely my pleasure." Miss Young nodded. "This is so exciting, and I am so glad that I am a little part of this."

The phone rang, and she answered it. After a few seconds she hung up the receiver. "Okay, I have a parent meeting in a few minutes, so congratulations once again. I am so proud for you, Chen!"

Chente got up to leave. He walked past her desk and gave her a big bear hug.

"I think this is amazing, and I want to announce this to the student body. Is that okay?" asked Miss Young.

"Really?" Chente chuckled as he gave Miss Young an odd look. "You're asking me whether it's okay to make an announcement over the school intercom? Are you serious?"

Miss Young rolled her eyes and started to laugh as well.

The next couple of days blew by like a West Texas whirlwind, and Chente was relieved that all the commotion was almost over. Even though he enjoyed celebrating a state championship with his friends, he was also having to deal with the exposure of coming out on national TV, and that had been quite challenging—even for Chente.

On Wednesday morning, Chente and Victor pulled up to school thirty minutes early because Victor had to attend tutorials to complete a quiz for his World History class. Chente was going to take the extra time to clean out his locker and get ready for the spring tennis season.

Chente entered the gym and walked up to the locker room door; it was locked. He noticed the lights were on in the coaches' office. He knocked on the door, and Coach Doss answered with a cup of coffee in his right hand.

"Hey, Chen, come on in," Coach Doss said as he returned to his desk. "Coach Alvarez is running a little bit late this morning."

Chente hesitated but walked into the office and sat down. "Actually, I wasn't looking to bother either one of you," he said. "I just need to get into the locker room, and it's locked."

"Oh, okay. Give me a second to complete this, and I will open up and get out of your way," answered Coach Doss as he finished grading what looked like a world geography quiz.

There was a chill in his voice Chente couldn't ignore. "Coach, it's not like that," said the senior class valedictorian as he shook his head. "I was—"

"You don't have to explain," interrupted Coach Doss with a hint of edginess in his voice. "I understand that we have to keep our distance."

Chente couldn't handle the intensity in the room, and he exhaled. "Look, maybe it's better that I wait outside."

He got up to leave, but Coach Doss grabbed his hand and motioned him to stay. "I'm sorry," Coach Doss said with a sigh.

Chente locked eyes with Coach Doss and noticed the dark bags under his eyes. It was apparent Coach Doss hadn't been sleeping well. "I just don't know how to act around you anymore," mumbled the coach nervously.

"I know. Me too," agreed Chente with a heavy heart.

Coach Doss had a desperate look in his eyes, and he began to fidget with his hands. "I know that I'm a teacher, and you're a student, and this is wrong, but I can't help the way I feel. I really can't," he whispered.

It was painful to see Coach Doss like this—hopeless, frustrated, and defeated.

"I just don't want you to get into trouble," replied Chente as he put his hands on his head and sighed.

Coach Doss nodded, closed his eyes, and took a deep breath. "All of my life I have done what my parents wanted me to do," he said. "I was a good student, a good athlete—I always followed the rules."

Coach Doss slowly shook his head and exhaled. "I went to college and graduated. I got engaged to a beautiful girl—your all-American boy. Picture perfect from the outside, but inside it always felt like a winding road to nowhere."

Silence filled the office.

Coach Doss sat motionless in his chair, like a lifeless puppet. "And then I met you, and for the first time in my life, I felt alive. You were like oxygen. You breathed life into me. Everything made sense." He opened his eyes, looked at Chente, and smiled.

Chente smiled back and nodded. He felt the same way.

"And then you come out to the entire high school, and you didn't flinch." Coach Doss shook his head in amazement. "And then you revealed yourself to the world on national TV—and when the smoke cleared, you were still standing tall."

Coach Doss's voice began to tremble, and he cleared his throat as he reflectively paused on those memories. "Chen, do you have any idea what that did for me? Every day I loved you more," he whispered. "You are my heart, my hero, and my fearless inspiration."

Chente slowly shook his head in disbelief and swallowed hard. "And every day I thought I was pushing you further away," whispered the high school senior.

Coach Doss slowly took Chente's hand and kissed it. "Not even close. You are intoxicating. Don't ever doubt my love for you, Chen."

The first-year teacher continued to quietly play with Chente's fingers as a peaceful silence enveloped the coaches' office. "Next to my grandfather, you have been the most important person in my life, and I know I love you. I love you so much, it hurts."

The assistant coach sighed heavily and wiped away the tears rolling down his cheeks like raindrops on a windowpane.

Chente was speechless. He could barely breathe and was unable to think clearly. This was what he had been waiting to hear for weeks. He was in love with Coach Doss, and he didn't care whether anyone approved.

"But the truth of it all is that I will never be able to act on my love for you. I could never hurt my parents like that," said Coach Doss as he let Chente's hand go free. "I am not brave like you. I am scared of what people will think … I have to get married now …"

He got up from his chair and began to pace back and forth in desperation, and like a programmed robot, he began to speak. "I will marry Bella in June, and you will go to college, and what might have been will be nothing more than a faded memory. That's just the way it has to be."

Chente shook his head in disbelief. "No. It doesn't have to be that way," he insisted as he shook his head. The high school senior felt like someone had kicked him in the stomach and started to breathe heavily. It felt like the office walls were slowly caving in and burying him alive.

"I will wait for you … I will wait for you," whispered Chente as he desperately reached for Coach Doss's hands. "We can be together after I graduate," continued Chente. "That way you won't get into any trouble."

"No, Chen. That will never happen. I just can't do this," replied Coach Doss as he pulled his hands away, looked down at his shoes, and shamefully shook his head. He put his hands over his face to hide his disgrace and hurt. "You and I will never happen," he whispered as he almost choked on his words. "It simply can't happen."

"Don't say that," lamented Chente as he fell to his knees and pleaded like someone was holding a gun to his heart and about to pull the trigger. "Please, don't say that. I love you," pleaded the high school senior as he reached for Coach Doss. But the teacher pushed him away.

"Please don't do this," begged Chente. "Please."

The bell sounded, and Coach Doss quickly gathered his belongings and ran out the door, trying to escape the pain in his heart. But he left Chente all alone—broken and shattered into a million pieces.

"Chen, quit picking at your food and eat something. You look dreadful," said Haven as she played with Beau's blond hair. "Are you feeling okay? Are you coming down with a cold?"

Chente looked up and nodded slowly. No one could ever know that he'd had his heart trampled on this morning—no one. "I'm just a little tired," he lied. "It's been a long week. You are such a mom." He tried to smile to hide his torment.

Carlos studied Chente's body language. He sensed it was more than that, but he wasn't going to question his best friend in front of an audience. "Maybe you should just go home and take a nap before the pep rally tonight."

"Like, skip school?" asked Felipe as he perked up. "Maybe we should all go home and take a nap." Felipe winked at Christina, who was sitting across from him, and blew her a kiss.

Christina rolled her eyes and continued to file her fingernails. "Hey, Chen, is it true that you are going on *Ellen*? I love *Ellen*," asked Christina as she let out an extremely dramatic sigh.

Chente chuckled and shook his head at Christina. "No, Christina. Don't believe everything you hear. That is just a rumor. But if she were to invite me on her show, I would insist on taking my friends to sit in the audience."

"Woo-hoo! That's what I'm talking about!" replied Christina as she blew Felipe a kiss. "Chen don't forget his friends."

The cafeteria table friends started to laugh again and cut up like usual. Carlos and Felipe continued to harass Christina, and Haven's new relationship with Beau looked like it was exactly what she needed. Chente needed his friends to distract him because his gas tank was on empty, and he felt like a walking zombie.

"Seriously, Chen," continued Carlos. "You look like you could use some sleep. You need to be on your A game tonight at the pep rally."

"Maybe you have a point," agreed Chente as he grabbed his food tray and got up. "I will text Vic and leave the car keys at the front office for him to pick up after school."

"Why? What? You're going to walk home?" asked Carlos.

"Yeah, I think I am," replied Chente as he perked up. "It's nice outside, and I haven't walked home from school in a long time. The air might do me some good."

"You know that Principal Timms will let you go home—without

question." Carlos laughed. "Just show him your state tournament MVP medal, and you can do no wrong in that man's eyes."

Everyone at the table laughed.

"Okay, see you guys tonight," said Chente as he waved and walked out of the cafeteria and into the hallway. He was walking directly to his locker to grab his letterman jacket when Ricky exited the boys' bathroom halfway down the hallway. There was no avoiding him. They were the only two people in the hallway.

"So how is Mr. Gay America doing today?" sneered Ricky.

"I am doing great," answered Chente with an extra pep in his step. "How are *you* doing?" asked the high school senior as he gave Ricky a big smile. "Who have you blamed today for your obvious shortcomings?"

Ricky grunted and rolled his eyes.

"Oh, be sure to thank your dad for the anonymous Facebook posting." Chente laughed.

"I don't know what you are talking about," replied Ricky.

"Sure, you do," replied Chente. "Everyone knows it was you and your dad who outed me on Facebook and then leaked it to the media."

"Well, prove it," said Ricky.

"Listen, I'm good with it." Chente grinned as he extended his arms wide and celebrated. "ESPN wants to do a documentary on me throughout spring tennis called *Gay Athletes in Action*."

Chente gave him a little laugh. "Y'all actually did me a favor," he said with a wink. "So be sure to tell Daddio thank you."

"That's so disgusting," said Ricky as he shook his head and growled. "My dad is speaking to the school board about having you dress in a separate locker room during tennis season."

Chente didn't flinch. "Cool. I'm good with that, too," he replied, unfazed. "Besides, my focus is on winning a state title and not on which locker room I use to get dressed."

Chente turned and started to walk away but hesitated instead and began to laugh. "Oh, and one more thing, Daddy's Boy," he said with a smirk. "I think you are giving yourself way too much credit."

"What does that mean?"

"I just mean that you're safe," Chente said plainly as he bit his bottom lip to keep from laughing. "You are *very* safe—I promise!"

Ricky became visibly more irritated. "Safe from what?"

"Dude, what I mean is that no girl or boy will ever find your tiny penis hot. I promise." Chente laughed as he waved at his rival with his pinky finger and casually walked away.

Ricky's curse words followed Chente down the hallway.

A few minutes later, Chente walked into the front office and quickly checked himself out. He was feeling a little claustrophobic and eager to escape through the front doors of the high school and to find the freedom of the gentle northern breeze.

He meandered through the elementary playground and reminisced about all the good times he and his friends had shared playing on the swings and climbing the monkey bars when they were younger. He remembered riding the merry–go-round and playing hide-and-seek before school. He missed the innocent laughter of childhood, and a part of him longed to return to the past, to appreciate what he had taken for granted.

When Chente finally made it to the safety of his home, he was relieved to have the house to himself. He longed for peace and solitude. His mother was away, helping to clean the church, and wouldn't be returning until later in the afternoon.

He walked over to his mother's religious altar and began to pray for peace, strength, and clarity.

Dear Lord, please give me the courage to get past this. Take away this pain … please … He made the sign of the cross and wiped away the hurt rolling down his cheeks.

Chente walked into his bedroom and set his alarm clock for 5:00 p.m. He got into bed and pulled the covers over his head as the tears came steadily, like a faucet, slowly dripping. He begged for sleep to steal away the acute pain he felt inside his chest. And with a heavy heart, he drifted away.

"Chente, *mijo*, wake up," said Mrs. Jimenez as she turned off the blaring alarm clock. "Are you not feeling well? *Qué te pasa*?"

Chente rubbed the sleep away from his eyes and yawned. "No, Mom, I'm fine," he said. "I was just tired, and so I came home to get some sleep." He got out of bed, scratched his head, and stretched his arms.

"Oh, okay." She sounded relieved.

Chente slowly looked around. "Where's Vic? He has the car, and I need to be at the football field by five thirty for the pep rally."

"He said he would be here by five thirty," replied Mrs. Jimenez. "He had a lot of work to make up due to his suspension." She shook her head as she exited the bedroom.

Chente chuckled under his breath. He got up, went to the restroom, and brushed his teeth; then he splashed water on his face. He glanced at the clock; it was 5:10. He decided to walk to the football field. He went the living room, grabbed his letterman jacket, and opened the front door.

"Mom, I am going to walk to the football field. See you later," shouted Chente.

"Okay, *mijo*. I'll see you in about thirty minutes. Remember to enjoy the moment, Chente," she said, waving at him, and returned to the kitchen.

Chente put on his jacket and began to walk. The power nap had rejuvenated him. He felt a little bit better. He felt rested and strangely reassured.

A blue Toyota Tacoma truck pulled up beside him. The window rolled down, and a familiar voice spoke to him as he walked down the street. "Hey, little boy, you want some candy?"

Chente stopped and looked inside to find Henry Hamilton laughing hysterically.

"What are you doing here?" asked Chente as he laughed. "You're crazy!"

"What do you mean?" said Henry with a silly grin. "Of course, I am going to the community pep rally to cheer for you."

Henry was happy and full of energy. There was a sparkle in his eyes.

"Come on, Chen, get in, Mr. State Tournament MVP," he teased. "I'll give you a lift to wherever you are going."

Chente hopped in the truck and strapped on his seat belt. Out of the corner of his eye, he saw Henry smiling at him. "What's the matter? Why are you smiling at me like that?"

Henry just shook his head and casually shrugged as he drove away. "It's just really good to see you," the boy from Kress laughed. "That's all."

"Hey, my mom and dad are coming to the community pep rally as well," Henry said, smiling, as he patted Chente's knee. "They are so proud of you."

Chente was a little surprised to hear that, but it would be good to see them again, and he was touched that they would drive in from Kress to support him.

"It's been a super crazy week," said Chente as he looked over at Henry. "There has been a lot of media exposure."

"Dude, I can only imagine," replied Henry with a little awkward chuckle under his breath. "But of course the media has been crazy—y'all only won state! Okay? Where am I going?" asked the red-headed boy.

"To the football field," said Chente. "Just keep going down this street. We can park in the Baptist church parking lot."

"You got it," replied Henry as he gripped his steering wheel tightly. "Hey, have you thought about going skiing with us next week?"

"I have," said Chente with a hint of energy. "I would love to go if the invitation is still good."

Henry's grinned and nodded excitedly. "Absolutely. Mom and Dad rented this amazing three-bedroom cabin in the mountains. It's going to be insane. You just made my day!" replied Henry as he playfully nudged Chente's shoulder. "We are going to have a blast. I promise."

"Well, thanks for the invitation," replied Chente. "Just pull in here and park over there by the red convertible. I will introduce you to my friends."

"Cool," said Henry.

All eyes were on Chente when he got off the truck with Henry. The shock on his friends' faces was amusing.

"Hey, guys, this is Henry Hamilton," announced Chente. "He drove in from Kress to come to our community pep rally."

Nobody moved. Nobody said anything. There was complete silence. Henry nervously began to shuffle his feet and looked at Chente for some reassurance.

"Hello, Henry, so nice to meet you. I'm Haven, and this is Beau," said the pretty blonde-headed girl as she reached out and gave him a friendly hug. "So glad you were able to make it tonight."

Beau followed suit, shook Henry's hand, and welcomed him.

"Are you kidding me? My team lost to you guys twice this year," Henry said, smiling, as he bashfully glanced at Chente. "I'm just glad to be here on friendlier terms this time."

Everyone laughed, and the introductions continued. Carlos was first, and then Felipe followed. Henry congratulated them on their state tournament win, and it ignited a healthy conversation between the guys.

Haven looked at Chente and smiled. She gave him a thumbs-up.

Chente shook his head and looked away.

"What's the matter with you? He's nice." Haven winked.

"Haven, he's just a good friend." Chente sighed as he rolled his eyes "I have known him for years. I don't think he likes me that way."

Haven gave him a shy smile and carefully watched the boy from Kress from afar. "Really? I think you're wrong, Chen," she whispered as she squeezed his hand and walked away. "Please keep an open mind, sir."

Christina mindfully inspected the lanky, red-headed boy from top to bottom. She paused and nodded confidently. "So, Henry, how tall are you?" asked the high school fashionista.

Henry glanced at Chente with intimidation on his face. "I'm six-three. Why? Would you like my weight too?"

Christina brushed back her long, black hair and grinned mischievously. "Wow! Good for you, Chen," replied the head cheerleader as she snapped her fingers and walked away.

Chente wanted the parking lot to open up and swallow him as he stared at his friend from Kress and embarrassingly shook his head. "Well, we … uh … we … should get going," stuttered Chente. "Coach Alvarez is super strict about punctuality."

"Y'all go ahead," said Henry. "I want to get a light jacket. It will probably get a little chilly later on tonight." He jogged back to his truck to retrieve it.

"I'll wait for you," said Chente.

The Avalon point guard looked at his group of friends, and they were all staring at him—smiling at him. He gave them a desperate look and motioned them to leave. "Y'all go on. We will catch up." Chente smiled.

Felipe laughed under his breath and gave him a big wink. "Uh-hmmm … you better."

Carlos slapped Felipe on the shoulder, and the group left. Beau turned around and gave Chente a little smile.

Henry returned with a light-blue jacket in hand. He was still grinning from ear to ear. "You have great friends, Chen."

"I agree. I would have been lost without them this year. That's for sure," admitted Chente. "We have been friends since kindergarten."

They started to walk to the football field and stopped to wait for traffic to clear so they could cross the street.

"I'm glad you're here, Henry," said Chente as he gave him a little, playful nudge.

"Really? You are happy that I'm here?" asked Henry as he gazed at Chente.

"Of course, I am, and I can tell that my friends like you too," remarked Chente as he chuckled under his breath.

Henry didn't say anything for a couple of seconds. He just smiled and exhaled. "Well, I'm simply happy to be here with you. I think you're pretty awesome."

Chente froze. Was Haven right? Did Henry actually like him? Up until that moment, Chente hadn't really considered that a possibility. He didn't know how to feel about it either.

The Avalon point guard could see his friends waiting for them to cross the street.

"Hey, isn't that one of your basketball coaches?" asked Henry as he began to zip up his jacket.

Chente turned around and saw Coach Doss standing outside his house, holding his briefcase. He had just gotten home and was looking at them from a safe distance.

Henry smiled and waved at him. Coach Doss nodded and waved back as Bella's car pulled up and parked behind his 4Runner in the driveway.

Chente and Coach Doss stared at each other for a few seconds. Chente felt a rush of sadness invade his broken heart.

"Come on, Chen, let's go," said Henry as he smiled and gently grabbed Chente's hand. And with no hesitation, he helped Chente cross the street.

ABOUT THE AUTHOR

A. G. Castillo was born and raised in a small West Texas town. After graduating from Texas Tech University with an English degree, A. G. Castillo began his career in public education, serving as an English teacher, high school basketball coach and principal, and as a superintendent of schools. When he is not traveling the world, A. G. Castillo resides in San Antonio with his partner, Tim, and their incorrigible dachshunds, Puppy and Penny.

He is the author of the ***Valiente Series***:
Valiente: ***Courage and Consequences***
Valiente: ***Tattoos and Temptations***
Valiente: ***Flames and Fury***